THE GALLERY OF STOLEN SOULS

HELEN MOORHOUSE

POOLBEG

Published 2020
by Poolbeg Press Ltd.
123 Grange Hill, Baldoyle,
Dublin 13, Ireland
Email: poolbeg@poolbeg.com

A catalogue record for this book is available from the British Library.

ISBN 978178199-381-1

www.poolbeg.com

About the Author

The Gallery of Stolen Souls is Helen Moorhouse's fifth novel. *Ever This Day, The Dead Summer, The Dark Water* and *Sing Me to Sleep* are also published by Poolbeg.

Helen works as a freelance Voiceover Artist and Writer. Her interests include reading, cinema, TV and things that go bump in the night.

Originally from County Laois, she lives in Dublin with her husband and four daughters.

For more, see www.helenmoorhouse.com

Acknowledgements

My deepest thanks go to Paula Campbell and the team at Poolbeg for a wonderful ten years of patience, support, guidance and faith, and for making a dream come true from the very start.

To Gaye Shortland, my editor, for her positivity, patience, caring and dedication and for taking this stream of words and moulding them into a story that I hope my readers will enjoy.

No thanks at all go to my children for their help with anything related to the writing of this book – however, for everything else they've brought to my world there simply isn't enough appreciation and love in existence to acknowledge how wonderful they are, and what an exquisite joy it is to watch them grow.

To my husband for his undying support and encouragement in everything.

To my family – sisters, brothers, nieces, nephews, in-laws, cousins – and my friends, for always having my back and giving so much support and encouragement.

To my readers for reading, sharing and keeping me going when the page seems too blank to fill. I hope you enjoy stepping into the dark again.

For Bea and Holly, my wonderful distractions

Prologue

London, 1872

The gallows beam at Newgate could fit four, if necessary. There would be room to spare in the morning, in that case.

Albert Bridgman consulted his pocket watch – one of the few souvenirs that he had kept for himself over his career – most of them he had sold on, and he would do the same for those he would receive tomorrow.

In half an hour, the clerk of St Sepulchre's would make his lantern-lit way along the tunnel under the street to the condemned cell at Newgate to ring his famous handbell and issue his edict.

"All you that in the condemned hole do lie
Prepare you, for tomorrow you shall die.
Watch all, and pray, the hour is drawing near,
That you before Almighty God will appear.
Examine well yourselves, in time repent.
That you not to eternal flames be sent.
And when St Sepulchre's Bell tomorrow tolls.
The Lord above have mercy on your souls."

Within, the prisoner would wash the wholesome advice down with a little water and brandy as the day of their death began.

Bridgman would not have minded a brandy himself, but what was granted to the prisoner was denied to the executioner. How short a time it seemed since all had changed – since he would have spent a comfortable evening in a tavern, regaling his fellow drinkers with tales of hangings past, pleasantly passing the hours before he would appear in front of the crowds gathered at Tyburn and the cry of '*Hats off!*' would go up in order that all might see him at work.

Nowadays, however, he, too, spent the night as guest of the prison, lest, they said, he become intoxicated and fail to carry out his duty – a preposterous accusation. And the business at hand on the morrow would be carried out in a shed within the prison walls, observed only by two reporters, with steady hands and strong stomachs, one hoped.

It would be done quickly, the rope returned to the prison shortly after nine. Brisk and efficient. There was a certain ceremony – theatre, almost – to the old ways which Bridgman had to confess he missed. His mother had always accused him of being a show-off and he had to admit that she was probably right.

Still, late as the hour was, there was still work to be done. He had yet to set eye on the prisoner and, despite the fact that weighing and measuring had been completed, and the drop table consulted, the final preparations could only be made after observing his charge in the flesh. The thickness of the neck, for example, the particular build – every subject differed, some in ways that he couldn't describe, but which he instinctively understood.

Bridgman quickened his step. If he hurried, then he could be done by the ringing of the execution bell, and there would be time for a few hours' sleep after a final check on everything. At least having to lodge the night before in the prison meant less of a rush in the morning. He could rise after six, enjoy a leisurely breakfast, sparse as it might be (he would make up for it afterwards – his job gave him an enormous appetite), and be waiting in place at half past seven when the prisoner would be brought from the condemned cell along Birdcage Walk, the mesh of the tunnel overhead affording them their last look at the sky. Their arms would be pinioned en route, their legs strapped to prevent bridging the drop with outstretched feet, and then they would be helped to the scaffold, hooded in linen immediately prior to the lowering of the noose in order that they might take in the last sight of this world, as grim as it was, and truly feel repentance.

Then, and only then, would he see them face to face, and they him. He would look into the eyes of yet another who had taken life – was there truly a difference between their deeds and his, Bridgman wondered, and not for the first time. There would be a handshake, a final prayer, last words ... and then he would pull the bolt and the final, brief struggle would begin and end.

It would be the short drop – Bridgman did not yet trust this notion of the longer one which was being trialled in Ireland – some said it was faster, more humane, but he had no desire to see a head ripped clean off, as he had heard was possible. If it seemed the process was taking too long, then he would apply his tried and trusted method of adding his weight to theirs, pulling on the legs until it was over. It had never failed him.

After that, it was procedure and paperwork. The taking down, the washing, the handing over for inquest. On a good day, burial would be complete by lunchtime, the lime at work, and Bridgman off for a feed of pie and ale and then to sleep in his own bed. And while he would record it, of course, in a matter of days, he might have no memory of the name of person whose life he had just taken. He wondered if this prisoner could say the same of their victims, for there had been many.

The notice of execution would be displayed outside Newgate for a time, as testament that the deed had been done, that justice had been served. And then the name would diminish and disappear out there in the world, like so many others. Hanging them was one justice, alright, but that no one would ever call their name to mind again was another. On that, Albert Bridgman, Lead Executioner, was rarely wrong.

Not *never*, however.

Chapter 1

DUBLIN, 2018

"Good morning. I'm Kate Harvey, and these are Monday's headlines. Outrage this morning as a list of politicians to travel abroad for St Patrick's Day is published. News that single-use plastics are to be banned by 2030 is welcomed by environmental groups. The public has been asked for their assistance in locating a Clontarf teenager, missing since Monday last. And – Trump in excellent health, says his doctor ..."

The January morning was cold but frost-free, vibrant reds and pinks and deep, ominous purples fringing the velvet navy sky as dawn broke.

Joe Davis cut the engine of his van, silencing the eight o'clock news, before peering through the windscreen at the terraced houses with their small, orderly gardens nestled in a circle around a well-kept green. It sang of contented community – organised litter-picking, tidy garden initiatives, a summer fun day. There were pretty little pockets like this all over Dublin, quietly occupied by old folks who had lived here all their lives, and the new arrivals who snapped them up as previous owners sold on

– young couples who built bright extensions, and knocked through rooms and installed Velux windows, the occasional thirty-something unfettered by partners and kids, like himself, putting years of hard savings into a doer-upper starter home.

That's what this gig was going to be, he guessed, as he studied the front doors to find which he should knock on. The woman who'd booked him to come round said there were just the two of them and that everything needed freshening up – walls, ceilings, woodwork.

Joe stepped out of the van and zipped up his jacket, sucking in his stomach a little as he did. Still a bit of festive damage to undo, he acknowledged, but a few runs would sort that out soon enough. He glanced at his reflection in the car window, smoothing down his thick, dark hair and pretending he didn't see the new grey just at the temples. A haircut and a shave wouldn't go astray either, he thought, rubbing a hand over his chin. His grey eyes were tired too – he couldn't get his sleep patterns back to normal after Christmas. He sniffed and dug his hands into his pockets. The houses weren't the only doer-uppers around here.

No. 17, from the outside, was a prime example. The black paint on the front door had bubbled and peeled, and the brasses were tinged with green. He pressed the doorbell, and waited, double-checking that he had, indeed, the correct house. No 16 and No 18, however, were very clearly marked – 16 with a plaque, and 18 with trendy, oversized floating numerals – so it stood to reason that 17 was between them.

There was silence for a few moments, then the mumble of voices within before the door was suddenly swept open by a tall, muscular woman in her thirties dressed in Lycra cycling gear. "Hi – Joe, isn't it? I'm Ros. We spoke on the phone." Briskly, she ushered him in and bade him wait, pointing into an adjacent room and telling him she'd be back in "two shakes" before disappearing down the hallway.

Joe did as he was told. It was a sitting room – shabby, and much in need of a good dusting. The brown sofa and the standard lamp with a fringed shade, the rug riddled with burn-holes from the open fire which cast the metallic tang of cold ashes into the air, all looked as if they had been in situ since the 1970's at the latest. It had potential though, he thought, as he tapped the original wooden floor with the toe of his work boots and ran a finger along the cracked paint of the shutters on the window.

He shuffled uncomfortably as voices travelled down the hallway.

"It's a painter," he heard Ros say brightly. "I took some initiative and booked a guy to come and give the place a lick – *ta-daaah!* You can thank me later!"

Another woman – an unhappy woman – responded in a low voice. "You never said anything about a painter!"

Joe squirmed internally.

"I know. Because it's a surprise. Anyway, he's here – in the front room."

"I wasn't planning on having the place painted. Why would you even get someone to come in without saying it to me first? Why ... what made you even ..." The woman stumbled over the words, unable to finish what she was saying.

Joe raised his eyebrows in alarm.

"Evelyn at work got her place done – this guy was round there the time I called over – do you not remember

I told you? Sure why wouldn't you want a lick of paint round the place?"

"It ... it ... it doesn't ..."

"Oh, it does – that bit out in the hall where the wall is all black ..."

Joe glanced out the sitting-room door. There were, indeed, filthy streaks on the wall corresponding to the handlebars of a bike that rested against it.

"... and once you do one bit, then the rest starts to look shabby. It hasn't been done in how long? My mam always gets the house done every two years."

Joe inhaled sharply through his teeth.

"Look, I'm paying," he heard Ros add. "Least I can do. That's what mates are for."

"But ..."

"I gotta head on. You can show him around. Now ... have I got everything ... keys, wallet, headphones ... where are my bloody headphones ... ah, here. Gotta split. Catch ya later."

Footsteps scurried down the hall and Ros appeared back into the sitting room.

Joe gave a half-smile, adopting what he thought might be an innocent expression that said, '*Didn't hear a thing*'.

"I gotta leg it to work," she said apologetically. "But Lou will show you what needs doing. Have a good one, bud." And with that, she inserted a pair of headphones deeply into her ears and flung open the front door, then dragged the handlebars of the bike along the wall as she wheeled it outside. Joe watched her bump it down the front steps before swinging her leg over and sailing off into the sunrise, leaving the front door wide open behind.

Unsure what to do, he glanced down the hall toward

what he could see was the kitchen. When no one emerged, and Ros didn't return, he closed it gently himself and stood in the gloomy hallway for a moment before concluding that the onus was obviously on him to go in search of whoever this Lou was.

He found her in the kitchen. Small and slight, with wide anxious eyes and lank bobbed hair, he understood her likely reticence in coming to greet him as she gripped the collars of a fluffy dressing gown tightly around her throat.

"I'm sorry," she began. "Ros – my housemate – never told me you were coming."

"No worries at all," said Joe, dismissing the apology kindly. "I'm Joe Davis." He thrust out his hand.

The woman regarded it with some dismay, clasping the gown, which was beltless, even tighter around her.

"Actually ..." Joe said, retracting the hand to scratch an imaginary itch on his cheek. "I have to get something from the van before I have a look around. Do you mind ...?"

He gave it ten minutes before he returned, holding his measuring tape aloft.

"Found it!" he announced with a smile, as he re-entered the kitchen where Lou was now standing at the sink, this time dressed in jeans, a baggy red jumper and a pair of sloppy Ugg boots, her hair pulled into a ponytail.

Her expression still couldn't be described as friendly, but she seemed a little calmer than at first.

"Do-over," he grinned. "I'm Joe Davis."

She took the proffered hand this time but didn't return the smile.

"Louise Lacey," she replied. "I'd better show you around then."

Abruptly, she charged past him and out into the hall.

9

The tour was brisk, no more than five minutes upstairs and down. His hostess barely spoke as she led the way, pointing into rooms for him to glance into, before charging on to the next. Joe followed quietly along.

It was a pretty standard house for the area, he observed. Two bedrooms and a bathroom upstairs, kitchen extension and living room downstairs, along with a third room – a dining room, he assumed – in between, but Louise simply strode past that door without opening it.

It wasn't just the sitting room that needed a little TLC either. The place was shabby all over, inhabited rather than lived-in, and badly in need of a dusting, a good tidy and some basic repairs – a couple of the kitchen-cupboard doors hung at an angle off their hinges, bathroom tiles were missing, tangles of wires rested on the floor beside piles of magazines in the living room, and one bedroom was carpeted with discarded socks, jeans and underwear. Catching sight of her flushed cheeks as he turned away from that doorway, it struck Joe that some of Louise's brusqueness might be down to embarrassment more than anything else. She clearly hadn't had a clue he was coming. No wonder she was annoyed.

"Cool," he remarked as they descended the stairs back to the hallway. "Looks straightforward enough. I'll get cracking then – Ros texted me a list of colours but I'll need to do some measuring before I nip out for the paint. You sure you're good to start with this today?"

The woman looked at him, her lip curling slightly. She sighed and thought for a moment before glancing over her shoulder to the dirty black streaks along the wall. She frowned, and then nodded.

"I suppose," she said. "I just wasn't expecting … sure.

Go ahead. Knock yourself out." With that, she turned abruptly and padded into the kitchen.

"Okay then!" Joe called, as the door slowly closed over behind her.

This was a small house, Joe concluded, but it was going to feel like a very long job. Very long indeed.

Chapter 2

Bloody Ros. Bloody stupid bossy, bloody Ros and her bloody nerve.

Louise sat at her desk, immobile with rage, and fumed. The absolute *cheek* – the entitlement, the damn brass *balls* on her. How dare she? Making decisions like that without even checking it was okay first. Who the hell did she think she was?

Steamrolled again. *Why* did she keep allowing stuff like this to happen? How hard would it have been to point out "*Sorry Ros, but it's up to me to deal with the house maintenance,*" or "*No thank you, Ros – when I need a painter, I'll organise one myself.*"

Louise buried her head in her hands. It wouldn't have been hard at all – what it would have been was pointless. As quick as a flash, Ros would have shot back with something cutting, demanding to know that if it was up to her, then why didn't Louise ever *do* any house maintenance or call a painter, or a plumber or a tiler or any tradesperson at all, in fact, because they had need of all of them. And, damn her, she'd have been right – but even if she wasn't she'd have argued back in that booming voice anyway, managing, as usual, to shut Louise down completely.

What was it about bloody Ros?

Louise was fully aware, and resigned to the fact, that she just wasn't an outgoing person. To be truthful, she sometimes thought that she could happily live without other people around at all – but she could still manage to get by day-to-day perfectly well with most of the human race. She could deal with clients, even the troublesome ones, although it gave her no pleasure, she handled disputes with the broadband company peacefully and even maintained an entente cordiale with her neighbours, Gerry and Pam, who would have lived in her pocket if she'd allowed them. But Ros – it was as if her housemate triggered some sort of immobilisation switch in Louise which rendered her barely able to construct a reply, never mind tackle her overbearing behaviour. Arguing with her left Louise feeling like a fish on a riverbank, and so, over time, Louise had learned to capitulate rather than confront. She just couldn't win.

Which led to situations like this – an uninvited tradesman plodding about her house on a Monday morning, singing to himself, while she sat, stuck in her office to avoid him, in the blackest of moods. All because of Ros.

She should have seen the red flags rise the day Ros came to view the place – that whole, long year ago. Louise had put it down to her simply being assertive and practical – the way she had sized up if there was enough space for her bike, pointed out the shelves in the living room which she would allocate to her games collection – especially the way she had dropped heavy hints that the larger of the two bedrooms would suit her better because of the rowing machine and exercise bike she planned to buy – thank heavens she had stood firm on that. But still, she had allowed her to move in – Ros was cash-ready, and, at that point, Louise was cash-desperate.

Sighing again, she flinched suddenly as a loud crash came from outside the door, followed by swearing. The damn painter. Someone else taking up her space and her time. During the day, when Ros was at work, was the only peace and quiet that she could get – and now this.

Louise clenched her fists and squeezed her eyes shut. It wasn't the painter's fault that she was so angry. And she'd been rude to him that morning – which wasn't like her – she'd nip out and get some nice biscuits or something in a bit to say sorry. No, he was just doing his job – not his fault that he'd caught her unawares in her dressing gown. That was bloody Ros again, of course. It was all *her* fault.

Except it wasn't, was it? There was only one person to blame for her current predicament. The fault was hers and hers alone. Sure, allowing Ros to move in in the first place had been a mistake – but it was way past that now. It was she who kept her there and she who continually failed to stand up to her. There *was* of course something that she could do – but she was just too gutless to do it. She could just tell her to move out.

She had to admit that on the plus side, the rent Ros paid – albeit well below market rate – was very handy indeed. And, at first, it had kept her alive when she'd suddenly found herself jobless and with bills to pay. That, at least, had been a plus.

The minuses, however – dear God, the minuses. The mess. Those morning smoothies which left the countertops strewn with kale leaves and slivers of avocado and dollops of fromage frais – the hairs that required clawing out of the plughole – the tangled balls of wires strewn everywhere from her game consoles. And *her* – the very Ros-ness of her – the overwhelming, uncompromising personality, the space she took up – physical and emotional.

Louise was exhausted by it all, and exhausted by the excuses she kept making to herself not to ask her to move out.

But there was no excuse for her excuses anymore. She didn't need the money, Ros's trips away with work weren't frequent or long enough to make it bearable, she couldn't 'wait and see' if things would settle down – she could no more make Ros change than she could turn down the sun ... no, no excuse was good enough, especially when it all boiled down to one true reason. She was just too scared.

She rolled her shoulders and stretched. Wouldn't it be wonderful to just be free? To be alone? To go to bed knowing that no one would wake her banging about the house in the morning, or by playing video games or talking on the phone half into the night while she tried to sleep? To have a clean and tidy house, filled with her things alone – to know that the only key opening and closing the door was hers.

Another clatter came from the hall, along with a fresh burst of tuneless song.

No. She was just going to have to do it. Finally, Ros had taken things too far – after all, who took the decision and paid money to redecorate someone *else's* house anyway? Someone who planned on never leaving, that's who. She blinked. That was unthinkable. How much further could Ros push her dominance? And how much more could she tolerate – no, how much more was she going to *allow* herself to tolerate?

She sat upright suddenly. That was it then. It was truly now or never – and never was unthinkable. She gulped and took a deep breath. She had to get it together – to finally grow the nerve.

Maybe this was finally the time she'd actually do it.

Chapter 3

London, September 1860

The first – his first – was Alice Digby.

It was a Monday evening when the photographer rang at the front door of the Digby household in Portman Square and was admitted, unaware that he stepped into a home where a pall of despair and desperation and futility had permeated everywhere, and everything that little Alice had touched in her short life.

In her nursery, each small item took on a new, bleak significance, sucked of joy, of their everydayness. They were all significant now, tainted – her spinning top, her rocking horse, her cup and ball, the new button boots that would never step outside. It was as if the very walls seeped desperation and distress now that Alice had died.

The dread calmness had descended that very morning, at that bleak hour just before dawn, when little Alice Digby stilled on the lace-trimmed pillow. She looked as if she should soon wake after a restful sleep and pad across the nursery to eat her egg and soldiers, her white-blonde curls tousled, her demeanour bright and full of the prospect of mischief. The servants wept openly, comforting each other in the passageways. They avoided the room where she lay, too devastated to see their beloved Poppet so still, so *wrong*, then cried with guilt for leaving her so alone. She still needed to be cared for, but who among them would do it?

It was Mrs Watson, the housekeeper, who took it upon herself to bathe and dress Alice, and lay her down among clean sheets, as if she were asleep.

And, choked by the sight of her pale beauty and flooded with memory and grief and the desperation to never forget it, it was Mr Digby who suggested gently to his wife that perhaps it was pertinent to consider a keepsake. He had of late, in fact, encountered another family who continued to draw immense comfort from that very thing long after they had committed their child to eternal rest. Might it be in order to have a photograph taken? Alice's image preserved forever?

Mrs Digby, torn asunder, agreed. She had already taken a precious lock of hair but would have agreed to anything, *anything* more that would keep Alice with her.

Samuel Temple came as quickly as he was summoned – the timing was fortuitous, he reflected as he made his way on foot from his studio in Wigmore Street. There had been no clients that day, nor any in the previous week and, stretching back a month, he could count only three. In fact, he had been puzzling over his accounts when the messenger had arrived with the briefest summons to come as soon as he possibly could. Eagerly, he had gathered the equipment he would need and set off. A client, at last. Just what he desperately needed.

On arrival, he was shown into a small drawing room which was entirely devoid of opulence. The households in this area were like that, Temple knew. Genteel, sometimes with even distant connection to royalty, but often of – albeit well-disguised – slender means. If, however, respectability and propriety were currency, they would be rich as Croesus.

He wasn't waiting long when the door to the room opened quietly and a woman dressed in black swept in.

"Mr Temple," she said. "Thank you for coming at such short notice. I am Mrs Watson, the housekeeper. Mrs Digby asked me to see you, as she is, understandably, indisposed."

"Quite," replied Temple, unsure why it would be understandable. "My pleasure, Mrs Watson. My studios are nearby so it was a short trip. How may I be of service to the Digby family today, summoned as I am at such haste? Has there been a happy announcement, perhaps?"

The woman frowned, quite taking Temple aback. She was an imposing figure, tall, deep-voiced and with that air of authority that a good housekeeper exudes.

"Quite the opposite, Mr Temple, I'm afraid," she replied. "A member of the family has sadly been taken to her eternal rest. Little Alice – a fever has taken her. That is why you were called to come urgently. Her parents wish for a portrait to be taken as soon as possible ... before ... while she is still ... *herself*, or as much herself as she can be."

Temple wilted under the woman's stare and went pale. "Are you saying a post-mortem portrait is required, Mrs Watson?"

The woman tilted her head a little to the side, fixing her stare even more forcefully on Temple. "Is that a problem?" she asked.

Flustered, he shook his head. "Absolutely not, Mrs Watson. Little Alice, you say?"

She nodded. "Almost three years old. Her parents are

grief-stricken, Mr Temple." She paused. "I believe such portraits are quite commonplace, am I not correct?"

"They are ... indeed ... many see them as a great comfort," he babbled.

"Indeed," replied the woman calmly and authoritatively. "We shall proceed, then, without delay. Let me show you to where Alice is."

With that, she turned and, without waiting, strode toward the door. Nervously, Temple stooped to pick up his camera box and followed.

By the time they reached the top of the stairs, he had composed himself and asked to be left alone in the room to carry out his business, with an authority that the housekeeper didn't question. With a nod, she opened the door to the room where he should go and stood to one side. "I will be here," she whispered. "Should you require anything."

Mr Temple, however, merely required solitude to calm his racing heart as he stepped into the dimness and prepared to accustom himself to the subject of the portrait which, he felt sure in advance, would be abhorrent. Many of his contemporaries had taken the opportunity to record such events, and did so as a matter of course, but this was to be his first. Such things were ... distasteful to him, and a little frightening, truth be told. To photograph the dead – and a child at that. But the money – he could not ignore it. He could look the grocer's messenger in the eye, and perhaps replace the boots that allowed the rain and filth of the streets to seep in through the worn soles. Times had been hard for Samuel Temple and his business.

Motivated by the prospect of at least temporary solvency, Mr Temple took a deep breath and lifted his head to confront his subject. Dread weighed heavy in his stomach, and nausea fluttered at his throat as he cast his eyes to the bed. Only to find himself touched, and – dare he say it – pleasantly surprised.

The sight wasn't repellent at all – in fact, to his photographer's eye, it was oddly beautiful. There was a serenity to it – and the stillness ... my God, but it was beauty frozen in time.

The child was pale as porcelain, and perfect – her features like those of a doll, devoid of suffering. He drew closer to where she lay for a better look, to take in the rosebud lips, the button nose, the closed eyelid, its lashes resting against the soft cushion of her cheek. All of it perfection – except for one thing – the smooth skin of the crater where the child's other eye should be, the eye she had been born without, the eye that was, no doubt, usually covered by the clean, white patch which lay on the bedside table, discarded now for there was no need to protect her from the gaze of others. The angel sleeps, he observed, as an idea grew within him. An idea for something very special indeed.

Inspired, he set to work.

Flowers, he decided, opening the door to quietly speak to the housekeeper who studied him sternly as he made his request. At first, he thought that she might refuse – that the moral rectitude of the household might render his request unacceptable. However, Mrs Watson merely nodded in reply and went downstairs. Within a short time, she returned, bringing what he wanted – as many as she could lay her hands on – gardenias and dahlias and carnations and Baby's Breath – little Angel Alice would be remembered for all time in a bower of blooms, as befitting her own beauty and purity.

And when they were arranged to his satisfaction, Temple studied them, thoughtfully, finally selecting a single white rose, which he tenderly placed in Alice's lifeless hand before settling her little body, like a doll, against the pillows. *Glorious,* he thought, as he cast a final eye over the tableau.

With a now-sure hand, he smoothed the counterpane at her feet and then stepped away from the bed where she lay, taking a final look before crossing to the windows and opening the curtains a little, not so much and for so long that it could be deemed disrespectful but just enough for what he needed to do. He turned to check the bed and gasped as a shaft of sunlight fell on Alice's face, illuminating her in what he knew could only be a heavenly glow. "*Don't move,*" he murmured – to the light, of course, not the child – and moved hastily across the room to assume his position. A final glance, a fortifying breath, and he crouched, bending behind the camera and pulling the black cloth over his head. This would be glorious, he knew.

Verging on perfection.

Perhaps the start of something new ...

Chapter 4

2018

Louise didn't usually feel excitement at having to leave the house for work, but when she woke on Tuesday morning to the ping of an early e-mail begging her for a 'dig-out', she replied instantly that yes, she could be in the recording booth at Armitage-Kelly Advertising at 9.30am to voice some scripts, then lay back on her pillow, stretched, and smiled.

She was up and showered before Ros roused, and out the door just as Joe pulled up outside. She greeted him with a wave and footed it down the road as quickly as she could. Ros could let him in today and he could have the whole house to himself while she was gone, to get on with his clattering and trudging about and the endless, tuneless singing.

It was a twenty-minute walk into town, and a dry, crisp winter's morning made every second of it enjoyable. She loved the city first thing – she'd forgotten how much – the smells of petrol and bus fumes, coffee, wafts of aftershave, the snatches of conversations. And through it all she moved as if in a bubble, unnoticed and anonymous.

Two hours later, she emerged from AKA feeling even better. The commercial was for both TV and radio, all stations, and with a UK version too. "*Ker-ching,*" the producer, Declan, had said with a grin as he ran through the script with her. It had required a few takes, but Louise was happy to do as many as he wanted, all the while mentally calculating her fee. It was big. Really nice. Time to treat herself to breakfast, she decided, as she stepped up out of the basement studio on Merrion Street into the bright winter morning.

She went first to the ATM around the corner and withdrew some cash, way more than she needed, but she was feeling quite flush, then chose a window seat in a café called Steamy Beanz and settled herself in a glass-warmed sunbeam, ordering a bacon sandwich and a coffee. A man in a suit tapped at a laptop nearby, devouring some toast, while two manicured women sipped herbal teas at a table beside a small fireplace over which the specials were written in coloured pen on a mirror.

At the counter, a man and a woman, in suits and coats, sporting lanyards bearing a company name she couldn't make out, stirred sugar into takeaway coffees and fitted lids to their disposable cups. A little way behind them in the queue stood a woman, equally well dressed and wearing an identical lanyard, studying her phone as she waited for her order. She didn't see the man nudge the first woman surreptitiously and make a face in her direction as they went out, to which his colleague responded by succumbing to silent, helpless giggles. Louise did, however, and a wave of unease rolled over her. The woman followed after a moment, her face still in her phone, but as she passed outside the window where Louise sat and watched, she glanced at the pair ahead, her expression anxious. She knew, Louise realised. She

knew damn well what they were at, those bloody bullies
– and it wasn't the first time they had done it either.

A sudden, intense flush of gratitude flooded through
Louise at the fact that, somehow, it had come to pass that
she was self-employed. She worked only for herself, and,
better still, *by* herself – a state of affairs that she had never
imagined would come to be, and which suited her so much
better than her previous working life. Ten years she had
done it – straight out of college and into the office – and
she'd have done it for another ten, she knew, and beyond,
and known no better, if she hadn't been laid off on that
dreadful afternoon almost two years previously. The exact
moment of it suddenly flashed back into her mind and she
was, for an instant, there again, feeling the disbelief, the
intensity of the rejection. Back then, it had been the
absolute worst thing that could have happened to her. Her
job – her wonderful job. What would she do? It was only
with the passage of time, in retrospective moments such as
this, however, that she saw her time in Emerald FM –
Dublin's All-Ireland Radio Station – whatever that had
actually meant – for what it was: ten stifling years of
pressure and stress that had built and bubbled and
expanded until she had been unwittingly on the verge of
blowing apart.

In many ways, being let go had been the best thing
that had ever happened to her. It hadn't felt like that at
first, of course. It had broken her completely, in so many
unexpected ways. She had nothing. No back-up plan, no
savings. Unable to afford her rent, she'd had to move out
of the apartment she shared in town with a flight
attendant who was hardly ever there – her perfect flatshare.
Back home to her parents she went, crushed. And it

wasn't that she had ever lived, and now lost, a wild social lifestyle – nor would her folks have prevented her from doing so under their roof – within reason – but at thirty-four years old, opening her eyes in the morning to the same Fatboy Slim and Robbie Williams posters that had greeted her the first morning of her Junior Cert certainly made her reflect on where she was in the world. And it was not a good place.

But how unexpectedly things had turned. How one minute, hopeless and helpless, she was hiding under her duvet in her childhood bedroom, losing herself slowly to a depression that turned the world dark, to the next, when she was forced to focus on something she had dreaded – being by her beloved nana's bedside as the old lady slipped away – to the next, where she was entirely unexpectedly the owner of property – a small house near the city centre. That was the point when the world suddenly became tinted again with colour, and hope, and opportunity.

"It's official in the will," the old lady – sharp until the very end – had told her. And it was. 17, Maryborough Gardens, was hers. She was laid off on a Friday, lost Nana six months afterwards and moved in a fortnight later, like a hermit crab, taking shelter in a shell that didn't belong to her. What a time. Thank God it was over.

And it *was* over, she reassured herself as she tucked into her food. All past. And at least some good had come from it all. Without that awful job at Emerald, she'd never have met Amy, the Production Manager, in whose studio she'd taken refuge from the Sales room so often. Amy, who had liked Louise's voice and asked her to record some ads, Amy who had taught her the basics of the production desk, and who, after Louise had been let go, had called round to the little house for coffee and admired the dark dining room, suggesting that it would make a cracking little recording studio with some rudimentary soundproofing, and wouldn't it be a great idea if Louise had a simple set-up with a computer and a mic and could voice and record ads for her at home and make a few quid in the process? Lovely Amy who had been the glow that started the thaw, who had believed in Louise, and encouraged her and helped her with all the technical stuff that she didn't understand, and taught her the basics of what was now her living. Louise glanced at her watch. It would be the early hours of tomorrow morning in Brisbane now and Amy would be asleep at home. Louise allowed herself a moment to miss her, and then silently thanked her friend for saving her.

And now – Louise Lacey, *Self-Employed Voiceover Artist and Audio Producer*, her Facebook profile read. She supposed that some people would call what she had done 'setting up her own business', but that didn't feel right to her. She had pictures in her head of what people who set up their own businesses looked like – an artisan chocolate-maker holding out a tray of rich treats, a wood turner, head bent, carefully hollowing out a smooth, rounded piece of oak. People who set up their own businesses had stalls at farmers' markets on Sunday mornings, they met with suppliers and distributors, they had loans and business advisors, projections and targets – they didn't sit at a computer, alone, in the former dining room of their shabby little house, reading special offers into a second-hand microphone.

But that's what she did. And she was good at it. At least once a day, she worried to herself that it might be time to get a proper job, something reliable, with a regular, consistent paycheck coming in. But then something like today would happen – a new client – she had *clients!* – and a hefty cheque and she'd suddenly realise that she had come a long way.

Louise set the sandwich down and rolled the crumbs between her forefinger and thumb as she thought. Yes. She really had come a long way, and, if she really put her mind to it – perhaps she could go further? Her current set-up was extremely basic – and a lot of the time she felt as though things were out of her control – a hangover from that hideous dark time of self-doubt. But she had to admit to herself that deep down, more often than not lately, she had felt a stirring of something – of a new confidence. She had been thinking of getting a business loan – investing in some more equipment – doing some advertising online – branching out to do copywriting, podcast production – perhaps growing this little business of hers.

She'd never had an intention to work for herself – not in a million years. What she did now had simply started as a stopgap to earn some extra money after ... well, after everything. She'd been sure that she didn't have the discipline and looked at those who did in the same way as she looked at surgeons, and marathon runners and reality-show contestants who were, to her mind, simply made of different stuff. But it had turned out she was perfect for this – and it was perfect for her. The solitude required posed no problem – she loved it – but she wasn't so misanthropic that she was off-putting to clients. She was merely an introvert – a characteristic that seemed to confuse and even frighten Ros.

That was something else she'd have to tackle, of course.

But it was time – beyond time – for Ros to go.

A slow smile crept over Louise's face as she gazed out the window, her eyes suddenly wide with possibility. She'd do it. She decided. All of it. Right away. She'd go and make a plan – an actual plan – and stop daydreaming and start doing. She drained her coffee and stood up, swinging her coat around her as she did and glancing again around the café. The same people sat in the same places, doing the same things as they had been doing when Louise had got there first. Everything was the same, she observed, except her. Beaming, she approached the till to pay, and allowed a whole new feeling to wash over her. A feeling of change. Change, of which she was entirely in control.

Chapter 5

The Cotswolds, October 1862

The second was Alistair White.

Twenty years old, and always a sickly child, when the priests of St Mary's College near Gloucester decided that there was no hope, permission was granted for Alistair to be sent home to die. Home to his parents to spend his final weeks in the bosom of his family. They would pray for him, they assured him. God was always with him, and soon he, Alistair, would be with God, to rejoice forever with the hosts of angels. Two of the household staff came to collect him – his father's manservant Mr Hodges, and the housekeeper Mrs Watson who, in her last position, had also nursed a dying child, experience for which Alistair's mother was truly grateful.

When he was twelve years old, Alistair was already almost six feet tall.

He towered over his playmates, who mocked him, calling him names like 'Long Bean' and 'Pillar'. By the time he was sent to the seminary – the only place he would be protected from the derision, his parents had decided – he was close to six feet nine inches, and always poorly. Thin, pale and breathless, he watched from afar as his fellow seminarians played boisterous, muddy games of football, and went on long, cross-country runs to keep their minds and bodies pure. Alastair could never have hoped to join in – his back ached constantly, and the feeling in his legs was often unreliable, but he carried on as best he could about his daily business, painfully aware that he was too long for every bed and chair, and that he could go nowhere where he wouldn't be seen. He dreaded the day he would be ordained and sent to a parish where his visibility would increase. The Giant Priest, they'd call him. Father Beanstalk. In his heart, Alistair longed for one of two things to happen to him – the first being that God would perform some sort of miracle and he would wake in the morning the size of a normal man, his feet in the bed with him instead of sticking out over the end, numb and blue with cold. The second simply that God would just take him. He'd known his whole life that death was coming, and he prayed long and often for forgiveness for wishing that it would just hurry up.

When the time came for him to go home, it was a relief in many ways. At least he could stretch full-length in the bed that his parents had commissioned especially, and he no longer had to wear the stifling, hard fabric of his cassock. He could also be alone, and silent, with his bible and his beads to keep him company.

And, of course, the ministrations of Mrs Watson who clucked and fussed about him, favouring his care over all of her other duties. Her comforting ways were a relief in those last days when he lay threading his brown wooden rosary through his long, elegant white fingers, his soft, dry lips moving wordlessly in prayer. She plumped his pillows, tempted him to eat – she even went so far as to rub soothing balm into his skin, and give him her secret tincture in his bedside water – "My special poison," she joked as she administered a few drops and then helped him to drink it all without spilling a drop.

It was she who closed his eyes for the final time, and also she who, afterwards, wrote urgently to summon a man she knew who would be sympathetic and trustworthy in carrying out the task which the White family desired.

Time was of the essence, she insisted in the note, and she hoped that he would be able to find enough to undertake this extremely personal and special task in his busy schedule. Samuel Temple, at the sight of her neat and ordered hand, had felt his heart give an unaccustomed skip, and rearranged his diary without delay.

What a woman Mrs Watson was, he thought to himself as he settled in his seat, watching the grime of London recede and give way to glorious English countryside – he had missed her in the six months since she had departed. She had, after all, a hand in the turning of his fortunes. Her endorsement of his extraordinary portrait of little Alice Digby had rippled through the serving community of the city, and soon his reputation as a sympathetic and creative portrait artist of the recently deceased had spread far and wide, bringing more business. His work with the dead was soon so highly regarded that commissions of the living followed soon thereafter.

He and Mrs Watson had become friends and had regularly taken tea together at his home on her days off, discussing between them all sorts. He had never encountered a woman like her, he mused, as the train rattled on through fields and over bridges. She was quite wonderful, really. Always listening, always encouraging – proud almost.

There was some quality to her that enabled him to open himself up, to speak as frankly as he had ever done to another soul in his life. It had been quite the blow when she had informed him that she was to depart for Gloucestershire to take on a new post. She had been widowed but three years, she explained, and longed for a change of scenery away from the grime and the memories that she encountered on every London street. A fresh start, she had told him, but she had promised to keep in touch – particularly if she might encounter something that he would find of interest. That was something else entirely surprising and delightful about her. That she understood what he liked to call his *special* interest. Not everyone – not anyone, come to think of it – would appreciate his particular tastes. But Mrs Watson did, and never questioned them. What a woman, indeed.

The photographer had set to work the moment he had arrived at the house where the body of Alistair White lay, ably assisted by the housekeeper who had proudly shown it to him, laid out on the impressively long bed. The undertaker had been told his services would not be required until after the official portrait had been taken.

"Look at his *height*, Mrs Watson," Temple enthused. "I've never seen anything quite like it – magnificent!"

"I thought it might please you, Mr Temple," she replied. "Something different. Like you talked about in our tête-à-têtes."

"Such a beautiful thing, really," Temple observed. "Skin so smooth and powder-pale, those cheekbones – that extraordinary chin. And so peaceful – a vision of piety. I'm so glad you called me."

"To think that you once were squeamish about such

33

things," remarked Mrs Watson with a smirk, picking a piece of lint from Alistair's arm. "Who would have thought you could become such an expert with the recently deceased, so very comfortable in their presence?"

Temple shrugged the thought away and bent closer to peer at Alistair's hands, the fingers waxen and drained of colour and artfully interlinked, the fingernails spotless.

"There is beauty, too, in death, Mrs Watson," he said.

"Oh, I agree wholeheartedly," she replied, with conviction. "More than I could have imagined myself, you have made me realise, sir. How goes business with you these days?"

Temple turned briefly and beamed. "Quite marvellous, Mrs Watson," he replied, careful to check his tone, not wishing to sound inappropriately joyful on such an occasion. "My appointment book is quite overflowing – although it was a pleasure to rearrange a day or two for you." He turned back to the body and resumed slowly travelling the length of it, hunched close to observe every minute detail.

"How wonderful!" replied Mrs Watson. "To see you prosper gives me great joy, Mr Temple. And what excitement it must be to still live in the city. I shall have to contemplate a return some day."

"Do, indeed," replied Temple, distracted.

"I do miss our little exchanges," continued Mrs Watson. "Especially your fascinating thoughts on the art of the post-mortem portrait, and your interest in ... the *unusual* ... in society."

Temple nodded, his focus on the young man's ears. "Quite," he said.

Mrs Watson paused and, in turn, watched Temple for a few moments, her eyebrows raised.

"The Whites know that you've had to travel such a long way at short notice and have gladly agreed to cover the costs," she said eventually. "They know also that you are the best in your field, Mr Temple – I have assured them of that, and that such excellence comes at a price – so you will be rewarded well for this trip."

Temple glanced up over Alistair White's crown and saw that Mrs Watson was watching him. "Yes," he said. "I'm very grateful indeed." He returned his attention to the body.

Mrs Temple smoothed her skirts and continued. "So, if you'll pardon my directness, you won't forget that there is a matter of my commission to be paid, will you? The Finder's Fee, as it were, which I suggested? Our little arrangement for this particular job of work?"

"And well deserved it is, every shilling. Mrs Watson, are there any roses to be had in the garden?"

The housekeeper watched him for a moment, while he was transfixed by the deceased's nose. "I shall see to it right away," she replied before gathering her skirts and leaving the room quietly.

Temple barely noticed she was gone, so absorbed was he in continuing his examination, making a series of admiring noises at everything he saw there.

Momentarily enraptured, the housekeeper temporarily forgotten, he retraced his now familiar steps on such an occasion. On silent feet, he crossed to the window and opened the shutters very slightly. There was no glorious sunbeam this time – such a pity the day was overcast and gloomy, although it did create a certain atmosphere – but a shaft of low daylight fell across the bed, nonetheless – cradling the body of the unnaturally long man, chalk-white and stiff, brown wooden beads laced through his waxen fingers. It seemed sombre and fitting. And it would do very nicely indeed.

Taking a deep breath, Temple walked reverently toward his camera.

Chapter 6

2018

Louise's heart felt lighter as she stepped out of the café onto Baggot Street. The fresh cold, raw with a hint of snow to come, shocked her momentarily and she wrapped her scarf tightly around her nose and fished in her handbag for her sunglasses. Had she just experienced an epiphany, she wondered? She suddenly felt more purpose – verging on optimism, *excitement* even, dare she say it? – that she'd felt in as long as she could remember. She'd ask Ros to move out tonight, give her a few days to get her stuff together – there was no formal rental agreement in place between them so she could be gone very soon. She felt herself almost float with anticipation as she set off briskly in the direction of home.

As she walked, she fished in her pocket for her phone. Time to check her emails, see what was on the agenda for her once she got back to her desk.

It was nothing, however. Louise swiped down on her screen again to double-check – **Updated Just Now,** it reiterated. Louise paused for a moment. Her gut reaction to 'nothing' was usually to worry that nothing would ever come her way ever again, but, for a change, a small smile spread across her lips. She had just done a really nice job and made some pretty big decisions into the bargain. She was her own boss – if there was no pressing work to be done, then what was the rush to get home? It was such a gorgeously sunny day – why go home to the painter – awkward encounters in the kitchen, him accidentally rattling the doorknob of the bathroom when she was trying to pee – the infernal singing? She slipped her hands into her gloves and turned in the opposite direction. She wasn't going home then. Not yet. Instead, she was going to stroll through the city and simply see what she could see. Window-shop, saunter through the park, idle in a bookshop – all those wonderful, solitary, soul-refreshing things. *Then* she was going home, and she was quietly and efficiently going to evict her unwanted housemate and get her space back, and her peace, and put her plans into action.

As she walked, Louise's brain raced ahead with constructive, positive thoughts for a change. Ros could be moved out by the weekend, hopefully. Louise wasn't sure where she'd go – frankly, she didn't actually care, if she was completely honest with herself. She thought about her little house, her precious little refuge – back to herself again. Her poor, neglected little house. It was because of Ros, she realised – or at least her attitude to Ros – that it was in the state it was in. She was ashamed to admit to herself that she simply hadn't done anything cosmetic to it for fear of causing disruption of any sort and also – this was worse – she simply hadn't wanted it to be *nice* – hadn't felt that she deserved it to be while Ros was there. But she'd change that now. After the painting was done, she'd see what she could do to dicky it up a little. She'd have tons more space everywhere too – wardrobes, drawers, shelves – she could do a proper tidy-up, and then maybe nice curtains or blinds? And she could pick up some pretty things – cushions and candle-holders – all the things that Ros would break or rip or spill things on because she didn't care about them, denouncing them as "girly" or "unnecessary" or "stupid". And then Louise would fix all of those things that needed fixing – the flush handle on the toilet, for instance, the door of the saucepan cupboard ...

She walked in the direction of the Liffey, peering into windows as she passed, her head whirring with plans. There was the issue of the painter to be solved, of course – Ros certainly wouldn't be paying for him now. She *could* save a few quid and paint it herself, she supposed. Her lip curled at the thought. She *wanted* to be one of those people who could shrug when people complimented their beautiful home, using phrases like 'just a lick of paint' and 'did it in no time'. She even liked the idea of herself in paint-spattered dungarees, a scarf tied around her hair, and a streak of emulsion across her cheek. But she'd have to get all the gear – ladders and sheets, not to mention the bloody paint – and then put masking tape everywhere on the woodwork – and – *ugh*, gloss the bloody woodwork. Before she'd reached College Green, she knew for certain that she wouldn't be taking that task on any time soon. Especially not when there was a painter currently on site. No. She hated having him around, but a professional could finish the job – she'd work it into the improvements budget.

She crossed the road at Dame Street, and meandered on, down through Temple Bar, feeling uncharacteristically light-hearted, strangely high, almost, smiling at passersby and even saying the odd 'hello'. She stopped to study windows and menus, popped in and out of shops that just took her fancy – revelled in the feel of the bracing air, and the smells that manifested around her – coffee, baking, spices, leather, oils. It felt somehow important to be doing this. It felt like a significant day – a sort of Independence Day.

She crossed the Liffey at the Ha'penny Bridge, contentedly carrying on with her browsing and window-shopping. She'd pay a visit to that little deli down the side street, she decided – the one with the fresh mozzarella and the pesto ... my God, the pesto! Her mouth watered at the thought of it as she turned to take a shortcut, then froze momentarily. It would, of course, mean passing the old Emerald FM office – something she'd assiduously avoided since she'd been let go. Today, however, somehow, she felt okay about it. She'd ride the wave she was on, she grinned – confronting fears here, banishing demons there. What did she have to worry about anyway? The radio station had moved to the Docklands a year previously after it had been taken over by a big media group, so there was no chance of bumping into any reminders from her past.

A move had been long overdue, she mused, as she resumed her route. By the time she left, Emerald FM was still crammed into its original studios and offices – where it had started life as a pirate station in the 1980's – over a fishing-tackle shop in a Georgian house on Quaker Lane, which had itself closed during the recession. She cast her eyes down the street ahead of her, in search of the familiar, now-deserted building.

Except it wasn't deserted. She approached the entrance

curiously, taking in what she saw – the front steps scrubbed clean – the railings outside gleaming with a fresh coat of gilt paint, the front window filled with a display of knick-knacks and curios, and a new sign – black with gold lettering: *Temple Antiques*. So – Emerald's old home had a new tenant. Impulsively, she climbed the steps and entered.

The smell was the first thing to greet her – it wasn't strictly musty, but there was a distinct aroma of age – of other people's homes and histories. It looked completely different from how she'd remembered it. The walls were papered in a dusky blue, and beneath Louise's feet was an Axminster rug – faded now, but rich once with reds and blues. Soft lighting glowed throughout, from lamps of all sorts placed on shelves and occasional tables, atop cabinets, standing alone. The quiet was punctuated by soft ticking from clocks hung around the walls. She glanced from one to the other – at pendulums swinging, second hands ticking their way around – at cuckoo clocks, Georgian and Victorian style clocks, Art Deco pieces – a large grandfather clock which stood against the wall.

On her right, a glass case displayed silver jugs and cups, a porcelain figurine, a crystal bon-bon dish, a doll with a cracked face under her lace bonnet. Chests spilled over with faded books and long strings of costume pearls. A dressmaker's mannequin stood inside the window wearing a hat with a voluminous purple ostrich feather and stabbed through with a long emerald-topped pin.

Louise scanned the room trying to take it all in – a washstand with a pristine bowl and jug, with a chamber pot underneath, beside stacks of old vinyl records, locked wooden cases with rings nestled in velvet, silver photo frames, candlesticks, an abacus – a polished, wooden

41

rocking horse with a red saddle. Toby jugs watched from a shelf on the wall, and from beams across the ceiling hung birdcages on long chains, copper pots, a bouzouki and a saxophone.

The faint crackle of music rang low in the background. She followed the sound to a portable record player, on which the Glenn Miller Orchestra played softly. The warm smell of the revolving vinyl filled her nostrils, prompting her to crouch down to casually flick through a box of LP's – more for the pleasant sensation of pulling them toward her one by one, and reading the titles, than with the intention of buying anything – Ros owned the turntable at home, and had forbidden anyone to touch it but her. It would soon be gone, in fact, if all went to plan, come to think of it.

Louise's thoughts turned to the space that would be free in the living room once Ros had left – and she suddenly stood as an idea hit her and her eyes swept the glorious clutter of the room with intent. Here – right here, maybe there was a thing, *something* that stood out, that perhaps she might use to fill one of those spaces? Something significant, that was hers, and hers alone? Something to mark the day – the decisions she had made ...

It was the glint of sunlight on brass from the camera that caught her eye – the briefest flash – *look at me!* She went to it, where it stood inside the window, reaching out to lightly touch the extension of the reddish-brown leather bellows before suddenly withdrawing her hand and glancing around. Was she allowed to touch it? There was no one in sight to admonish her, so she reached back and gently slid a finger through one of the folds, taking a light layer of dust away on her finger, which she rubbed against the tip of her thumb. She reached then and stroked the wood around the lens, tracing around the brass and down to the tripod underneath, her heart leaping as it gave a little wobble and she thought for an instant it might fall.

It was beautifully imperfect, scratched here and there from use but still somehow proud. Somehow, it looked *alive* to Louise, as though it was watching out the window, waiting for an opportunity – for something, or someone interesting to happen by. Watching the passing of the days along narrow, quiet Quaker Lane – every sunrise and sunset, the comings and goings of the little street. She imagined it performing the same task at her living-room window, peering out at the street outside – observing the changing seasons, her neighbours, the trees around the green, cats, dogs – the occasional fox. It would look perfect, she thought, visualising her living room cleared of the clutter, the camera standing there majestically.

She stared, imagining it keeping watch for her, elegant and steadfast, imagining it being in her possession – but more than that, imagining what it could represent – a life, lived on her own terms, in her own, reclaimed space.

A blur of movement out of the corner of her eye made her turn. A man stood at the record player, gently lifting the needle and turning the disc.

"Excuse me!" she called.

He concentrated on replacing the needle, until the faint background music rose up into the air again, before he turned to her.

"Can you tell me how much this is?" she asked, pointing at the camera.

He came and stood beside her, crossing one arm across his chest, twisting a strand of what was a pretty impressive auburn beard, complete with handlebar moustache, with the thumb and forefinger of the other.

He was a lot younger up close than he initially appeared, Louise noticed, taking in an overly sculpted hairstyle and slim frame under a houndstooth jacket and fashionable skinny trousers.

"*Umm* ..." he began, leaning his head to the side, and studying the camera very intently – a bit too intently, in fact.

Louise suddenly realised that while he might look the part of seasoned antique dealer, he was very much winging it, more style than substance.

"So sorry. I found this piece in the storeroom just this morning, actually. Let me check?" he said, suddenly disappearing.

She heard the tapping of computer keys somewhere behind, before he reappeared.

"*Umm* ... I think it's two seven five?"

Louise looked at him. His expression was uncertain – she imagined the glance that he threw in her direction was hopeful that she would just thank him and move on to the next thing. Which is usually what she would have done. Today, however, she stunned herself.

"I'll give you two-twenty for it," she said. She felt her cheeks flush, and a prickling sensation in her head.

This wasn't at all like her. Her voice even sounded distant, as if it belonged to someone else. To her amazement, the man in the shop looked as if she had slapped him.

"I ... *uh* ... I'm not sure ..."

"Does the tripod come with it? Because I'll give you two-thirty if you throw it in too." She wasn't entirely sure what she was doing – she had never bargained, negotiated or haggled on a price in her entire life. But somehow, his lack of knowledge, his discomfort, was *driving her on.*

His face was purple with discomfort in the spaces that weren't obscured by facial hair. "*Emm* ..." he composed himself slightly. "I'm not sure I could let it go for less than two hundred and sixty, to be honest ..."

"Two-fifty." Louise swallowed, her heart pounding and her resolve wilting slightly. What if he just said no? What if he asked her to leave? Or worse, called his boss, who would order her out of the shop, and then what? She'd never be able to come in again – not that that should matter seeing as she'd probably never come in again anyway – but the *shame.* The experience would stay with her, she'd relive it every time she walked near the shop – near Quaker Lane, in fact.

"Okay."

What?

"*Emm* ... just let me – I'll need to fold it, and get it packed up for you."

She stood back as he gently picked up the camera with both hands and disappeared toward the rear of the shop with it, before returning for the tripod, giving her an embarrassed smile as he did so. She watched, her heart thumping in her chest. She wasn't sure what had just got into her, but it had worked – at least she thought it had. She had no idea if she had struck a fair deal in the slightest. Had she just been fleeced? Or had she somehow fleeced *him?* Did the damn thing still work? Did it matter a jot if it didn't? Or had she struck a deal that would make her a fortune in the future if the *Antiques Roadshow* ever rolled into town? She was clueless – but

elated – well, she would be, if she made it out of the shop
with her purchase – if no one emerged from the back and
told her to hold on, that she should, in fact, have paid
two grand for it – in which instance, she probably would,
just to avoid the embarrassment of giving it back.

A cough for her attention came from the rear of the
shop.

"Sorry," she said, and approached it.

The man was standing at the same counter that had
served the fishing-tackle shop, she remembered, in front
of a pair of black doors, one of which led through a
beaded curtain into a small office and toilet that served
the shop, the other through to the stairs and up to the
offices and studios – or had done in her day, at least. On
the table was a large, wooden box with a carry handle.
She eyed it nervously. It looked extremely heavy.

"So, two-fifty," he reminded her.

It took moments for her to hand it over from the extra
cash she'd impulsively withdrawn earlier, then she fled,
carrying her purchase awkwardly, to make her way as hastily
as she could back out toward the quays and flag a taxi.

She almost – *almost* – regretted the purchase, as she
sank into the back seat.

What had she done? There were impulse buys – she
understood that – understood the momentary high, and
the comfort and pleasure to be drawn from them – and
then there was this. She'd just spent two hundred and
fifty euro of her hard-earned, self-employed cash, on
something that she knew nothing about and would never
use – why hadn't she just gone to Penneys and bought
some new pyjamas if she needed a little treat so badly? A
muffin, or a pain au chocolat – the damn mozzarella and

pesto that she'd set out for in the first place and which she'd totally forgotten? She glanced down at the box which she held safe with one arm on the seat beside her, expecting to feel regret, or guilt. She was surprised, and relieved, however, to feel that she didn't. She was thrilled by this thing – this bizarre gift to herself. Even in the box it was beautiful, she thought. She giggled quietly, still on an out-of-character high. She had been *right* to buy it. Damn the expense – it might be an investment and, even if it wasn't, it represented something. It would stand in *her* space, because *she* chose it, and because *she* wanted it, and because it had been *her* decision and bought with *her* money. There was a change in her today, a huge change – and this would serve as a reminder of that. She smiled and stroked the wood of the camera box as she might a pet or a child, advising the driver to take a right turn, heading toward home.

Chapter 7

Joe was just opening the back doors of his van outside No. 17 when he heard the taxi pull up behind him. From the corner of his eye, he saw Louise trudge past him into the house, lugging something heavy and awkward, just as it drove off again. She was clearly in a hurry, and didn't acknowledge him, which didn't surprise him in the slightest. She wasn't what he'd call rude, but she certainly wasn't the warmest homeowner he'd worked for in his time.

She was nowhere to be seen by the time he re-entered the house. Presumably back in that little private room – the one he'd yet to see inside because she kept the door constantly closed. He wasn't sure if he should take that personally – as an implication that she didn't trust him. It worked for him, though. It meant he could just quietly get on with the job, undistracted by unsolicited cups of tea and cake and chats about the weather and the state of other places he'd worked in.

His view obscured by the bundle of dustsheets he carried, Joe almost tripped on the large wooden box which was dumped right in the middle of the hall floor. He spotted it at the last minute, under the vast ball of paint-spattered fabric in his arms, and veered to avoid it, raising his eyebrows at the near-miss. With some effort, he pushed it out of the way with his foot and had just laid the sheets on the ground when he heard the toilet flush and then the bathroom door open.

Louise bounded down the stairs with an energy that surprised him. Even more surprising, she stopped halfway down and smiled. "Hi Joe, all good in the 'hood?"

He hesitated before answering, wondering if he were imagining the exchange, or being confronted by a friendly, identical twin of the woman whose house he was painting. She even looked different, her hair shining and styled, her make-up done, and she wore a knitted black dress and funky biker boots.

"All – all good," he replied. He felt suddenly suspicious. Was she setting him up for something? Like firing him on the spot, or accusing him of damage to something? He racked his brain – he had knocked over a lamp in the last house he'd done, and accidentally sat on a cat hidden under a cushion in another, but no – he had harmed nothing here.

"I was just in town there for a bit – gorgeous day. Did you get yourself a tea or a coffee while I was out? There's a packet of Toffypops in the tin too – I should have told you to help yourself ..." Her face fell suddenly as she looked past Joe toward the wall. "What the hell is *that*?"

He followed her gaze. "Oh those," he said. "Tester pots. Ros liked a particular shade from the colour chart but I ... wasn't ... I didn't ... I hope you ...."

"They look like *poo*," Louise blurted flatly.

Joe recoiled in shock before a surprised guffaw burst from him. "Well ..." he began, searching for a more diplomatic phrase. "Yes," he managed.

Louise snorted in disbelief and began to giggle, shaking her head.

"This one's *Decaying Leaves*," he said, introducing the smears on the wall one by one with a grin. "*Mouldy Bread, Toddler Snots* and *Autumn Slug*."

Louise giggled again. She leaned over the bannister for a better view and rolled her eyes. "Ros is colour blind," she said. "She would have had no idea what those colours are."

"That explains it," replied Joe, smiling.

"It looks like a dirty protest," replied Louise, as she took another couple of steps, still gazing at the patches of colour on the wall.

"She got the living room okay," offered Joe.

"Even a stopped clock gets it right twice a day." Louise grinned back. "It's only certain colours she can't distinguish. I can't believe I didn't think to check what she'd picked – I totally didn't add two and two together and think that letting her loose with a colour chart was *not* a good idea – not that I'd win in an argument with her anyway."

The painter smiled. "I'll make sure to go through the rest with you – I think there's some doozies in there. I can show you a few options before committing."

"She's the one needs committing," mumbled Louise. "Sorry. Look, I was going to talk to you about this later but, as I have you, Ros is going to be moving out but I do want you to finish the job – can you let me know the price that you agreed? And I guess – yes – any sort of colour stuff that needs to go down from now on, you can check with me first – is that okay?"

"Are *you* colour blind?" Joe replied, straight-faced.

Louise laughed out loud again. Joe was taken aback

for a moment at how much her smile changed her face. Normally it was small and pinched, as if she were in pain, but when she laughed it opened and transformed completely, illuminating her eyes and making them dance. "Nope," she replied. "I can tell my ... *Spring Sludge* from my *Butcher's Block*."

"That's actually a real colour," Joe said, and she curled up her small nose in disbelief. "It is, I swear, look!"

"It *isn't*," she said, chuckling, as she began to descend the final few steps.

He pulled a folded colour chart from the top pocket of his overalls. "Cross my heart!" he said as he glanced at the chart in search of the colour, then back at her, his face suddenly dropping. "*Stop! Careful!*" he yelled as he saw what she was about to do, but his warning was too late.

Her own expression changed from mirth to panic as she reached the bottom step, missed it, and tripped right over the box she had carried in, the box he had slid out of his way to prevent himself from doing the very same thing.

The fall happened, as all falls do, in slow motion. Her expression was helpless and terrified as she lurched over, unable to stop herself, her foot twisting as she went. Joe reached out to try to catch her, but it was too late. She screamed as she landed, smacking heavily down, cheek first.

"Jesus Christ, stay there!" Joe ordered her. "Are you okay, can you hear me?"

Louise bit her lip and groaned as she lay where she was, her head against the hard floor. Her right foot was still caught around the case at a painful angle and she seemed stunned.

Joe knelt beside her. "Don't move – did you hit your head?"

51

Louise made an attempt to nod, then to shake her head. "My foot ..." she managed, before a whine escaped her.

"Okay, okay." Joe's voice was reassuring, although his breathing was fast. He turned his attention to her foot, and gently touched it in an effort to free it.

"*No!*" she screamed as he made the lightest contact.

He pulled his hands back, as if burned, and looked at her in concern. "I think you might have broken it. We're going to have to get you to hospital."

Chapter 8

Louise's eyes flickered open and she grimaced.

Her body had stiffened overnight, and her ankle ... dear God, but it felt like it had expanded to twice its normal size. She'd never felt anything like this before.

Just a bad sprain, the doctor had said it was. Not the worst he had seen, but enough to put her out of action for a few days. He'd mentioned something to do with RICE which she recalled involved compression and elevation and ice and, presumably, rest. She raised a hand and gingerly touched her cheek which throbbed where she had smacked it off the floor. At least she didn't have a broken nose on top of it all, as Joe had pointed out. He had been so helpful – wrapping ice in a tea towel, helping her out to the car and taking her to A&E. And he'd stayed with her the whole time, cracking jokes and fetching coffee and chocolate – then he had popped into the pharmacy for her painkillers on the way home and made her tea and toast when they got there to boot. She really owed him.

She rolled herself into a sitting position and glanced at the clock. It was 8.30am – to think that only twenty-four hours before she'd been striding confidently into town, brimming with purpose and enthusiasm. What a good start to the day it had been. Everything had felt so *easy*, so *enjoyable*. It was the first time in an age that she had felt normal – better than normal, in fact. And now – here she was with a gammy leg, a face the colour of plums and a foggy head. So much for setting to with her grand plans as soon as she got home. She hadn't even seen Ros, never mind given her marching orders. She'd pull herself together and do that later.

As if on cue, the boom of her housemate's voice suddenly rose up from outside, greeting someone as a vehicle pulled up. Joe, Louise assumed, puzzled, as a muffled exchange took place, then a car door slammed and drove off. Maybe Ros had sent Joe away or something? Taken a notion to give her peace and quiet? Surely she hadn't stayed home to 'mind' her? *Please, no!*

Louise's ankle gave a sudden, savage throb. She needed painkillers.

Cautiously, she pulled on a pair of leggings and a hoodie and made her way down the stairs using the crutch the hospital had given her. Coffee, she decided. Coffee and then painkillers. She'd be able to think straight then. She groaned at a painful twinge as she hopped into the kitchen and over to the countertop.

Ravenous, she toasted thick bread in Ros's four-slice toaster – at last, a use for one of her many gadgets – and washed it down with a huge cup of coffee. Thankfully, she had the kitchen to herself while she ate. There was no sign of Ros, and Joe's voice could be heard from inside the sitting room crooning along to something on his headphones. She guessed it might be Radiohead, but she couldn't be sure. For a change, however, it didn't bother

her. The sound of him working away was quite comforting, actually. Or maybe that was just the pills kicking in.

Louise's laptop sat, closed on the kitchen table. Sliding it toward her, she opened it to scan her emails, and then flicked on to Facebook, to check in with the outside world, her brain entering a state of numbness as she scrolled down through her newsfeed. Here and there she 'liked' the occasional post – Katie, her friend in Cork, had posted a large gin and tonic the night before, held in her perfectly manicured hands, captioned '**Who said anything about Dry January?**'. Aaron, who worked at Spaced Advertising, had contributed a shot of a glorious pink-and-orange sunrise taken over Dublin Bay from the DART that morning.

Impulsively, Louise glanced down at her ankle, and pulled her phone from her dressing-gown pocket, sliding the camera setting to active. She snapped the injured limb three or four times, before selecting the best and posting it, checking in with the comment '**Housebound**'. Within seconds, she had a list of sympathetic responses – sad face emojis, 'wow' reactions and 'feel better soon' comments. She engaged with a couple of them, explaining to her cousin Marie that she had tripped on the stairs, but it would be fine in a few weeks and to Ken from Vocal Voiceovers that no, she wouldn't be holding out much hope this transfer season.

Louise smiled guiltily. She used Facebook a lot to check in with others, but rarely posted herself. There was something vaguely self-indulgent about it, she felt, but she still did it from time to time. She refreshed her feed and was taken aback by the first new post that popped up. A check-in from Ros at Dublin airport. '**Silicon Valley** here I come! See you next Tuesday, suckahs!' she'd posted, accompanied by a series of emojis – the Stars and Stripes, a plane, a hotel, the Statue of Liberty and a series of dollar banknotes that ran across two lines of the post, followed by the 'crying laughing' emoji repeated six times over. So that's where she was – off on one of her trips to California with work – the ones that had even made having her as a housemate seem tolerable for a while. Louise frowned. She'd be gone for a week. *Dammit.* She'd really wanted to get the ball rolling on getting her out and now it would have to wait. She scrolled past the post without 'liking' it, and clicked through a news site – there had been yet another school shooting the States, the Gardaí were renewing their appeal for the public's help in finding a missing teenager, and a rural politician had made an unpopular suggestion that the legal age to drink should be lowered to fourteen. She snapped the lid of the laptop shut and took a large swig from her cup, only to immediately splutter it back in. The coffee was cold. So was the entire house, come to think of it – it was turning into a bright day outside, but the temperature must still be below freezing. She shivered and leaned back on her chair as far as she could in an attempt to reach the 'boost' switch for the heating from where she sat.

"Morning!"

Louise's heart leaped, and she turned, her chair crashing back down onto four legs and jolting her ankle. "*Jesus!*" she shrieked, as much at the fresh burst of pain as the fright.

"Oh my God, I'm so sorry!" Joe looked horrified as he hurriedly approached her. "I thought you knew I was there – here, let me do that for you!"

56

Louise stayed still, waiting for the pain to subside, as he reached behind her and pressed the heating on. They listened, nervously, as the ancient boiler made a worrying series of clicks and groans before going completely silent for a moment, then kicking in. At the same time, both Joe and Louise slumped with relief.

"I can take a look at that boiler for you, if you like?" he offered, turning to face her. "Try and prevent that threatened heart attack every time you switch it on. Especially when it's this cold." He exhaled a puff of mist to demonstrate just how cold it was.

Louise raised her eyebrows. "*Wow!*" she said. "It must be really freezing outside – what, minus one or two?"

Joe shook his head. "That's the thing – it's a balmy five Celsius outside – at least that's what it said in the van on the way over this morning – it's just in here it's like the polar ice cap. Have you got insulation?"

Louise frowned again and nodded. "This place might be falling apart on the inside," she said. "But it was my nana's and the one thing she couldn't bear was being cold – she had the external walls insulated about five years before she died, and the attic is lined – she had an unhealthy obsession with double-glazing and she couldn't pass a hardware without checking for draught excluders – I'm not exactly sure how it's so cold."

Joe shrugged and rubbed his hands together. "Maybe some of the rads need bleeding or there's a window open or something. Mind if I make myself a cuppa?"

"Of course not."

Joe beamed gratefully and headed straight for the kettle. "Would you like a hot cup yourself? Have you eaten anything actually? How's the foot today?"

"Large and painful. I've had a bit of toast to keep the painkillers down."

"I could throw together some scrambled eggs for you if you wanted? Would you eat some if I made them?"

Louise was taken aback and considered the offer. "I actually would," she replied. "Do you mind?"

"Say no more. Ready in five!" Joe cut her off with a sweep of his hand, and turned to the fridge, taking out three eggs before heading back to the worktop and setting to.

Louise felt herself relax a little as she watched him. She'd normally never ask anyone to do anything like this for her, but, despite her breakfast, she was still starving.

"Ros got off okay earlier," Joe remarked as he poured the eggs into the hot saucepan. A sizzle rose into the air from it, and subsided, just as two golden slices of toast ejected themselves from the toaster. The smell was delicious.

Louise grunted in response. "Was that her taking a cab earlier?" she asked.

Joe cast a glance over his shoulder at her. "It was. She was leaving just as I arrived – she gave me a loan of her key while she's away and while you're incapacitated, as she put it." He laughed. Louise didn't.

"That's okay, isn't it?" he asked.

"Of course. Sorry. I didn't know she was going, that's all. Look – thanks a million for all this – there's no need."

"No worries," Joe replied. "I'll run through those colour charts later with you, if you like? I'm going to start on the hall in a bit and leave you in a bit of peace in the front room. I can go back and gloss the woodwork there when you're back on your feet – remember now, the doc said to keep it elevated as much as possible and the front room's the best place to do it. In the meantime,

I'm just going to nip out after my tea for a bit – I need to pick up a couple of rawl plugs and some putty, if that's okay with you?"

Louise smiled as she watched him leave, carrying his cup of tea in Ros's *Archbishop of Banterbury* mug, and was struck by his thoughtfulness. There was no need for him to vacate the sitting room, of course – she'd be getting back to work straight away – it wasn't like she was sick, or anything – but how considerate of him, making her breakfast, taking her to the doctor, bleeding the radiators. She really wasn't used to it, especially not from a stranger. She finished the eggs in contented silence and sat back in her chair. A long yawn crept up on her and she rubbed her eyes, suddenly sleepy. That would be a combination of the food and the drugs kicking in. Maybe she'd take Joe's advice after all and just have a little rest on the couch. The front room would be warm, too – the sun in the mornings made it really pleasant, not that she spent much time in there when she could be at her desk. Still, today was an exception – she was *incapacitated* after all. Slowly, she pushed her chair back and gripped the crutch, hearing the front door slam shut as she exited the kitchen and made slow progress along the freezing-cold hallway into the front room.

She settled herself on her armchair, lifting her leg onto the coffee table and settling herself as comfortably as possible under a tartan rug that she used as a throw. She lay her head back, suddenly feeling utterly exhausted. She'd just close her eyes and bask in it for a moment, she decided. Then back to her desk – she had plans to make, things to be getting on with ...

Within minutes, she was in a deep, painkiller-induced sleep.

Chapter 9

London, 1864

On reflection, Mr Temple was well aware that he had tipped the driver of the hansom cab a little excessively.

It was the excitement, you see. The bubbling well of anticipation as he rolled through the streets of London, his photographic equipment held secure on his knee, and the prospect of Mrs Watson's smile at the end of his journey. Or Mrs Fields as she was now known.

"It is the privilege of my years, Mr Temple," she had informed him over tea in his study shortly after her return from Gloucestershire, during one of their assignations, "that change can be made freely and often, or not at all, depending on my own desires. I am a lady who follows those desires, and will make changes as they suit my fancies, my requirements or, indeed, my prospects. Goodbye to Gloucestershire, says Mrs Watson, and, lo, to London goes Mrs Fields!"

Sometimes he didn't fully understand the marvel of her mind, but she was a woman of firm conviction, and he dared not question it.

It was not to one of their ordinary assignations that he travelled now, however. His trek across the capital was made in response to a *special* summons. For business, not pleasure – business that differed somewhat from his usual subjects. And what a special one it was, indeed. That parents of a deceased child required a memento was not, in itself, worthy of note. But that the child was ... *different* ... from others, and that the parents lived at an exclusive address was good fortune indeed. She had not informed him exactly what form this difference would take, which heightened his anticipation. He trusted, however, that it would be greatly to his satisfaction.

The best fortune, of course, was having the acquaintance – the *friendship* – of such a splendid woman as Mrs Watson – Fields – of course. To benefit from her caring, professional nature and her vast knowledge of the human race, from the highest to the very lowest was a gift. That they shared similar sensibilities, and a broader outlook on life and fortune was a blessing, however. How rare a flower the lady was! They had so much in common ... what possibilities on both professional and personal levels ... well, a man could dream.

A wreath of yew, tied with black ribbons on the front door, clearly identified the Talbot residence. Mr Temple stood across the street for a moment, having disembarked, and composed himself before crossing over and closing his hand around the bell pull. There was a time when he would have been nervous at the prospect of being admitted to such a place lest they spot his threadbare jacket or his leaky shoes. Not anymore, however. He was a man of considerable substance nowadays, his business considered the finest, the most suitable and, indeed, prestigious in the field. His sympathy and artistry were simply unparalleled. Samuel Temple, they said of him, was a man who truly cared.

He was admitted by a footman dressed in black and instructed to wait in the hallway where he stood, absorbing the absolute silence of a house in mourning, to which he was now accustomed. After a time, his peace was disturbed by the brisk rustle of silk.

He turned, smiling, at the familiar scent of lemon and bergamot.

"Mr Temple," she said, her voice barely more than a whisper, "good day to you. It is very good of you to come."

"Always my pleasure, Mrs Watson," he replied, giving his customary comical bow. When he stood, he expected her usual smile, and the deep, ironic curtsey she always performed.

Her face, however, was stone. She gritted her teeth and glanced around her as she hissed at him. "*You mistake me for someone else, Mr Temple!* My name is Mrs *Fields*. I am the housekeeper here. I do not know anyone by that other name."

Temple recoiled. "My deepest apologies, madam," he spluttered, glancing about. "A slip of the tongue, I assure you. A previous client who ... suddenly came to mind at an inopportune moment."

Mrs Fields cleared her throat and nodded her head in acknowledgement. Mr Temple felt his cheeks colour as a glint of steel in the housekeeper's eye served to warn that he should be very careful not to err again.

"The mistress, Mrs Talbot, asked me personally to show you upstairs," she continued, as if nothing unusual had passed between them. "She and Mr Talbot are busy preparing for their portrait."

Temple raised an eyebrow. "The parents of the deceased wish to be photographed also?"

With a nod, Mrs Fields indicated that he should follow her as she began to ascend the marble staircase. "The Talbot family is ... was ... very *close*," she said. "Mr and Mrs Talbot have a very specific interpretation of the memory they wish to keep."

Puzzled, Temple fell into step behind her. "They must be devastated," he observed. "You never mentioned in your correspondence ... was it sudden?"

"Terribly," came the sardonic reply, as Mrs Fields stopped suddenly and turned to address him. "One day George was quite his usual self. Gallivanting about, always seeking out fun and games and companionship. And then ..." She snapped her fingers, her expression cold and hard. "Just like that he was gone. There was no rhyme or reason to it – it was almost as if he ate or drank something ..." Her voice trailed away as she continued to fix Mr Temple with her stare.

"What did the doctor say?" he asked.

Mrs Fields shook her head. "No doctors, Mr Temple. "*'Theirs not to reason why'* – is that not what Lord Tennyson said? The parents are distraught at the loss of their son. What good would it do, I asked them, to have yet another doctor poking and examining and asking more questions? George was the recipient of more medical attention than most throughout his life, you understand. It was a consolation to his mother to forego yet more in this dark hour. It will not, after all, bring him back."

"Quite, Mrs Fields," replied Temple who found himself momentarily discomfited by the tone and expression of his friend. "The family are lucky that you are such a profound part of their lives."

"Indeed," she sniffed, observing him coolly and

authoritatively for another moment, before turning and proceeding up the stairs.

Temple followed faithfully behind.

"They will miss poor Baby terribly," she said as they proceeded along the landing,

He stopped suddenly. "Mrs Fields ... an infant?"

The housekeeper raised an eyebrow as she turned to face him. "Come now, Mr Temple," she whispered. "It is hardly rare for one in your profession to have to – sadly, albeit – capture the memory of an infant? Surely you've seen one before?"

Aghast, he stared at her. She was correct, of course. Much of his work involved the photography of babes in arms, but it was the one thing he had never been able to fully come to terms with. He could not photograph an infant up to the age of one year old without feeling deep discomfort and upset. This she knew from their talks.

And then he frowned, baffled and horrified as he observed the faintest hint of a smile form on her lips.

"Have courage, Mr Temple," she smirked. "All is not as it seems." With a sweep of her arm, she indicated the door through which he should enter. "Meet Baby for yourself."

Reluctantly, Temple twisted the knob and pushed the door open gently. Mrs Fields nodded in encouragement, her finger placed to her lips, as he glanced at her, his eyes filled with trepidation. Slowly, he opened the door further, employing his tactic of gazing first at the floor, and slowly raising his eyes to take in the room piece by piece in order not to be shocked or frightened when finally encountering his subject.

To his relief, there was, in fact, no body to be seen – it wasn't even a bedroom, in fact, but a closet of some sort, on which children's clothes hung on racks, and shoes were lined neatly side by side in pairs. Temple frowned as he looked at them more closely.

Velvet suits, sailor suits and hats – even little fancy dresses such as boys wore before they were breeched. A little boy's wardrobe, then.

"This is Baby's dressing room," she said, her tone mocking.

She led him to an inner door.

"And this," she announced quietly, "is the main event."

With that, she swung open the inner door, smiling as she hummed a snatch of a jaunty circus air. Temple regarded her with a mix of horror and curiosity. What was the woman doing? He had never seen such disrespect before.

Such a black sense of humour, Mrs Fields had. Yet another thing that many would not understand.

"Oh, Mrs Fields!"

Temple could barely speak as he took in the sight before him. The dressing room had led through to a bedroom. A four-poster bed, empty, formed the centrepiece and was surrounded by a dressing table, a washstand, a chair, a writing desk and the other furnishings that might be required by a gentleman. Except it was different from any other bedroom that he had visited in the past – and he had been admitted to many – in that every piece of furniture was child-sized. A short, low bed, a miniature jug and basin.

Temple was baffled. "What is this, Mrs Fields?" he asked. "Why is everything so small? And where is the infant that I am to photograph?"

Still she maintained her enigmatic smile as, with an elegant swoop, she stepped aside only to reveal behind her, positioned with its back to the window, a miniature armchair which contained, slumped to one side, the body of a man, the head large, the limbs short, his appearance showing that he was fully grown in years but his stature that of a child of no more than, say, four years old.

Temple gasped.

"Do you like it?" Mrs Fields asked.

Temple found the question jarring but was too taken aback to address it.

"Twenty-eight years old at his next birthday, with the mind and intellect and sensibilities of a normal man, but only three feet tall. Say hello to George Osborne III – or 'Baby', if you will. They say his great-grandmother was a Cornish pisky and his father is so embarrassed by him that he's only allowed outside in a carriage, disguised as a small child for the past twenty years. Our very own Tom Thumb!" Her tone verged on gleeful.

Temple placed his camera box on the floor and crouched before the figure which was slumped to one side of the chair and resting against a cushion as if simply napping.

"His clothes!" he gasped, reaching out to finger the lace-trimmed gown – like that which would be worn by a very young child. "Why did they dress him so?"

Mrs Fields bent to retrieve a matching ruffled bonnet from the floor which she placed on the arm of the chair.

"His mama's wishes," she replied. "His papa's embarrassment is outweighed only by her immense grief. It is a delicate thing, but she has spent her life convinced that George – her only living child – never grew because he was destined always to be her baby – to somehow make up for others she had lost – hence the affectionate term by which the household knows him."

"But he is a man!" gasped Temple.

"Very much so," replied Mrs Fields, sweeping across the room to the small dresser and reaching underneath it to press something which triggered the opening of a panel on the side.

She stood back to reveal to Temple the contents – a number of miniature men's suits on small hangers and two pairs of boots such as any adult would wear but in child's sizes. Tucked away behind them was a half-filled decanter of golden liquid which Temple took to be brandy or whisky.

"As his trusted companion, it was my responsibility to keep this stocked for him," she said. "And it was also my duty to ensure that he was able to slip out unnoticed once his mother had retired for the evening, suitably attired. Quite the co-conspirators we were. I understand that he was a prolific gambler and a regular client of certain discreet houses of ill-repute. Our little Tom Thumb over there was on a road to ruin, Mr Temple, I have no doubt, whether it would be the alcohol, Venus's Curse, or an angry debtor. Baby by name, he was, but far from it by nature."

Temple exhaled. "Goodness!"

"Not one of his virtues," said Mrs Fields with a smile. "Another irony of the situation is that while he lived in this magnificent house, with the lavish furniture and servants galore, he was entirely penniless – his parents refused to give him an income of his own – thought that his small body meant that he had a small mind and would never know what to do with money. And, after all, did they not cater for every one of his needs? His mother at least – all that concerned his father was that he remained invisible in society – I'd swear the man would have drowned him in a sack at birth if he'd been let. If our Baby had been born into squalor, however, he could have probably clawed himself upward and earned a small fortune working for the likes of your friend Mr Crick."

Temple shook his head. "No, no, Crick is no friend of mine," he stated, lowering his voice to a whisper. "Ignominious wretch!"

Mrs Fields emitted a tinkling laugh. "Oh-ho, Mr Temple! And what exactly is it that Mr Crick did to you since last we spoke on the subject?"

Temple wore an expression of deep offence as he replied. "Accused me of terrible things, Mrs Wa – *Fields*. Had the audacity to show me the door of his grim establishment, said I was trying to benefit from the misfortune of others ..."

"And would not allow you to photograph the Dragon Man with his tattoos from head to toe, am I correct?"

Temple coloured. "I had offered Mr Crick a once-in-a-lifetime commemorative portrait of his star attraction, so cruelly taken from this life by that assailant in darkest Whitechapel. Crick –" flushed with outrage, he sought the correct words, "*shooed* me out of his ... *human zoo* like a street urchin who had ducked in without paying. Horrid man. As if I sought to exploit the freaks more than he already did."

Mrs Fields regarded him with curled lip, suppressing more laughter. "Goodness me. *As if!*" she said sarcastically.

"Regardless, the experience taught me a lesson," continued Temple, oblivious to her mocking tone. "People of his nature do not deserve the opportunity for their deceased to be honoured with portraiture of the calibre which I provide. And, on further ponderance, what, indeed, remains remarkable about such exhibits when they have been seen already by most of London for a few bob in half a dozen sideshows better and worse than Mr Crick's *Spectacle of Curiosity?* Such a grandiose title for what is little more than an outhouse full of the deformed and demented ... oh, my goodness, I beg your pardon!" He flushed again, his eyes catching sight of the purpose of his visit.

"Between you and me, Mr Temple," said Mrs Fields, her voice dropping to a stage whisper as she glanced, smirking, from the photographer to his intended subject and back again, "I think he cannot hear you."

Struck with dread, the joke sailed over Temple and he bowed his head toward the little body.

"It is *this* which is extraordinary," he whispered, pointing to George Osborne. "Wonders such as this – a grown man, kept forever as a baby by his mother, hidden in plain sight by his father and living a secret life of his own – which I have come to realise, thanks to my unpleasant encounter with Crick, is what I wish to commemorate. Ordinary people, *broken* and different, unacceptable to polite society – the too tall, the too small –"

"*The fat, the thin, their eyes turned in!*" interrupted Mrs Fields in a sing-song tone. "I could listen to you orate on the matter all day, Mr Temple. However, there is the small matter of a photograph to be taken – and I am sure that by now even the mother of this boy, as grief-stricken as she is, is wondering just what exactly we are doing up here in preparation. Erecting a tent, perhaps, or taming some lions ..."

Temple regarded her with a quizzical expression. "Quite," he managed. "Let me tarry no longer, then, madam." Chastened, he bent to unbox his camera and set it up, all the while wondering if Mrs Fields wasn't being quite as darkly playful as he liked to believe, but instead a little cruel. She gave him no time to ponder, however, and instead swept to stand behind the chair where George's body rested and pulled herself to her full height.

"Mrs Osborne requires the set-up just so," she explained briskly and authoritatively, her tone that of a business-like stranger, replacing the confidante who had engaged in such disturbing conversation only moments before. "Mr Osborne is to stand here, while Mrs Osborne will be seated, the body of her son held in her arms, like a babe at rest. You can manage that, Mr Temple, can't you?"

He nodded meekly, overcome as always with an awe of the dominance she exuded. Such an enigma, that woman, he reflected. Catlike. Toying with the mouse one moment, dispatching it the next with a single blow of its paw. Metaphorically, of course. She was of the gentler sex, after all.

"Why, of course, Mrs Fields. That should be no problem. I will set up accordingly."

"Very good, Mr Temple. I will go and inform the Osbornes that you will be ready for them soon. And perhaps, when you are done, you will pay me visit downstairs in order that we can complete our agreed arrangement?"

"Very good," replied Temple. "The fee for this remains as per the previous occasions, am I correct?"

"Quite," she replied with a nod of her head. "I will leave you to get on with it, then."

He nodded in return and was about to bid her good day, but she was gone, the only sound the retreating click of her heels outside the bedroom door.

"Extraordinary woman," Temple said suddenly, addressing the lifeless body before him.

Chapter 10

2018

It didn't feel right letting himself in. Joe glanced over his shoulder around Maryborough Gardens in the early-morning darkness to see if anyone was watching and if he looked dodgy, then checked himself and stopped, conscious that doing so made him look even dodgier. All he needed was a well-meaning neighbour to get the wrong impression.

There was a knack to it, but he finally got the key to work and pushed the door open, calling gently from the top step to alert Louise to his presence. He wanted neither to alarm her by suddenly appearing, nor to wake her if she were resting. She had been completely knocked out in an armchair the previous day – even when he had left. He had debated whether or not it might make him look creepy but had left her some tea and toast on the coffee table. It seemed like a responsible sort of thing to do.

The house was entirely in blackness, the only sign of life the rattling of radiators as the heating cranked to life. He stopped and listened. There was no sound – Louise was in bed, he guessed. She was such an odd cookie, he reflected, as he flicked on the hall light and then returned to the van to bring in what he needed. Sullen and reserved one minute, absolutely furious the next – although that Ros probably certainly had something to do with that. *She* was a piece of work. And then Louise would be friendly and funny – with that smile – the way it transformed her whole face like that ... Joe pushed the thought to the back of his mind.

He set to work quietly, listening to music on his headphones as he scrubbed the woodwork clean. This could be a cracking little place with a bit of care, he reflected. Near to town, a lovely area with everything you could need. He hummed quietly to himself, scrubbing and swabbing his way along the skirting, pausing to stand for a moment and shake out the pins and needles in his feet. It struck him as he did how cold the place felt as a sudden prickle of goosebumps broke out across the top of his back and upper arms. He shivered and made a '*whooo*' noise as he rubbed his hands together to warm them. It was even cold enough to see his breath manifest in a cloud before his face again. He recommenced scrubbing vigorously, to try to warm himself as much as anything but it didn't work – a chill gripped him down along his spine and up through the soles of his boots. It seemed even to get colder as he moved down the hall.

Joe stopped what he was doing. This house was cold, no doubt about it – but this – it really didn't feel right. He decided to investigate and headed toward the kitchen but stopped as he spotted something along the way. The door to the little room along the hall was slightly open – unusually – and icy air blasted from the room. "*Ah-ha!*" Joe muttered to himself as he made to enter, but he paused on the threshold. That door was never open – and he had never been invited in or shown around. It was clearly private. He was freezing, however – and it wouldn't take long before the entire house was too, which he was sure Louise wouldn't be happy about when she awoke. What should he do, he wondered, one foot on the saddle board, ready to enter.

He marvelled at just how concentrated the air coming from the room was – and that it wasn't just cold either, but almost damp, like a fog. It was the sort of cold that settled in your bones, slowing your body down, pervading every inch. So unnaturally cold, in fact, that he wondered if it might be air conditioning or a fan? At the thought, he made the decision to enter, and went to reach inside the gap between the door and the frame, into the darkness of the unfamiliar room, when a dark shape in his peripheral vision made him jump. He gasped as he looked up with a fright that subsided instantly as he saw a slow-moving Louise turning on the landing and commencing a laboured descent of the stairs with the help of her crutch.

She smiled as she glanced at him and then returned her focus to the steps. Joe pulled his headphones from his ears.

"You need a hand?" he asked.

"Just heading out for a jog," she replied drily, and he grinned in return.

"You're getting the hang of that," he remarked, nodding at the crutch.

"Just about. Need my drugs though, man. I'm strung out."

Joe grinned. "Are you feeling any better today?"

She nodded. "I am, actually. Almost twenty-four hours sleep can do that to a girl. I could eat a horse though – just going to see what's in the fridge and then consume the lot."

"I hope you don't mind, but I actually brought you something – I just picked it up on the way – it's nothing much, just a sausage roll ..."

"Oh, thank you," she said gratefully.

"Like – a baguette with sausages in it – not one of the pastry ones," he continued.

Louise's eyes lit up. "You're kidding me?" she said.

Joe shook his head. "No. And I got one of those apple Danishes too – the ones with the icing on top."

Louise rolled her eyes in excited disbelief.

"I didn't know which you might like. There's a ham and cheese crown too – but they're all probably cold by now ..."

Louise couldn't contain herself. "You're a bloody genius, Joe – thank you *so* much!" she exclaimed, turning awkwardly as she reached the bottom step.

"And a cappuccino – but that's cold too ..."

She beamed at him. "I can heat it in the microwave. You have no idea how grateful I am."

And there was that smile again. Joe looked away, feeling his cheeks colour.

"Speaking of cold, however," he said, indicating the studio, "I think there's a window open in there – I wasn't sure if I could go in or not."

"Of course you can go in," she replied reassuringly. "There's no window though – what made you think there was?"

"Air conditioning then?"

She shook her head. "No. Why do you ask?"

"Oh, because there's this ... hang on ..." He raised his palm to the open doorway again. "That's weird."

"What?" Louise limped alongside him.

74

"Well, there was this cold air coming out of there – I felt it when I was working – like, a really *really* cold blast ... but it's not there now ..." His entire face wrinkled in puzzlement as he felt the air around him. "Or have I just got used to it – can you feel the cold?"

Louise shrugged. "No more than usual – you're sure it was coming from my studio? That's actually the warmest room in the house." She leaned against the doorframe.

Joe shook his head, defeated. "I could have sworn ... anyway, you really *are* strung out, aren't you?"

She grinned through the pain and leaned on her crutch heavily, starting to make her way past him. "I absolutely am," she replied. "Gotta get those drugs." Her crutch thunked along the hallway as she laboured toward the kitchen, everything else forgotten.

Joe reheated her cappuccino and made himself a cup of instant as she ate the food he had brought with him. He was sure he could actually see strength returning to her as she devoured it unselfconsciously, and he placed a fresh glass of water in front of her when it was gone in order for her to take her painkillers.

She gulped it down. "New woman," she sighed appreciatively.

"Feeling better now – here, I'll wash those," he said.

She nodded. "Thank you so much – and for that tea and toast last night and breakfast yesterday too – I was a bit short with you then, I'm sorry."

"That's okay," he replied. "You've had a stressful few days."

Louise snorted and pushed herself upright. "And then some. Now. I think I need to sit down for a bit after all that."

75

Joe followed her as she hobbled out to the hallway, stopping again at the door to her office and putting her hand to the open door.

"Do you mind if I just take a look inside there?" he asked.

Louise nodded and pushed it open.

She went in ahead of him, exclaiming as she struck something with her crutch. "Bloody *hell!*" she yelped and she fumbled to turn on the light.

He peered in behind her.

"This stupid thing again!" she said angrily, tapping the crutch against something solid.

Joe glanced down to see the famous wooden box that had caused her downfall, sitting directly in front of the doorway, ready to be tripped over again. He used his foot again to slide the box into the space between a small couch and the wall beside the door, out of the way.

"That thing sure is heavy," he remarked.

Louise nodded. "It is. I'm actually not sure why I bought it. It's an old camera thing I found in an antique shop. Thanks a million for moving it." Her tone verged on apologetic. "I know it's not in the job description. Neither is making me meals, mind, and bringing me to A&E – I really appreciate it."

He turned to her, smiling. "Seriously, it's not a problem, none of it! What is it you do in here again?"

"Voice-overs," she replied. "Commercials, e-learning, video narration, a little bit of audio production."

"Interesting." He looked approvingly around the small room. "This is normally a little dining room in this type of house."

"Yes – it was my grandmother's dining room actually,

until they extended the kitchen across the back of the house and popped the dining table in there. My grandparents hadn't used it for years. It was perfect for a studio."

"Why does it have to be so dark?"

"Oh – it doesn't," she replied. "It has to be soundproof – well, at least as soundproof as I can make it. The rugs on the floor and the carpet on the walls? They're to muffle sound to prevent echo – that one there ..." she pointed to the wall behind her desk, "blocks the serving hatch through to the kitchen which was originally a window looking out into the back garden and normally where you'd get your light from but there's no natural light in here anymore. The carpets and rugs and whatnot also keep things toasty warm, which is why I'm confused that you thought it was cold in here."

He nodded and ran his hand over the panel of cream carpet on the wall. He looked from there to the matching panels on the other walls, and the thick, red rug on the wooden floor.

"It's really nothing too advanced," Louise explained. "I have a very simple system – just a Mac, mic and mixer, really. I'm going to invest in some new equipment though."

"It's all double-dutch to me," he grinned. "Handy little set-up though. Do you like working from home? Must get a bit lonely at times?"

"No," she answered without hesitation. "Not lonely at all. I much prefer it this way. No one in your face all day, wrecking your buzz, wanting to talk, picking rows ... I much prefer things this way. Being my own boss. Like you, of course, you're your own boss too."

He shrugged. "Sort of. This is really my dad's business but he had a stroke a while back and I stepped in just to keep things running while he's recovering. I like meeting new people, though. Seeing how other people live, learning about their lives. Everyone's got a story to tell."

"Or a comment to pass. Or a criticism to make ..." Louise shook her head. "Not you, of course. Just ... I just prefer to keep myself to myself. It's a lot easier that way. Anyway – I'd better let you get on with it. Thanks for moving the camera box for me."

With that, she turned, and hobbled out of the room and out along the hall into the sitting room.

Joe watched her go, then turned back to examine the studio room again, frowning. She was right – it was far from cold in there.

Carefully, he studied the walls – there were no gaps anywhere, no vents, no breezes coming from the skirting, the serving hatch or behind the couch and desk. It was well insulated – positively cosy.

So how on earth had he felt a bitter breeze blowing through the door and out into the hallway beyond. How was that possible?

Perplexed, he took a final glance around before flicking the light off. Must have been a draught from somewhere else maybe? These old houses, no matter how well insulated you thought they were, every winter revealed a surprise.

Shivering despite himself, he left the room, making sure to close the door firmly behind him.

Chapter 11

London 1865

It was at times like these – when her patience was stretched tight as the string of a violin – that the erstwhile Bridget O'Dowd wondered if this was why people prayed.

Behind her – for she couldn't face the girl without wanting to slap her silly – her charge licked and slurped and sucked her way through the vast dish of trifle. Bridget tried not to picture her but couldn't help it – the sight of that long, cow-like tongue encircling the serving spoon – an ordinary spoon was not big enough to shovel sufficient amounts of sweets and cake into that great, gaping maw – was burned into her brain and she pictured it now as she failed to block the accompanying noises, the moist suction as the jelly was inhaled, the slurp of the custard. The spoon scraped insistently against the bottom of the dish, ensuring nothing remained – the signal that the trifle, an entire bowl, was almost gone.

Bridget braced herself for the bread and butter pudding which would be devoured next.

Yes, prayer. That's what the people did in trying times. That's what Kitty would do if she were here in her place. She'd sit here, patiently darning this enormous stocking, muttering the 'Memorare'. As if that had ever done her any good.

Bridget felt her mind drift away from the revolting sounds behind her and toward the uncomfortable, familiar shore that was thoughts of her mother. A sharp prick of the darning needle into the purlicue of her right hand pulled her back to the here and now and she cleared her throat and settled again in her seat.

"Everything alright, Adeline?" she called over her shoulder.

The response – she assumed in the affirmative – was thick with nutmeg-laced cream and chunks of moist day-old bread. Bridget's stomach lurched as she visualised it involuntarily and she gagged, despite her best efforts to restrain herself. Adeline. Such a beautiful name. But the creature who bore it was *vile*.

At least the dwarf – when she could bring herself to look at his oversized head and his short limbs – had amused her almost as much as he had disgusted her by playing at being a man. Of all of them, the giant had been her favourite. He had simply got on with the business of dying, cleanly and quietly. But this one – this great hulking jollocks, this fat simpleton – needing to be fed more often than a fire – she was foul indeed. It was surely a test of will for Bridget to endure her – maybe her mother had been right and there was a God after all, and this was her punishment for misdeeds past.

Bridget turned, her lip curling as she took in the sight before her. Adeline sat in her habitual way at feeding time, her legs opened wide to enable her to get her enormous upper half as close to the food as possible. That it might take less time to reach her mouth, Bridget imagined. And what a mouth that was – the thin upper lip, the determined jaw – like a cavern in the bottom of her face which needed constantly to be filled. Adeline's focus had to be admired, Bridget admitted, as she watched her devour the bowl. It was as if she existed in a world of her own – forgetting everything else but that which she could eat. Forgetting Bridget, the latest in a line of constant companions, recommended to Adeline's parents along a chain that began with none other than Mrs Osborne who had no use for her now that Baby had departed this life.

"A wonderful woman is Mrs Fields," Adeline's mother had been assured. "Kind and patient beyond belief ... an angel on earth ... discreet and loyal ... in possession of infinite patience ..."

Of that, Bridget was no longer sure.

She wondered if Adeline understood that her behaviour was at best impolite and socially unacceptable – at worst, abnormal. She was simple, of that there was no mistake – it was impossible to understand her when she spoke – as if the capacious mouth had been designed to remain slack to allow food in, but distort any words that might come out – although, when the chief utterance from it was simply the command "*More*", it presented less of a problem than one might have thought. Yet she had a skill for jigsaw puzzles and would assemble them with great speed and dexterity between meals. In short spurts, in other words. Her parents had insisted that she be fed if she wished it, fearing that to stop her consumption of food would somehow cause her to starve and die abruptly.

Did Adeline know that she was a woman, for instance? Eighteen years of age. The daughter of wealthy parents, of inherited money – at her age she should have had no end of suitors for whom she would dress in an array of pretty gowns. She should be presented at court even. Bridget snorted and turned back to her task. Inconceivable. Even if her whole body had not disappeared under the layers and folds of fat, even if her thighs were not so enormous that they had to be rolled and lifted and hefted apart to sponge between them, even if her pendulous breasts did not require cleaning out at least once a day to divest them of the great quantities of scraps that had fallen between them, she would not be considered a match, must less a catch for *any* man. Her repellent face with that downturned mouth and the bulge at the bridge of her nose, her oddly dainty hands, and skin that bruised if she so much as leaned against the arm of her chair. No. Adeline would forever require a patient, constant nursemaid. She would never be a wife, never bear a child.

It struck Bridget suddenly that, as a childless widow, there was a possibility that they had that in common. She blanched at the thought as it dragged her mind to her own circumstances.

Would she forever be in this state, she wondered with a sigh, and her hands dropped to her lap as she studied a spot on the wall. Childless, unmarried, in servitude. True, being a companion of sorts was better than being a housekeeper, and being a housekeeper was far better than being a housemaid and being a housemaid was better than being a scullion which, in itself, was infinitely better than being a barefoot, lice-infested, starving daughter of an immigrant Irish prostitute – but still, when would it be her time to finally step onto the path where she longed to walk – where she *strived* to walk?

When would she possibly ever be her own woman?

She chewed her lip as she remembered, ruefully, how she'd tasted it for the briefest time with Watson, damn and blast him! And damn and blast herself for falling for his patter, the skilamalink. He'd played her like an old fiddle, alright. Set her up just the way she wanted – what luck – pulled from the gutter to the little house, the promise of a family, the steady income – and all of it lies. To think her hand had trembled as it poured those drops from the little bottle she got from the apothecary into his tea of an evening. To think she had wondered if she would burn in eternal damnation, consoled only by the thought that there was a while before that would happen – when he was gone – and he deserved to be gone – that she'd at least have it all to herself – Watson's worldly goods – only to find that all had been lost on the poker table, and back out on the streets she'd have to go. That's when scrubbing flags and carrying slops became her preference, although she tended to omit that part of the tale in polite conversation. It sounded far smoother to simply jump from when she was ... *widowed* ... to her first post as a housekeeper – a necessary measure for one alone in the world if they did not wish to fall foul of the trap of poverty, you understand.

She had told the tale so often by now that she quite believed it herself, relating it along every step of the ladder upwards, and now she was tired of climbing, always climbing, yet getting no higher. Each household, each charge, a step closer to the top. Then on she would go – a new woman again, sometimes a new name just to be safer than sorry, sometimes a new part of the country – what a long journey it had been. She was quite exhausted.

And still, she was not there. She glanced around the room where she spent her hours confined with the enormous, insatiable girl-child and made a face. True, it stank of riches – although it stank of Adeline, mainly, her sweat and flatulence – but wealth seeped from every inch of wall, every fold of fabric. But that was not what Bridget wanted. Such fortune would be an unattainable goal for her.

Instead, she craved something more basic, something which had been denied her from her very earliest days. Solidity. Stability. Respectability. Things that she thought she might never experience in a past of which she had never uttered a word.

Bridget O'Dowd had never described to anyone, for example, how she had been unable to close her father's eyes when he died because he lay out of her reach, dead in a frozen Irish field eighteen years previously, when she had been ten years old – his body fiercely guarded by a bone-thin mongrel who first bared his teeth at Bridget before turning to gnaw at the corpse. Nor, when asked if she had family living nearby, did she ever mention her five dead – starved – siblings, the youngest a boy of eighteen months, nor the grandmother they had been forced to abandon to the workhouse, nor the uncle who had stolen their passage money to America whom she cursed in the darkness at night, praying – against her beliefs – that he had died in horror on a coffin ship. That her mother and herself had escaped what they called The Great Hunger and made it safely to London was a miracle in itself, but not one on which she cared to dwell, or even remember if at all possible. The image of Kitty O'Dowd's ancient, hollow, terrorised face, even though she had been not much older than Bridget was now, flashed before Bridget's eyes and she shook it away. Not now, she told herself. Not ever.

She wondered for the briefest of moments what had become of her mother when she had left, if she survived or if she died of a disease contracted from her filthy tricks, or if one of them beat her to death, or if she starved – despite the fact that she now lived in a land of plenty – or was found destitute in an alley or a sewer.

Bridget stood briskly, to physically shake away the image and the accompanying thoughts. It never did to think of these things too long.

"*'ore!*"

The 'm' of 'more' was never pronounced, the wide, limp mouth instead emitting a round, hollow sound.

"Not now, Adeline," Bridget retorted sharply. "You've had quite enough. There's a good girl."

"*'ore.*"

Bridget bit the inside of her cheeks.

No. This would not do at all. It had been a bad move coming here, to this house, to be maid to this creature, despite the comfort of the quarters and the tidy wage. It was not enough, however. She, too, needed more. So much more, despite all the years of squirreling away what she could here and there, despite those few extra payments she had received from Temple, it was never enough. She could not do this on her own.

It irked her immensely that this was the case, but it was true for every woman in this day and age. If she were to go anywhere in life, to rise above any station, then, unfortunately, all the saving and squirrelling and plotting and scheming and planning in the world would mean nothing without the use of that which she swore she would do her best to avoid. A husband.

"*'ore.*"

Bridget felt a flare ignite inside her. The girl had turned to look at her, her expression demanding and determined. Thus it was with Adeline. She would consume and consume and still would never be filled. She remembered who Bridget was now, alright, all of a sudden. She was her feeder. It was her task to bring Adeline more, to try to fill her, to quench this unappeasable beast that was her appetite.

"*'ore,*" she said, angrily now.

"*You – have – had – enough,*" Bridget said, her voice low, her teeth gritted.

But Adeline had not. For such a thing was impossible. The thick curve of her second chin wobbled as she shifted in her seat, alarming Bridget, who stepped back, feeling her way toward the door, just to be on the safe side.

"*'ooore!*"

It was a roar now, and she was trying to stand. She could not move quickly, the lumpen thighs obstructing her as they slapped and slid against each other, each unable to get out of the other's way, but if she reached Bridget, there was no doubt that she would be in danger. With Adeline's girth came enormous strength. Bridget had heard from the staff under-stairs that Adeline had almost smothered her companion once by sitting on her. To have survived all that she had – famine, poverty, destitution, widowhood and the subsequent years of servitude – and then to die, suffocated under a simpleton – well, that simply would not do.

Especially as a new plan had of late struck her. A way out. A way up. It would take strength of will, and all of her persuasive wiles – but rather that than spend another moment under threat from this idiot beast, feeding her and washing her and drowning in her repugnant stink.

"Alright, Adeline, calm yourself," she instructed.

There was no time like the present to set a plan in motion, she decided. She had done it before, and she would do it again. Hopefully, on this occasion, for the last time.

"Let me speak with Cook," she said, her tone both authoritative and placating. "See if we can't find you some of that blancmange you like, eh? See if we can't find something special to put in it for you." She tapped her pocket to reassure herself. The bottle was there, where she liked to keep it safe from enquiring eyes. It was time, she decided.

She would need Temple to put her plan into action, she thought to herself as she stepped outside the door and locked it to keep Adeline contained in her absence. Another fool, that Temple, but a prosperous one – albeit with her help. So in a way, she was entitled to a share.

How convenient that she had no doubt she would see him soon. Without question the household would require his services very shortly. But first things first. It was time to get Adeline something to eat, and something to drink.

Chapter 12

2018

"Good morning. It's Saturday, it's ten o'clock. I'm Brian McElhatton. Here are your headlines. Winter Wonderland – Ireland is blanketed with snow – more is forecast for later, so the country remains predominantly in shutdown, but a thaw is expected as early as tomorrow. More upheaval in the White House as Trump fires another key staff member. And the gardaí renew appeals for help as the search for Dublin teenager Dylan Fogarty enters a third week ..."

On Friday, it had snowed.

It started with hail showers early in the morning. Joe had arrived bearing the now customary cappuccino and Danish pastry with the broad shoulders of his coat sprinkled with perfect white beads.

By elevenses, the hail and sleet had turned soft and persistent. Louise had stood at the sitting-room window leaning heavily on her crutch, sipping a coffee and staring upwards into it, mesmerised by its dizzying descent, white against the greyish sky, flakes spinning and twirling and drifting. They seemed endless, the clouds thick with more and more to come.

By lunchtime, Joe popped his head around the door of the sitting room where she was dozing on her armchair. "Have you seen?" he asked, nodding at the window. She levered herself up out of the seat and limped to join him at the window. Outside was entirely white – cars stood in snow to their hubcaps and the road was indistinguishable from the pavement.

"Christmas card stuff," observed Joe joylessly.

Louise glanced sideways at him and saw that his mouth was set in a line of grim concern.

"Oh my God!" It suddenly dawned on her why. "Of course – you should go – it'll be unsafe. Sorry – I'm so dim. I don't drive, so it doesn't occur to me."

"Would you mind?" He met her gaze, his expression timid, as if he would be letting her down.

"Absolutely not – get home before it gets worse, and dark – honestly."

"But what about you?" he asked. "What are you going to do over the weekend?"

She shrugged and smirked. "Skiing, bobsledding ..."

He frowned. "No, seriously – have you got a friend or someone who could come over? I mean, going by the forecast, you're going to be trapped indoors?"

She grinned. "That's not a problem for me – I'll be fine – I had a big shop delivered yesterday so the cupboards are full, the heating's working – just about – and I have my anti-bear rifle locked in the gun cabinet – I think I'll survive a bit of Irish snow."

"But you'll be completely alone!"

She nodded. "I know," she replied, smiling. "I'm good with that. I'm still slow on my pins, but I'll be absolutely fine. You're the one who's facing into who-knows-what out there – you know what people get like when there's a centimetre of snow on the ground. Complete panic! Nuclear wasteland! Stale bread!"

He regarded her with concern. "If you're really sure you're okay?"

She laughed. "I'm fine – seriously – *go*. I'll see you Monday morning – if we survive."

"I'll bring a breakfast roll," he replied.

"And a foil blanket," she quipped, following him as he left the room.

"Very funny," he replied, stopping to retrieve his heavy jacket from where it hung at the end of the stairs.

"And a Saint Bernard with a little brandy keg!" she called as she clumped past him and down to the kitchen. She heard him snigger and then, moments later, the front door close.

She was completely and utterly alone.

It was absolutely delicious.

Louise woke on Saturday morning, refreshed, to a world transformed, and a whole day to herself ahead. It had stopped snowing at some point overnight – the sun beamed down now, but it was still freezing outside on the deep drifts that had formed in the gardens. In the distance outside, she could hear the scrape of shovels on cement as the neighbours set to clearing pathways and pavements. She checked the news website – everywhere was closed around the whole country – it was like some sort of involuntary Christmas Day.

At the kitchen table, she drained the dregs of her coffee and poured herself a glass of water to take two painkillers. Even after almost a week she felt the need for them at least once a day. At least the filthy bruise on her face had subsided. And the throb in her ankle was definitely less noticeable than it had been a few days previously – but it was still there.

What to do, what to do, she wondered, as she rinsed her glass and left it to drain. A quick check outside, she decided, and limped down the hall to peer out the front door.

Her front steps were thick with snow, at least four or five inches, she reckoned, testing it by sinking her crutch into it. She cast her eye around the Gardens – completely silent, the entire green around which the houses sat covered by a smooth white blanket. Smiling, Louise took her mobile from her pocket and captured some photographs – trees with their black arms carrying snow raised upward, her bins with a neat layer on their lids and, prettiest of all, the Volkswagen Campervan in which Gerry and Pam next door embarked on their regular early retirement adventures. It looked so cheerful in the crisp sunlight, covered in souvenir stickers, bright yellow in contrast to the dazzling white.

A bracing gust of cold air enveloped Louise suddenly as she snapped, and she shivered. Time to retreat, she thought, and 'bunker down' as the internet kept suggesting she should do. The thought of that felt nice. Safe.

She shut the front door, and trudged back to the kitchen, hitting the 'constant' setting on her overworked heating – the house just couldn't seem to warm up properly. She studied her photographs while she waited for the kettle to boil and, on impulse, set Pam and Gerry's van as her Facebook profile background. She'd light the fire, she thought, and later, when it got dark and cosy, she'd just chill out and binge on that Danish drama series that she'd been saving. She usually couldn't watch anything subtitled without a barrage of questions and comments from Ros, so it would be a real treat. What now, though? Aimlessly, she picked up her coffee and wandered from the kitchen.

Taking her time, she idled in the hallway, transfixed for a moment by dust motes circulating in a beam of sunshine that came through the fanlight over the front door and splashed onto the wooden floor. The painkillers were kicking in, she realised. Everything felt relaxed and simple, all of a sudden. There was no pressure on her time or her patience, the world had stopped for a break and she was alone. It was Louise's idea of perfection.

She pushed open the door of her office as she passed, and limped in, pausing in the doorway to flick on the light-switch and observe the room – she was unsure exactly why – it wasn't as if anything would have changed since she'd last been in there. Everything was as she had left it – the two-seater sofa covered with a shabby red throw, the floor-to-ceiling IKEA shelving on the opposite wall, the tall lamp in the corner, her notebook, and the mug where she kept her pens and some rolled-up receipts on her desk. Aimlessly, she clumped over to her chair and lowered herself down onto the crimson seat and sighed contentedly. She put her cup down on her desk and contemplated turning on her computer but decided against it – she knew from checking both her laptop and phone earlier that she had no emails – and, anyway, it was the weekend. Absent-mindedly, she pushed her chair back and did a slow, full rotation in the middle of the floor, only to immediately regret it as the slow spin made her dizzy. Using her crutch as a brake, she stopped herself and saw that she had come to rest facing the wooden box in the corner. The camera. The Declaration of Independence.

What had she been thinking, spending all that money on something about which she knew absolutely nothing? All the plans, the decisions that she had reached about her future – that the impulse-purchase of the antique symbolised – they seemed very far away just now. Had she been realistic with herself about what she could really achieve, she wondered?

She closed her eyes and squeezed them tight against the self-doubt that she could feel creeping in. She mustn't allow that. She must stay positive.

Here – she'd have a look at the damn thing and see if it might inspire her once more.

She transferred herself from the desk chair to the small, low sofa. Gingerly, her sore ankle stretched safely to one side, she reached over and slid the box around toward her, undoing the catch and carefully opening the lid. A musty smell immediately filled her nostrils, a cloud of thick air. She sat back as it reached her as if to get out of its way, then peered into the case and examined the contents of the green baize-lined container. On top lay a square canvas satchel, underneath it the tripod. With both hands, Louise carefully scooped the satchel out and brought it to rest on her knees, where she undid the strap and reached for the contents. First, she withdrew the camera and set the satchel aside. She studied the camera, gently undoing the brass clasp so that it expanded and revealed itself. She ran her fingers over the mahogany and the brass around the lens, before delicately teasing the leather of the bellows. It really was beautiful, she acknowledged, but what was *she* doing with it? In her head, in the little cavern of wonders that had been the antique shop, she had visualised how appropriate it would look in her sitting room. But here, on her lap, in her house, in her possession, she felt no affinity with it, and without some sort of relationship with such a thing it would just look and feel ... she couldn't think of a term to describe the *wrongness* of it. Fake? Pretentious?

She was assailed suddenly by a series of sneezes, brought on by the dust emancipated from the box, waiting for a final sneeze that threatened to explode. When it didn't, she closed the camera up carefully, and set it beside her on the seat, wondering what to do about it. Next, she picked up the canvas satchel and examined the contents, drawing them out one by one – three perfectly intact glass plates, in pristine condition, a flat piece of wood she identified as the baseboard that sat on the top of the tripod, on which the camera would sit, and finally a flat box, smooth, and beautifully finished in a gorgeous reddish wood, lacquered so that it felt like silk to the touch.

It was roughly the length and width of an A4 sheet of paper, and the depth of a book – like a jewellery box, she thought, or a cigar case, but slightly more functional. She shook it gently, and heard something rattle softly within – nothing hard, she noted – more muffled, like paper. Letters perhaps? Or a manufacturer's manual? She studied it closely, comparing it to the camera and plates. It didn't match them exactly – the colour of the wood, the smoothness of the finish – it was altogether more recent. She rattled it again, feeling the soft shift of the contents inside, and felt around the edges for a catch or a release button, but all that she could find was a keyhole. Gently, she tried to prise it open, but it wouldn't budge. Resting it on her knees, she reached again for the canvas satchel and fumbled around inside. Empty. She checked the front pocket – also empty. Finally she turned the bag upside down and shook it but was disappointed to hear no *thunk* of a key hitting the floor. "*Hmm*," she said. "Little mystery box, huh?" Carefully, she laid it to one side at her feet, and turned her attention back to the other contents which she had taken from the bag, replacing them in the satchel where they were stored.

A sudden *whoosh* from her pocket made her jump. An email. She was pleasantly surprised by what she read.

To: Louise

From: LK Sedgewick

Subject: Is anyone in Ireland at work?

Hi Lulu – greetings from the US – has your country really closed down because you guys got a foot of snow? And does snow in Ireland mean that people can't speak anymore or can you dig your way to your desk to voice something for me? Sorry to ask at a weekend, or The Day After Tomorrow as you guys seem to be treating it, but I need a lady to talk real fancy on a script and have it back on my desk asap – you think you could do that for me? Client in a hurry enough to ask at stupid o'clock on a Friday night so I'm just sharing the love. Script attached, let me know your availability. Over.

Louise grinned. Luke Sedgewick ran a small studio in Florida, had found her online and regularly threw work her way. He was a good payer, and a prompt one too. In return, he expected a speedy service which she was glad to provide. She opened the script – a nice long one – something medical, which she didn't understand, but it was work – easy work – and almost three thousand words. She replied on her phone.

To: LK Sedgewick
From: Louise
Re: Subject: Is anyone in Ireland at work?
Am down to my last supplies. Have been forced to eat the rest of my team. Tell my mother I love her – I may not see the dawn. And yes – will have this back on your desk right away.

She pinged it back and received a thumbs-up emoji almost instantly. 10.30am in Ireland, she noted. So it was what ... 5.30am in Florida? Luke sure liked to get started early.

Her mood lifted as she turned on her computer and set about the job at hand. Of all days, she was delighted to finally have something to do – even if the job didn't require huge amounts of concentration. All the better for that, actually, considering the numb state of her brain.

Louise tested her audio levels with a couple of 'one two's', and, satisfied that they were where they should be, she slid her headphones on, opened the document on her phone and held it at eye-level to read from it as she leaned toward the mic and began to deliver.

She could always relax with one of Luke's scripts. With typical American efficiency, he would write the phonetic pronunciation of anything he felt she might find difficult in brackets beside the word, along with little warnings and reminders of the difference in pronunciation for an American audience – like '*aloominum*' and '*vite-a-min*'.

She was an efficient sight-reader, operated quickly and with a low rate of error. She finished the first read-through of the piece and then immediately went back to the start to do it again in a slightly different style to give Luke a choice.

She had just finished a third read-through, when she was struck with a sudden urge to use the loo and, with a sigh, manoeuvred herself upwards and out the door as quickly as she could.

The toilet trip took her a while – her leg was stiff from sitting. She deliberately took her time coming down too, as she had done all week – one slip, and she could fall again, with no paintbrush-wielding White Knight to rescue her this time. Once down all in one piece, she decided to fortify herself with a mid-morning coffee before sitting back down to finish the job. She carried it carefully, along with a packet of chocolate biscuits, back into the studio room and settled again at her desk, popping on her headphones.

She tutted as she realised that she hadn't stopped recording when she'd gone upstairs – there would be a big gap between a third and fourth reread now that she'd have to edit out. Taking a sip of coffee, she did a final read-through, then stopped the recording before clicking back to the start to begin editing.

She worked steadily, highlighting the small wave forms that indicated breaths and deleting them, along with some errors she knew she had made along the way, grabbing herself another biscuit as she reached the section where she had gone to the loo. There would be nothing to listen to for a little while, so she pulled her headphones down to rest around her neck – she also couldn't bear the noise of herself eating amplified in them – and worked by sight instead, highlighting the flat line that the long silent section made on screen in order to delete it. It was the simplest task in the world, but tedious, and she knew there would be a lot of flat line to cover before the wave forms would indicate again the point where she had resumed speaking.

She was just about to reach into the pack for another biscuit when something on screen stilled her hand – a brief thickening in the line of the silence. Some sort of sound had been picked up while she was out of the room. She thought back – she'd left the door of the studio open, of course, so it could be something like the toilet flushing. It was very brief, however – if it was a toilet flush, then the chunk of sound would appear a lot longer. She frowned, and, curious, slid her headphones back over her ears, hitting the space bar on her keyboard to play the audio.

She listened once, and paled, before playing it again – and then again. Something had recorded while she had been out of the room alright, except it wasn't any noise that she had made.

It was a voice.

"*Hello,*" it whispered, distant – as though it were present, yet not present.

Louise played it again.

"*Hello …*"

Puzzled, she allowed the file play on. The silence continued, on and on, until … *there* … there it was again.

"*Hellooo …*"

A chill ran the length of Louise's back and down her arms.

Then silence again. A long silence this time.

Louise, her eyes fixed to the screen, watched the flat

line travel across the screen, her body rigid, her knuckles white around the mouse. Still silent. Just the low hiss of atmosphere. Silence, followed by more silence. She relaxed a little. She had reached the end ...

"*Halloooo!*"

Louise's entire body spasmed with shock, and reflexively she pulled the headphones from her ears and flung them on the desk, pushing herself back from the screen as though it might harm her. The final one had been unlike the others – the first two distant, sound picked up from somewhere else. The last one had been closer, much closer – sounding exactly, in fact, like a mouth pressed up to the mic. Louise stared, wide-eyed and uncomprehending at the screen, the shout still echoing in her ears. What the hell was it?

It must have been something outside – but how? The recording hadn't even picked her up going upstairs, opening the bathroom door or flushing the toilet inside, so how could it pick up a voice from outside like that?

But the alternative to that meant that the person was ... but it couldn't be ... *inside* the house?

But she was alone. She *knew* she was alone, was certain. So that meant ... what exactly?

Her phone suddenly gave another loud '*whoosh*' and she jumped at the sound, reaching for it immediately. It was an email.

Hey, Irish, assuming you must have been eaten by bears but, on the off-chance you haven't, any chance I could get that VO pronto? Client's on an all-nighter and has lit a fire under my ass and hidden the extinguisher.

Louise took a deep breath. "Okay," she said to herself,

refocusing. She had to do this now – she'd get right back to work. It was the best thing – something tangible, something immediate, something *real*. Anything so that she could block the sound of that *voice*.

She forced herself to concentrate on editing the piece she had recorded for Luke. Leaving her headphones off and being careful not to hit 'play' again, she went back to the start of the silent section – the silent, interrupted section – highlighted it and quickly pressed 'delete'. She didn't want to hear it again, whatever it was.

She needed air, she decided, whizzing the audio off to the States via a transfer app with a comment that she had wrestled the bear, won, and he was now her slave. When it was gone, she closed all of the open tabs on her computer, especially her recording program, and shut it down completely. Then, as briskly as she could, she stood, shoved her chair against her desk and left the room, glancing behind her briefly – and fearfully – before flicking off the light-switch and closing the door firmly behind her.

She made her way to the front door and pulled it wide open. The house was stuffy with the heating on all day and her head throbbed a little. This would do her good. She took a deep breath and closed her eyes.

"Still chilly all the same."

The voice came from the garden next door and she looked over the hedge to see Gerry of the campervan standing in his garden, dressed as if he were about to take on Everest, and leaning on a shovel, observing the road.

"Oh, hi. More to come, I believe." Her voice sounded strange out in the open air.

"You didn't get a chance to ... you know ..." said Gerry, lifting the shovel and waggling it in her direction.

It was an admonishment, she knew. She raised her crutch and waggled it back at him. "I'm out of action, I'm afraid. And Ros is away until Tuesday."

"Oh no!" Gerry looked genuinely surprised and sympathetic.

He was a bit of a busybody, but a nice man underneath, she knew, a self-styled community prefect for the whole of Maryborough Gardens and was often to be seen picking up litter and peering into some of the more unkempt gardens with distaste. The uncleared pavement outside her house would have driven him to distraction. So perhaps ... could it have been Gerry that had been picked up on the recording? She wouldn't have put it past him to take it upon himself to ensure that all the residents were doing their bit for safety. And if the doorbell had taken one of its notions not to work, as it was wont to do, then she wouldn't have put it past him to start yelling for her attention. It seemed to make sense. Sort of.

"Why didn't you knock on the wall? Have you been stuck at home with nothing? Are you alright, you poor cratur?"

Louise laughed. It felt nice to laugh. To interact with another human. She'd never have dreamed of knocking on the wall or asking them for help in any way unless she was completely stuck. And by stuck, she meant physically. As in under some fallen bookshelves or something.

"Not a bit of it, Gerry! I have the house stocked and the heating on – I've been cosy as a bug in a rug. Happy out."

"So long as you're sure – but you should always call if you need anything – we didn't know at all – is it broken?"

"Just badly sprained," she replied. "It'll be fine. Just

needs rest."

"Well, go in out of the cold. I'll clear your path for you, don't be worrying a bit. If I had known I'd have done it yesterday when I was doing my own."

"Sure it would have just snowed fresh on all your hard work. Thanks a million, Gerry. I really appreciate that. I'll get in and get my foot up again now."

"Mind yourself!" Gerry waved the shovel again, in a friendly manner this time, and start to shovel along his own pathway.

The regular scraping sound was muffled as she closed the front door behind her and leaned against it for a moment. Back inside, she thought. Alone again. It was ludicrous to think that she was, in any way, not.

Chapter 13

Ben Daly was bored. So bored. Off his game bored, in fact. The whole country was thigh-deep in snow and here he was, home alone, on the third floor of an apartment block, with nothing to do. Normally at this time on a Saturday, if he had the day off, he'd be on the bus into town for brunch, followed by some record-shopping and a browse in Oxfam, maybe a trip to the barber to get his beard – his pride and joy – trimmed properly. If he was working, however, like he was supposed to today, he'd be stuck in that stuffy, smelly antique shop listening to the seven million clocks tick-tock endlessly, waiting, hoping, praying, for as much as a single customer to come in, which was infinitely more boring that being stuck at home in the snow so, he guessed, he'd grin and bear it.

Without much thought, he closed Instagram where he had been spying on his ex and was just about to tap the Tinder app open when an alert flashed up on his phone. He brightened immediately – there was someone at the door. "*Yess!*" he whispered in delight at the interruption and swiped the alert message. Who could possibly have braved that weather to come to his rescue and whatever had they planned? A long walk in the drifts? Sledging? He quite liked the idea of that. There had been tons of pictures on the 'gram of people sledging – dogs and grannies and everything. Excitedly, he watched the screen for his caller to appear, ready to shout '*Rapunzel here!*' as soon as he saw who it was.

Instead, he saw at first only blackness, and then, when it pulled back a little, a nostril. Ben recoiled in disgust. Gavin. It had to be Gavin. Thinking he was being funny. He supposed he was lucky it was an orifice on his face, he guessed, knowing what Gavin was capable of in a playful mood.

"That's disgusting, Gav," he said, hitting 'accept' so that he could be heard by his caller and hear them in return.

The nostril withdrew further, revealing a nose, and then a mouth, and then a full face – one which Ben had absolutely not expected to see.

He sat bolt upright and pulled the phone down toward his chest to hide his horrified face. "*Shit,*" he whispered. "*Shit, shit, shit.*" What in the name of God was *he* doing here? And he looked furious.

Ben was in deep trouble, he was sure of it. Maybe he shouldn't have just assumed this morning that he had the day off, like everyone else in the country. It had just seemed obvious at the time – the whole city was shut down – who the hell would be going antiques-shopping on a day like today? There was a red weather warning for God's sake – didn't that make it, like, against the law to commute?

"*Hello.*"

The tone was gruff.

Ben swallowed and made a hurried Sign of the Cross. Deep breaths, he told himself. Tough it out.

104

"Boss!" he exclaimed, pulling the phone back up to his face and adopting an expression of surprise. "What has you out in this weather?"

And what was he doing here anyway? How had he made it all the way out to Inchicore from the City Centre when the roads were like glass and no public transport was operating?

Adrian Temple was peering into the doorbell camera, looking like a Labrador trying to identify it by smell. Ben suppressed a giggle, which vanished as Temple through his milk-bottle glasses finally identified the small lens of the camera and fixed it with a glare. Ben gasped in fright and leaned back. There were three storeys and two locked doors between them, but it still felt as though his employer was glaring directly at him.

"*You can see me,*" Temple said.

Ben watched his boss watch the camera and wondered if it was a question that had been posed, or simply one of his statements. Why did he work for this weirdo anyway?

"I can," Ben replied. "Can I help you at all?"

He realised that he should probably invite Temple inside, out of the cold. The idea made him squirm.

"*Did you take her?*" came the voice from outside.

Ben frowned. "Sorry? I didn't quite catch that."

Temple pursed his lips and scowled at the camera.

"*Did – you – take – her?*" he repeated, elucidating every word.

Ben gave a weak smile. He'd been afraid that he'd heard right the first time. And he had.

"Sorry, Mr Temple, did I take what?" he asked, keeping his tone light, all the while regretting fiercely ever answering the door alert.

"*My camera!*" Temple exploded.

Ben dropped the smile. "What are you on about? I didn't take anything – I wouldn't dream of it."

"*Then where is it?*" snarled Temple, his thick lips curling upward with rage.

Ben considered how freakish he appeared as he tried to think what next to say. "Your camera?" he tried, innocently.

"*Where is it?*" yelled Temple.

Ben jumped and hoped that none of his neighbours could hear. He really had to get rid of the awful man.

"I don't know what camera you're talking about," he said.

"*My* camera," responded Temple, before taking a breath and rolling his extraordinarily strange eyes upward. "*Bellows camera. Late 1850's. Mahogany with brass fittings. Heavy. It was kept in a wooden case which also contained other items. It was on a high shelf in the storeroom, out of the way. Now do you know which camera I'm talking about?*"

Ben racked his brains ... suddenly it came to him. "Oh, I know the one!" he chirped. "I remember it from a week or so ago. Found it on the top shelf in the back room. It was snapped up the minute I put it on display. A woman bought it – she paid two hundred and fifty euro for it ... oh God, it was worth more, wasn't it?" His face fell. There he was, thinking he was great to have solved the mystery of the missing camera only to realise that he'd absolutely cocked up.

Temple stared, wide-eyed. He didn't look so angry anymore. It was hard, in fact, to tell by the quality of the video and through the thick glasses, but he looked as though he had got a fright. It was as if the colour had drained from him very suddenly. Ben even thought for a moment that he saw him sway a little.

"It was," Temple said quietly. "It was priceless in fact. What in the name of all that is holy have you done?"

If he had appeared pale before, he certainly didn't now. In fact, he was turning red, redder than Ben had ever seen. Panic washed over him.

"I ... I ..." he tried, but no words would follow.

Temple's voice rose to a bellow. "*What have you done? Why did you touch it? The camera was not for sale! It had a note attached to that effect!*"

"There wasn't any note –"

"*There was!*" Temple roared. "*This note!*" He shook a sheet of paper violently in front of the lens. "*I found it still on the shelf!*"

"I d-d-didn't s-see it!" Ben stuttered. "It m-must have f-fallen off!"

"*You must have seen it! But you sold my camera regardless! My camera – my own personal camera! A family heirloom! And I need it ... I need it!*"

Ben gasped for words, watching his boss all the while become more incandescent with rage.

"*I cannot do this without it!*" Temple continued. "*It is necessary! It is essential! What am I supposed to do without it there to complete my work?*"

Ben continued to flounder. He couldn't even understand what Temple was talking about now, never mind compose a response. "I'm so sorry –" he managed before Temple cut him off again.

"*Who?*" he bawled. "*Who bought it? Who is this woman? Where can I find her?*"

107

"I don't know!" yelped Ben. "I remember her – small, shiny dark hair ... a bit pushy ... she paid in cash ... I don't *know* ..."

"You ... you got no name? No record? Then how am I supposed to find her?" Temple's rage was weakening, turning to desperation.

"I'm so sorry," Ben repeated, and a fraught silence fell between them.

"You are an idiot," said Temple suddenly.

Ben blinked as if he'd been hit. "What's that?"

"*Idiot!*" spat Temple.

"Here now, you can't be –"

"*Idiot! Fool! Moron! Cretin! You're sacked, do you hear me? Gross incompetence. That was my prize possession and you ... you gave it away. Never come near me or my shop again, do you hear? Never!*"

And with that, he was gone.

Ben blinked. There was something comedic about it – the dropping of the word '*never*' like a panto villain, before swooping off and disappearing. Under other circumstances it might be funny.

Except he'd just been fired for selling a piece of stock – for doing his damn job – he should be getting a bonus, not the sack. How dare that little fish-faced freak fire him? He'd take him to an unfair dismissals tribunal, so he would. Drag him through the courts. How the hell was *he* supposed to know not to sell a fecking antique in an antique shop? Damn him anyway. Glancing again at the screen of his phone and on it the empty doorway to the apartment building, Ben blinked in disbelief. He was fecking-well unemployed now. And the gig had been handy in some ways – handy in that once he turned up to work looking the part, it was half the job done. He fingered his beard and frowned. Where the hell was he going to work now?

"Oh fuck it!" he said into the air and flung his phone on the sofa beside him. He'd have loads of money once he took Adrian Temple and his shitty shop to the cleaners. He'd just get himself a shit-hot lawyer – a shark, isn't that what they called them on TV? Once he could afford one. He'd definitely do it then. He'd just need to find a new job first. One where his boss wasn't a bug-eyed creep who was never around yet expected him to know the inner workings of his brain. "*Cretin*," repeated Ben, fumbling around the sofa for the remote control. What did that even mean anyway?

Chapter 14

By Sunday evening, the rain had started, a sweeping downpour that pelted steadily against the windows, growing heavy enough from time to time to thunder against the roof like showers of pebbles. The sitting room, lit by soft lamplight and with pillar candles flickering on the mantelpiece, was cosy, the curtains drawn against quickening storm.

Louise turned on the TV, and flicked through the channels, coming to rest on a comedy. It would do nicely, she thought, settling to watch, while simultaneously scrolling on her phone, reading the fresh warnings. The Met Office was certainly busy this weekend. It was a storm this time, coming from the west, due to hit Dublin overnight with gales and torrential rain. That would surely wash the rest of the snow away. Gerry should have just waited it out and conserved his energy instead of doing all that shovelling.

She was just about to click into a video of stupendous waves crashing over a pier in Galway when suddenly the screen went blank. Dead battery. Louise swore – the charger was on the kitchen countertop. She slid the phone into the pocket of her dressing gown. She was planning on making a hot drink in a while. She'd take it out and charge it then.

It had been a funny old weekend, she mused, sliding her finger under the foil wrapping of the bar of chocolate on the arm of her chair. She'd loved it, really – all the peace and quiet, space to breathe. She needed that so badly – more than most, she knew. Being around others sometimes drained her, and other times it made her feel saturated, overloaded, overwhelmed by the need to interact, to do and say the right thing – to do and say *anything*, for that matter. She knew that other people thought her antisocial and odd – she couldn't actually think of one other person that she knew who would look on two days trapped indoors, completely alone and with an injury, as a lovely break, but she had.

Still, it would be nice to have the world back to normal in the morning. You could have too much of a good thing – and even though it meant a day closer to Ros's return, it meant a day closer to finally asking her to move out. It was a conversation that Louise was dreading, but the benefits of it would far outweigh the discomfort. She was looking forward to Joe being back at work too. It was strange for her, but she had really grown used to him about the place, with his broad smile and his repertoire of hits.

She lasted half an hour before the drowsiness crept over her, as it did without fail lately. For a while, she drifted in and out of a half-sleep, coming to, to stare befuddled at the TV, only to drift off again moments later. It was the violent scream of a sudden gust of wind which eventually woke her fully.

She shot upright, her heart pounding with shock, her

skin prickling as she blinked herself awake. There was another howl from outside which rattled the window – the storm was growing in force – as the forecasts had said it would. She shivered, feeling disoriented. It sounded a bit scary out there, actually.

Time for bed, she decided, glancing at the clock. It was early, but at least tucked up under her duvet, with the last couple of those painkillers on board, she might conk out again and miss the worst of it. And if not, then she could listen to it howl and rage from the safety of her bed. With care, she lifted her injured foot down to the floor from the coffee table and waited a moment for the throbbing to subside before easing herself forward and reaching for her crutch.

When something made her stop.

The wind gusted again just as she moved, distracting her momentarily, yet Louise was sure that she had heard a noise coming from just outside the sitting-room door.

She craned her neck to listen more closely. It sounded like ... of all things ... *whispering* ... but that was impossible, of course. She held her breath. All was silent, but ... *there* ... she was sure ... yes, there it was again. What was it? Frustratingly, just at that moment, the wind chose to gust forcefully against the front of the house, blocking out the sound. She frowned at the interruption and sat forward in her chair, tilting her head so that she might hear better. And for a while, all was quiet, long enough for Louise to conclude that she had imagined it.

Until she heard it again.

For sure this time – a low susurration, for all the world as if someone was speaking, but slowed down. There were no distinct words, just murmured, elongated sounds – like a chant – whispered prayer.

Her blood turned to ice suddenly and her eyes widened in alarm. Could there be someone in the house? Ridiculous. The front door was chained and locked and the back ... she had peered out into the back garden at the last of the snow earlier, but she was sure that she had locked it ... hadn't she? What if it didn't catch, though? What if someone had forced it and got in? Someone seeking shelter from the freezing cold? Were they whispering to themselves? Or to someone else? Was there more than one?

Fear was replaced by a bolt of alarm – she could hear the whispering clearly now – she wasn't alone in the house anymore. She gripped the crutch tightly, as much for defence as support – and stood as quickly as her injured foot would allow. She craned her head toward the door again to listen. It was silent just now – but did that mean that they had become aware of her? Thank *God* she had woken up – or was that a good thing? Would it put them on the defensive? Had they fallen silent because they knew that she knew, that they – she kept thinking *they* – were there?

And there it was again – the long, slow murmuring chant. Louise flushed hot with fear and then prickled with cold again. It was such an unnatural sound – what on *earth* was it? She squirmed, her mind racing. She was in no fit state to protect herself from intruders. She'd have to call for help. Heart thumping, she reached into her pocket and withdrew her phone to call the Guards, pressing the home button, but the screen remained black. *Fuck it,* she swore under her breath – the damn thing was dead, of course. A fresh wave of dread hit her. This felt really unsafe now.

As silently as possible, she limped across the room toward the door, terrified of making a sound. Her stomach churned

113

with each step, and lurched as she got closer. The whispering had started again, except it seemed faster now, and a little louder, growing in speed and volume as she crossed the room. The wind surged outside against the window.

She limped the last few steps, stiff with terror.

She stopped when she reached the door and, trembling all over, pressed her ear to it. Again came the noise. Louder, and closer, and louder still, until suddenly, without warning, it stopped.

She tensed.

Silence.

Then a low moan from the wind outside.

Barely able to control the shaking, she slid her hand toward the doorknob.

But before she could turn it, she tensed and froze. There was something else ... from the corner of her eye, she saw something ... it couldn't be ... something emerging *through* the wall by the fireplace.

At first, she couldn't bring herself to look, instead squeezing her eyes shut, hopeful – sure – that when she opened them again, the dark shape – an optical distortion, surely – would be gone. It was a simple trick of the light, of her eyesight.

It had to be – a combination of shadows thrown by the flickering fire, and dim lamplight – and the stress, overloading her brain, brought on by what she was hearing on the other side of the door – *that* was what she needed to focus on, confronting whoever was out there and getting them – or herself – out of the house.

When she opened her eyes again, however, and blinked to clear them, her chest tightened as she saw that the shape was still there. And it was *moving*.

Her brain scrambled to make sense of what she was seeing.

It was a shadow – a person-shaped shadow. At least it would be if it were real, a tiny voice told her – and it couldn't be – it was impossible for one thing, and for another, it was too tall, impossibly so – no *person* was that size ...

She took a step backwards as the shape seemed to turn and glide along the wall toward her. Horrified, she followed its progress as it approached, sliding along. Silently, it grew closer, towering over her by at least a couple of feet. She pressed herself against the wall behind her as the shadow slid over the door and closer to her, and closer still ... and then *over* her, bringing with it a momentary damp coldness, like a freezing fog.

She gasped, and her entire body went numb as she watched, immobile, the room darkening, like a cloud passing over the sun, as the shadow passed over and *through* her, and then glided on, rippling with the folds in the heavy curtains, then into the corner and along the bookshelves before turning again back onto the wall from where it came, fluid and smooth. Louise watched, incredulous, as it then vanished, disappearing into the wall as if sucked through to the other side.

For a few moments, she simply stared, aghast, her mind blank.

Her heart juddered in her chest and her breathing came heavily as she stared at the space over where the shadow had travelled. It was just the same now as it always was, buttercup yellow, bare of pictures. Just an ordinary patch of very familiar wall ...

Like an explosion in her brain, terror suddenly

flooded every part of her body at once. Her shaking hands reached out and gripped the doorknob, twisting it as fast as she could manage. As if her body was moving independently of her mind, she flung the door open and gasped as the dim light of the sitting room spilled out into the dark of her hall. A colossal surge of adrenaline roared through her body, blanking any coherent thoughts. Preparing ... preparing for ...

Nothing.

She stood there, trembling silently, every nerve-ending in her body tingling, looking around and above her. But there was no one – and nothing – there. Even the wind outside seemed to have paused, waiting, waiting ... for what?

Suddenly her body spasmed with shock as a thunderous bang echoed through the house. She shrieked, her heart galloping against her ribs. She spun around, and around again, her chest tight, as she checked all around her and her brain attempted to process what she had just heard. Was it something outside – a car backfiring? A gunshot? She'd never heard a gun being fired close by before, so maybe ...?

It wasn't any of those things though, was it? Her heart sank, and she peered upwards again. It hadn't come from outside ... it had come from upstairs.

Feeling as though she had no control over her movements, she slowly limped toward the bottom step and began to ascend, terrified that the noise had been what she thought it was. But there was no logical way *that* could have happened. So had it ...?

It had.

She gasped as her eyes proved what her gut knew as she reached the top stair and was confronted with her worst fear at that moment. The bathroom door was shut – something that only happened if either herself or Ros were in there. It was one of the few, possibly the only habit that they had in common. Unless the bathroom was in use, the door was left ajar for ventilation.

Louise stared at it for a moment, dizzy with disbelief. If someone had been in the hallway – whoever had been whispering – then they were now in the bathroom, cornered. But how? How could that be possible? Louise squeezed her eyes shut. *Think*, she commanded herself. *Breathe. Use some bloody logic here.* How could it be another person? It couldn't have been possible for someone to stand outside her living door whispering and then to almost instantaneously get to the bathroom and slam the door shut. No. That made no sense. None of it did. It was all in her mind – it had to be. She'd been in a deep sleep, after all, and had been woken abruptly. There was a storm raging outside – she'd been on heavy duty painkillers for a week. All of that was taking its toll. None of this was real – that was completely impossible. She opened her eyes and stared at the bathroom door. It had been the wind that had slammed it shut … somehow. Of course it had. There was no other explanation.

With a juddering hand, she reached out and grasped the doorknob to open the door.

Which didn't budge.

She tried again, gripping the old-fashioned brass knob more tightly.

Yet again, defying her, it refused to turn even a millimetre. A hot wave of fear prickled its way down her back. She tried turning the knob the opposite way. It remained resolutely in place. The slam must have broken it, she rationalised. Because the other reason in her mind was too impossible ...

That it was being held from inside.

At the thought, she yanked her hand back. That was ridiculous, she chided herself. It was impossible – truly impossible. It was something wrong with the mechanism, that was all. A screw that had been dislodged with the impact of the slam ... which must have been caused by a draught ... *must* have been ... there could be no one here – she'd have heard them run up the stairs. This wasn't happening – it *couldn't* be. It was just broken somehow. Everything in this house was dodgy – from the heating to the damn cupboard doors. It was just a stupid *doorknob*.

Louise took a deep breath, then another, and then reached out and grasped the handle as firmly as she could once again. She paused, then set her jaw and prepared herself to give it a final, vigorous twist.

Before she could, however, it did something unthinkable ... without her control, it twisted violently in her hand, pulled away from her, and the door was flung wide open.

Louise screamed, both with terror and in pain, as she staggered backward, forced not only by the fright of the door opening by itself, but by the force of what emerged, purposefully rushing past her and whooshing down the stairs. She staggered backwards across the landing, unable to stop herself, and unable to prevent her full weight going down on her injured ankle before losing her balance. Louise cried out in pain as she landed hard on her backside, a flare of hot pain erupting in her coccyx.

She sprawled there, numb to all thought, save what she had just seen and felt. It was like a person, rushing past her and down the stairs – except it wasn't – there had been nothing human about it whatsoever – it was a mist, a *mist* ... that had knocked her over and rushed down the damn stairs.

Louise looked around her, stunned, entirely unsure of what to do next, until something broke inside her. Before she could stop them, the flood of tears overwhelmed her, and she wrapped her arms around herself. What the hell was happening to her?

Chapter 15

Outside, the storm had finally arrived, the heavens releasing rage on the city, bearing down on streets and lanes and parks. The wind was furious and sent the rain to beat down like millions of angry fists.

Louise drifted deeper and deeper into sleep, into another world, through which she raced against time in a dream, although she didn't know why. In it, she tried to pack suitcases which emptied themselves again as soon as the task neared completion. She struggled to reach unknown destinations without knowing why, running down endless corridors, climbing stairs, travelling up and down escalators that led nowhere, all the while in a state of panic, fearful of something, she knew not what.

Until once, in the early hours, when she was woken – at least she thought she was awake, although she knew for certain afterwards that she couldn't have been – by a sudden sense of calm, a strong smell of flowers – and a presence in her bedroom. She propped herself on one elbow and sat up to see. The curtains were open, letting a shaft of moonlight fall across the end of her bed. It was remarkably bright, she observed. And calm. Hadn't a storm been forecast? And why were the curtains open? What matter. She was safe and it was beautiful – that soft light, tinted with blue.

And there, sitting on the armchair beside the window, was the figure of a girl. Louise knew it should have alarmed her, but it didn't. In fact, she could feel a warmth radiating from it – a kindness, a protectiveness. Wasn't it wonderful the way that dreams could make you feel that way? Could fill you with such pure emotion, such love? She smiled at the girl, who turned slowly from where she had been watching out the window, her face pale and beautiful in the light. She was dressed in a long white gown – a shroud? – reddish hair twisted into elaborate knots and coils. She was beautiful, just on the cusp of womanhood – too young, thought Louise, wondering how she knew that.

She felt no fear as the girl's eyes met her, nor when she whispered to her – at least, the sound of words travelled across the room, although it didn't appear that the girl moved her lips. "Help you," she said, and suddenly Louise felt overwhelmed with kindness. She smiled again and watched as the girl slowly moved to the end of her bed where she raised her arms, as if to show Louise something. But something wasn't quite right. The lace of her sleeves gently slipped back a little further than usual, revealing two stumps just below the elbow. The girl wanted Louise to see that she had no hands.

And then Louise was drifting off to sleep again but, unlike before, it was calm and natural and comforting. And as she descended again into a peaceful slumber, it finally registered with her what the girl had actually wanted her to see. It was so glaringly obvious, but she was very tired. And everything was so fuzzy lately. How could she had missed it? It was right there in front of her the whole time. That the girl had wanted to show her she was special.

Chapter 16

"*Louise!*"

At first there was no response. Louise's body simply flopped from side to side on the studio sofa as Joe gripped her shoulder and shook.

"*Louise ... please wake up ... are you okay?*"

Joe felt relief as her eyelids fluttered and a small moan escaped her. He wasn't prepared, however, for the look of absolute terror on her face as she opened her eyes wide, looked straight at him, and screamed.

He retreated, startled. "Louise ... it's me, Joe ... are you okay?"

The scream turned to a groan, and then faded to a whimper as Louise looked around her, puzzled by her surroundings. She attempted to sit up straight again, and grimaced in pain as she did, leaning forward and grasping her head in both hands.

"Jesus, Louise, what's happened?" Joe asked, kneeling down in front of her, his voice filled with alarm.

Louise released her head and looked at him through red eyes which she could barely open. She clenched her teeth as she unfolded her leg – the injured one – and tried to straighten it.

Beside her, on the small sofa, Joe noticed an empty bottle lying on its side. He recognised it – River Barrow Gin. He had removed it, half full, from one of the top bookshelves in the sitting room when he had cleared them to paint and had wiped the dust from it as he returned it afterwards. An empty coffee cup lay on its side on the floor nearby. He picked it up and sniffed it, recoiling from the bitter smell.

"Louise ..." Joe squatted before her, trying to make eye contact.

Weakly, she opened her mouth as if to speak but suddenly gagged.

He stood sharply and ran, returning in seconds with the washing-up basin from the kitchen. His timing was fortunate. Louise vomited just as he handed it to her. As she retched, Joe turned away. When he thought she was done, he glanced over his shoulder to see her, eyes closed, holding herself stiff.

"Sorry," she managed.

"Hopefully you'll feel a bit better now," he replied brightly, and swiftly took the basin from her juddering hands and left the room. He returned a few moments later, the basin empty and clean, and set it on the floor beside her feet. He leaned over and retrieved the gin bottle from where it had slipped behind a cushion and gently placed it on the floor too.

Louise grimaced at the sight of it.

"Did you drink all that?" Joe asked, squatting down before her and regarding her with worried eyes.

Louise nodded. "What time is it?" she croaked drily. "Why are you here at night-time?"

Her words were a little slurred, Joe noticed, and he frowned. "It's a quarter past eight on Monday morning," he said gently.

She raised her eyebrows in surprise, and nodded, taking a deep breath.

"Are you sure you're okay? You were alone all weekend, in the snow – did you spend the whole thing drinking?"

"*No*," she replied sharply. "Something happened ... something weird ..."

And then she stopped herself.

"I hurt my leg again," she said. "I ... I lost my balance and came down on it hard, and I finished my painkillers ... all I had in the house was paracetamol – may as well have been taking Smarties. It got really bad last night so I ..."

"Self-medicated?"

She nodded. "I fell asleep here ..."

"Sitting up, with your foot in that position, all bent up on the couch? How did you even ..."

She shook her head a little. "Not sure. I feel terrible. I don't drink very much as a rule."

Joe sighed. "I'm sorry. It's none of my business. But, Jesus, I thought you'd maybe tried to – I dunno – end it all, or something. You were completely out of it. Was there no one you could call for help? Why did you end up in here?"

"It happened late last night," she answered. "I didn't want to ... I ... I wasn't thinking straight."

Gingerly, Joe peered at the ankle, reaching out his hand slowly to touch it.

She recoiled at even the prospect. "*Don't!*" she barked, fearful of his touch.

He pulled his hand back. "Sorry – again. It looks a bit swollen alright, from what I can see. Can you move it at all?"

"A little. I just need to loosen up first – I'm completely stiff all over. I'll get to the doc later, now that the roads are clear – they are clear, aren't they?"

"Yeah. I brought your morning coffee and a croissant – do you think you could manage it?"

Louise made a face. "Probably not."

"How about some dry toast and tea, then?"

Louise grinned at him gratefully. "You wouldn't happen to have a Diet Coke and a huge bag of Hula Hoops too?"

Joe snorted. "Baby steps with this hangover, I think," he advised. "If you start with the tea and toast and we get some strength into you, and you keep it down, and you're a very good girl, then we might get you a little treat on the way back from the doctor, alright?"

She managed a laugh. "Okay, Dad. Hang on, what do you mean 'we'?"

He made a 'duh' face as he stood. "Well, how the hell else are you going to get to the doc? Drone delivery?"

"Well, maybe after I've had your miracle tea and toast. You don't have to, though. I'll get a taxi – my GP does a walk-in clinic until half ten –"

"You'll need a limp-in clinic," he interrupted. "Or a crawl-in, looking at the state of you."

Louise's hand flew to her hair which stood completely upright around her head, and then down at the dressing gown she still wore. "Oh my God," she gasped. "I must look a state!"

Joe responded with a smile. "Well, at the moment, if Ken Dodd and Ronnie Wood had a lovechild ..." he said dryly. "You're grand. Have you got health insurance?"

She nodded.

"Then I think you might be better going to one of those Urgent Care clinic places run by your insurance company rather than your GP. I mean it's up to you but, if you go to your GP, then you're going to get sent to A&E, aren't you? And that could take hours and hours, and still no relief."

Louise nodded, then closed her eyes and sighed. When she opened them again, he was staring at her.

"I mean, I'll drive you wherever you want to go – no problem – your call."

She smiled. "No, you're dead right. Make me that tea and I'll ring for an appointment when my bones warm up a little."

"Tea it is. And then let's get you fixed up – I wouldn't be much of a mate if I just stood there splashing paint on your skirting while you dragged your zombie ass off to the doc, now would I?"

Louise smiled again. "Thanks, Joe. You're so kind."

Smiling back, he stood, giving her two thumbs up as he retreated to the kitchen, wondering what, exactly, she was hiding.

Chapter 17

London, 1865

Bridget – she had reverted to that now that they were alone – leaned across the hearth to take from Mr Temple that which he held out for her perusal.

"Thank you Mrs ... *Bridget*," he said, smiling coyly. "I do find it difficult to become accustomed to such informality."

His smile was not returned. Instead, his companion sighed heavily, a weight upon her.

"What of it, Mr Temple? If I am Bridget or Jane or Anne or anyone? At present I am Miss No One from Neverland, it seems."

Temple regarded her with furrowed brows. He had not previously seen – nor indeed conceived of – such a side to the lady. Awkwardly, he sipped his claret and a silence – not entirely comfortable – fell over them, disturbed only by the shift of logs in the grate and the slow tick of the grandmother clock. The parlour was growing dark with the November afternoon.

"Quite," he replied eventually, shifting in his chair. "Perhaps if you were to take a look ..." he leaned forward to indicate the photograph that he had just passed across, "it might ... *cheer* you ... somehow?"

She scowled, and he recoiled, taken aback.

"A picture of a dead girl?" she bit back.

Temple floundered for a moment as he sought the correct words. "A ... a ... *portrait* ... of your charge ... of poor Miss Adeline ..."

Bridget immediately straightened and adjusted her features, as if suddenly remembering where she was. "My *former* charge – of course," she said apologetically. "I shall look right away. Why, Mr Temple –"

"*Samuel*," he interrupted. "If you are to be Bridget, then I am to be Samuel and that is that."

She glanced at him, her eyes momentarily hard, before looking back down at the picture.

"Why, Mr Temple – *Samuel* – you have such a skill," she enthused. "Indeed, it often seems to me that you capture the very *soul* of your subjects."

Temple blushed and affected modesty, but couldn't conceal the broad, proud grin that spread across his face.

"Why thank you, *Bridget*," he replied. "To capture the soul indeed is a privilege, but there is no soul without a ... a subject and that, my dear woman, is where you come in, time and again it seems." He raised his glass in a toast, and accepted the photograph which Bridget returned to him, a little disappointed that she did not spend more time studying it.

Instead, she raised her teacup in return – no liquor touched her lips – and took a demure sip, before leaning back in her chair, sighing again and staring into the flames.

"It's my privilege to be able to recommend your services to my various employers," she said. "Although it seems, as I look back, to be a great misfortune that I have had to do it so many times. Poor Adeline and Alistair and Alice. Why, if it weren't for George I should wonder if it were time to move on to the letter 'B's'. Indeed, if I were of paranoid disposition, I should begin to think that *I* had something to do with it all." She glanced at Temple from under her lowered eyelids. "Although, whatever you want those pictures for, I shall never know. Especially that one – great, fat thing like that simpleton girl ..." She indicated the portrait that she had just handed back with disdain. "Such trouble we had with her. Couldn't keep her out of the larder, sneaking down at night, spying on Cook to jump in and gorge herself when she thought no one was looking. Such gluttony I've never seen. It's no wonder she was that size, that Adeline. She'd have gone sooner or later – her heart would have given up, or she'd have choked on a chicken bone. Between you and me, her family is better off without her – whatever took her did them a kindness. And her too. Poor Adeline – gone – and with her my position. A perfect subject for your tastes, however, although sometimes even I don't fully grasp your choice of subjects in the slightest."

Temple *tsked*. "Why, Bridget, have you not heard that beauty is in the eye of the beholder?"

"Why, of course, Samuel. But beauty ... is ... *beautiful* ..."

"And don't you see beauty in the peaceful, sleeping form of poor Adeline? Released from her earthly bounds? I do. Something rare and magical – the same quality in all of them. Peace at last."

A silence fell between them for a moment as they watched the logs crackle in the fire.

"Don't you think that there can be a beauty in broken things?" Temple asked after a while.

"I do not, to be frank," she replied. "It is my firm opinion that there is far too much sentiment in this world. That when something is broken, it is broken, and unfit for purpose and should be disposed of in favour of something functioning, something useful. If a bucket can't carry water, or a cup is chipped, then they are of no use."

"And the same goes for people?" Temple probed. "Are they the same as buckets or cups? Are they to be disposed of? If a simple girl cannot control her compulsions? Or a man cannot grow? A husband cannot give a wife a child?"

Her eyes flicked to his face and back to the flames and she shifted in her seat.

"I think otherwise," he said. "That there is something ... irresistible ... about that which is not as it should be. You cannot deny that when you see something – some*one* who is different, that you are filled with a desire to look more closely. To see more, to see *why*. To wonder what could possibly have gone wrong to turn something as simple as a human being into a living anomaly. Was it witchcraft, perhaps? Faulty workings in a mother's womb? An imbalance in the humours, as they'd have said in the olden days? Can you not admit that you find the deformed irresistible? And how difficult it is to look away – yet, how impolite to stare. For me, there is never enough time to study what made me at first gasp and look away – to dare myself to look longer and harder, to make sure that every single terrible, horrible component of such a sight has been absorbed, never enough time to sate my scalding curiosity."

"Really, Samuel Temple. There are plenty of places where such atrocities can be viewed at your leisure. Why, they are ten a penny – bearded ladies, Siamese twins, midgets and giants abound – mermaids, even!"

Temple wrung his hands. "Mermaids indeed. But the moments granted for my penny are never sufficient. I find myself tantalised by the mere glimpse – and you know my feelings on such amusements. So imagine then, a gallery – a private, decent gallery where these fascinating, scintillating abominations that exist, barely seen among us, could be viewed and analyzed in detail, at one's leisure, time and again as desired? Imagine such a thing?"

Bridget stared at him, baffled.

"*That* is where my interest lies," he said. "Not in a tawdry, noisy travelling show, but in *art*. In preservation, forever, of people like my subjects – those who stay in our society, but who move in the shadows, who must not be seen for fear of offending the delicacies of the normal, yet will never be reduced to outcasts hidden behind curtains, save for glimpses afforded to jeering drunken wastrels and swooning slatterns. But what is more, not only shall I preserve them, but I shall elevate them! That is the power that I possess. It shall be my life's task to grant them eternal dignity. With my skills, I will make their lives worthwhile. Preserve them in order that they will no longer be derided, but ... but ... *enjoyed* for generations. Grant their greatest wishes – have I not already made a giant a priest? And a mongol girl a *beauty*? And that is how they will appear forever. Someday, I might well be hailed as a genius. An anthropologist of note – wouldn't that be amusing, and I with no education but that which life and experience has brought me? Oh, I have such plans, Bridget. Such plans!"

Bridget continued to observe him, flushed as he was between the fire and the wine and his growing enthusiasm. She cleared her throat to remind him of her presence.

"Indeed, I had plans myself once," she said, somewhat timidly.

Curious, Temple looked at her.

"But the Good Lord saw fit to take Mr Watson too soon – goodness me, there is another to add to my list ..."

"Nonsense," said Temple, in a tone that suggested reassurance.

"There I was, a widow at such a young age, my life before me," Bridget continued, eyes downcast as she watched the flickering flame. "My years in service, in all of my houses, as I call them, to all of my charges, were fulfilling in their own way, although never quite the same ..." She allowed her voice to trail away.

Temple watched, horrified, as, behind a handkerchief she produced, she seemed to succumb to emotion.

"My dear Bridget," he began, but was silenced as she continued.

"Never the same as caring for someone of my *own*." She paused to blow her nose loudly, causing Temple to flinch and the claret to jump in his glass. "Oh my goodness – such lachrymosity! Why, you must think me quite hysterical. It is just that ... throughout my life, I have observed on more than one occasion that I appear to be a woman who has been blessed and cursed at once by having simply too much *love* to give. The love I gave to my poor, departed husband, that I have endowed over the years to my charges, to my work – that indeed I know I possessed in my boundless heart for my own children – the children that never were."

Temple observed her heaving shoulders in horror. Then, with a great, deep breath, she composed herself and within a moment had lifted her face from her kerchief to reveal that she had so fully suppressed the tiresome crying that it now appeared that she had not so much as shed a tear. *What an incredible woman*, he thought, yet again. *Such fortitude!*

"You'll pardon me, Samuel," she said, her voice low. "I am terribly out of sorts today. I fear it must be the weather – the cold grip of a winter without employment for one such as me brings no joy. I am also finding it terribly difficult to sleep at the moment. The mattress at my lodgings is somewhat lumpen, and the pillow hard. And outside on the street ... well, I am a woman of the world, but there are such noises and utterances late into the night as would made a sailor blush. I lock my door, yet still fear for my safety. Silly of me, I know. But I am used to different things. I have grown soft in my old age."

Temple's eyes had widened in outrage. "Well, I ... firstly, you are not, indeed, so much as on the steps of old age, my good woman. And secondly, I shall not permit you to spend another night in tawdry lodgings such as you have described. You simply must come and stay here – I have plenty of rooms with soft mattresses and without fear of disturbance – you can take your pick!"

"Why, Mr Temple!" Bridget's response was filled with outrage of her own. "I simply could not be seen to do such a thing. A respectable woman in the house of an unmarried gentleman? Imagine the scandal, and I in search of employment as soon as I can cast aside this dreadful ennui that assails me since my departure from the Browns! There would be talk!"

Temple was sitting on the edge of his seat now, his earlier enthusiasm returned threefold.

"Why, let them talk! For it would be nothing more than a

respectable widow staying with an old friend. You know my reputation, Bridget – any impropriety would be completely out of the question, and my staff will vouch for that."

"It is very kind of you, Samuel ... but ... I couldn't possibly ... not with you ..."

"Well then, let me be the one to vacate the premises."

Bridget's eyes widened. "Wherever would you go?"

Samuel waved her words away. "That would be for me to figure out. And, besides, it would be my hope that my absence would be temporary. No longer than, say, a month ... that should do it."

"Should do what?"

Bridget watched, incredulous, as Temple suddenly set his glass and the photograph down on the table beside him and suddenly dropped from his chair onto one knee and reached his hands out for hers. In disbelief, she observed his observance that he was wide of the mark, and subsequently had to shuffle, still on his bended knee, closer to her. A spark flew at him from the fire as he did so, and he dodged it, finally grasping her hands and puffing out his chest.

"If we go about it immediately, it should be sufficient time to have a suitable dress made," he said. "And have banns read ... what do you think, Bridget? I am but a humble photographer, but I have great plans, as I already mentioned. And I have no doubt but that I will achieve those plans – but imagine how much faster and better I could do that with a partner by my side? Benefitting from that great surfeit of love of which you spoke. I know you may not feel it now – I would be arrogant to believe that I was deserving of even a morsel of it – but I would make a good husband, Bridget – loyal, considerate, fair. I would never so much as lay a hand on you nor drink to excess nor play cards ..."

At this she went rigid.

"I would provide for you – already I have this house and my business and plans to grow and make my fortune. But what a lonely fortune it would be if I was to have it all to myself, and you out there – toiling away for no greater reward than perhaps clean sheets at night? You would be mistress of my house, Bridget – Queen of my little Kingdom. What do you say? Oh, please say yes!"

Bridget pulled herself upward and fixed him with a firm stare, as if perusing goods in a butcher's shop. Silently, she looked him over – his balding pate, the beginnings of a pot belly, the chemical stains on his fingers.

"I admire your vision and determination, sir," she replied. "Your honesty and the integrity and kindness that you have shown not only to me, but to your subjects over the years. It would be my absolute honour to accept your proposal."

A hush descended as Temple looked back at her, his eyes searching her face for confirmation, for an assurance that he had heard what he had heard, waiting for the caveat that he was sure would follow. When none came, he grasped her hands and jumped to his feet.

"I assure you, Bridget, I will make you happy as best I can," he said breathlessly. "As happy as you have just made me ... let us celebrate!" He swung around in search of his glass and plucked it from the side table, swinging it violently in an upward arc and spilling a drop on the front of his shirt. "Oh that it were champagne!" he lamented. "I shall have some on our wedding day, my dear – to properly toast the moment that you agreed to formalise our perfect partnership. You, too, will be glorified, my dear. No longer a widowed housekeeper, but the *wife* of Samuel Temple, the greatest photographic artist in all of London. We will do great things together, my dear. Such plans, indeed!"

Bridget watched as her future husband drained his glass in one gulp and immediately scurried to the sideboard to pour another. His cheeks were flushed and his eyes gleaming with excitement. It seemed that he had their future laid out far in advance, a future that would lead him to glory.

She smiled at her fiancé, a smile that slipped when he turned his back. It wasn't that the engagement was problematic for her, of course, or that she necessarily disliked Mr Temple. It was that perhaps she would have to set to work quietly to modify his ambitions somewhat, to mould and *direct* him in a direction she wished to go. There was time for all that yet, of course.

She smiled again as Temple beamed at her and raised his glass. Patience, she urged herself. Patience and fortitude.

This was but the first step on the journey. There was a way to go yet.

Chapter 18

2018

Louise woke with a start to a bright bedroom, and the sound of the front door slamming.

Then voices – a man and a woman. *Shit*, she thought. *Ros is home.*

She pushed herself up on her elbows and reached to her bedside locker to check the time. Her eyes widened – it was half past ten in the morning. She had been asleep since the previous afternoon. She relaxed back onto the pillow, and realised that she felt rested for the first time in days.

She supposed she should get up and go say hello, politely ask Ros about San Francisco. Instead, she reached for her phone and pulled the covers up under her chin.

She had no sooner tapped into the news – Brexit, famous actor outed for sexual harassment, teenager still missing – than the emails started to whoosh in, one after the other – seven in all – from a client she wasn't fond of, but who paid excellent rates. She typed back frantically as she swung out of bed. **On it**, she replied.

Ros and Joe were in the kitchen when she got downstairs, Joe standing politely, arms folded, and Ros talking at him.

"Here's old clumsy clogs!" Ros yelled cheerily as Louise appeared.

Louise responded with a polite smile and crossed the kitchen to the kettle.

Ros slouched at the kitchen table, scrolling through something on her phone. On the table was a cup from Grounds, the café where Joe bought the morning cappuccinos, and an empty croissant wrapper.

He flashed Louise a sheepish look. "Brought you a coffee," he said meekly, indicating with his eyes that it was the empty one, as Louise flicked on the kettle and put two slices of bread in the toaster.

"Yeah – cool, thanks, mate," replied Ros without looking up.

Louise closed her eyes and took a deep breath, opening them again to see Joe smirk. She smirked back and turned back to the toaster.

"So I have a ton of work to do for a lunchtime deadline," she announced as she buttered the toast. "Could you guys maybe just keep the noise down a bit this morning?"

Joe responded by saluting. "Yes'm! I'm going to make a start on the kitchen."

Ros stretched and yawned. "I'm going to get some kip anyway. The old red-eye takes its toll – got me a case of the j-lags."

"You do that," Louise bit, before leaving the room, carrying her breakfast to the sanctuary of her office.

The work was marvellous. Feeling invigorated after her night's sleep, Louise lost herself in it, blocking out everything – the handicap of her injured foot, Ros, and the ... happenings in the house over the weekend. It felt liberating to be too busy to think about them, to puzzle over them, trying to understand how such impossible things could happen.

It was after four when she eventually emerged, ravenous and exhausted, but rewarded. The job was done, pick-ups sorted, and the first of the next phase of scripts recorded. Daylight grew dim outside as she entered the kitchen, to see Ros busy at the cooker.

The kitchen was, of course, in its post-Ros state – the fridge ajar, strips of carrot peel stuck to the surfaces of the kettle and the bread bin, tiny pepper seeds formed a trail to the sink, and the wooden breadboard stained where chillis had been chopped on it. The floor crunched underfoot as Louise crossed to the fridge, and she glanced down to see bits of dried noodles spilled from the packet all the way from cupboard to cooker.

"Good to get back on the health saddle. Those American portion sizes – *whooo!*" Ros announced cheerily, as she energetically shook the wok and flicked at it with a spatula. A clump of beansprouts flew over the edge, followed by some pepper on the next stir. There was a loud sizzle as the pot of noodles boiled over onto the hob. "Did you get your bit of work done?"

Louise couldn't help herself and sneered at her back. "It's a big contract actually," she said. She watched a piece of onion take flight across the kitchen floor.

"That'll be great for you, won't it?" Ros said.

Louise didn't reply, instead opening the fridge and peering inside. "There was a quiche in here," she said. "Did you eat it?"

"Oh that? Chucked that out, it was out of date."

Louise turned, her lips set in a thin line. "It wasn't," she said.

"It was use by today," Ros said, poking a fork at the noodles.

"Yes," Louise replied. "So it was still edible."

Ros's eyes widened as she shook her head. "No. Use *by* today – which means it had to be used yesterday."

"Seriously?" Louise said, her temper rising. "It was use by *today*, which means it was still fine to use *today*. If it had to be used by yesterday, *then* it would have had yesterday's date on it!"

Ros didn't answer, suddenly absorbed in draining her noodles and transferring them back to the wok.

Louise sank her teeth into the inside of her cheek and slammed the fridge door.

It was only then that her eye was drawn to the freshly painted walls at the far end of the kitchen, but nowhere else.

"Where's Joe?" she asked. "He doesn't finish until half five at the earliest."

Ros took her time about answering, carefully spooning her meal into a dish. "Oh, I sent him home," she said casually.

Louise frowned. "Why?"

Ros placed the spatula directly down onto the countertop and looked around at the walls. "He was doing the walls in here the wrong colour. This is a really shitty shade of brown. I just said to him to finish up and to start again with the right one tomorrow. He's done the hall all wrong as well." She waved a fork in the direction of the front door as she sat down and started to tuck in. "That's not the colour I told him to do at all," she observed through a mouthful of stir fry.

"No, it's not!" Louise snorted. "Damn right it's not –

that colour you picked was horrendous – these are the colours *I* picked."

Ros glared at her. "They're not the ones *I* told him to use," she said angrily. "Why did you go and change them behind my back?"

"You're colour blind," Louise retorted. "The colours that you picked – they were all wrong."

Ros suddenly slammed her fork down. "I didn't have to help you out with painting the house," she said, "but I thought I would, because you were always complaining about how rundown it looked – so I decided to *do* something about it. And instead you have to go behind my back and change it all!"

Louise stared back, open-mouthed with disbelief. "Because ... because, for starters, it was *horrible* ..."

"Jesus wept! Is this the thanks I get for doing something *nice* for you? It's not cheap, you know!"

Louise could feel heat rise from her chest into her face. "Well, you won't have to worry about spending a cent of your hard-earned money," she said. "*I'm* paying for it!"

Ros looked as if she had been smacked. "Since when? With what? You're broke?"

"*With my money that I earn from my job!*" Louise was yelling now. "What I do in that room isn't a 'little bit of work' – it's an actual job, that pays real money! So that I can eat, and buy clothes, and pay bills and get the painting done in *my* house!"

There was a sudden silence between them, broken sharply by the scrape of Ros's chair against the floor.

"So that's how it is now?" she said bitterly as she leapt to her feet. "*Your house* ..."

"Well, it *is* my house!"

Ros suddenly roared at her. "*I've got that! Loud and clear, okay?*"

An electric silence fell between them, each regarding the other contemptuously.

"What's that smell?" Ros asked suddenly, out of the blue.

"What smell?" Louise snapped.

Ros sniffed the air, frowning. "It's like shitty flowers or something – maybe it's that shitty paint that ... *Jesus!*"

They both jumped at the noise – the scrape of metal against metal, and then the swoosh and crash of the wok falling – no – *flying* off the cooker and crashing against the floor. They stared, incredulous, at where it had landed, a good four feet away from where Ros had left it on the cooker hob.

"*What the ever-living fuck did you do that for?*" yelled Ros, jumping to her feet.

Louise looked from the wok to her, eyes wide with shock. "What do you ... *I* didn't do that – how would I have done that? *I'm nowhere near it!*" she yelled back.

"*Well, it didn't do it by itself!*" Ros roared.

Louise, infuriated, opened her mouth to reply and then all of a sudden stopped, raising her head instead to sniff the air. That smell ... *shitty flowers* ... she could get it now. Lilies. For some reason, the kitchen smelled of lilies.

A strange feeling overtook Louise, as if the scent in the air somehow emboldened her.

"I need you to go," she said.

Ros stopped midway through bending down to pick up the spatula and stared at Louise.

"Sorry?" she said. "Go where?"

Louise shifted nervously but held her resolve.

"To leave. To move out. It's not working out, you living here."

Ros opened and closed her mouth, speechless, outraged. Then she slammed the spatula down on the kitchen table, turned, and stormed out into the hall.

Louise followed, and saw her put on her jacket and grab the bike. She contemplated, for the briefest instant, asking her where she was going, but she really and truly didn't care. She simply stared as Ros fumbled in her pockets, checking for wallet, and phone.

"I ... I just can't, Louise, okay?" she mumbled, before turning and opening the front door. "I'll talk to you when you're over ... whatever's going on with you. You've just lost your head or something." And with that she bumped the bike down the steps and reached back to slam the door behind her.

Louise basked in the silence as the echo of the bang receded. Finally – after putting it off for so long. It had actually been easy to get the words out when she needed to. Although she wasn't entirely sure Ros believed she was serious, she'd actually done it – kicked her out.

For a moment, a flicker of fear rippled through her at the sudden silence of the house. She was alone again. After the weekend and all it brought with it. What if ...

What if indeed, she thought suddenly. She'd cross that bridge when she came to it. Right now, she felt strong enough to take on anything. Turning slowly, she limped her way back to the kitchen where, with another loud, long sigh, this time of relief, she began to clean up.

Chapter 19

Joe turned off the engine and slumped back in the driver's seat, despite the fact he was late.

On purpose, mind, in the hopes that Ros would be back at work today and would have left by the time he got there. He shook his head in disbelief as he recalled her tone the previous day, stating how unhappy she was to come back and see the state of things, dismissing him as if he were some sort of servant. And now he was just bloody confused – Louise had said that Ros was moving out and that she'd be paying the bill, but Ros had breezed on back and assumed control – he hadn't known what to say to her, so he'd just left, as instructed, unwilling to wake Louise who had conked out on her new painkillers when she'd gone up for a nap.

Joe rolled his eyes at himself. What a mess. And here he was, back for more, in the confusion up to his knees. What was he doing getting so involved with all this Louise business anyway?

If he was honest with himself, she baffled him. And that shouldn't be a problem, he thought, grunting as he stepped out of the van and slowly approached the front door. Because she wasn't his friend, after all, just the lady whose house he was working on. No different to any of his clients. And if any of his other clients were giving him the runaround like these two, he damn well wouldn't be here until he'd had a call from one or other of them to clarify what his position was. So why was he so caught up in Louise's seemingly over-dramatic life? The leg injury, the shitty-flatmate trauma, the binge drinking – the fright he'd got the previous morning finding her like that. If it had been a bloke, he admitted to himself, he'd probably just have left him there. And another woman? Mrs Purcell at his last job? Well, he'd probably have sneaked back outside and vigorously knocked and rung at the front door until he'd roused her without actually having to wake her, and pretended that he hadn't seen anything amiss.

But Louise? His heart had been in his mouth when he'd seen her passed out on the couch like that, sure that something terrible had happened. He was probably foolish to believe her when she said it was only a once-off, mind. She'd been in a right state – and she'd got through those painkillers pretty fast, hadn't she? Had it been a ploy of some sort to get new ones, stronger ones from the doc? Bloody hell. What the hell was he doing?

It had been a bit scary in fairness, he admitted, inserting the front door key into the lock as quietly as he could manage, unsure if it would open at all. To find her lying in the dark like that on the couch in her office in the freezing cold ... what was it about this bloody house anyway, he wondered. It was like the walls were lined with ice.

To his surprise, the lock yielded to the key as easily as any other morning and the door opened – Ros hadn't changed them then or put on the safety chain or a deadbolt or anything against the errant painter. That was something, at least, he supposed.

The bike was gone too, which lightened his mood no end. Presumably Ros *had* gone to work, then. So hopefully Louise would be up and about – and sober – and he could maybe chat to her and try to figure out where he stood – whether to keep going or not. Cautiously, he cast an eye into all of the rooms downstairs. She was in none of them, in which case, he concluded, she was either gone out or was still asleep. He glanced at the stairs, contemplating seeing if she were up there, but instantly deciding against it on the grounds of over-familiarity. He sighed. Why did he feel he had to overthink everything about this bloody job? Casting an eye around the place, he laid his eyes on a tin of white gloss. That was it, he decided. He'd start on the woodwork. He'd be safe with that. Ros, surely, couldn't mistake white for anything else and cause another fuss, could she?

He rubbed his hands together to warm them before setting to work, laying out his dustsheet and prising open the tin, wiping at a streak of paint that transferred itself from the lid to his hand with a rag that he stuffed in the back pocket of his overalls. Then, calmly, he began to paint. And think.

Louise. He felt sorry for her, really – although he'd never say that to her – wouldn't know how, without sounding patronising. She'd lost her job, she'd said – he wondered what had happened there? And then moved in the first housemate who'd answered the ad. He shook his head. What a mistake that seemed to have been. So what would she do when Ros moved out? Move in a new housemate? Or live alone completely? Judging by what she said, her life seemed fairly isolated – not much in the line of friends, working from home, no boyfriend ... which wasn't a bad thing? He allowed his thoughts to stray for a moment to how pretty she was when she smiled, and the fact that she was funny, and he wondered suddenly, more than anything, what she'd be like if she wasn't stressed out, like she always seemed to be?

He swore under his breath as, distracted, he dripped paint onto his hand, and sat back on his heels, reaching around to his back pocket to grab the rag which he had stuffed there only moments before.

Except it wasn't there.

Puzzled, Joe, felt around his back to his other pocket for it, then swivelled around to check the floor behind him, but it wasn't there either. "What the fuck?" he swore quietly, as he frowned and stood up to get a better look. But the rag was nowhere to be seen.

"*Fucking house*," he hissed under his breath as a fresh blast of cold air wafted from the direction of Louise's studio just down the corridor. That damn breeze was something else he just couldn't figure out – now where was the *damn* rag? He shivered and pulled his glasses from the top pocket of his overalls to get a better look but there was still no sign. But he was *sure* he'd put it in his pocket – it wasn't like he didn't have other rags, but where the hell was this one gone?

Baffled, he rolled his shoulders back to stretch them and turned around fully to face the front door, stopping abruptly and staring in complete disbelief at what he saw.

How? How could that have happened? He was completely alone, and he hadn't done it, so how? It was completely impossible ...

Joe stared and stared at what he knew couldn't have happened – but had.

The rag, that he knew for certain he'd stuffed into his pocket, was dangling – impossibly – from the catch of the Yale lock on the front door.

He blinked and looked over his shoulder expecting to see ... what, exactly ... someone who would verify that he was seeing what he thought he was seeing. Was this really happening, or was it a hallucination ...

He glanced upstairs again, his face pale at a memory from the previous day at the clinic where he'd brought Louise to get her foot seen to, of Louise asking her doctor if her painkillers could cause hallucinations, insisting when asked, that no, she hadn't been having any herself, she was just curious. But if she hadn't been having hallucinations, then why did she ask? Or at least *thought* she was having them ... because, for a moment, *he* had thought he was having one, but he wasn't, was he? The rag had really, truly, travelled *somehow* from his back pocket to hang on the front door.

Frozen to the spot, Joe stared at it, suddenly terrified to go and retrieve it, while all the while, around him, the hallway seemed to grow colder and colder.

Maybe he shouldn't have come in today after all, he thought, as goosebumps exploded all over his body.

Chapter 20

London 1865

The bride wore lavender – a colour deemed suitable based on her age and her status as a widow – and carried a modest posy of myrtle leaves and holly berries from the photographer's garden that she bound together herself.

"I have no time for fuss or fripperies," she told her intended in a businesslike fashion when he presented her with a wedding gift of a pair of pearl-drop earrings. "If we are to be married and to create a household anew, then income should be preserved for necessities, or kept safe for future needs. It is a partnership we enter, Samuel," she chided him. "Not a fancy-dress competition." Still, however, she kept them, and wore them as she made her vows to love, honour and obey, before two witnesses and the chaplain. It was the only sign of ostentation on a day which verged on puritanical.

There was neither wedding breakfast nor honeymoon – indeed, the bride insisted that her new husband keep an appointment to photograph a family of three in Mayfair.

"Business as usual, Samuel," she had instructed him, dusting lint from the shoulder of his greatcoat as he set off into the December air. "We must start as we mean to go on, you and I. Partners, with such plans."

Smiling, yet a little bewildered and disappointed, Samuel did as his new wife bade him. There was time yet, he decided, when the fire was lit and the evening dark, to enjoy a celebratory glass and mark the occasion. His wedding day – imagine! He couldn't quite believe his luck.

Alone in her house, the new Mrs Temple cast a fresh eye about her as she wandered through the rooms and began to make some mental notes. True, she had resided here for a little over a month now, and Temple, to his credit, had kept his promise and found himself lodgings elsewhere for the sake of propriety.

Now, however, with her simple gold band tight around her finger, things had changed. She was now mistress of this place and, as such, had a duty to make it as homely and suitable for their married life as possible. A lick of paint here, she thought, and fresh curtains there. It would just require some freshening-up for now – a woman's touch, for it had too long been the abode of a bachelor. There was no point in spending large sums on it, however. Not when it was a temporary arrangement.

There was much business to be attended to, in the meantime, however – she would have to look at the finances of the household and, possibly, the business – she had an excellent head, and years of experience at household book-keeping, of course – a weight that she could lift from her husband's shoulders. And there was planning to be done also. Temple had many qualities but thinking ahead wasn't one of them. Indeed, even thinking of anything beyond his ghoulish fascination with dead freaks seemed to be a difficulty when it came to her husband.

No, someone would have to take control of things if

everything was to go the way she imagined it, if she was to travel cleanly from step to step to reach her final goal. She was sure she'd been there before, but it was clear now: Watson had not been the man she needed him to be.

Temple, on the other hand. Well, he was a busy man, who had much to focus on that was not at all domestic.

Lucky for him, he had Bridget then. And lucky for Bridget, that she had him to work into her plan.

Chapter 21

2018

Louise couldn't say for certain, but for the next day and a half, she imagined that what she might be feeling verged on happiness – contentment, certainly.

Her mind was occupied with work, her ankle was feeling remarkably better and as for the strange happenings in the house? Nothing – unless you counted another of the vivid dreams with the girl dressed in white who came to visit her room. It had happened again the night Ros had left, leaving Louise with a lovely feeling of being protected and looked-after. She was fairly sure too that she understood now what it meant. Any amateur dream detective could figure out that the young girl was her own developing self-confidence – the sense of feeling loved and protected was simply the part inside her that was growing less fearful of taking care of her own life. And the missing hands? Well, that was easiest of all – once she had cut off the most obvious thing that was troubling her she felt proud of it, and wanted to hold it up and show it off, as it were, just as the girl did in the dream. "*Special. Darn tootin' I'm special,*" Louise whispered to herself as she thought about it. It was a sign, she was sure. That things were going to turn around for her. That she was over the worst.

There had been no contact from Ros either. Admittedly, Louise had kept half an eye on her social media to see where she was and, more importantly, if she was coming back. Ros had been unusually quiet, however – a photograph of traffic in the rain at dusk the previous day with the misspelled caption '**Curent Mood**'; and a **Watch Me Run** app map showing a route through the Phoenix Park, near to where her parents lived.

At lunchtime on Thursday, however, there was a knock on the front door.

Louise's stomach fluttered as she made her way down the hall – which, oddly, Joe hadn't finished painting yet – he had been in a funny mood for the past few days, in fact – and tentatively turned the latch.

Ros stood there, a suitcase resting on the step beside her.

Louise's heart sank as she looked from it to her.

"You're here," Ros observed gruffly.

Louise frowned. Where else would she be?

"I just came by because ..." Ros took a deep breath, as if to fortify herself, "I'm just going to have to leave, Louise." Her tone was matter of fact.

Louise frowned.

"I'm moving out," Ros clarified, as if Louise had a problem with understanding her.

"That's what ... that's what I asked you to do on Tuesday," Louise replied.

"There's no point in having any argument about it. I'm sorry, but I just can't stay here with you ... with ... *Jesus*, the tension, Louise!" She looked her deep in the eyes. "The *tension*!"

154

Louise stood back to let her in.

"Just to clarify, Ros," she said. "It was me who said that you –"

"I just need to go upstairs," Ros said, ignoring her completely. "I need to get my stuff. I'm taking everything now. My brother's here with his van outside. I've had to take the day off."

Bemused, Louise indicated that she could go ahead. "Knock yourself out," she said.

Ros responded by picking up the suitcase with ease – it was empty, of course – and starting up the stairs. Louise closed the front door over and watched her go, before heading to the kitchen to assemble a sandwich for lunch.

She ate without tasting, listening to the movement upstairs as Ros bustled and thumped about.

Fifteen minutes later, a scraping from the front door lock indicated that Joe was back after his own lunch – he had taken to eating elsewhere over the past couple of days, instead of grabbing a sandwich and bringing it back, chatting to her as he ate at the kitchen table as had been his habit for a while.

He entered the kitchen quietly.

"Okay if I make a coffee?" he asked.

"Sure," Louise replied, distracted. She paid him no attention as he gathered everything he needed – mug, spoon, coffee, sugar, milk and waited for the kettle to boil.

"There's a van parked right outside – guy sitting it. Thought it was a bit odd," Joe remarked as the kettle boiled.

"A white van? Maguire Shredding?"

Joe nodded.

She was just about to explain when suddenly a loud thump came from upstairs and Joe gave a start.

"*Jesus!*" he yelled. "Did you hear that?"

Louise turned to look at him, slightly puzzled by his reaction. "Sorry," she said. "It's Ros – she's just .... getting her stuff."

Joe clasped his chest. "*Fucking* hell," he breathed. "Sorry. I just ..."

Loud footsteps on the stairs interrupted his flow, followed by the noise of plastic rustling and a fresh set of thumps and bangs coming from the sitting room.

Ros appeared in the kitchen a moment later.

"I'm done ... oh, hi ..."

His voice trailed off as he noticed Joe standing at the countertop. He couldn't have looked any less comfortable as he nodded in greeting before leaving the room. "Just going to pop to the loo," he mumbled as he slid awkwardly past Ros.

She waited until he was gone.

"I'm done," she announced dramatically.

Louise stared, unsure if she meant the packing, or with her. She managed a nod in response.

"I'd give you back my key, but I never got it back from the painter," she continued. "Never even got the chance." She turned abruptly and headed down the hall.

Sighing, Louise stood to follow. By the time she stepped out of the kitchen, Ros was standing by the front door, a black refuse bag in each hand, surrounded by the rest of her belongings.

"I just have to say this before I go, Louise. I hope you find a good housemate to replace me, but I don't think you will. I was good to you – helping you with the rent, doing things around the house, being a friend."

Louise's eyebrows shot upwards, and a burst of courage came from somewhere.

"No, Ros," she replied calmly. "That wasn't the case. And to be fair, the rent was well below what you'd have been paying elsewhere. I simply don't want to share my house anymore."

Ros tilted her head to one side. "You know, Louise, that's just you all over. *I don't want to share.* I mean how hard is it? And what am I supposed to do now? Do you know what it's like out there? Am I to live on the streets? Get myself a nice, big cardboard box? There's a homelessness crisis, do you know that? Do you? And if you do, do you care about contributing to it? Do you?"

Louise rolled her eyes. "Come on, Ros ... it's hardly ..."

But Ros had turned her back, swinging the front door wide open, before storming out toward the van parked on the kerb.

Louise stood in the hallway, hands on her hips, and watched as Ros's brother Brian stepped out and slid open the side door for Ros to lob the bags inside before she turned to charge back toward the house.

But just as she reached the bottom step, something entirely unexpected happened. Louise gasped as the front door suddenly and without warning swung violently shut, slamming directly in Ros's face. There was silence for a moment, the sound of the bang reverberating through the house, and then Ros started to hammer the door knocker.

Louise stared for a moment, then rushed to open it. Ros's face was red with fury.

"*What the absolute fuck did you do that for?*" she roared.

"I didn't – I swear!" Louise replied, her heart racing, her mind playing over and over again what had just happened. "It must have been the wind or a draught or something." *But there had been no wind – and a draught strong enough to close it was only caused if the back door was open at the same time. But this – this was as if someone had pushed it with all their might, to slam it …*

"*I swear to God!*" Ros hissed. "Let me get the rest of my damn stuff out of this place. What kind of *bitch* slams a door in someone's face? You could have hurt me! After that business with the wok too – you need your head examined!"

Louise shook her head, her eyes wide. "I didn't, Ros – I swear!"

"She didn't, mate – I saw her."

Louise glanced over her shoulder at Joe who stood on the stairs, his face as white as her own. Ros, too, looked up toward the painter and gritted her teeth at the sight. "And you – you, *mate*, you can … you can *fuck right off!*" she spat, wagging a finger in Joe's direction.

Sullenly, she bent and picked another black plastic bag and the now-full suitcase and exited the house again, turning to glare once more at Louise and Joe as she strode down the path.

Louise swallowed, and looked back at Joe, who still stood halfway up the stairs, as unmoving as she was – and was taken aback by what she saw.

He was white-faced, and his expression was one of deep worry – or was that fear? But, instead of watching the scene of Ros's departure played out, his gaze instead was turned toward Louise's bedroom door. A surge of fright suddenly ran through Louise as she watched him. Why was he doing that?

And then, as she tried to sort her jumbled thoughts, and regain some control of her emotions, there was an unusual shift in the atmosphere. She couldn't describe it, could barely acknowledge it, but something ... something *changed*. She listened as the side door of the van outside slid shut, and the engine started, chugging loudly. A door slammed, and it revved, and drove away.

And – again. Louise sniffed the air – it was unmistakable, the heavy perfume of blooms billowed through the space, coming from upstairs, and clouding around her, like a cloak.

Or an embrace.

Chapter 22

Kent 1865

From the time she was a tiny child, Maud had nursed one desire over all others, and that was the desire to be of help to someone.

And from the time she was a tiny child, that very desire was denied to her.

"Let me, Mama," she would beg, as the chickens were fed and eggs collected, dishes washed and puddings stirred. The response was always the same – "How?" – the tone of delivery derogatory, and Maud would be brushed aside so that the task at hand could be completed effectively – always without her.

And so it was that Maud came to grow up as an '*other*'. Present, at the centre of the trio who existed together on the small holding – mother, daughter, son – the father had been lost to them many years before – yet sorely absent from the *life* that was lived there. She grew up surrounded by love, but distant from participation – always apart, a watcher in the heart of her own family.

So she contented herself with that – keeping a keen eye from her perch on the hearth in the kitchen, or from the window seat in her tiny bedroom, watching through the glass for the comings and goings of her family.

She knew she was lucky in many ways – her mother always reminded her of that, and never let her fall asleep at night without first thanking the Lord for her blessings – a roof over her head, bread on the table, a fire at night. And God had blessed her with good health overall – what he had not given, he had compensated for by never laying her low with a cold or a cough. But she longed to do more, to bid her exhausted mother sit by the fire a while to sup tea while she weeded the herb garden, or carried a bucket of milk on the crook of her elbow, or pummelled the dough to make a loaf. How she longed to see how that felt, plunging into the soft, sticky mixture and beating it into shape, tossing it in flour, turning it and kneading until her muscles ached.

And so she would sit and observe, and keep an eye, and from time to time she'd see that perhaps her mother needed something – a drop of milk, a spoon, a cup – and she would nudge it toward her, to put it at hand, and if her mother were in a good mood she would be rewarded with a smile, and if not, a '*tsk*' or a 'for heaven's sake, you'll break it!'. But, regardless of this, she would do it again the next time in expectation of the warm smile and the elation of feeling useful at last. And then she'd return to her thoughts and lose herself, become someone who could make and do, could pluck at loose hair and slide it satisfyingly against her cheek, or even summon delicate sound from a harp. And often, when she lay in bed at night, she would try to imagine what it would feel like to wiggle the fingers she had never had, to run the pad of an index across the silk of her eyebrow, or scratch between her shoulder blades when they itched.

God may not have given her hands, her mother reassured her, and that was, indeed, a burden – to both Maud and to the household – but he had given her a beautiful soul instead, and so she must be happy with that, because it meant that her entry to heaven was guaranteed, her spirit would never wander the earth in despair. And Maud, good and gracious and loving to her mother as she was, would agree, and bow her head as if saying her prayers, when instead she would lose herself in dreams of scooping up handfuls of clear stream water and drinking from her cupped palms.

Chapter 23

1866

Samuel Temple grimaced in disgust as the air coming through the carriage window gradually acquired a body to it – a sweet stink that offended his nostrils. The great jolt he experienced as the wheels lurched through a pothole further distressed him, and, as he righted himself, grateful that his camera was safely at home, he glared at his travelling companion who continued to snooze undisturbed, and wonder why on earth he had allowed such a disagreeable trip to be taken.

The sight of Mrs Temple, dozing, her chin resting against her chest as her body bounced with the movement of their transport, irked him. And he had to confess – to himself only, of course – that it was not entirely as pleasing as he had once found it. He took a moment to study her – at her finest, she had been handsome indeed – there was no denying that – but hard, her cheekbones set high in her face, her lips pursed and her jaw firm. He found her eyes the most unsettling thing. Green and narrow – reminiscent of those of a snake he had seen once at the Zoological Gardens. They were at once alluring in their rarity – but repellent, like a barrier to keep anyone from seeing what was inside, what was her true nature, something of which he still wasn't sure, despite the six months of marriage and cohabitation which he had found, to his inner dismay, he was enduring rather than enjoying.

The reality of their union, he found, was – despite his best efforts – not quite as idyllic as his vision of it had been. He was no fool, mind, and had known better than to *expect* fawning poetry and stolen kisses. He was a pragmatic man, after all, who had realistic requirements in a wife – companionship, of course – practicality, excellent housekeeping skills, a strong work ethic – all of which Mrs Temple possessed in spades. She had undertaken her duties as the manager of the Temple household with enormous energy and commitment – the trouble was, it was almost too much energy and commitment for his liking.

She had commenced by donning an apron herself and embarking on what she called 'a good clean' which involved a vigorous decluttering that resulted in the loss of many of his lifetime acquisitions – inherited, gifted and purchased – and the rearrangement of many more, that left him entirely at sea in a home where practically everything was dusted, beaten, plumped, polished or replaced. Indeed, it seemed as though Mrs Temple could not rest until it was just to her liking, even then declaring only that 'it would do for now'.

Once pleased with the aesthetics, he felt sure that she would relax a little – he understood it was the prerogative of a lady to nest – perhaps not as thoroughly as his wife had done, but if it made her happy then he was content to comply, on the basis that it would free her time and energy to embark upon the course that he envisaged – namely that she would become a companion in his work as much as in his domestic life. He envisaged her coming with him as an assistant when visiting clients, patiently arranging flowers and comforting distraught relatives; serving tea perhaps to those who came to his studio to have portraits taken – fully participating in his day to day, and then spending cosy evenings by the fire engaged in long discussions on his work and his plans. Such encouragement, he felt, would help him to flourish, to thrive.

It was not given, however. There was no time to do so, if his wife were to be believed. So much to do always – "A house does not run itself, Mr Temple," she clucked at him. She continued to use his full title, instead of an affectionate 'Samuel' or even – he dared to dream – 'Sam', which was what his mother had called him. It stung, somewhat, although not as deeply as another change that he had not expected, that of her complete apathy to his special work. It had been one of his favourite visions of their time together in the run-up to their union – hours lost in the study of his portraiture, imagining the future of it, figuring ways to make it better, more beautiful, more striking and honest – all of it done together. "I am too busy," she would tell him, before scurrying off to beat a rug with a duster. Or a somewhat dismissive "You are the expert". Once, he was sure he had caught a glimpse of disgust flicker briefly across her features when he had suggested they might look together at some of the finer points of the portrait of Adeline Brown – she had by no means paid it sufficient heed when first he had shown it to her. Although, he recalled, that was the night he had asked her to become his wife. In such a case he would forgive her, he decided. It had not been the best evening to examine the nuances of light and shadow falling on the ample wealth of flesh that it had been his fortune to capture.

And so he left her to it, as he always did.

And still, once the house had finally reached her standards, there was still to be no rest for Mrs Temple as she leaped headfirst from the physical cleansing into the administrative. Away went the feather dusters and out came the ledgers – goodness gracious, the ledgers! – accounts for the kitchen, lists of food for the household – what was needed, used and wasted. Lists of medicines and bandages and tinctures and potions, incomings and outgoings, an inventory of every item in the place from forks to furniture. Everything printed down in tidy rows and all of it – every last item, every last catalogued piece – all of it to be signed. In she would sweep – always in the midst of his working day – in a businesslike fashion with ledgers and notebooks piled open in her arms, all to be thrust at him for his mark. Only once, with a great sigh of frustration, did he challenge her. "Why on earth is there always to be a requirement for my signature? I seem to spend half the live-long day scribbling my name on your ridiculous household books and manage to use half the ink in London in doing it." Suffice it to say that her response – that icy, unforgiving stare, reminding him coolly that it was now "the system of the household of which he was head" – rendered any future complaint unthinkable, lest there be serious domestic consequences. From then on in, without outward complaint but with inner reluctance, Samuel complied with the system of the books, and although he eventually gave up examining the tiresome content, he patiently and clearly put his name to everything that his wife commanded.

And it seemed, he thought, to make her happy. She

fulfilled her domestic duties with the efficient zeal that she had learned from her days in service, those days from which he had rescued her, he noted on occasion; and he had plenty to eat, clean clothes to wear and a home so pristine that it would pass muster with the most fastidious military general. She seemed almost content – certainly busy enough – and he, well, what had he expected at his age? There was no room for the sentimental notions that rose in him now and again, the thought that he might turn and suddenly catch her admiring gaze upon him, or that at some unexpected time on a walk outdoors perhaps, or as he gazed through the windows out into the rain, that he should feel her hand slip into his and her head rest on his shoulder in search of comfort or protection.

There were often times when he didn't know what next to expect from his wife. Such tender moments were not among them, however.

It was the pregnancy that he expected least of all.

She had softened with it, all over her body, not just around the belly where his child – the idea of it made him queasy – grew and kicked, but everywhere, her face especially. The carriage jerked from side to side, and with it went the second chin which was rounding beneath the first, the jowly, puffed-out cheeks – even her lips were almost twice their size, not to mention her wrists and ankles. She stirred, as the driver relayed that they were almost at their destination, and an involuntary belch escaped her. Temple's lip curled in disgust, both at the sight of what this incubation had done to his handsome wife, and the prospect of what lay ahead of them in the months to come. The child was due in the autumn, she believed. And it was summer now. He had best make the most of it. Once this infernal vacation was finally over, this delayed-honeymoon, she had described it, then he would do his utmost on their return to perhaps capture some of the moments that he had foreseen when he had contemplated this marriage. What a magical prospect it had seemed, he recalled ruefully. How different the reality, but then, was that not life?

His musings were interrupted by the carriage rolling to a halt in what seemed to be the middle of nowhere. Their stop, the driver informed them, and offered no hand to assist with the removal of luggage from the roof, nor the removal of the disconcerted, swollen woman down the step. Temple managed it all, cursing silently the fact that they had come to this place – so wild, so uncivilised that trains did not run there yet, with porters, and platforms not made of mud, and regular return schedules.

A boy of eighteen or nineteen waited to then convey them, once they had disembarked at the coach stop, in what he could only describe as a haycart to their final destination. Caked in damp muck to his shins, Temple worried, as they clopped along what seemed like interminable mucky lanes, that he might die of shame should anyone encounter them. It was impossible to maintain dignity in this manner, he fumed, outraged, wisps of hay clinging to his jacket as he clutched his hat lest it be blown halfway across the county as he was bounced about. Resentment bubbled through him as he caught sight of his wife, upright and regal beside the boy as he *hoo*-ed and *haa*-ed the lumbering carthorse deeper into the countryside. Her head was held high, and she seemed to be sniffing appreciatively, inhaling great draughts of air before half turning and speaking over her shoulder to him.

"*This is Jasper, by the way, Mr Temple!*" she yelled in a most unladylike fashion over the clatter of the wheels. "*He is my nephew of sorts. The son of my husband's sister – oops, my late husband's sister.*"

He regarded her in surprise as she turned her face to the sunlight again and gave a great wobbling jolt as they rolled over a stone. Whatever sort of a thing to say had that been?

"We won't be long now," she added calmly, as they rounded a corner, and he suddenly had to scrabble for purchase to keep from sliding off the back of the cart. And she was correct because, before he could compose a response, the boy *whoah*-ed the horses to a standstill outside a thatched house which looked as old as the Bard, and a flurry of activity came from within. So they had arrived then. And this was to be their lodgings.

It looked a pleasant enough place, thought Temple, even if it were in the middle of nowhere. Charming, even. He could endure it, he was sure, although he wasn't entirely sure that he had brought adequate footwear. They were to visit for only a few days, however, in order for him to meet his new wife's family, such as they were, and then they would be gone, back to the city, back to the murk and the grime and the opportunity. Home, where heaven knew what you could possibly encounter under a hood on a street corner, or spot through a window at dusk. A city full of secrets, of potential for his gallery of wonder.

He stood a little away from his wife as she stiffly kissed the cheeks of a ruddy-faced matron who emerged from the house, dressed in her finest, no doubt, yet still to Temple's eye looking like a scarecrow. He observed the reunion. It was a pleasant one, nonetheless – the boy busily carrying the bags inside, Mrs Temple and her Country Mouse sister-in-law remarking on the weather and enquiring about the journey respectively, until suddenly Country Mouse was distracted by a dark shape shooting through her legs and causing a great fuss amongst a sisterhood of chickens who plucked and squawked a little distance away.

"*Puss!*" the country sister exclaimed. "Oh my goodness, pardon me, Bridie – *puss!*" – and she was away after the cat, flapping her skirts and yelling.

Temple raised his eyebrows and took the opportunity to slip alongside his wife. "You go by Mrs Temple and Bridget in the city, and Bridie in the country, then?" he smirked. "Another alias for the woman of mystery?"

"And what of it?" she bit back.

Temple was immediately chastened. The pregnancy made her quick to anger sometimes, of course. And no doubt she was tired after the trip. He would pedal back to ensure that he kept her temper moderate.

"It is a beautiful name, and a beautiful place to go with it," he reassured her, glancing once again at his surroundings. "And the sooner we are here, then the sooner we can get home, eh? We have much to prepare for, many plans to make."

"Why, Mr Temple, a trip to the countryside benefits us in so many ways – cleanses the lungs, refreshes the brain, invigorates the spirit." The erstwhile Mrs Watson breathed deeply, turning toward the house and indicating with a nod that he should do the same. "And, besides, plans can be made in places other than murky old London town, is that not so?"

Temple followed the line of her gaze, confused, as still the ruckus between the cat and the chickens behind him carried on.

"I am eager for certain things in life, Mr Temple," she continued in a serious tone. "As a widow, I was at a huge disadvantage in this world. Yet now I am a wife again, and soon to be a mother. I have new responsibilities to consider and, as such, I thought it time, perhaps, that we should explore the possibility of existence outside the gradual degradations of the city to experience a life more ... *pure*, more pastoral."

She glanced at her sister-in-law and Temple was surprised to observe what he was sure was a flash of ... could it be ... *envy*?

Turning back to him, Mrs Temple began to scratch her swollen belly absentmindedly.

"As you know, Mr Temple, my wants in life are few. That does not render them unimportant, however. As your wants are yours, my wants are *mine*, and dear to me. As is my future ... *our* future, as we are one – husband and wife together, is that not so?"

Temple opened his mouth to speak but couldn't think what to say, temporarily winded as he was by her talk of their union in such terms. She took another of her long inhalations as the belly-scratching lessened in intensity and became a gentle tracing of circles around her distended midriff with her fingernails.

"It is beautiful here, do you not think?"

Again, he spluttered, unable to think what to say. She carried on regardless.

"A most suitable place to bring up a child, wouldn't you agree? Clean air, fields to run in – perhaps with siblings – wouldn't that be wonderful? A village to frequent, a church to attend – with a pew of our own, perhaps – a plaque with our name 'Temple' to identify it as our seat, our rightful place near the altar and near to God. There is a status to be had in the countryside that simply does not exist in the city, I believe. Once out here with the woods to one side and the harvest to the other – well, it is easier to stand out, to be seen, and respected – to take one's place that one deserves."

Temple studied her as she spoke, her bright eyes, her eager expression. It was quickly beginning to dawn upon him what she meant as she continued.

"You cannot possibly mean that we should ... that we are to consider ... *living* here, my dear Bridget, now are you?" he asked in disbelief.

Her response was an unfamiliar charming, tinkling laugh. "Goodness no, you silly thing!" she replied. "Not *here*. Not in this crowded little ... *hut*, as suitable as it is for our visit, of course – with my wastrel husband's family. But elsewhere – nearby, perhaps. There is a house – my sister-in-law wrote to me of it – with some land – a fine place – a *Hall*, no less. I thought we might pay a visit while we are here. Please say that we can. Just a look ... there are gardens, and room perhaps for some pets – a pony, even. It would be perfect – idyllic – just you and me and baby of course – *our* baby. Our little family."

Temple stared at her, trying to figure out if this were another of her mocking games, this new way of speaking, the almost coquettish expression on her face. "I suppose ..." he replied, realising that she awaited a response – and the right one, at that. He was rewarded – most unexpectedly – with, of all things, a kiss on the cheek, before she turned, beaming, to pay attention once more to her sister-in-law who returned carrying the cat – a filthy, mange-ridden thing with one milky eye and a leathery ear. Together, the women clucked and cooed over it, as though it were a kitten, and paid no heed to Temple whose expression of stunned delight at the kiss slowly melted into something different entirely: one of absolute disbelief that, in turn, became one of horror.

Surely not, he thought. This must be some trick of hers, some game, some tease with which she meant to badger him for reasons yet unclear. It wasn't, however, was it? She had tricked him into coming to visit her family when, all the while, it was a more permanent move she had in mind – did she truly? Could this really be her heart's desire? This soft, fat, cat-stroking stranger who wanted to spawn more offspring to run in these godforsaken shit-scented fields? To leave the city and move to the countryside? Who was this stranger? Some changeling replacement for the woman with whom he had fallen in love? That sophisticated, mysterious, urbane, formidable woman – what had happened to her? What had happened to their partnership? Their meeting of minds? How on *earth* would he live in the countryside? How would he survive out here? The isolation, the quiet – how would he go about his business? And *who* would be his business? Should he photograph the trees? The peasants? The damned *pony*?

Absolutely not, he fumed, as his wife continued to ignore him, having moved on to some pleasantries with the boy – a gangling, malnourished creature. Was that what his own son would look like at his coming of age? Dressed in rags, working amidst beasts and filth and a savage, unfamiliar landscape? Good God, but that would not happen – never! He had little interest in the arrival of an infant, but the infant would grow to be a man – a man to take on his father's name, his father's mantle. His son would be the second finest photographer ever known in London circles, and he would be groomed and trained in his father's image, ready for the day when he would take up the reins – not of some lumbering hairy carthorse, but of the most remarkable gallery in all of England. And that – that level of training, of sophistication – that would not take place in the godforsaken countryside.

He blanched a little as Bridget turned suddenly and smiled at him. He gazed at her, transfixed for a moment by the softening of her expression, by the calmness in her smile. He felt himself soften, and begin to melt toward her. Perhaps ...

No.

He straightened his back and looked away from her. She would not have her way this time, he told himself. Not with smiles, nor with kisses, nor with any romantic gesture that he had been sure was impossible between them. He would stay firm. For the duration of their visit, he would remain calm, aloof. He would see what she wanted him to see, and then, when they returned to London, she would be told, in no uncertain terms that such a move was a sheer impossibility, and that it was impertinent of her to even consider such a thing. He would put an end to it once they got home. If he was head of the household, as she was so fond of saying every time she produced a journal and a bottle of ink, then he would damn well act like it. These women and their notions. What possessed them? And why, oh why, had he married such a one as this? Cruel one moment, downright silly the next. Temple cast his eye over the bushes in the garden and toward the house – anything to avoid catching his wife's eye – and sighed heavily.

His attention was suddenly drawn to movement in an upstairs window, and then down to his wife and her sister-in-law who were also looking up and smiling.

"Why, there she is – goodness, she's grown!" exclaimed Bridget.

"That she has," replied her sister in law. "Your little niece – she was ever so small when last you saw her."

Temple frowned. A niece as well as a nephew. How many more were there? Presumably they would all want to come live in this 'Hall' of Bridget's. Happy families, all under one roof. Clucking hens, ganging up together, while he, the proud rooster, stayed apart from them all, isolated and ignored. Damn them to hell. How would he possibly endure these next few days? Perhaps he wouldn't have to stay – now there was a thought. He could be called back to London for urgent business ... no, that wouldn't do. No one knew where he was. No – he felt uneasy about leaving the business for so long. He'd return early to keep an eye on things, to prepare the house for Bridget's return – perhaps that would get him out of it. Without him here, she might even abandon her plans to visit this Hall and reconsider the notion of becoming the wife of a country squire. That should do it, he thought. He'd have some supper and then outline his plan – he'd do it in front of the Country Mouse too – there was less likelihood of Bridget growing angry with him if they were not in private.

He frowned more deeply as the women as the women began to 'coo-ee' and wave at the figure in the window.

How unseemly, he thought, regarding with disdain their flapping hands and shrieking voices. Glancing upward, he tried to make out what the shrew above at which they hollered might look like.

"*Yoo-hoo, Maud!*" called Country Mouse. "Come down and meet your auntie and uncle!"

The shape stepped closer to the window, close enough for Temple to fully make her out. Close enough for him to pause for a moment – in his thoughts, his plans – his breathing even.

Then he gasped, and all the angry thoughts and ideas that had been formulating in his head moments before dissipated immediately.

Because the girl waved back.

And when she did, it suddenly became clear to Mr Temple that there was something of interest for him here after all.

Chapter 24

2018

Joe hesitated for a moment outside the front door before letting himself in. He was starting to really have second thoughts about this job. This house – that thing with the rag the other day – it was freaky, and freezing cold all the time too. It made him so jumpy just being here – every noise and creak and bang.

And ... the other thing ... the front door, and then ... that thing on the stairs ... had that been for real?

No. He wasn't going to think about that now, he simply wasn't. If he did, he'd never be able to get on with the job and get it finished.

He swallowed, toying with the door key as he glanced up the road where three men in hi-vis jackets unloaded plastic barriers and set them around a tree, the roots of which had caused undulations and cracks in the surrounding concrete. He could just walk out, of course – refer Louise to someone else. He could just put that key through the letterbox right now and walk away – away from that weird house and the weird stuff he'd felt and seen – *the way it had just ... just ... floated past him on the stairs and into that room* ... but really – would he really? What would he tell people – what would he tell Louise? They'd think he was insane.

Reluctantly, Joe slid the key into the lock. Nah. He'd have to suck it up. Just get over himself – it couldn't be real, after all, could it? Maybe it had just been a reflection of something, some weird optical illusion.

He shuddered again at the memory of it, then pushed the door open. He had to stop thinking about it right now, had to stop letting his imagination lead him astray. He was only getting himself all worked up over what had to be absolutely nothing.

He worked as quickly as he could through the morning, heading straight to Ros's now empty room rather than to Louise's which had been next on his list. He wasn't entirely sure he was ready to go in there yet.

By noon, the walls clean with their first coat of palest blue, Joe stood back to survey what he had done, his mind blank and calm, his focus on his work. Suddenly, an unexpected movement at his back made him jump, and he turned with a sharp gasp only to see Louise's familiar face peering around at him.

"Sorry," she said.

Blushing, and with his heart still racing, Joe popped his headphones from his ears and took a breath to calm himself.

"I've been stuck into some work all morning – only emerging now – I thought you'd hear me clopping up the stairs like a lame horse," she said, smiling.

He held up his headphones. "Just had music on." He didn't add that it was to block out anything else that he might hear around the house. If he couldn't hear it, then it couldn't make him edgy. Although, if he couldn't hear it, he couldn't tell if it was sneaking up on him ...

Louise tilted her head and looked at him. "You okay?"

He nodded. "All good," he replied, hoping that he sounded convincing.

"*I'm* just going out," she announced brightly.

"You're what?"

"First time since the fall – I'm making a break for it! Well, to McCarthy's – do you know the little old shop on the corner of Arden Road there? It's just a lovely day, and the foot doesn't feel too bad, so I thought I'd give it a shot. Would you like me to get you anything?"

"*Ooh* – that shop that's travelled through time? Let me see … a quarter of Bull's Eyes and forty Capstans, please?" he said and laughed.

Louise smiled back. "Alright then. Keep your phone handy in case I need rescuing again," she replied, and started down the stairs.

Joe stood, listening to her slow, careful descent, and then to the thick silence filling and settling in the house once the front door banged shut. Outside, a jackhammer rattled sporadically against the pavement. It was the sound of civilisation, but it seemed very distant.

Hi skin began to prickle immediately. Fuck that, he thought. He wasn't staying here alone. He'd take his lunch break early – nip off and grab something quick and eat it in the van until he saw Louise come back. He blushed at himself. What a bloody wuss he was! A grown man, afraid to be on his own in a little terraced house. But there was no denying that this place freaked him out.

He shed his overalls quickly and jogged down the stairs, feeling more relieved the closer he got to the front door.

Then his phone rang, just as he reached for the latch. He answered immediately, without looking at the screen, sure it was Louise ringing for pretend assistance. "Are you lost already?" he said with a smile, a smile which turned to a frown as soon as the caller at the other end responded.

"Is that the painter?"

It was the voice of an elderly woman. Joe grimaced. "Sorry about that, I thought you were someone else. It is, what can I do for you?"

"Do I have the wrong number? I was looking for the painter?"

"No – you have me," he replied.

"So you're not the painter?"

Joe rolled his eyes. "No. I mean yes ... yes, *I* am the painter. Can I help you at all?"

"I need some painting done," she began, and with that, she embarked on a description in her crackling old voice of where she lived – including directions – what she might want painted, and also what she might not. "It all depends, you know?"

Joe rolled his eyes. He'd just go, he decided. He could listen to her banging on in the car as easily as here. Quickly, he shrugged on his dark grey reefer jacket which hung on the bannister, and opened the front door, only for all sound to be immediately drowned out as the thundering of the jackhammer struck up again. He slammed it shut immediately as a screech of "*What in the name of God is that!*" pierced his ear, and tried to reassure the lady that it was all fine and that, yes, he was listening.

The interruption, however, served only to make her start over from scratch. Joe closed his eyes and balled the fist of his free hand in temper and frustration. On and on she rambled, describing rooms, where she'd like the furniture placed for safekeeping while he painted, telling him about the time her niece had left an important piece of Chippendale something or other to the mercy of her builders. And still, outside, the continuous clatter rumbled on. With a sigh, he turned and wandered aimlessly back down toward the kitchen, the phone pressed to his ear.

As he passed the open door of Louise's studio, he idly reached his hand inside the doorframe and flicked the light on to peer inside. No breezes today. In fact, it looked cosy in there. The heating on, and the big office chair waiting invitingly for someone to sit into it.

Nodding and '*mmhmming*' as Sheila – he'd got her name and family history – began to describe colours she liked, he strolled in and eased himself down into the chair with a quiet sigh. Sheila had a long way to go before she ran out of steam so he might as well rest his legs while he was here. He fidgeted as he sat, scanning the equipment on Louise's desk, tapping the space bar on the computer, clicking a pen, squeezing the foam around a set of headphones. Then, as was the temptation in a swivel chair, he completed a couple of lazy rotations. On the third, facing the doorway, he stopped dead, and went pale.

"I'm not mad on green now," Sheila wittered in his ear. "It reminds me of a dress my great-grandmother sewed me once, rotten old thing ..."

Her voice faded away, as his ears inexplicably started to ring, his body flooding with adrenaline as he stared at the open door.

Something ... someone ... stared back.

Something he couldn't comprehend ... something terrifying ...

Joe dropped the phone, his brain simply too confused to maintain hold of it against his ear, Sheila's voice growing tiny as it fell to the floor.

Chapter 25

Louise saw Joe's van as she turned back onto her road. She smiled at the familiar sight of it and immediately felt silly. The truth of it was that she was proud at the small achievement of getting herself to the shop and back and was childishly eager to share it with him.

As she grew closer, she spotted him sitting behind the wheel. He must be heading out for lunch, she thought, and was surprised to feel disappointed at the thought. She increased her pace as best she could, keen to present him with the bar of chocolate she'd bought him, just as a completely unexpected gust of wind pelted her face with freezing raindrops which seemed to come from nowhere.

She smiled to catch his attention as she drew level with him, then winced as a fresh assault of raindrops came at her horizontally, harder and colder. What was it with this stupid weather? It had been sunny half an hour previously. She frowned, and then hunched over to tap on the van window. She expected a response from Joe – that he might get out to say hi, to even tell her to go in out of the rain, or to wind down the window to say where he was off to and share one of their little jokes.

But he didn't budge. Instead, he looked directly at her and then looked away, toward the front door of her house. His expression was one of deep discomfort – alarm, even. Louise was taken aback.

She fished in her pocket for the chocolate she'd bought him and held it aloft, nodding toward it and then toward Joe, just as another hard drop of rain hit her right in the eye. She reflexively squeezed her eyes shut and rapidly blinked away the sting, opening them again just as she saw his window glide open.

"I bought you a Twix," she blurted. "It's best before June 1977, but I didn't think you'd mind."

He didn't laugh, much to her surprise.

"That's cool," he said instead, his voice weak. "I'm ... *emm* ... just going to ... actually I need to finish early today ...." He fired another look back toward Louise's front door.

She frowned. "So ... would you like it?" she offered tentatively, balancing herself as the wind drove another surge of rain against her.

Joe managed a feeble, polite smile as he took the bar in through the window. "Thanks," he said, dropping it onto the console between the seats, before gripping the steering wheel again. His hands were trembling, his knuckles white.

Louise remained where she was, unsure what to do next. "Okay then," she said, after a moment. "I'm going to ...." She left the sentence unfinished, instead indicating with another nod of her head that she was headed inside.

Again, Joe looked from her to the front door, but this time his face showed panic. Louise, baffled, turned to head in, when suddenly the van door shot open behind her. She turned sharply. Joe had half-emerged into the rain, one leg still in the driver footwell, the other on the pavement, gripping the door.

"You can't go in," he said, his voice low and frightened. "There's something ... please, don't go in the house, Louise. Just *don't* go in."

Her logical thoughts turned to Ros first – had she come back for something? Taken stuff? Or completely flipped her lid and *destroyed* something? But that was ridiculous, wasn't it? Ros was a pain, but she wasn't that kind of person. And for Joe to be as ... as *disturbed* as he was just now ... well, Ros would have to be in there with a weapon, or petrol and matches or something to warrant such a reaction.

"Just get into the car for a minute," Joe commanded.

Louise did as she was told.

They sat in silence. Joe's breathing was rapid, the only sound apart from the rain pelting tinnily off the roof. Louise looked at him – he was ashen, his lips clamped shut. Every few moments he'd glance at the house, and then back out the windscreen, where the street was growing ever more wet and bleak. Maybe there was a massive rat in there, she thought, out of the blue. Or a flood ... or a fire ... her studio – might he have done some accidental damage to the equipment? Or spilled paint everywhere?

"You're going to think I'm mad," he began in a shaky voice.

No, she thought. *Not this. Not him too.*

He fell silent again, trembling, as if the act of speaking had sent a surge of uncontrollable fear through him. She stared out the windscreen, pleading with herself not to speak but resigning herself to the fact of what had to be said.

"You've seen something in the house, haven't you?" she said.

In her peripheral vision she saw him turn to look directly at her, his eyes saucer-wide. Her heart flip-flopped. She closed her eyes for a moment, sighed, and turned slowly to meet his gaze.

He continued to stare at her, his expression one of horror mixed with confusion and something that resembled blame. She looked away from him, studied her hands.

He released a noise – an exhalation of juddering breath mixed with a strangled sigh. "You know about it?" he managed.

She nodded without looking up.

"You *know* about it?" he repeated, a trace of anger creeping into his tone.

She turned her gaze deliberately away and stared through the passenger window out at the green without replying.

"You know that there's ... something ... in there and you never said?" He paused, waiting for a response that didn't come. "You never warned me, or ... could I have been hurt? What *is* it? I thought I was imagining things – thought I was going mad or something ..."

"Why don't you drive?" Louise suggested suddenly.

Joe fell silent and looked at her in surprise.

"Why don't we just go somewhere – away from here – and talk. I think I need to know what you saw or felt or whatever."

He took a breath, as if to reply, but then pressed the ignition button and scraped the gears clumsily into first.

Within minutes they had pulled into a car park along the coast nearby. The light grey sea churned dismally before them, raindrops hitting the water like pellets. Joe turned the engine off and leaned back against his headrest for a moment, eyes closed, as if shutting it all out.

They sat like that for a while, Louise silently watching the miserable day through the windscreen, until finally she reached into her pocket and produced her own bar of chocolate. "I'm going to eat this," she announced. "I'm starving."

"You're always starving," came the reply.

Louise paused, mid-bite, and glanced at him. His eyes were still closed, but a half smile played on his lips, as if it were as much as he could manage.

He opened one eye and peered at her. "Does nothing stop you eating?" he asked, sitting forward and leaning his forehead against the steering wheel. "I mean, I haven't a clue if I'm coming or going and you're tucking into a Snickers?"

Louise took a bite. "I'm not myself when I'm hungry," she quipped, her mouth full.

He gave a small chuckle and then sat up and took a deep breath.

"Feels better out here," he observed. "Your house, it makes me jumpy. I guess it could make you imagine things, although ..." His voice trailed away.

Louise frowned. "What happened?" she asked quietly. She wasn't sure if she wanted to know, but then again if someone else was in this too ... she wasn't alone, was she? The thought made her feel oddly braver.

Joe shook his head. "It wasn't just this morning," he said. "There's been stuff before but I didn't want to ..."

186

"Acknowledge it?" Louise offered.

He nodded.

"Well, it just seemed impossible, and I was sure that there was ... that there *had* to be logical reasons for the stuff."

"Like what?"

"I don't know – tricks of the eye, creaks in the floorboards, old house – the usual stuff."

"No, I meant what sort of stuff?"

He thought for a moment, then started to speak, the words tumbling from him faster as he told her about the icy spots along the hallway, and about finding his rag dangling from the latch of the door. Louise listened intently, the colour draining from her face as she struggled to take it in.

"I'm probably talking nonsense – now that I hear myself say it out loud," Joe said. "I'm sure I must be. I mean, there could be logical explanations for all that stuff, couldn't there? You know none of that in itself is proof of anything out of the ordinary ..." He paused.

"But ..." prompted Louise.

"But ... there was something else ..."

Her heart gave a thump.

"That day ... you know when Ros came back to get her stuff? And you guys ... I'm sorry if it came across like I was eavesdropping – I wasn't, but there was a bit of yelling and I wanted to make sure you were okay ... I mean, I know it's not my business ..."

"It's okay, Joe – go on."

"Well, anyway, I was on the stairs and then the front door slammed on its own – you saw that too, didn't you? But you went to the door to open it and let her back in,

187

remember, and when you did, well, this is crazy but something *rushed* past me ... like ... just, *whoosh* – like someone running, but *faster,* even, and at first I couldn't see anything until ... a few seconds later, Ros came back in and you were arguing ..."

"And you were looking up at something? I saw you. What did you see?"

Joe inhaled deeply and blew the air out in a '*whoo*', as he steeled himself.

"It was a ... shape ... it's really hard to describe because it was blurry, and sort of insubstantial – it was a sort of misty white shape, a person-sized *blur* – and it was sort of *hovering* outside the airing cupboard for a minute ... this sounds so weird, but it's as if it were *watching* what was going on – and then, it went *whoosh* again – straight into your bedroom. Like it was sort of blown in, or sucked in maybe, I dunno."

Louise felt queasy.

"I know I should have gone after it, just to check it out, but truthfully, I couldn't. My legs just sort of *froze* into place, and I couldn't move. They felt like jelly, and I was shaking all over."

They were silent for a moment as Louise digested the information, and Joe paused for a moment to fish in the driver's door pocket from which he withdrew a half-drunk bottle of water and took a long swig.

"Then there was today," he said. "I'm sorry, but I couldn't stay there. I didn't know what to think, or what I'd just seen, and I was – I was too scared to go back in, which is stupid – I'm a grown man, and I shouldn't be frightened of stuff but ... I'm actually not really sure I should tell you this ..."

Louise's eyes grew wide in alarm. "You have to, now."

He gave a nod. "Okay. I mean, I genuinely have no explanation for this – I don't understand it, but I'm sure of it. I'm sure of what I saw, I'm not making this up, I swear – I'm not trying to scare you or anything ..."

"I believe you."

He studied her for a moment, as if to see if she could take it, then continued. "But ... well ... I was taking a call in your office – I wasn't snooping, I swear – I didn't touch anything, well, a couple of things, but I didn't do any damage. It was just that there was this old lady wittering on on the phone and –"

"Now *you're* wittering, Joe," Louise interrupted softly.

He rolled his eyes and nodded, before taking another deep breath. "Well, what happened was that I sort of spun around on your swivel-chair while she was going on and on and on, and when I stopped I was facing the door, looking out into the hall, and when I looked at it ... well ... there was something there, something ... someone ... looking back at me."

Louise stared at him, sure that she had never felt so cold in her entire life. It gripped her entire body, freezing her blood, her muscles, petrifying her.

"It was only for a split second," he continued. "But there was a face ... and it was smiling – sort of *leering* directly at me ..."

"A *person?*" Louise gasped.

Joe paused, searching her face as he thought about replying. "I'm not sure," he said.

Louise recoiled as if she had been punched in the chest. "What do you mean?"

Joe chewed his lip as he thought about it. "All I saw was a face ... it was a man's face. I'm sure of it – although it really was very fast. It was sort of peering around the door. The thing was, though ..."

Again, he hesitated.

"Go on, Joe," Louise urged, her heart hammering in her chest.

"It ... it was the *height* it was at – that's what was so terrifying. It was a man's face, but it was ... *low* ... like, below the doorknob low, like a man's face on a child's body or something? Or some sort of ... I dunno, *goblin* or something. Now that's ridiculous – I shouldn't have said that, because I absolutely don't believe ..."

But Louise had stopped listening, and her heart had almost stopped beating. This – she couldn't take this in. All of the other stuff he had told her – she knew what he meant, could identify with it all because she had seen or heard similar. But this ... this was new. This was terrifying, more so because if Joe had seen it all, experienced it all, then it all had to be *true*. It couldn't be her imagination, or her drugs, or the stress, or anything she wanted to pretend it was.

"I didn't think you'd believe me," he said quietly. "I didn't think anyone would believe me. But you do – and you know about this stuff too, don't you? You know what's going on there? It's not just me?"

Louise shook her head. "No, Joe, it's not just you. Not at all. And yes, I believe you – of course I believe you."

"What's happened to you?" he asked.

Louise pondered for a moment, trying to think where to begin. And then she told him.

By the time she finished, she was exhausted. In a

single gulp, she drained what was left from the stale bottle of water and wanted more.

They sat there in silence for a long time, not knowing what to say, until the cold got to them, and they acknowledged that they couldn't stay there much longer. By the time Joe dropped her home, an early, dank, winter dusk had fallen. They sat again, parked outside, studying the front of the house, the simplicity of the red-brick edifice, just like all the others on the road. Just an ordinary house.

"I don't think you should go in," Joe insisted.

Louise didn't reply. Instead, she continued to study her house, her eyes flicking from window to window, with almost an expectation of seeing something, something that she now was certain was actually there.

"It's fine," she replied, surprising herself. Because, suddenly, it was. "I've really got nowhere else to go anyway." She turned to him and smiled reassuringly. "I'll be grand."

He looked at her anxiously.

"I swear." She smiled.

Joe nodded hesitantly, and she opened the car door. "Rain's stopped," she observed, as she extended her crutch and balanced against it to push herself out of the car.

"You'll call me if anything happens, won't you?" said Joe. "You'll make sure your phone is charged, right?"

"Much use you'll be," she sniggered. "What'll you do, sit in your van and wait for my bloodcurdling screams of terror?"

"I will arrive in an instant," he joked. "Bearing all manner of wooden stakes and garlic and silver bullets."

"That's vampires and werewolves. You're no bloody

help at all! You'd be more use with a bottle of white spirits and some sandpaper!"

"White spirits for the white spirit," Joe replied, but without smiling. His expression switched back to worried again. "You're sure you're okay?"

"Go on, get away," she said warmly.

He gave a weak smile. "Just call," he urged.

"Go home."

She slammed the door shut and watched as he drove away.

When he was gone, she made her way up the path, inserted the key in the lock, and slowly let herself in, stepping into the gloom of her hallway, and closing the door gently behind her.

It was cold, but no colder than it should have been. It smelled normal – fresh paint mixed through with a faint hint of the curry that she'd made the previous evening, and that tiny hint of damp that always pervaded the old bricks on a cold, wet day.

She stood still – defiant – her back to the front door and waited.

Nothing happened, of course. No noise, or movement, or cold spot, or sudden wind, or shuffling or sound.

She made her way to the kitchen, flicking the kettle on for a cup of coffee and pausing to lean against the countertop to close her eyes and take a breath. There was so much to think about – she almost felt herself bend under the weight of it. What they – because it was a shared experience now – had seen and felt. She could scarcely begin to make sense of it.

The sound of the kettle clicking off suddenly roused her and she swore under her breath – lost in thought, she had forgotten to actually make the cup of coffee that she wanted so badly. Tutting at herself, she reached up and removed the jar of instant from the cupboard, before limping gently to the fridge, careful not to put too much weight on her leg. She stopped to pull a teaspoon from the cutlery drawer on the way back to the counter, swearing again as she dropped it on the floor and bent to pick it up. Then she made her way back to the countertop – where she stopped suddenly, her eyes widening. The jar of coffee had moved.

She had left it just under the cupboard where it lived.

But now it sat beside the kettle. It had moved – had *been* moved. And certainly not by her.

She held her breath. There was nothing around her but silence, and stillness. Without knowing where her own voice came from, it was she that broke it.

"I know you're there!" she called, feeling her courage dissipate the second she did it. Her legs felt suddenly weak, and she stood, petrified, waiting to see what would happen. Nothing.

Taking a deep, fortifying breath, she continued with her task. She tried to maintain composure but found that she was barely able to open the jar of coffee for trembling. When suddenly she was overcome with the oddest feeling. Her entire body turned cold as if she was engulfed in dry ice, and it tingled, yet it wasn't entirely unpleasant – not dissimilar to the feeling she'd had when the long, dark shadow had drifted over her, but without the despair. And then the feeling grew more intense – intense to the point where she was certain that someone was standing behind her. Someone who smelled of lilies.

Louise inhaled deeply, and contemplated turning, but a

jolt of fear overtook her, fear that she would *see* someone there, someone close enough to touch her, to put their arms around her, or whisper in her ear. Her entire body stiffened in anticipation of such a thing happening and she trembled even harder, spilling granules from the coffee jar onto the countertop, but then, within seconds, the feeling was gone again, without warning or explanation, the scent dissipating into the ether, the room feeling immediately empty.

Louise exhaled slowly. Contact. She had just had contact with whatever inhabited her house. It had been as close to her as a live person could possibly be – closer – it had permeated every inch of her – yet it had done her no harm. Gently, she lowered the spoon into the cup, and grabbed the edge of the countertop for support, washed over suddenly with a wave of relief.

"Thank you," she said aloud, quietly. Then a second time, louder. "*Thank you!*" she called, so that she might be heard out into the hallway and up the stairs to wherever – and by whatever – it was that now shared her space.

Chapter 26

Kent, 1866

From her spot in the shade, Bridget watched the summer's afternoon unfold before her.

The heat was quite overwhelming. She was glad of the coolness of the stone seat beneath her, and the protection of the trees underneath which she sat a little way from the cottage, which formed a welcome barrier against the relentless glare of the sun. It was one of those days, those rare and perfect English summer days that seemed to happen so infrequently, yet made it difficult to imagine that there could be any other kind of day. Away into the distance, the fields of ripening barley swayed in the warm breeze, the air was loud with birdsong and thick with scent. Bridget felt the child flutter within her and rubbed it with a protective hand, and for a moment imagined that it could always be like this.

How wonderful that could be, she thought. To have at your window the expanse of green that rolled around them, the song of the blackbird as your good morning, and the whoosh of swallows' wings rushing home to roost your goodnight. She sighed, content at the thought. There was a steadiness to a life like this, she reflected. A calmness, a safety that one just didn't find in the city with danger on every corner. It was a life lived at a peaceful pace, in a bounteous place where there was no worry, no want. It was as far from her upbringing as the earth from the sun.

If only she could get that useless dreamer she called husband to agree with her. What frustration. To get the horse so close to the trough but be entirely unable to convince it to drink.

She had been sure it would be a simple matter of convincing him again, the same as she had convinced him of so much before – to overcome his fear of the dead to photograph them, to grow his silly business, to marry her, for heaven's sake. All it had taken was – well, it hadn't been difficult. A man such as him – short, balding, downright *strange* – would likely never have found a woman to live with him in all of London, so she had done him a favour by taking such an interest, by marrying him and now – the ultimate – by bearing him a child. She had come so far, and given so much, when you considered it. And now, surely he had to see that it would only be fair and right to give her something in return.

Yet he would not budge. She'd had a week to try – to nudge first this way, and then that, to no avail. They finally had taken the stroll to Redtrees Hall on the third day of their visit – seeing it would surely turn him, she had been sure.

She had been wrong.

He had remained implacable, unmoved by the lyrical picture she had painted of their lives as the Temples of Redtrees. "What ostentation, Mrs Temple!" he had scoffed at first sight of it, much to her frustration. Resilient to the last, she had carried on, appealed to his sense of history by describing the original twelfth-century hall around which it was built, led him through the gardens, throwing suggestions hither and thither of what they might like to plant there and how gay it would all be in the summer with plenty of space and fresh air for their child and its siblings to run and play. She had treated the gazebo hidden among the rhododendrons as a surprise. "A lovers' nook," she had described it, with one of her coquettish smiles. Yet he remained singularly unimpressed. In fact, it seemed to Bridget that he couldn't wait to leave the property and return to the infinitely shabbier Thistle Farm and its trio of residents – her scruffy sister-in-law who reminded her so of her wastrel first husband, her dullard son and her daughter – that hideously malformed creature.

Bridget mopped her brow with her kerchief and shifted position, her discomfort growing as quickly as her disgruntlement at the thought of her husband and his complete lack of interest in their future. For every advantage she had served him, he had parried with a disadvantage.

Yes, they could afford it – *but it would need repair and refurbishment.*

The price of the London house would more than cover such costs – *but that had been his father's house and he would never sell it as long as he lived.*

What a wonderful, calm life they could give their children in the countryside – *all well and good but how would he ply his trade so far from London?*

Photographers were required in the countryside too – *but by so few – he had not come to where he was today on three family portraits a year.*

197

And so on, and so forth. As she bowled, he batted – it was unheard of between them that this should happen. Why would he not *see*? It was as plain as the nose on his stupid face that this was what she wanted. So why was he being so obtuse? Why would he not do as she wanted?

The child rumbled within again and sweat trickled between her shoulder blades. She shifted in her seat, stretched her back, but still there was little comfort to be found in any position. Still, she would not complain. How full she felt, how swollen her belly. It was a good thing this time – she sometimes had to remind herself of that. It was full and swollen with life and goodness – not like before when it was distended by hunger. She had been young then – so young – but the sensation of it had never – could never – leave her. That indescribable hunger, that emptiness, as if her insides were eating themselves, all the way through to her soul. She would never be that hungry again, she had sworn. Would never feel such darkness and ... *despair* was too small and soft a word for it. The things she had seen and felt, such horrors, such inescapable atrocities everywhere you turned. Never again, she told herself her whole life. She had been one of the lucky to escape it and she had vowed on her own life that she would never go back again to such deprivation and degradation. Never. If she had to beg, crawl, steal or kill for that to happen then that is what she would do. If that meant forsaking or betraying those she purported to love, then so be it. There was no price too high to pay to keep free of it all, even if she were to spend eternity in hell.

She had no fear of hell, as it happened, because as far as she was concerned she had been born into it.

A sultry breeze rose from nowhere and kissed her cheek, rippling through the trees above and on to the surrounding garden and beyond to the ripening crops. *There, there*, it seemed to say. *You're safe here*. That was better. Even the wind knew. So why didn't he? Why couldn't he tell that if he just came here with her, then she could finally stop? Here was home – she was sure of it. Here was Arcadia, her promised land. Here, the relentless flight, the escape could finally cease and she could settle, draw Redtrees Hall like a cloak around her and never fear again. No more hunger – apples on the trees, wheat in the fields, fish in the stream – and no one to take it from her. Not as long as she was provided for – or provided for herself, if it came to it. She had managed before – one last time could do no more harm. But that was not what she wanted. What she truly desired – all of that was within reach – a husband, a house, a child – a life without fear, without longing. All of it required just one word: yes. 'Yes, Mrs Temple, you are absolutely right and you shall have what you want, one final, perfect, glorious time!' It was so close – she could smell it, tantalising her, teasing her – why oh why was he so against it?

A painful thump reverberated through her belly, followed by squirming – the child was turning, shoving – anything to push through the restrictions that she found suddenly she was placing on it, hunched over in the seat as she was, her body taut, her fists clenched. She straightened, to give it more room, and took a deep breath, prising her nails from her palms. In the distance, there were voices – a man and a girl, chattering. A peal of laughter rose and carried into the air and away. Bridget visualised it – a rainbow-coloured cloud, dissipating in sparkling dust into the air. She frowned. So that was where he had been. She had wondered alright – not for long, albeit – but he had disappeared after lunch when she had said she would go to the garden to sit and take the air. And instead of joining her like any loyal husband would, so that she might entreat him yet again to perhaps think a little longer, a little harder about how idyllic a life in the country could be, he had vanished. And with him – there they were now, clucking like chickens yet again, as if such a thing were normal with one such as her – was her niece. Maud.

Bridget watched them as they appeared around a distant corner, and trudged along the laneway toward the cottage. Samuel, fanning himself with a large leaf as if it were a ladies' fan, his cheeks – and his pate – turning pink in the heat. He would have a headache later, no doubt. And rightly so.

And then the girl. Bridget's lip curled in disgust – she simply couldn't help it. That useless cripple, that limbless freak. The very sight of Maud was abhorrent to her – those stumps, one crossed over the other in imitation of two hands being clasped as she walked. Broken, broken and useless, and disgusting. No use to man nor beast and yet here she was, audaciously walking with *her* husband – with a gentleman who should, in Bridget's opinion, not be seen dead with such a flawed thing. How people would stare if they saw them, stare and then turn away at the ghastliness of it. It quite made her shudder.

Another rainbow laugh ascended as they strolled, growing closer, close enough to greet with a wave. Bridget adjusted her features and fixed a smile into place and returned the salutation, making sure to wiggle her fingers as she did in a base attempt to show her advantage over her niece. The girl acted so normally. As though there were not a thing in the world wrong with her – like that dwarf used to. And who did they think they were, behaving like that? When they were *wrong*, when they were abominations?

"Enjoying the shade, my dear?"

Her thoughts, growing angrier and darker the more she watched, were disturbed by her husband's cheerful tone. She fixed her eyes on his face as he grew nearer. Not that she wished to gaze upon it, but because it was less repugnant that those terrible rounded stubs that Maud possessed in place of hands.

"Quite," she managed, dabbing at her upper lip with her handkerchief. "It is quite stifling today, don't you think?"

"Oh, but the breeze when it comes is heavenly!" Maud exclaimed.

Bridget forced herself to look at her. That face – so normal – freckled and framed by copper hair held back in a braid that had come undone.

"What is seldom is wonderful, as the Irish say, eh?" chuckled Temple, rubbing his hands in glee and looking at Maud with a great idiot's grin on his face.

His wife stared at him, puzzled, before she seized her opportunity.

"So you are coming around to the notion that it is beautiful here, Samuel, are you not?" she said, smiling upward at him.

He glanced again at Maud, and then back to Bridget, grinning idiotically.

"It has its share of pleasures," he replied.

There was a silence between them for a moment, broken only by the chirrup of a sparrow overhead.

Bridget's face darkened.

"Your child is a busy one today, Samuel," she said eventually, extending a hand pointedly in his direction. "And it's rather tiring. I should be very grateful if you could assist its mother indoors to rest – do you think you could do that? You look like you could do with some shade yourself, in fact, while we are at it."

"Oh," replied Temple, a disappointed look pulling down the corners of his mouth. "Of course. I am a little warm, I suppose ... here ...."

Accepting the proffered hand, he pulled his wife to her feet. She watched, frowning, as he released it immediately, and wiped his palms along his trouser legs, turning to Maud as he did so. "Very well then," he said. "It's been such a pleasure taking a constitutional with you ... *Maud*. Perhaps we will manage it again before I leave for London."

The girl responded with an odd little twist of her head and bobbed a small curtsey. "I should enjoy that very much, Mr Temple," she replied. "I found it most fascinating to hear all about photography – I never imagined quite how interesting it would all be. And Aunt Bridget, I hope you have a lovely rest and that my little cousin may nap along with you." She finished with a giggle and a warm – unreturned – smile.

Instead, Bridget took her husband's arm and turned him, quite forcefully, in the direction of the house and, with a barely discernible shudder, walked away from the little stone seat and the smiling girl who, in turn, knelt to examine a buttercup nearby. And in doing so, quite missed the look that her aunt-by-marriage threw in her direction when she slowly turned to look at her. A look of revulsion, cast by eyes as cold as stone.

Chapter 27

2018

Saturday morning dawned after a blessedly uneventful night.

Distraction, Louise decided. There was so much rushing around in her head – so much to understand that she couldn't possibly know where to begin. Inspired – and shamed – by the brightness of the winter sunlight filtering in to reveal layers of dust and grime around the house, she decided to occupy herself by giving the place a good clean. That, at least, was manageable.

She began downstairs, working her way as vigorously as she could manage around the sitting room and along the hall with the vacuum cleaner, drawing satisfaction from seeing the place transform. She was just heading upstairs with a duster and polish when the doorbell rang. She glared at the door, running through the possibilities of who it might be and whether or not she could be bothered answering. It was probably someone from an electricity supplier, trying to get her to switch, or local kids with sponsored walk forms – or Gerry, checking up on her. Oh God – what if it were Ros?

None of these possibilities appeared anything but annoying or potentially awkward. So would she answer or just leave it? She didn't *have* to answer it, she told herself. She didn't have to do anything she didn't want to, but then, if she didn't ... what if it were something important? What if they just came back later – she knew herself, knew that she'd spend the day in anticipation of their return, whoever it was and whatever they wanted. It was so stupid that this sort of thing set her into a frenzy of overthinking, but it did, she just couldn't help it.

The doorbell rang a second time.

"*Louise, are you there?*"

She slumped with relief. It was Joe. She grinned. Good old Joe, probably terrified she'd been murdered in her bed. Reliable Joe who, for some reason, seemed to really care that she was okay.

"*Louise!*"

He rang again, alarm in his voice, and hammered with the knocker.

Louise rolled her eyes good-naturedly and put the duster and spray down on the bottom step of the stairs. "*I'm coming!*" she called, checking her appearance briefly in the hall mirror and smiling as she pulled the door open.

Joe stood there, wearing a heavy coat and scarf, with his now-familiar worried expression.

And behind him stood a girl in her early to mid-twenties, her full figure swathed in black with a long scarf and chunky boots. Louise was reminded of a young Dawn French but with heavier make-up – thick eyeliner and dark purple lipstick. As soon as the door opened, she peered inside, making no effort to conceal her curiosity.

"You're okay? Is the doorbell busted again?" Joe said.

"Don't sound so surprised, I'm grand," Louise reassured him.

He looked relieved "Sorry for calling on a Saturday –"

"I put the lid back on the open tin in the bathroom," Louise interrupted, "and washed your brushes so they wouldn't go hard."

"Oh – thank you. That's not why I called though." He turned slightly and indicated the girl. "I hope you don't mind, but I brought my sister with me – Tash, this is Louise – Louise, Tash. *Emm*, I wanted to check you were okay but as well as that, well, Tash ..."

They were interrupted by the girl rudely pushing her way past Joe and stepping into the hall.

"Hi," she said. "Sorry, but I'm really curious – do you mind ...?"

Louise stood back, surprised, as the girl strode past her down the hall, peering in through the studio door and then curiously scanning the kitchen.

"Oh shite, sorry about that," said Joe, stepping inside after her. "We won't stay long, only I asked Tash to come along because I thought maybe she could help."

"With what?" asked Louise gruffly as she observed Tash open the door to her under-stairs cupboard and poke her head in as far as she could.

"The ghosts," came the muffled voice from within.

Louise whipped her head back to Joe for an explanation.

"I know I should have asked you," he said. "But last night when I left you I called in to my parents' house and, well, I was so freaked out I told Tash all about everything and ... well ..."

"*I* love ghosts." The girl smiled broadly as she shut the cupboard door. "And we brought biscuits – Joe says *you* love food."

Louise raised her eyebrows at Joe who pulled a packet

of chocolate digestives from his jacket pocket and shrugged.

"Alright then," Louise said resignedly, shutting the front door. "I suppose you had me at biscuits. Come through, I'll put the kettle on."

Louise prepared hot drinks, all the while watching over her shoulder as Joe's sister scoped out her surroundings. At first, Tash stood near the door, peering out into the hall, as if expecting to see something, until Joe instructed her sternly to sit down, as if she were a child. Reluctantly, Tash did as she was told, but even then she continued to fidget, looking behind and all around.

"Nice day –" began Joe, before he was interrupted.

"Joe says you have loads of ghosts, and that you've seen loads of stuff," Tash blurted enthusiastically.

Taken aback, Louise stirred the drinks in silence.

Joe clumsily tried to change the subject. "Tash is in college," he said lightly.

Louise glanced at him. He looked uncomfortable, and a little embarrassed.

"Oh really?" she replied. "Whereabouts?"

"UCD," Tash answered. "Folklore."

Louise nodded, placing steaming mugs in front of her guests. "That sounds interesting," she said. She eased herself down into a chair and took a biscuit.

"It's grand," Tash replied. "So is the place really quiet now? Can you feel it when the spirits are around – like physically? Joe says there's cold spots and that?" She teased something from the corner of her heavily made-up eye with a long, copper-painted nail which resembled a penny attached to the top of her finger. She regarded Louise expectantly, silently demanding an answer.

"Tash ..." warned Joe, glaring at her.

Tash looked at him, sighed, then picked up her cup and blew on the hot liquid, before turning her attention back to Louise. She wasn't giving up on a response.

"*Tash!*"

The girl rolled her eyes in a way that made Louise giggle.

"Alright, alright, alright," Tash said resignedly, reaching out for a digestive and slumping in her chair.

Joe threatened her with a look and shook his head.

She glared back resentfully. "*You* brought me," she said quietly.

"*But you don't just start demanding stuff the second you walk in!*" he hissed, exasperated.

Louise suddenly burst out laughing. The girl's determination was funny.

"I'll show you around when I've had my coffee," she said calmly.

Tash's eyes went wide with hopeful excitement. "And do you think we might see something? Like how often do you see stuff or hear stuff? It sounds really active here – are the chances good do you think?"

Joe groaned.

"I can't promise anything," Louise replied.

Tash's face fell a little.

"Is it something to do with your coursework?" Louise asked.

Tash wrinkled her face and shrugged. "Not directly, no," she replied through a mouthful of chocolate and crumbs. "I just really like the paranormal and stuff."

"Tash knows a lot about the area," said Joe.

Louise turned to him, puzzled. "Maryborough Gardens?"

He shook his head. "Sorry, no – ghosts and spirits and that sort of thing. Ever since you were little, Tash, am I right?"

Tash swallowed and wiped a crumb from her lip with delicate fingers. "Always," she nodded emphatically. "Got hooked on the *Goosebumps* books when I was a kid, I've been fascinated ever since." She dropped her voice and widened her eyes. "*Be-weahhhh, you're in for a scare!*"

Louise grinned. "Have *you* ever seen anything?" she asked tentatively.

Tash shook her head.

Joe cleared his throat. "Tash is bonkers," he explained, "but she's read a lot about this sort of thing. I brought her along today to see if we ... you ... could figure out maybe what to do next. To help, like ..."

Louise looked across the table at him in surprise. She had to *do* something? She hadn't thought of it that way before. Up until now, her thoughts had been entirely consumed by wondering if something was actually happening, or if she were simply losing her reason. It was only this morning that she was actually coming to terms with there being something in her house.

"What do you mean?" she asked, looking from one to the other. "What does a person *do* in this sort of situation? What *can* you do?"

"Loads," said Tash brightly. "You can start to document the evidence, try to record or take pictures or video and send it to paranormal groups for authentication. You can run all sorts of experiments and tests to try to prove that it's all actually supernatural and not just natural phenomena –"

"Like what?" asked Louise.

"Your wiring for starters," Tash stated matter-of-factly. "Old wiring can make you feel very uncomfortable, like being watched or as if there's a presence. It can emit a high EMF."

Louise stared at her blankly.

"Electro Magnetic Frequency?" Tash explained.

Louise nodded, as if she understood. She didn't.

"Other things can be as simple as draughts – old houses move and shift all the time so you might have a draught that you didn't have last winter ... *or*, let's see .... animals in the attic – mice, rats, a trapped bird, that sort of thing. There's often a logical explanation for everything."

"What about the stuff we've ... you know ... *seen*." Joe whispered the last word, throwing a glance toward the open door of the kitchen.

Louise gave a small start and looked over her shoulder, relieved to find nothing there.

"Well, that's difficult to quantify," replied Tash, sitting forward in her seat. "Eyes can play tricks – we all know that. At night-time or dusk or conditions of artificial lighting, you could experience pareidolia – that's where something that you're familiar with resembles something it shouldn't – like, seeing your dressing gown hanging on the door of your room and convincing yourself that it's a person, or seeing Jesus in your coffee or Elvis in your toast – the mind sees a pattern where none exists, basically."

Louise listened intently.

"It's very easy to spot a shadow and think it's something it's not," continued Tash. "Or catch something out of the corner of your eye and your brain then interprets it as someone or something that shouldn't be there. That can set off a chain reaction where you begin to ascribe paranormal reasons to everything. The mind is a funny place."

"Yours is for sure," said Joe. "But what I saw – I told you – that was in daylight – clear as anything."

"Well, that's a bit harder to figure out," said Tash. "Word of mouth is one thing – but I pretty much believe you cos I know you."

"What do you mean 'pretty much'?" asked Joe, in mild outrage. "When have I ever lied to you?"

Tash tilted her head to one side and pretended to think, tapping her nail against her cheek. "*Hmm*, let me see – melted Barbie head ..."

"I was eleven."

"Too old to be melting your sister's doll with a stolen lighter and lying about it. Then you broke my Biffy Clyro CD ..."

Joe shrugged. "What's the problem there?"

Tash frowned and glared at him. "And *thennnn* .... denied having a pop off Liam O'Connor for calling me Miss Piggy ..."

"Little bastard was asking for it!!"

"I'll forgive you that one." Tash smiled coyly.

"Is that it? The sum total of my deceit?" Joe grinned.

Tash tapped her cheek again. "Oh – and becoming a stand-up comedian."

Louise burst out laughing and turned to Joe, but he wasn't laughing. Instead, he looked sheepish and had flushed red. Before his sister could continue, he stood up abruptly.

"We'll head on, Tash," he said. "Louise has stuff to do, I'm sure."

Puzzled, Louise looked from Joe's embarrassment to Tash's annoyance. "I don't, really," she protested. "Tash, would you like to look around?"

The girl's face brightened and she nodded emphatically.

Louise turned to Joe. "If that's okay with you – you're not in a hurry or anything, are you?"

Joe bit the inside of his lip. "Fine. Just a quick look, though, alright?"

Tash clapped her hands like a child and jumped out of her seat, grinning.

"I'm actually genuinely interested in hearing what Tash has to say," Louise said, giving Joe a reassuring grin, which he returned after a moment.

"Lead on," he sighed.

Louise showed Tash the upstairs rooms at first, while Joe loitered on the landing. With some prompting, she soon found herself describing everything that had happened while Tash studied the layout of the rooms, asking question after question about the conditions at the time of various events. Had the window been open? How about the doors? Were the floors straight and even? Did Joe have a spirit level in the van – at which she bellowed with laughter – "a *spirit* level!" – and could he get it, then please?

The trio descended then to the hallway, where Tash had insisted on opening the front door wide while she ran through the house, opening and closing windows and doors in an attempt to create a cross-draught whereby it would slam shut. She failed. This was followed by opening and closing the curtains in the sitting room for a while before emerging into the hall where Tash fell to her knees and attempted to move a dishcloth from the kitchen by blowing on it. When that failed too, she stayed on her knees and ran her hand along the length of the skirting board on either side of the hall, followed by feeling underneath each door and around each doorframe. After a while of this, Louise's interest began to wane. Joe's patience was already clearly thin.

"*Tash!*" he barked eventually. "Is all of this really necessary?"

"I just want to see ..." she abandoned the sentence midway through to concentrate on the cupboard under the stairs, before indicating to Louise that she'd like to enter her studio room. Louise stifled a yawn to grant permission with a nod, and they followed Tash inside, where Tash perched herself on Louise's chair and turned her attention to Joe, demanding that he describe how he had been sitting when he saw the face at the door – at what height the chair had been positioned, how many rotations he'd completed before stopping – had he felt dizzy? Could it have been an afterimage of something he'd scanned in the room as he'd spun around?

Louise sat, slumped, on the small sofa and watched, joined eventually by Joe when Tash was satisfied.

"Are you under stress at the moment, Louise?" Tash asked suddenly, spinning herself slowly around to face her, in the manner of a Bond villain.

Louise blinked, and spluttered. "I ... maybe ... I suppose ... I mean, I've hurt my leg, which was pretty stressful. And ... I just kicked out my housemate ..."

"Who bullied you for two years." Joe said it quickly, and looked down at his knees, as if he felt it was somehow inappropriate to say so, but he couldn't stop himself.

Louise coloured. "Yeah," she agreed. "I also ... I suffer from anxiety a bit. Not full-on panic attacks ... not anymore, anyway ... but yeah, you could say I'm a bit stressed."

Joe turned to study her intently. Louise looked flushed and uncomfortable.

213

"Okay." Tash took a deep breath. "The rag and the slamming door – I'd have initially said poltergeist. The shape on the walls – Stone Tape."

"What the hell is that?" asked Joe, making a face.

"It's a theory that energy and emotions can be stored in solid things and then replayed – like as if your house had a memory and kept repeating it over and over, as if it had been recorded to a tape. Does that make sense? How old is this place anyway?"

"Early 1900's, I think," Louise replied. "It was my grandmother's house – she left it to me when she died. I spent a lot of time here all my life, though, and it's really only recently that all this started. Really recently, actually. Since Christmas."

Tash nodded thoughtfully. "The stress and turmoil in the house – your energy – it could be causing the playback."

Louise stared at her, eyebrows raised. Tash wasn't joking.

"Then again, maybe not. If it's only been happening recently – well, there's one more thing I think it could be." She paused. "Did you bring anything new into the house recently? Did you .... get something second-hand or replace something with something old – like a door, or a piece of furniture or something?"

Louise stared at her blankly, and racked her brains for a moment, shaking her head slowly as she failed to recollect anything.

It was Joe who nudged her and pointed toward the box on the floor.

"What about that?" he said.

Louise felt a thrill of electricity through her body as she

followed his finger and her eyes fell on the box camera.

"Oh Jesus, yes," she said breathlessly. She stared at it for a moment. "That ... it's a camera," she explained to Tash. "I bought it a few weeks ago – it was a complete impulse buy – I don't even want it anymore – I had a notion ... do you think it could have something to do with what's going on?"

Tash looked thoughtfully at the camera box and shrugged. "I'm not an expert, but it's certainly worth consideration," she said.

Louise shook her head in disbelief. "The timing," she said. "Everything started around the time when I brought it home. Do you remember, Joe?"

Joe nodded, his lip curled as he looked from his sister to Louise to the camera. "Are you being serious?" he asked Tash.

She shrugged again. "It's a theory."

"So you're telling me the camera is haunted?" Joe's voice indicated that the boundaries of his belief had been pushed.

"It's called Spirit Attachment," Tash replied authoritatively. "It's pretty self-explanatory – a spirit attaches itself to something it had particularly strong connection with in life. I mean, if you've got a better theory, let's have it."

"What do I do with it?" Louise's eyes were wide as she looked at Tash. "I mean, do I have it blessed or exorcised or what?"

Tash blinked. "You could just get rid of it?" she suggested. "You said you didn't even like it, so can you sell it or something?"

"I could bring it back to the antique shop," Louise said, excited. "I'm sure they'll take it back – in fact, I don't think I paid enough for it – I think I was undercharged – maybe that's why it's ... *bothered* – do you think? Maybe it feels that it wasn't treated respectfully or something?"

Tash scrunched her face into a 'maybe' expression, while Joe cast a sceptical eye toward the box. "Are they open Saturdays?" he asked. "I can give you a lift into town with it today if you want to be rid of it quickly?"

Louise turned to him and beamed. "Could you? I mean, would you? That would be fantastic."

"Of course," he said, practically jumping to his feet. "Do you want to go now? We could get some lunch in town ... if you wanted ..."

With a smile, Louise nodded and stood up herself. "Let me just get my coat," she said.

"I'll pop this in the van – oh, crap, I won't be able to fit both yourself and Louise in, Tash."

Tash shrugged. "No bother," she said. "Don't worry about me, your sister, who you forced out of bed this morning to solve your problem."

"You demanded I bring you! And I called you at ten!" Joe snorted.

"Crack of dawn," Tash replied. "I'm a student. Anyway, it's all cool. Glad to be of assistance. There's a bus into town from around here, isn't there? I could meet you in there."

"Just out on Arden Road," said Louise from the hallway as Tash and Joe emerged, Joe carrying the camera box. "You'd be in town in ten minutes – are you sure that's okay?"

"No worries."

Joe was holding the box away from himself, as if it were somehow contaminated. "Is my van going to be haunted now if I put this thing in it?" he demanded over his shoulder as he headed for the front door.

Tash rolled her eyes. "Thanks for letting me look round, Louise," she said, ignoring him. "Sorry if I came across as a bit weird. I'm just really interested in this sort of thing. It'll give me something to discuss with the paranormal society at college at the next meeting. Will you let me know if the activity stops?"

"Absolutely," Louise replied. "Thanks so much, Tash. You've made me feel there is a solution to my problem. Hopefully that camera is the cause of it all."

"*De nada!*" Tash called back, following Joe out onto into the front garden, scanning her phone. "Right, bus in five according to the app. Later, losers!"

In the hall, Louise hastily double-checked the presence of purse, keys and phone in her handbag. Satisfied that she had everything, she followed, reaching for her crutch which was propped beside the front door. She contemplated how very straightforward the whole thing now seemed, as she draped her handbag over her shoulder. It all made sense, too – in as much as something like all this could actually make sense. It was true that all the ... oddness ... had begun when the camera came into the house. How clever of Tash to spot that – Louise would never have thought of it in a million years – she might not even have been inspired to *do* anything about what was going on. And how far could it have gone? Her mind flashed back to the previous evening, to the feeling of being suffused by that electric coldness. If they ... it ... whatever the hell was in her house, could do things like that, then what was next?

Out of habit, she glanced over her shoulder from the front door up the stairs. Nothing. There was nothing there. Of course there wasn't.

"Are you coming?" Joe called from the van.

She smiled and carefully hopped down the step.

Chapter 28

The antique shop was darker than Louise remembered it. Colder too. And the smell was different – still musty, but with an unpleasant undertone, as if there was something very old, and very dirty, somewhere. There was no jazz today either. She jumped and ducked instinctively as something moved near her head – a birdcage, containing a live budgie, pale blue, fluttering and panicked.

Her mind rolled back to her previous visit – the day she'd bought the damn camera. Bartering over the price – what had she been thinking of? Who had she even been? Confident, enthused and brave at the decision she had made to finally ask Ros to leave. She remembered how freeing she'd thought it was all going to be. How all her stress would immediately evaporate, and how the camera was supposed to represent that change. She snorted disdainfully. Things had changed alright. Except she'd exchanged the stress that the living caused, for the stress of the dead.

Louise shivered. Could it really have happened to her? That there had been actual real-life – or death – spirits of the dead – *ghosts* – in her house? A part of her was still

219

telling herself how nonsensical that was. If the experience hadn't been shared by someone else, in fact, she'd still be at home wondering if she were losing her mind.

She looked up at Joe gratefully, standing beside her, gallantly carrying the hefty box. If it hadn't been for him she would never have acknowledged what was going on. And if it hadn't been for him bringing Tash around, then she'd never have known what she could do about it. She gave him a grateful smile, which he caught and returned.

They stood in silence for a few moments before someone appeared through the bead curtain that led through the door at the back of the shop. It was a girl today, dressed modestly in a floral long-sleeved dress, thick black tights and wine-coloured Mary Janes, her hair pulled back in a high ponytail.

"Can I help you?" she asked.

Louise took a deep breath. "I bought something here a while ago. And I wanted to see if I could return it ... if that's okay?" Her heart sank as the girl's face dropped. The shop must have a no-returns policy, she thought, feeling panic rise in her. The girl was going to speak to her now like she was stupid – and she probably was. Who had she thought she was, buying something like that anyway? The camera – things like that were for people who really knew about antiques, not people like her who couldn't distinguish between something from Sotheby's and something from B&Q. The girl was going to tell her no, and she'd feel ashamed, and embarrassed, and look like a fool in front of Joe.

"What is it?" the girl asked.

"Oh. It's this actually," Louise said, pointing to the camera which Joe held up for the girl to see.

Immediately her expression changed. Her eyes widened and she bent down to look more closely at it.

Oh," she replied. "*Oh*. Yes. Could you ... wait a minute? I have to talk to my boss and he's just stepped out, but he won't be long – I'll just ring him, is that okay?"

The sudden change in her demeanour puzzled Louise. She thought she heard a tone of panic in her voice.

Louise nodded. "Sure." She turned to Joe. "*I* can wait anyway – if you want to go on ...?"

He shook his head. "Lunch, remember?" he said with a smile.

Louise nodded and grinned, turning back to the girl. "Yeah, we can wait."

"Great," the girl replied, and fled back through the beaded curtain, leaving Louise and Joe alone in the silence, broken only occasionally by a chirrup from the budgie in the cage.

"Poor little thing," Joe remarked. "It looks agitated."

Louise nodded. "I know how he feels," she remarked, without thinking.

He looked at her, frowning. "You do?"

She nodded sheepishly and looked at her feet. "I get very stressed out doing this sort of thing," she said shyly, her cheeks flushing at the admission. "It's pathetic, I know."

"No, it's not," countered Joe. "You just don't look stressed at all – you appear to me to be calm as a breeze. You're either a fabulous actress or a complete woman of mystery."

Louise smiled. "I'm neither, but thanks for thinking that I'm calm. Fake it till you make it is working today then."

"What stresses you out about this?"

Louise shrugged, and avoided his eyes. "Dunno," she

replied. "Just dealing with other humans, I guess. Just afraid that she'll tell me to feck off with myself. Stupid, I know."

"You seem very together overall."

It was an observation, rather than the type of challenge she was used to if she dared mention her anxiety: "*But you had no problem talking to me?*" – "*Why would you be scared to just talk to a stranger?*" – "*But you run your own business? You record ads that thousands of people are going to hear on radio?*" This was why she didn't tell people when she didn't feel brave. Because different things – smaller things – by their standards – terrified her. The prospect of asking for directions, or a hot refill of coffee.

She searched inside her brain for a response to Joe.

He spoke first, however. "My mam suffers from anxiety too," he said. "It's really tough for her – simple things are just hard to do – yet she'd have no problem, say, reading at Mass. When my Dad got sick, she got really bad. Panic attacks about leaving the house for a while, that sort of thing."

Louise studied his face, searching for any sign that he was about to give her a helpful tip, or tell her to feel the fear and do it anyway. He did nothing of the sort, however.

"I had panic attacks for a while too," she said quietly, leaving the sentence hanging in the air, as if it was an admission of weakness. She waited for the inevitable response: a '*Do you know what you should do?*'

Instead, Joe tutted sympathetically, and poked his finger in through the bars of the little cage where the budgie squeaked and hopped.

"It was after I left my job," she said.

"What did you work at?" he asked casually, waggling his forefinger at the small bird who went still and rested on its perch, staring at it, head to one side.

"Radio," she replied. "In the sales end of things. This building was my office actually – upstairs. Emerald FM."

"I know it – 'All Irish Hits *ar feadh an lae, ar fud na cathrach*.' What a coincidence the offices were here!"

"Well, not really – I only bought the camera in the first place because I was passing, and I wanted a peek at what the old stomping ground looked like now."

"Cool. Your job must have been really interesting?"

Louise made a face. "Nope. Not really. And very stressful. High targets, tight deadlines – it was all about the money, money, money end of things. More money, right now. Huge pressure, long hours, a lot of socialising."

"Oh, nightmare," he observed. "If you get stressed out by that sort of thing."

"I wasn't as nervy back then. But I am introverted so it used to exhaust me, and I didn't know why."

"That's tough going when it's not your thing," he remarked, turning his attention to a beaded necklace that draped from a trunk beside him.

She watched him, marvelling at how easy it felt to talk about this with him. How *safe* she felt in this conversation. Unlike back then, where every conversation was a one-sided demand. Why hadn't she got new clients this month? Why hadn't she exceeded her target? Why was she leaving the office at five thirty? Everything was a criticism.

Her thoughts were thankfully disturbed by the rattle of the bead curtain again and the reappearance of the girl. "I can't get hold of him just now, but I'm sure there's no problem at all in returning *that*." She pointed to the camera box.

Louise raised her eyebrows at the response. "Oh, great," she replied, glancing at Joe who beamed at her reassuringly. "I have the receipt here."

The transaction was completed quickly, the cash counted and handed back to Louise with a smile.

"I'll just get you a new receipt to show you've returned it," said the girl, pulling an old-fashioned receipt book from a drawer beside her. "What's your name?"

"Louise Lacey."

The girl scribbled it down, along with the date and the amount refunded before ripping it from the book and handing it over to Louise. "That's super," she said. "Thank you *so* much for that."

"That's that then," said Joe as they turned to go.

Louise giggled, feeling suddenly giddy, suddenly free.

"Right then, lunch!" said Joe loudly, rubbing his hands together. "Back home towards Maryborough Gardens or stay in town?"

"Oh, stay in town," replied Louise, laughing. "Let's celebrate."

Chapter 29

London, 1867

Bridget could hear the commotion the moment she closed the front door behind her. Muffled voices, the wail of a child, reassurances – her husband's voice making apologies. She stood and listened but didn't have to wait long to see the cause.

The door to Samuel's studio further along the hall was flung open abruptly and out marched an aggrieved gentleman, followed by his wife who scurried down the hallway, trying to soothe a red-faced infant in her arms. Temple came after them, uttering more apologies and reassurances that if they just came back in and posed again they would see it was all absolutely fine, that his assistant had meant no harm.

Bridget frowned. Assistant? She smiled politely as the family brushed past, but they paid her no heed in their haste to leave. The smile dropped immediately when she turned to look back at the studio door.

There she was. The cause of the kerfuffle, no doubt. It was clear to her now what had happened as she glared at Maud who stood there, looking sheepish – cheeks red, and eyes downcast, trying to hold back tears. Assistant indeed, thought Bridget crossly as the front door slammed.

Her husband stood there, staring helplessly at the door and shaking his head.

"I don't understand," he muttered. "What was there to be upset about? It would all have been perfectly fine."

He turned and sighed, only to be greeted by his wife's dour expression.

"I take it your clients were unhappy with something, Samuel," she said.

He shook his head again. "They were too hasty to judge the situation," he replied. "The child, if they had given it but a few moments, would have stopped crying ..."

"And why was it crying in the first place, may I ask?" Bridget's tone was ice-cold.

Her husband shrugged. "If they had just ..."

His wife cut him off with a look, before turning to the meek girl who stood watching them. "Go to your room, Maud!" she snapped abruptly.

Her niece complied, almost gratefully, turning and running quietly up the stairs, avoiding their gaze. When she was sure that they were alone, Bridget turned her attention back to her husband.

"If they had just what, Samuel? Might it be that it was not their fault at all, but that something ... or someone ... might have put them off? Could that be it, perhaps? *Hmm?* The reason why *paying* customers are marching out of this house and taking their custom elsewhere? Could it be that your ... *assistant* ... may have disturbed their child? Frightened it even?"

Temple glanced up the stairs where Maud had scurried and then glared at his wife, pressing a finger to his lips. "Quiet, Bridget," he commanded, an instruction that merely caused her to roll her eyes.

"What in goodness' name are you thinking of, having her in the room when people come for their portraits? *Nobody* wants to see her. There is no need for anyone to be forced into looking at *that*."

He frowned more deeply, exasperated. "*Bridget*," he bit out, "you must not ... you *cannot* say such things!"

"She is grotesque, Samuel," Bridget insisted. "She is ... *hideous* to the eye ..."

"Your niece is a very attractive young woman."

"You *know* that is not what I am referring to." Bridget fixed him with a glare. "She is missing *limbs*. Those ... what remains ... it is *hideous*."

"They see worse as they walk down the street any day," retorted Samuel. "Men – servicemen – amputees among them. They meet soldiers without legs, without arms at the houses of their friends, at dinners, encounter them at the theatre. They see cripples on street corners with a stick to balance on. Does their child cry at every single one of them? Why on earth would an innocent young girl with a similar affliction terrify them so? It is nonsense."

Bridget shook her head, frustrated. "That is precisely the reason why it is so unpalatable. To be exposed to those *stumps* – the shape of them, in one so young, so normal in all other ways – why, it is unnatural! Imagine being a child and having those great ugly things coming at you – you would think you were in a nightmare. It is bad enough that you insisted on her returning to London with us –"

"To help with the baby, Bridget, and well you know it."

"What a clever idea that was, eh? A nursemaid who cannot even lift? Who cannot push a perambulator?

Shame you didn't think of asking me before you extended your generous invitation. Her mother thought that Christmas had come early, I'm sure – rid of her at last, someone else to take on the responsibility of putting food in the mouth of the girl who cannot as much as lift a cup."

Temple closed his eyes and shook his eyes. "You are cruel at times, Bridget, do you know that?"

Bridget snorted. "I'd call it practical, Mr Temple. For what use is she exactly? Eh? She cannot feed the child, nor bathe him as she will drop him when he grows slippery, nor can she stroke his brow nor minister to him when he is ill."

"She is a good companion," he countered.

Bridget sniggered. "To whom, pray tell?" she asked snidely. "I don't see her at my side, whiling away the hours with embroidery and light conversation, as we womenfolk are meant to do. And I simply *cannot* have her along when I make my afternoon calls – the embarrassment of bringing her to the drawing rooms of polite society where I make such effort for the sake of my name – of *your* name, as it happens. Imagine how it would go down for me to be known as the woman who wanders about with a handless freak as her only friend? Is that how you would like the name Temple to be recognised among our peers and prospective clients?"

"It is not like that –" he began, only to be cut off again.

"So if she is no nursemaid to your son, and no companion to your wife, then she must be yours, Samuel, am I correct? What tasks exactly does she assist you with at your work? Lifting glass plates, pouring those chemicals about? Horrifying small children and disgusting their parents?"

"You talk of her as if she were a *monster*, Bridget."

"*And she is.*"

The sharp hiss of her tone struck Samuel dumb and they stared at each other, Bridget's eyes narrow and burning, Samuel's wide in disbelief.

"You are filled with unnatural hatred," he managed eventually. "She is a sweet, innocent thing, denied every opportunity by an accident of birth. If our son had been similarly afflicted, would you stand before me and call him a monster too?"

She flinched, but only barely, and then composed herself to reply. "Our son is perfect," she replied calmly. "But if he were the same as *her* then he, too, would have no place in society. He would be useless – worse than useless because he would require the expense of feeding and educating, assistance to wash and dress and remain unable to contribute in return. He would be a burden until the day he died, as she is a burden. One who has turned your soft head with her angelic face and '*Oh, how wonderful, Mr Temple!*' and '*Gracious, I have never in all my days, Mr Temple!*' and whatnot. She is a strain on our household – a needless strain. One which we wouldn't have to suffer if you had only listened to me when I urged you to purchase Redtrees Hall and take your family to a life and status of which we are deserving. She would have had no opportunities at our expense less than three miles along the road from her own hovel, where it would be best she stayed. But no, you knew best, husband, did you not? A new nursemaid, a new assistant for the business, here in filthy London. All will be well, you said."

"And it will," he urged.

"When?" Bridget demanded. "When she grows hands? When she can stitch a tear, or lift a kettle? When she no longer frightens our customers away and our income with them?"

"An income that we would have lost in the countryside," argued Temple.

"An income that we – you – will lose in the city too if you continue to give your customers a portrait sitting with a freak show thrown in for free. That is the second we have lost in as many weeks, am I correct?"

Temple paused for a moment and then sheepishly nodded his head.

Bridget shook hers and tutted disapprovingly. "And us with another mouth to feed. The 'son' of 'Temple and Son' who would starve because his father showed more sympathy to a fawning curiosity than to his own heir and successor. Call me filled with unnatural hatred all you will, Samuel, but you are the one who is consumed with something unnatural – an unnatural fascination with the abhorrent. And it is one thing to fixate upon them as subjects, to dream of your monsters' gallery but it is quite another to bring one into our home to eat our food and warm herself by our fire. There is no place for her here, Samuel, and well you know it."

Temple's brow furrowed with hurt. "These are harsh words, Bridget ... I understood ... I thought that you shared my passion with me ..."

"Not this one!" she snapped. "Not when it will cost us and is already costing us in more than matters monetary. You know what you have to do, Samuel. You know that it is time for her to go."

She could see that, for a moment, he contemplated

replying, but the slight slump of his shoulders showed that he had decided against it. He made no sound as he turned away from her and went back into the portrait studio, quietly closing the door behind him, leaving her in the hall.

Victory, she thought, but a hollow one. It was not the victory she desired – none of this was what she desired, of course. He had flatly denied her of that. What a life she had dreamed of for them! It was by far the best way, but Temple – that stupid, soft fool couldn't – or wouldn't – see it.

Her lip curled in disgust at the door behind which she knew he worked, tidying up the setting he had created for the commission that was now lost. Carefully putting away the glass plates, covering the lens on the camera. Shut into his dark little room. Yet what about her? Shut into this house, this life – trapped, forever, with no prospect of escape. And, thanks to that idiot, trapped with that awful disfigured girl – Bridget shuddered as an image of those incomplete arms flashed across her mind. She simply couldn't bear to look at the damn things – those useless, useless, broken appendages – the very thing that so fascinated the man she had married. The idea of them disgusted her, and by extension, so did he.

Bridget turned and made her way up the stairs as quietly as she could, slipping into her room and turning the key in the lock so that she could not be disturbed. She had some time before she would be needed again. Dolly, the housemaid, had taken Samuel Junior for his daily air in his perambulator, a task *she* was equipped to perform – and Samuel Senior would busy himself at his work for as long as he could, now that he was in her bad books.

The girl would never dream of approaching her unless asked to. Useful solitude then, space and time to think and decide. There was paperwork that she would need to consult, lists that she would need to make. So much planning, but she must do it right, must have everything perfectly in order. This time there was too much at stake to act hastily or be slipshod. There were decisions to be reached, huge decisions, not just for herself, but for her boy, because there were two of them to consider this time.

And she would. She was an excellent planner after all. Meticulous, measured and patient. With a deep sigh, Bridget seated herself at her desk, unlocked it and rolled open the cover. There, everything was ready – a fresh sheet of paper, a pen, ink.

And in one of the small drawers – she opened them all until she found the right one – another bottle – smaller – the perfect size to fit, concealed, into a pocket, for use when the opportunity arose. With a steady hand she took it from the drawer and held it up to the light to see what it contained. It had been a while since she had used it, of course. And – yes, she thought right. It was almost empty.

Step one, therefore, on her to-do list: a trip to the apothecary for a refill.

She'd be needing it soon enough.

Chapter 30

2018

The knock on the door came the following Friday afternoon.

Louise, had been attempting to read a book, but instead was thinking about how much she'd enjoyed having lunch with Tash and Joe the previous week. They'd eaten antipasti and drunk Prosecco, they'd lingered at the table for a couple of happy hours, and she'd laughed properly, for the first time in – she couldn't remember how long – as Tash and Joe each told stories and teased each other.

She'd learned things about them too – how Tash wanted desperately to travel, and how Joe dabbled in stand-up comedy at open-mic nights – something she'd been keen to chat more about when he came to work after the weekend, away from Tash's quickfire interruptions. Except he hadn't arrived on Monday. He'd texted instead to say that his mother had taken a tumble at Mass and fractured her hip and, being Favoured Son, as Tash called him, he'd been forced to look after both parents for a few days.

So perhaps that was him at the door now? Louise brightened at the thought. It came as a surprise to herself, but she had really missed the company. The living company, that was – to her relief, it had seemed all week that her ... unwanted houseguests, she supposed she could call them ... were gone. The undesirable companions. Since Saturday, and the return of the camera to the antique shop, there had been no strange shadows, or whispers, or draughts. Everything was back to normal. Tash had been right. And while she didn't understand the why or how of it happening in the first place, she was content to chalk it down to just some weird episode that she was sure she'd process and understand some day. But, for now, she was just glad it was over.

Carefully, her ankle complaining as she limped cautiously across the room, she made her way out to the front door, and pulled it open just as a second knock sounded.

It wasn't Joe, however, who stood there.

Instead, a stranger waited at the bottom of her front steps, turning around to face her as the door opened. Louise instantly felt ill at ease at the sight of him – his ill-fitting crumpled brown suit was worn with a tan-coloured shirt and a burgundy tie. His hair, thick, brown and curly, had been wrestled into a side parting. He wore a pair of large, thick-soled white trainers, entirely incongruous with the rest of his appearance. But it was his smile that unnerved her the most. A broad, humourless, insincere spread of full lips across a weasel-like face. Her immediate instinct was distrust. She pulled the door over behind her, blocking the entrance to her home with her body as much as she could. She simply didn't want him to see inside.

Ascending the bottom step, the man removed his right hand from where it had been thrust in his trouser pocket and offered it to Louise. "Adrian Temple," he announced.

"Owner and proprietor of Temple Antiques."

She took the hand loosely, feeling it close over her own. He released it after a clammy half-shake, and stepped back down, his eyes roaming over the front of Louise's house.

"Is it you who returned a very valuable camera to my shop at the weekend?" His voice was thin and nasal, his accent a mix of Irish and English.

Her stomach sank. What had she done wrong? Did she owe him money? Would she have to take it back? Had she damaged it? For a moment, she contemplated lying. A simple 'No, you have the wrong house' would send him away on a fruitless search. And then what? She'd live like a nervous wreck waiting for him to come back – or move house so he could never find her?

"Yes, I did," Louise replied meekly before clearing her throat and taking a deep breath for courage.

She was rewarded with another of the wide smiles.

"Wonderful!" he replied. "You can't imagine how grateful I was to see her home."

Louise frowned.

"The camera," he clarified. "She should never have been sold, you see. She's an heirloom – belonged to my great-great-grandfather."

Louise's hand flew to her mouth. "I'm so sorry," she said. "I didn't know ... it didn't say ..."

"No, it didn't," replied Temple, shaking his head. "She was just stored at the shop but was put out front in error. And someone doesn't have a job anymore because of that. Still, all's well that ends well. She found her way home and that's what matters."

Louise smiled politely as he removed the other hand

from his pocket and rubbed his palms together vigorously, wrapping his hands around each other and blowing into them.

"So," he continued. "Why am I here, correct?"

Louise nodded faintly. She didn't want to appear impolite, but he was making her intensely uncomfortable. The urge to just slam the door was huge. But that wouldn't make him go away, would it? She'd have to stay and see it through.

"Well, firstly to say how grateful I am to you for returning her in one piece. You seem to have taken very good care of her."

"I barely opened it – *her*," blurted Louise defensively. She was sure that a 'but' was coming, some blame to be laid at her feet.

Temple nodded. "Very good. Did you not like her?"

The question was strange, accusatory, as if a response in the negative would be taken personally.

"It – *she* – was an impulse purchase," she said, her tone apologetic.

Temple seemed to think about this for a moment, before nodding again. "It's just ... I was wondering ... you say you examined her just the once, am I right?"

Louise nodded. "I was very careful. And I made sure that everything went back where it belonged – all the pieces."

Temple cocked his head to one side as he listened, and then nodded again, apparently thinking for a moment.

"All of them?" he asked.

"Yes," Louise replied. Of this, at least, she was sure.

"You're certain?"

He didn't believe her.

Louise nodded, more emphatically this time. "Certain,"

she said. For a second she thought to politely ask if something was missing. This, in fact, is what she would normally do. And then, if she behaved as she usually did, she'd convince herself that perhaps, yes, something *was* missing, and might go and check. And then what? She'd have to invite him in while she did that. And of one thing she was certain, she did not, under any circumstances want to be alone in her house with this man.

In response, he looked around him again, thinking, and nodding. After a moment of this, he wrinkled his nose and pursed his lips. "Very well. If you say so. I'm sorry to have bothered you, Miss Lacey. Thank you for your time. I'm sorry to have disturbed you. Enjoy the rest of your evening."

And with that, he turned briskly and padded halfway down the path in his oversized runners before stopping abruptly and turning back to her.

Louise's stomach knotted again.

"I just want to say thank you again, Miss Lacey," he said. "Returning the camera has enabled me to undertake a project I've been looking forward to for a long time now. I'm very grateful."

With that, he nodded briskly and turned, continuing along the path and out onto the pavement.

Louise watched him go, only closing the door when he was out of sight. She stood inside, baffled. What an odd exchange with a very odd man, she thought.

A very basic realisation suddenly hit her, and the colour drained from her face. He'd called her Miss Lacey. How had he known ... oh, she'd given her name for the receipt, so that was fine ... but how the hell had he known where she lived?

She felt a little dizzy. She turned quickly and, her

hands now trembling, fumbled the security chain into place on the door while peering out through the peephole onto the road. She fully expected to see him there again but, to her relief, it was deserted. Still, her hand slid down the door to the thick key which rested in the mortice lock and she turned it before resting her forehead against the door and closing her eyes for a moment to allow the rush of panic that had flooded through her to pass over. Yes, he was gone. But he hadn't believed her, had he? That she'd returned everything – what did he think she'd kept? What was he missing? Something valuable? Something irreplaceable? Whatever it was, she didn't have it – of that she was sure – but he'd clearly been unconvinced. What if he came back though? He was so creepy – would she put it past him to do something … desperate? Mentally, she ran through the entry points to the house in her head as her heart thudded wildly, ticking them off one by one as secure. She was safe, she reassured herself and breathed deeply in an effort to calm herself down. Maybe she should ring the Guards – or was that taking it too far? They'd just tell her that there was nothing they could do unless he tried something, wouldn't they? So did that mean she'd have to wait until he came back? *If* he came back? And what if he did? What if he caught her unawares? What then?

She took a deep breath, urging herself to calm down. Maybe she'd ring them anyway, just in case. No harm in having something on paper, was there? And what if, maybe, they were aware of him? What if he was a dodgy sort, and did this kind of thing a lot? What if this was his modus operandi for acquiring stock for his shop, for example? Perhaps others – elderly people, for example –

would allow him in out of the cold for a few minutes, and then he could have a good look around for any valuables?

So could she expect a break-in now? Or had her determination not to allow him in made his visit an unproductive one? Worry after irrational worry seemed to pile up, the more she thought about it. Instinctively, she tested the pockets of the tracksuit pants she wore for her phone before remembering that it was on charge in her bedroom. With a final test of the front door handle, she made her way across the hall and up the stairs.

With trembling hands, she unplugged the phone from where it sat on her bedside locker, and went to the window, studying the street outside in both directions. A solitary woman – who Louise recognised as the resident of a house further down – in a puffy coat with fur around the hood paused as her Jack Russell cocked his leg and left a scent on a pole. There was no one else in sight. Louise wasn't reassured, however. He could be watching from a car, or hiding in someone's garden – somewhere, watching the house. Take no chances, she thought, hurrying to the door, scrolling through her phone for the number of the nearest Garda station.

Just as she reached it, however, she froze.

There was something behind her. Movement.

She sensed it at first – a change to the atmosphere, a strangeness.

And then, from the corner of her eye, a flicker of something – something white.

Louise turned her head an inch and blinked, hopeful that it would be gone when she cleared her vision.

But it wasn't. It was definitely there. A shape at the window, something moving, shimmering almost, something translucent. Louise stood, rooted to the spot, unable to turn her head any further. Desperate to see – and more desperate not to. It was just her imagination – surely – it must be – there couldn't possibly be anything there.

But still it hovered in her peripheral vision. And it was not all – suddenly the room was filled with a strong smell – overpowering almost. And one she recognised.

Those shitty flowers, Ros had called it. She had smelled it too.

Lilies.

It was the scent of lilies. Again.

Whatever was in the house – whatever was here with Louise, on her own, had not gone after all, it had merely waited. And it smelled of lilies.

And now it was turning – Louise could just make out the shift in movement. What was it going to do? Come toward her? Glide into her again? Touch her? *Say* something to her?

The thought was unbearable.

With a strangled shriek, she found her feet and fled as quickly as she could manage. Away, down the stairs, away from it, whatever it was, and whatever it wanted of her.

Chapter 31

It felt like an eternity before Joe arrived.

Tash was with him – Louise saw them from where she stood, waiting at the sitting-room window as they both leaped from Joe's van and raced up the path. Rushing to meet them, she opened the front door before they could knock, where, much to her own embarrassment, she greeted them with a loud, uncontrollable sob.

Joe grabbed her and she fell into his arms, pressing her face against his chest to suppress more sobbing.

"What's happening?" barked Tash eagerly, pushing her way in past them and stepping into the hallway.

"Are you okay?"

Joe's voice was so kind that Louise felt she might dissolve entirely into tears.

Taking a deep breath to compose herself, she pushed herself away from him and nodded in response, unsure if she could trust her own voice.

"Oh yeah, that too," said Tash as she peered into the kitchen, turned the light on, and then retreated back to the hall before turning her attention to the studio. "Nothing doing here either," she called, her tone disappointed.

Joe tutted and shook his head, before turning back to Louise to look at her, his arm still reassuringly around her shoulders.

Tash shook her head as she turned her attention to the cupboard under the stairs, and then up and around at the landing, her face a picture of confusion and disappointment.

"I thought you said something was happening?"

"Bloody hell, Tash!" said Joe. "That's enough."

"So it wasn't the camera's fault after all," continued Tash. "If only I could just *see* something!"

"This isn't about you, Tash." Joe's voice was low and stern. "There's something not right about this house."

"Upstairs," Louise managed suddenly. "My room ..."

"Can I look?" Tash asked eagerly.

Louise nodded, and watched fearfully as Tash ran upstairs.

Louise turned to Joe. "The white thing ... the lilies ..." she began helplessly, her voice trailing off as Joe steered her back in the door of the sitting room.

"Sit down for a moment," he said. "You've had a shock."

She allowed herself to be guided to the sofa and lowered herself gently down, wrapping her arms around herself as she did. She smiled gratefully at him as he sat beside her, still watching her with a look of worry. She saw now that it was mixed with fear as he flicked his eyes toward the door and out into the hallway. He, too, was scared of what he might see, she realised, turning to look herself just as Tash bounded noisily down the stairs and back in.

"There's absolutely nothing there!" she wailed. "In any of the rooms – not a dickie bird – I'm raging!"

"*Tash,*" chided Joe, glancing sideways at Louise.

242

"Sorry," said Tash. "I just got so excited – I'm all carried away."

"We noticed," said Joe in quiet sarcasm.

"It's disappointing though, isn't it?" Tash looked hopefully at her brother and Louise. "I've never seen actual real-life proof before. I really wanted some evidence to show the lads at the next meeting."

"I'm not sure Louise wants all your ghost-hunting buddies to know about her private life," said Joe.

Louise lifted her head suddenly. "Actually, Tash, would you mind?"

Tash's eyes widened in surprise. "What, telling the Para Soc?"

Louise sighed and covered her face for a moment before continuing. "I wish more than *anything* there was nothing to tell. I tried to tell myself for so long that nothing was going on – convinced myself that because something *couldn't* or *shouldn't* happen, that it *hadn't*. Then you saw that stuff, Joe, and I couldn't deny it anymore. And I had really thought that returning the camera had sorted things – I thought it was that simple, but it isn't. I have to face up to this now. There's something really not right here. And it's getting a bit too much for me, so if there was *anything* that *anyone* could do to figure it out ... to make it just go away ... then I'd be so grateful."

She rubbed her eyes with the heels of her hand and sighed heavily.

"We could try to talk to it."

Tash's statement was given with her usual blunt delivery and greeted by stunned silence from both Louise and Joe.

"Bollocks to that!" replied Joe, shuddering.

Louise, however, looked at her quizzically. "What do you mean – just ask who's there and request that they leave me alone or something?"

Tash nodded. "Well, you could do that – but there's something else we could try if you were up for it."

"What's that?" asked Louise nervously.

"Well ... can I have your keys for a sec, Joe?"

She stood and Joe reluctantly withdrew a key ring from his pocket and handed it to her.

"Back in a mo," she said.

Joe and Louise heard her open the front door, apparently leaving it open as she did as cold air flooded into the house. Louise shivered and wondered momentarily if, somehow, whatever was in the house might just flood out just as easily?

Tash brought the cold into the room with her when she returned, a large, long-handled canvas bag slung over her shoulder.

What *is* that?" asked Joe.

Tash looked at them, her expression a mix of glee and hope. "I'll show you," she said, sitting down on the edge of the armchair and clearing a space on the coffee table, before extracting something from the bag.

"First things first," she said, brandishing a chocolate swiss roll. "Cake."

Joe stared at her in disbelief. "Did you ... do you just *carry* a cake around the place with you?" Tash looked back in surprise. "Didn't Mam ever tell you never to visit anyone empty-handed? Here you go, Louise. Now ... this is what we need."

With that, she reached back into the bag and produced something larger. It appeared to be a board game.

Joe groaned and sat forward as he recognised it. "*No fucking way*," he stated. "*Put that back*."

Curious, and a little alarmed, Louise sat forward too to get a better view. "What is it?"

"*Ta-daaah!*" said Tash as she laid it on the table and sat back.

It was a sepia-coloured board, covered in characters and numerals in a typeface reminiscent of an old-fashioned circus poster. The letters of the alphabet were written across the centre in two arches, A to M above, N to Z curved underneath, and under that again numbers one to nine, and then a zero, were written in a straight line. In the top left corner, a sun smiled – in the top right, a halfmoon watched it. Clouds with faces blew wind from the two bottom corners. Beside the sun was printed the word '**YES**' while '**NO**' sat beside the moon.

"This isn't happening, Tash." Joe was angry now.

Tash ignored him and looked expectantly at Louise.

"A Ouija board?" Louise asked.

Tash nodded. "Okay – I know that they aren't everyone's cup of deadly nightshade, but I'm just throwing it out there – if you want to communicate with whatever's in your house, then this could be the way."

"They're dangerous, Tash, and you know that," said Joe.

"Only if you're a bunch of teenagers on Halloween night," she replied facetiously.

"Come off it!" growled Joe. "Louise, you don't have to."

Louise continued to stare at the board, her mind blank and racing at the same time.

"How do we do it?" she asked suddenly.

Tash clapped her hands and made an 'O' of delight with her mouth. "You're in then?" she chirped.

Louise continued to consider the board. "I'm not sure," she countered rapidly.

"Good. *Don't*, Louise," said Joe.

"How does it work, Tash?" Louise continued, ignoring him.

"Well, basically the users try to communicate with spirits by combining energies that we channel into a device – a planchette, or a glass or something – that the spirits then use to spell out words and convey messages."

Joe sighed angrily. "All this, Tash, it's all absolute bullshit."

Tash froze and looked her brother directly in the eye. "Well, what do you suggest we do then? Just carry on pretending that nothing is happening in this house even though you've seen it yourself? Why are you so against trying to help Louise? I thought you, of all people, would want to be White Knight here?"

Joe went a deep shade of red before biting back. "I've never heard one good thing about using one of these." He pointed dismissively at the board. "Either they don't work – which they don't – or ... *they're* ... *bloody* ... *dangerous.*"

"Scaredy Cat Joe!" she sneered. "Afraid the boogeyman will come and get you!"

"*We're doing this!*" Louise spoke so defiantly that Tash and Joe were immediately silenced.

She was still staring at the Ouija board, her expression a mix of confusion and trepidation.

"I think we have to," she said, looking up. "I think Tash is right – it's as good a shot as we have to find out what's going on. And I *need* to know what's happening here – what's happening to *me*, if I'm to have any chance at making things go back to normal – if they can ever go back." She looked from one to the other. "I live my whole life scared of stuff, you see. I'm scared of answering my phone, or of bumping into the postman and having to chat to him. Every single day is just a bloody battle to get over my stupid fears – ordinary, everyday things – stuff that other people don't even think about. Some days it's like a war – like I'm just dodging bullets, imagining the worst, steeling myself constantly to cope. And today – suddenly – all this is just too much. It's just one thing too many for me to have to fight against – and it's in my home, where I'm supposed to be safe from all that. I've been trying to get stress *out* of my life – and instead it's quadrupled. And I'm sick of being scared all the time, sick of feeling ... *intimidated*, controlled by things that I'm not in charge of. Bloody sick to the back teeth of it. So yes – if this board is going to maybe, in some way, help me take back control then we have to do this."

She sat a little straighter in her seat and looked from Joe to Tash and back again. Joe shrank back a little and looked down at his knees.

"I'm not sure ..." he began.

"I know," Louise replied softly. "I know you're not wild on this idea and I have to respect that." Her hands trembled only slightly as she reached out and gently took his. "But if you could help me one more time, I'll be really grateful. I just don't know what else to do."

Joe's cheeks flushed again.

"I know you're ... uncomfortable," she continued. "And we're all scared. But I really want my home back to myself. And we'll all be together – and I'm sure Tash knows what she's doing."

"Oh God, no, I don't," said Tash.

Both Joe and Louise turned to stare at her, eyebrows raised.

Tash was wide-eyed, shaking her head. "I've never actually *done* a Ouija séance before, but I do know what's involved."

Louise's resolute expression wilted as she looked at Tash. "Oh," she said.

A nervous silence descended on the room.

"Fuck it. Fine, I'm in." Joe sighed and squeezed Louise's hand as he glared at his sister. "Not that I think it'll achieve miracles, but if it makes you feel safer, Louise – if you think it's the best thing to do, then I'll do it – *even* if Tash is involved."

Louise gave a weak, grateful smile and returned the squeeze before releasing his hand.

"So what do we do, Tash?" she said.

Chapter 32

Tash's excited face looked momentarily sinister in the flare of the match. She cupped her hand around it to let the flame steady, and then lowered it to the wick of the tealights that they had placed in small glass holders at each corner of the Ouija board. Louise looked around the room nervously as it gradually glowed brighter. Her studio, selected as a good location by Tash because the soundproofing would minimise noise from elsewhere, felt uncomfortably different.

Fortified first by tea and Tash's Swiss Roll in the kitchen, they had made a space for the session by wheeling the office chair out into the hallway and rolling up the rug in order to have a flat surface to use. Joe knelt on the bare floorboards, while Louise sat as comfortably as she could manage, her sore ankle extended along the side of the board, waiting for Tash to begin. She glanced at Joe, only to see that his face was a sickly white colour, which gave her no consolation.

Tash regarded them both with a grin. "We good?" she asked. "Ready for kick-off?"

Louise flinched and felt herself pale. She had a strong

urge, in that instant, to back out, to call a halt to the whole thing before it just got silly.

But then Tash blew out the match and, with the flame, seemed to go the chance of escape. A flare of hot fear ran through Louise.

Tash, on the other hand, was positively stimulated by the whole experience. She sat at the base of the board, facing the letters, one copper-topped finger extended over the upside-down glass, with an air of authority to her.

"Now remember, when we get started, to keep your fingers on the glass at all times," Tash instructed, wiggling hers up and down. "Right then." She shook out her hands. She inhaled deeply, centred herself and looked directly at the other two. "Whatever you do, don't ask aggressive questions and don't ask when you're going to d – i – e."

"Why in God's name would we ask that?" blurted Joe. "This is beyond ridiculous, Tash –"

She held her finger to her lips and shushed him. "Just gotta cover the bases. Most of all, don't get scared and bolt. Don't break the ring of protection, and don't run away. If you end the session without saying '*Goodbye*' – she tapped the base of the glass with her nail – "then you could release something new and we don't want that." She paused as Louise flashed her a worried look. "Most of all, try to stay calm. Close your eyes for a moment and picture a bubble of white light around us – a bubble of things that are good and positive and that will protect us. And stick together, okay?"

Louise did as she was told, and immediately closed her eyes.

Joe, on the other hand, continued to regard his sister with suspicion. "I'm assuming you learned all that at this

Para Soc, right? From people who actually know what they're talking about?"

Tash closed her own eyes and held her forefingers and thumbs together up in the air, as if meditating. "Mostly," she replied. "Some of it. Some from Googling ..."

"And the rest?"

"Possibly *Tales from the Dark*."

"The kids TV show? Jesus Christ!"

"Please, Joe," said Louise. "Please just do what she says. She *still* knows more about this than we do."

He grunted and, with a final glare at Tash, closed his own eyes.

"So. What we're going to do is place our forefingers on the glass on the board," said Tash. "And after that, I'll drive, okay? If you've got a question for the spirits, then you ask me to ask them. Don't push the glass – no trying to be funny, Joe – and try to stay as relaxed as possible and focus your energy. Are we ready?"

They all looked at one another, and then at Tash who lowered her finger and placed it gently on the bottom of the upturned shot glass. With a final, fearful, glance at Joe, Louise did the same and he followed suit. They remained in silence, until Tash cleared her throat and began to speak.

"We are here tonight to communicate with any spirits who may be present ..." her voice faltered, "in this house." She paused, and squeezed her eyes shut, swallowing deeply before continuing.

"We wish to communicate peacefully and respectfully. And if there are spirits here, we ask that you do the same."

She took a deep breath.

"Is there anyone here who would like to communicate with us?"

Louise felt Joe go rigid beside her, and her own spine prickled in anticipation. All three looked at their fingers resting on the glass.

It remained completely still.

"If you can, use the energy in the room to simply let us know if you're here," said Tash.

Still, nothing happened.

Tash looked at the expectant faces of Louise and Joe.

"Okay," she said. "Don't worry. It can take a bit of time to warm up. Stay focused."

They nodded.

"Have you lived in this house before?" asked Tash and stared down at the board. Everything remained in position. She shifted on her knees a little. "Are you, by any chance ... what was your grandmother's name, Louise?"

"Philomena. Everyone called her Phil."

"Is Phil here?" asked Tash clearly.

A wave of electric fear and disbelief suddenly shot through Louise as, slowly, the glass began to move beneath her finger.

"What the ...?" blurted Joe, his eyes widening.

"*Quiet, Joe!*" hissed Tash, her face a picture of amazement. The three of them watched as the glass slid slowly across the board from where it was positioned, at the letter 'G', down to the right until it came to a halt on one of the printed words.

Louise gasped.

NO, it said.

"You did that, right?" asked Joe, looking at Tash in alarm.

She shook her head.

Joe turned to Louise; "Did you?"

"No," she whispered, staring in shock at the board.

"Stay calm," ordered Tash. "This is what we're here for."

She flicked back her hair and took a breath.

"Thank you. Thank you for answering my question. Please remember that we mean you no harm – we just want to talk to you. Are you connected to Louise in any way? Are you family?"

The glass nudged itself to the right and then moved straight back to 'NO'.

"Okay, thank you. Do you think you could tell us your name?"

The glass was still for a moment, before giving a little nudge, stopping, then sliding slowly across the board and coming to rest again on 'NO'. Tash, Louise and Joe looked at each other, confused.

"I'm going to ask you again if you could tell us your name?" repeated Tash clearly.

The glass didn't budge.

Louise frowned. "Are you ... are there more than one of you?" she blurted out.

Tash glared at her. "*Let me ask the questions*," she hissed and addressed the glass. "Is that correct?"

The glass shot down the board. **YES.**

"How many of you?" asked Tash nervously.

With sudden great force, the glass swirled around in a circle.

"Shit," murmured Joe.

"So who am I speaking to now?"

Stillness. And then, without warning, the glass shot again around the board in a wide circle at great speed, before coming to an abrupt halt.

Tash looked around the group, worried.

"Alright. There's a few of you. Can ... can you tell us what you want in this house, why you're here?"

The trio tensed for a repeat swirl around the board, but instead the glass remained completely still.

"Can you ... can we help you at all?"

Again, nothing. Tash made a small grunt of frustration.

"*What do you want from us?*" she asked, a tone of impatience to her voice.

Again, the glass made no movement. Instead, a sudden noise came from just outside the door – a crash, the sound of crockery breaking against the floor, so unexpected that Louise squealed.

"*The bloody cake ...*" said Joe, his voice trailing away in disbelief as he peered through the dimness of the candlelight out into the hallway and saw the broken remains of the Swiss Roll, mixed with shattered pieces of the dinnerplate on which they had left it on the countertop in the kitchen. And above it, a huge shape hovering, impossibly darker than the darkness itself, moving and undulating like something underwater.

And then, another noise, sudden, strange and yet familiar – the low rumble of the castors on Louise's office chair as it moved by itself. They heard it gather speed, roaring on the wooden floorboards as it whizzed down the hall, coming to a stop as it crashed against the front door.

A hush followed, the only audible sound being Tash's rapid breathing.

Louise began to shake again and Joe looked at Tash, his expression asking 'What now?'.

"Is it wise to continue this, Tash?" he said.

She didn't reply at first, her normal cockiness gone. She chewed her lip thoughtfully.

"Do you mean us ... harm?" she asked suddenly, her voice faltering a little again.

She held her breath as she waited for a response.

But none came.

After a few moments, their fingers frozen on the glass, Joe, Louise and Tash looked at each other at precisely the same moment. There was a sudden, perceptible change in the atmosphere of the room. A different energy, an electrical charge. Louise looked around her, and out into the hall. All was still. No sound, no movement. Just the glimmer from the candles flickering on the floor and up across the faces of the three participants.

And then they went out.

Tash gasped as the room was plunged into darkness. They all sat, dumbstruck with fear, for what felt like an interminable time.

And then, without warning, a scraping, sliding noise came from behind Louise. In the dark, something shot across the floor and hit her extended ankle. She yelped in pain and shock, and scrabbled to stand as quickly as she could, leaning on Joe for support, desperate to get away from whatever it was and up onto the couch.

"Louise! What happened?" Joe steadied her as she swayed above him and, getting to his feet, he held her close. "Are you okay?"

"Yes, yes, but something hit me really hard on my ankle!"

"*Wait!*" barked Tash, her face suddenly illuminated as she lit a match and held it down to light the nearest tealight.

Together, they peered at the shape in the gloom of the single flame.

"What is it?" whispered Tash eagerly.

"Oh my God ... my God ..." said Louise in shock. "I know what it is."

"What?" said Joe.

"I *did* forget to put something in ..."

"What do you mean?" asked Tash.

"The camera. That box should have been with the camera, but I must ... I didn't see it ... and forgot about it ... Tash, can we stop this now ... please?"

Tash stood and flicked on the light. They blinked in the brightness, taking in each other's pale faces. With the lights back on, the room looked startlingly normal – a world away from how vast it had seemed in the dark, how filled with possibility it had been – the possibility of shadows becoming more than they should.

Tash stood, her hands on her hips, surveying Joe holding Louise, and also the box – the smooth, varnished case in the centre of the floor.

"*Wow*," she managed. "Everyone okay?"

Louise looked from the floor to Tash and nodded, her expression stunned.

Joe continued to stare at the box. "What's in it?" he asked.

Louise shook her head. "I don't know. I couldn't open it. It's locked."

"And it came with the camera?"

"Yes – it must be what that man was missing who called earlier – this must be what he meant."

"What man?"

Louise stood up and looked at Joe. "I forgot, with everything that was going on ... he's the owner of the Antique Shop – he was asking me if I'd forgotten a part of the camera when I returned it and I thought I hadn't but this must have got left under the couch ..."

"Guys," urged Tash. "We can talk lost and found later – maybe we should, you know ..."

Joe and Louise turned to look at her. She was pointing at the box, her eyes wide and expectant. "Oh Christ," said Joe. "Do we have to open it?"

Tash nodded and wiggled her eyebrows excitedly. The light had made her brave again.

"Who's up for it?" she asked enthusiastically.

Louise's lip curled with reluctance and she cast a glance at Joe, who looked ill. Overwhelmed with sudden disbelief, she sank down onto the couch.

"Not me," Joe said brusquely.

Louise looked up at him.

"I mean, not now," he said. "We'll do it, Tash – I promise. But right now? Right now I need a break. And so do you, and so does Louise. Just a breather. I'm going out," He drew himself upright. "I'm going out to get some fresh air and to have a think, and I'm going to the off licence. Because I'll tell you one thing, I did not enjoy one second of that and I need a bloody drink."

And with that, he walked out of the room, pausing for a moment to stare in disbelief at the mess of chocolate sponge, buttercream and shards of broken plate that lay on the floor, leaving Tash smirking in his wake, and Louise staring at the box on the floor, wondering what on earth it could contain.

Chapter 33

London, 1867

"Are you sure I can't get you anything else at all, Mr Temple? It's no trouble at all. I can carry quite well and even pour, once it's not too hot."

Temple could barely bring himself to look at her at first. Not because of her deformity, but because of her smile. There was something about Maud that touched his heart so very deeply that he found it almost unbearable. It was as if the girl glowed with kindness itself.

He held aloft the newspaper which she had just handed him, fresh from the paper boy's satchel. "I am quite content, Maud, thank you very much," he replied, finally bringing himself to make eye contact. There it was. The eager face, the wide eyes, filled with enthusiasm and hope.

"So long as you're sure, sir," she said, giving that awkward bow that was her habit. "I'm keen to help, and ever so grateful to you and Mrs Temple for this opportunity. Imagine, me being in London of all places. Never thought I'd see such a thing. I shall miss the hustle and bustle when I return home, but what stories I shall have ... oh, allow me ..."

At the sight of Temple feeling around his pockets for

his glasses, she turned and picked them up between her arms off the card table behind her and passed them to him. His heart dared to leap. He caught her scent as she bent to drop them into his waiting hands and he breathed it in, the very freshness and purity of it – her hair – the gleam of the light on it, like orange silk. He smiled in gratitude for the glasses and she beamed at him again. He looked away, suddenly ashamed. How could he possibly do what it was that Bridget wanted? How could he send her away? But he must. As cruel as she was, Bridget was his wife and he owed her loyalty. If only she could see Maud as he could see her – her capabilities, her warmth. Perhaps it would unite them – together they could defend the girl, elevate her. She was not so different after all ...

He dared to look again at her, just as she moved one of her arms and, helpless, he watched as she rubbed it against her cheek, completely unselfconsciously. My God, but she was magnificent, he thought. In that moment, the contrast that so fascinated him, between the perfection of her pale, pale, flawless skin and luminous features and the blunt brutality of the stump. It took his breath away.

For a moment, he contemplated doing something mad – asking her to hold out her arms so that he could examine in detail the places where both limbs ended prematurely. He itched to touch them, to run his fingers over the smooth skin, to rub it against his own cheek, to see how it felt. If he could just do that, then perhaps he could let her go? Let her return to her mother in the countryside, away from Bridget's cruelty. And he, too, could move on to something else – another subject of fascination – after all, folk without limbs were commonplace – why did he even want one in his gallery when such things existed as

Siamese twins, and fur-faced women, and people with spines that curved like question marks – surely these would make for more interesting models? Yet still, he ached to capture Maud – so unspeakably beautiful as she was.

As if she sensed his thoughts, she took the tiniest step back and folded her arms around herself, tucking each stump under the opposite armpit for a moment, before allowing them to drop to her sides and then crossing them behind her back.

"I'll be away then, sir," she said quietly, uncomfortably, and bobbed a little curtsey, before turning to leave.

Temple was struck immediately with dismay. "Maud!" he called.

She froze, her back to him, and he realised that he was just making it worse. He sought frantically for words to calm her. "Thank you so much for all your help since you've been here," he managed.

She rewarded him by turning her head to peer nervously at him over her shoulder. He smiled as warmly as he could and she returned it, shyly at first, then more enthusiastically and in a moment, she had turned fully and the wide, grateful grin was back.

"No, sir, thank *you*. It's really such an honour to be here – I can't tell you. You and my aunt have been so good to me, putting me up, allowing me to help you as much as I can. My mother doesn't allow me to do much at home, so it's a privilege to be useful – as much as I am allowed."

She flushed suddenly and looked down at her feet. Temple couldn't tell if it was because she had overshared – yet again – Maud loved to talk – or because she had made direct reference to her physical shortcomings. He thought to tell her that she should think nothing of them, that she was absolutely beautiful – magnificent, even, as flawless as a marble statue – the Aphrodite of Milos, no less. "*Venus* ..." he whispered under his breath.

She didn't look up and seemed not to hear him.

"Are there many things that you would like to do?" he blurted suddenly, regretting it instantly, expecting that it might drive her from the room back to whatever it was she did all day when she wasn't bringing him things. He had even taken to smoking a pipe of late, for heaven's sakes, purely so that he could ask her to deliver it to him by the fire.

He was surprised then, when she tilted her head to one side and thought deeply.

"I imagine, if you'll pardon my pride in saying so, sir," she said, "that I could probably do most things I'd put my mind to if I were allowed. But there is one thing ... you'll think me foolish ..."

She flushed again and cast her eyes downward, a movement so charming and sweet that Temple's heart leaped into his throat at the very sight of her.

"But I'd like to play an instrument. That's silly, isn't it?"

Breathless at her ambition, Temple shook his head. "Not at all," he murmured.

"I love music, don't you? And it would give me such pleasure to be able to make some of my own. I can sing a little – not very well – but when I see someone play music – the fiddle players at the village fair ... and the way that their fingers move with such speed and dexterity, making those glorious sounds ... why, it's magical, isn't it, Mr Temple? I can't understand how they do it – even if I'd

261

been born with fingers I doubt I'd be able to master such a skill but there's not much hope of me finding out, is there, if you'll pardon my saying so!"

With that, she burst into shy giggles, a laughter so innocent and infectious that Temple found himself chuckling along with her, until suddenly the door of the drawing room burst open.

Temple's face fell immediately at the sight of his wife, her expression stern and sneering. Not for the first time, he looked at the woman he'd married and wondered why, and how, he had done it. Her coldness astounded him anew almost daily. He glanced from her, with her neatly pinned hair and her thin-set, angry lips, to Maud who seemed at that moment like a most splendid angel and allowed himself to concede that perhaps he would be a far happier man were he married to a girl with no arms, instead of a woman with no heart.

Chapter 34

2018

Half an hour later, with the studio tidied back to normal while Joe tossed back two large brandies in quick succession, they filed back in, all clutching tumblers. Casting a filthy glance at the office chair, which Tash had retrieved from the hallway as if it were the Holy Grail, Joe sank down onto the couch and sighed.

Gingerly, Louise sat down at her desk, and placed her untouched glass beside her.

Tash, on the other hand, knocked her brandy back in one and leaned on the desk to get close to the screen. "Right then," she said. "Let's ask Professor Google how we pick a lock."

With a deep breath, Louise shook the mouse to wake the computer from sleep mode and opened the search engine. She typed the question in.

They stared at the screen while, from behind, came the sound of the brandy bottle being opened, followed by the thick *glug glug* as Joe poured himself another large measure, and moved something about at his feet.

"There's one," said Tash. "**Insert tension wrench** ... what the hell's a tension wrench?"

Louise ignored her and moved down to the next suggested site.

"*There!*" barked Tash. "**How to pick a lock with a bobby pin.**"

It was Louise's turn to be puzzled. "What's a bobby pin?"

"Oh, that's American for hairclip – the thin brown ones that come in packs of a million with the straight side and the squiggly side."

A sudden crash from behind them made them both jump and turn. What they saw, they hadn't expected. Joe had leaped to his feet and stood staring at the floor, dismay written on his face. On the floor lay the wooden box – open, and with its contents spilled across the floor. Louise and Tash looked down. A sheaf of pictures had spilled out and spread across the rug. Photographs.

"What the ever-living fuck, Joe?" said Tash, clutching her chest as she glared at him.

He didn't respond, just continued to stare at the mess on the rug before him. He was sheet-pale.

"What is it, Joe?" asked Louise cautiously, fresh fear creeping slowly through her body and along her limbs. "What happened?"

"I picked the lock," Joe replied, his voice quivering. "With ... with my penknife ..."

"Some photos, right?" said Louise. "They came with the camera – they must belong to whoever owned it ..."

She bent down to pick them up.

"*Don't do that!*" Joe yelled.

Startled, Louise shot back up again. "Why not?"

"Because I don't think you want to see them," he said, his eyes saucer-wide. "Seriously, don't look."

"But why?" demanded Tash, as she bent down and plucked one from the pile, turning it over. Her reaction shocked Louise.

Brave, excited Tash turned white and gasped.

"Because they're dead," replied Joe. "All of them – in the photos – they're all dead."

Feeling the ground shift under her a little, Louise turned, trying to process what she had just heard. She couldn't look – at either the photos, or at Tash and Joe.

She wasn't entirely sure she could take any more of this, In one sudden movement, she picked up the glass of brandy that she had left there and downed it, closing her eyes to it all as she felt her throat burn.

"Let's get out of this room," she said. "Can someone bring that stuff into the kitchen, please? I don't know whether I can look at it or not."

She stumbled out of the room as Tash began to gather up the photographs.

Chapter 35

London, 1867

Movement from the morning room caught Temple's eye as he passed on his way out the front door, camera in hand. He backtracked and peered in the door, unable to suppress the warm smile that spread across his face at the sight that greeted him. Holding a feather duster tightly and humming to herself as she flicked it about, was Maud, oblivious to his presence. The sunlight through the stained glass of the window poured purples and yellows and greens down over her and it seemed magical, as if she glowed like a colourful angel. He placed the camera box on the floor beside him and leaned against the doorway to watch her for a blissful moment until she turned and caught him staring.

"Oh my goodness, Mr Temple!" she gasped. "You startled me!"

He smiled paternally – at least he thought it might appear paternal. Although in his heart he hoped that it also appeared dashing – just a little. He couldn't hope for much – his hair was all but gone and his increased good fortune over the years had led to his waist straining a little against his belt. Nor was he as tall as he'd have liked, but he had retained most of his teeth and kept himself clean. Now that he thought of it, perhaps *dashing* was too large a request. Kind, then. He hoped he looked kind. That would have to do.

Maud giggled and blushed behind the feather duster.

"What is it that you're doing?" Temple asked.

She responded by holding the duster out to him for his examination. "I am helping!" she replied with a tinkling laugh. "Some dusting about the house. I have done upstairs and now I'm making my way about down here. Would you like me to do your studio for you? I'll be very careful."

"Oh my goodness, you are not here to be a domestic, Maud!" exclaimed Temple. "Tell me that Mrs Temple did not instruct you to do such a thing?"

"Oh no, Mr Temple," replied the girl. "I am simply passing the time. I found the feather duster while exploring and simply decided to help – it's so lovely and fluffy – am I doing something wrong? Will I get Dolly into trouble?" Her smile vanished, much to Temple's disappointment. "Why no, not at all, Maud. Don't worry yourself – please – if it makes you happy then you should do it."

She grinned shyly. "As I told you, I love helping. It pleases me greatly."

"And rightly so, Maud, rightly so," replied Temple. "Whatever makes you happy. You are far more capable of things than many would think, I am sure. I believe that anyway."

Maud looked at the ground and flushed. "Why, thank you, Mr Temple. How very kind of you to say so."

Temple shifted his position and stood straight. "I know that my wife ... Mrs Temple ... can seem a little harsh sometimes ... towards us all, indeed ..."

He paused as Maud reached one arm into the pocket of her dress and fumbled at something. "Pardon me for interrupting, sir," she said, glancing up at him. "But, as you've put me in mind of Mrs Temple, I must give you this ..." She nudged a small object to the top of the pocket, and deftly grasped it by pressing it against the stump of her other arm before holding it out to him.

It was a small bottle, which he accepted and held up for examination.

"I found it when I was dusting Mrs Temple's room – it had fallen beneath her writing desk. I kept it to give it back to her, but I clean forgot before she left this morning to run her errands. You'd better take it, in case I forget again."

"Quite," said Temple, reading the label and frowning. "Do you know what this is?"

Maud shook her head, her eyes wide. "No, sir. I cannot read well enough yet to know what it says. But I promise, I'm working hard on it, like you said I should."

"Goodness," he said, holding the bottle up to the light for a better look, "why did no one mention to me that we had rats in the house?"

"Rats?" asked Maud, puzzled. "There are no rats in this house, Mr Temple. It is too clean. Cook and Dolly make sure of that – they put down traps just in case but catch nothing."

"How curious," said Temple, turning the bottle over in his hand before slipping it into the pocket of his own coat.

"Are you on your way to an appointment, Mr Temple?" Maud asked.

Temple gave a start and reached for his pocket watch. "Gracious me, I certainly am, Maud. A poor bereaved family awaits and here I am, whiling away the time chatting with you."

She looked at the ground yet again, shamefaced. "I'm so terribly sorry, Mr Temple."

He glanced at her, his heart seized with sympathy. "Don't be sorry, Maud," he said softly, stepping into the room and reaching out to boldly lift her chin with his hand. "Not one bit. It is my pleasure to chat with you. I should do it all day if I could."

They stayed like that for a moment. Maud regarding her uncle-benefactor with wide, hopeful eyes. In turn, Temple was overcome with a flood of sensation – the thought of the softness of her skin against his gnarled finger, the sparkle of her cornflower-blue eyes, the sight of her flushed cheeks. For a moment, he was unable to move, captured entirely and totally in the moment and the madness of how it made him feel.

"Mind yourself while I am gone," he said, eventually. *Wait for me*, he meant. *Never leave, never change*. He cleared his throat. "I shall leave you then, Maud," he managed, his own cheeks reddening. "I shall be back later today. Perhaps you could show me then how well you're doing with your reading."

Her face brightened at the thought. "I should like that very much, Mr Temple," she replied. "Do take care."

"Until later, then," he said.

"Until later," she repeated gaily, immediately commencing her lilting song again as she went back about her business with the feather duster.

Temple's heart felt suddenly heavy as he picked up his camera and made his way to the hallstand to retrieve his hat and gloves. He shouldn't get too attached, he chided himself. He would have to ask Maud to leave soon – he had been delaying it, but there was no way Bridget would let her stay. But how could he let her go? How could he not see that smile, that innocence, that purity every day?

He sighed and let himself out the door. He would put it off as long as he could. There was work to be done first, and in that way he would forget about it.

And so he did.

And forgot also about the small bottle of arsenic that he carried in his pocket.

Chapter 36

2018

The first photograph Tash picked from the sheaf of pictures that fell from the box was a priest.

He was a young-looking man, bone thin, dressed in a black cassock and laid on a long, single bed. His head and shoulders were propped on pillows, affording a better presentation of his face to the camera. His cheeks were hollow, and his eyes sunken, his fingers, around which a rosary was wound, were bonelike.

On the left side of the narrow bed stood a table on which a candle burned beside a bible, and a single rose bowed its head mournfully in a bud vase. On the wall above the headboard hung a plain, unadorned crucifix.

"'*Alistair White, October 6th 1862.*'" Tash read the inscription in a curling script on the reverse of the photograph, and then looked at it once more before picking up the second. "'*Primogenitae. Alice Digby, 1860. Naturalis mortem.*'"

The child couldn't have been more than three or four and looked as if she were asleep. Like the young priest, she was propped against the pillows to better show a peaceful expression on her alabaster face.

Louise shuddered and took the photo from Tash to study it closer.

It was, undoubtedly, a beautiful photograph – had the subject not been dead. It was like a fairytale scene – a little princess, lying in a shaft of sunlight, slumbering in a glade of flowers. The girl was, for the most part perfect, save for the fact that she was missing her left eye – the angle it had been taken at made it difficult to spot at first. She lay, surrounded by blooms, clutching a single rosebud.

The strained solemnity of the moment was broken suddenly by a loud, hiccuping burp from Joe, who was sitting as far away from Louise and Tash at the kitchen table as he could, his large hand still loosely clasped around the bottle of brandy, now three-quarters drunk.

Tash made a face. "Sorry about him," she sighed. "He's not really a drinker, believe it or not." Louise glanced at him briefly, but her attention was back on the photographs in an instant.

"Look at this next one," she said. "'*Adeline. 1865. A lover of Mrs Fields's cake.*' Charming." The girl was large – obese – and dressed in a crudely made, shapeless smock. She was laid out on a four-poster bed, and there were no flowers this time, just her pudgy fingers entwined around each other as far as they could go.

Louise stared at it, and was suddenly startled by an unexpected, pungent breath on her ear.

"She sure liked her cake – like yourself, Tash – you look a bit like her actually," Joe observed casually.

Tash was outraged. "*You can eff right off!* Yes, I like my cake – but, seriously – in one go, you're fat-shaming me *and* a girl who's been dead for over a hundred years?"

"Hey, cool it! I just meant you have a look of her – a

272

general impression – the dark hair and stuff," Joe backtracked and then tried to deflect with "God, how are you even looking at those things?"

"Well, check out 'Baby'," retorted Tash.

Louise steeled herself.

There was no infant, however, on display in the image that Tash handed over, her lip curled in distaste as she did so. Instead, Louise found a family scene before her – a picture of a mother and father, seated, with the mother holding what appeared at first be a sleeping girl, dressed in a lace gown. Except ... the head was too large ... and, on closer examination, it became clear that it was not a girl – indeed, it was in no way a child – it was a man. She read the inscription. "'*George Talbot III, 'Baby', November 25th 1864. Homunculum.'*"

She flashed a look at Tash. "Did you see ... he's not a child, he's a dwarf."

"That does it," Joe slurred suddenly and stood, scraping the chair back across the kitchen floor and lurching out the door.

A chill crept over Louise as she continued to study the photograph – the expressionless face of the father, the eyes of the mother fixed on her child, her head tilted toward him, her hand placed on his in which was clasped a baby's rattle. *A child, with a man's face ...* Was that ... could it be what Joe had seen peering around the door at him? She glanced after him in alarm.

"*Eurgh!*" grimaced Tash, putting the photograph back down on the pile with the others as if it felt offensive. "There's way too much wrong with that last one."

"Just the last one?" smirked Louise.

Tash nodded. "I guess," she said. "I wouldn't fancy a

framed photo of my dead granny on the mantelpiece but whatever you're into. Lucky there wasn't Instagram in those days is all I can say. *Stiff-o-gram.*"

"Photo-kick-the-bucket," blurted Louise.

Tash sniggered. "Shut-her-eye. Flickr-out."

"Enough!" Louise covered her mouth to hide the fact she was sniggering hard.

"Sorry," replied Tash, smirking back. "Here – we've got a live one – '*Bridget, in sickness and in health*'."

A stern-faced woman dressed in black stood with her hands folded at her waist, glowering at the camera against a stark, plain background.

Tash shuddered. "She was a stunner all the same – some lucky man's wife obviously. The photographer's? *Ooh*, what about this last one though? '*Maud, 1867. With her goes my heart.*' His daughter?"

The subject of this portrait was a beautiful young girl in her late teens. Like Alice, she was surrounded by artfully arranged flowers – lilies – all around her, but unlike the others, she wasn't laid out in a bed. Instead, she had been posed on a chaise longue somewhere, her head resting on pillows, the body propped to make it look as though she was simply reclining. She was dressed in white, her hair laid in waves across the pillow beside her. Around her head she wore what looked like a laurel wreath.

"Oh God, look at her hands!" Tash said breathlessly, tapping a nail on the centre of the picture and holding the photograph up to give Louise a better look.

Louise gasped. Not at the instrument which had been placed against the girl's body to look as if she were about to play – Louise struggled for the correct name – a lute, she guessed – no – a *lyre* – but because it was held in place by the stumps of her arms which ended below the elbow.

The girl in the photograph had no hands.

Louise stepped back. No hands ... dressed in white ... this was her ... this was *her* – the girl from her dreams. *Maud* it said her name was. She had a name – she had been someone – she wasn't a dream – she was a *ghost* ... Louise bit the sides of her cheeks to keep herself from crying out.

"She's playing that thing hands-free," quipped Tash, oblivious to Louise's reaction. "Sorry, that wasn't called for. Gallows humour and all that." She yawned loudly.

"That's not funny," Louise managed to reply breathlessly. She sat upright in her chair and gathered the rest of the photographs together, placing them face-down again in the box and pushing it to the centre of the kitchen table, away from her. Her mind raced as it began to make associations, as realisation began to dawn on her. She needed to think ...

"Quarter to midnight," observed Tash, glancing up at the kitchen clock over the back door and standing up, oblivious to how unsettled Louise suddenly was. "I'd probably better start thinking about pouring his nibs into a taxi and getting him home. Although Mam will go bananas if she sees him in that state. She'll be thinking she needs to get his stomach pumped or something. Makes a change from how he normally is, I guess."

"What do you mean?" asked Louise, a little dazed.

"Well, he's so grown-up, isn't he? Responsible? Always looking after other people."

Louise looked guilty. "I think I'm one of those other people – he's been looking after me since the day he got here."

275

Tash grinned again. "Oh, he likes looking after *you*," she said wryly. "That's not a problem for him at all. It's just that he should probably look after himself a bit more too. He's healthy as a horse, mind. He needs to be just *Joe* for a while. Do what he wants to do instead of running round trying to please everyone else all the time. Give his comedy a shot, travel, get a girlfriend. His whole life he's been the responsible one – can't let anyone down. He's always got to be stepping up the plate, the bigger man. I'm telling you – your ghosts have done him the world of good. Haven't seen him relax this much in years, even if it is sponsored by Hennessy." She began to walk toward the door of the kitchen. "In the meantime, however, I'd best get him out of your hair and get home. It's been a long night. Leave you get some sleep or whatever."

Louise's stomach gave a sudden lurch as she followed reluctantly, bumping into Tash who had stopped suddenly as a loud growling noise suddenly came from the front room.

Tash puffed out her cheeks. "Well, that's a slight problem. He's in a brandy coma and snoring his head off."

She and Louise crept along the hall and peered into the living room. Joe lay sprawled on his back on the sofa, his mouth wide open, the brandy bottle on the floor beside him with the tiniest amber dreg left in the bottom.

"Why don't you leave him here?" offered Louise quietly.

Tash raised her eyebrows.

"And you too ... you could stay ... look, it's really late – and the spare room's made up and ..."

"And you're scared, right?"

"Well, yes – we all are, aren't we? And it's always

when I'm alone that things ... that they kick off again ..."

"You think they might kick off again?" Tash's voice was hopeful.

Louise ignored her. "And you're not going to get him into a taxi in that state, are you?"

Tash shook her head resignedly. "Plus we'd have to come all the way back over for the van tomorrow – whenever he's fit to drive it, which might be Sunday by the state of him."

"If you stay, we can talk in the morning – when it's daylight, and when we have clearer heads. And then maybe you can help me figure out what to do – if I need to call in one of your guys from college or something."

"Like a full investigation?" Tash's expression was like a child's on Christmas Eve.

Louise managed a chuckle. "We'll see."

Tash nodded. "Right then. I don't have my bedtime bear with me but ..." she paused as another yawn overtook her, "I think that brandy and all the excitement has knocked me out. Wonder if he'd get vodka next time – I can go for hours on voddie and Coke. Goodnight then, sleep tight, don't let the ghosties bite?"

"Thanks," said Louise sarcastically, and grinned at Tash she mounted the stairs. "See you in the morning." She stood at the foot of the stairs and watched her go out of sight around the turn in the stair.

Louise was left alone.

Maud.

She hadn't been dreaming after all – she had really seen her – and – my God, of course – the smell of lilies, that calming smell – it all made sense now – it was *her.* Had it been her then that had slammed the door on Ros?

Had thrown the wok on the floor when Ros got argumentative in the kitchen? Was she somehow ... *defending* her?

So who was it who played tricks? There was more than just Maud there, the Ouija board had told them. Who was it who had slammed the bathroom door, moved the chair ... was that ... was it the one called Baby? A child's body and a man's face – was that what had disturbed Joe so much that he'd blotted it out with the brandy? Had he recognised him? Or could it have been the little girl – was she the playful one? And the tall shape – which of them was that? The priest – he was the only one it could be, if she were to follow logic. But how much of this was logical? Was this actually happening? Was her house really haunted by the spirits from the photographs? And if so, how many of them were actually there? Was she suddenly living in a horror story?

Exhausted, she leaned against the doorframe and stared at Joe, so completely and utterly asleep, unaware of it all, his mind completely blank. She longed to sleep like that. Without dreams or disturbance, with no worries about anything. Just once – just one single night of fearless sleep – was that too much to ask?

With a sigh, she turned to follow Tash and make her way to bed. Maybe it would feel better in the morning, after she'd had some sleep.

If, after what she had seen that night, she could ever sleep again, that is.

Chapter 37

London, 1867

Temple scurried homeward, head bent against the rain that drove against him, eager to get home out of this filthy weather, yet dreading what would await there. The child, screaming – it never seemed to cease, despite the best efforts of almost the entire household. And then its mother, her harsh face always glaring at him, upbraiding him for what he had not yet done – what he had not the heart to do. The command that she insisted he give – she did not want to be seen as the one to displease her sister-in-law – hung over him like an executioner's blade. There was no respite from it – it waited for him in every room, shared every meal, stood between him and the person of whom he must be rid in their every exchange – those sweet conversations where she would share with him her day, or where he would, with authority, teach her something – anything – that she did not know, from photography to botany.

If only she could stay. He longed for it – some miraculous change of heart on the part of his wife. If only she would come to her senses and see what they could do for the girl. Already her reading was coming along by leaps and bounds, and she could fetch and carry most things with ease, once she was allowed to try.

And she was so sweet – so sweet and perfect – and how he loved to watch her, to see how she performed those everyday tasks that others took for granted without the use of digits. It was quite uplifting to see something – someone – so vulnerable, so different, try their very best to make their way. He could simply watch her for hours, in fact, and would if ever he were allowed.

She was wonderful with the boy too – the only one, in fact, who could, as if by magic, make the wailing stop in the simplest ways – a burst of song, a funny face – a game of peepo, but only when Bridget was absent from the room. The very sight of Maud wrapping her arms about her face to hide herself from the child before revealing herself to his utter delight seemed to trigger an unnatural reaction in his wife. It was quite noticeable, and it made Maud ashamed and nervous.

Temple hunched over further against a biting autumn gust. It was bitter and sharp, just like Bridget. What had made her nature so, he wondered, and not for the first time.

Bent low as he was, he failed entirely to notice the couple who came toward him, arms linked, their own heads bowed, and his thoughts were disturbed by the sudden and unexpected collision with them. There followed much surprise, and apology and begging of pardons. And then, recognition.

"I think we know you, sir," said the man, tall and thin.

His wife looked at him in surprise first, and then at Temple, peering at his face. "Goodness!" she exclaimed. "Mr Temple, is it you?"

Temple looked back blankly. "I'm afraid –" he began, only to be interrupted enthusiastically by the man.

"It is!" he exclaimed. "Oh, Mr Temple, how have you been? I think we've quite knocked you for six, have we? My name is Jonathan White, and this is my wife, Ada. You visited us in our home some time ago. You photographed our son, Alistair, after ... after he had passed away."

Temple nodded and grabbed his hat as it threatened to fly off with a gust. "I do apologise, Mr White, Mrs White. I am discombobulated by this infernal weather. Of course I can place you now. I remember, indeed, you were kind enough to host me in your home in Gloucestershire, am I correct? I remember your son very well indeed as a subject – very tall, wasn't he? I do hope that the portrait which I took was to your liking. It certainly was to mine, as I recall ... as an appropriate memorial image, of course."

His momentary excitement at the memory went unnoticed by his parents, who seemed pleased simply by Temple's recollection of the event.

"It has given us much comfort since then, Mr Temple," Ada White assured him. "Sometimes, when I cannot recall my son's features, all I have to do is gaze at the mantel, and there he is again. And such a beautiful likeness it is. I often think how terribly clever it was of our housekeeper at the time to summon you so quickly. She certainly knew that she was sending us the best in the business and for that we were ever so grateful, weren't we, Jonathan?"

Her husband nodded and righted himself against a particularly strong blast of wind that struck him off balance.

"I call her housekeeper," continued Mrs White, "but she was ever so much more than that, wasn't she? Nurse, carer, soother of pain – all those little tinctures that she used, a drop of his here, a drop of that there – a little bottle in her pocket. Alistair's passing was so dreadful yet, even still, I am sure that Mrs Watson eased it for him with her skills."

"Mrs Watson – yes," said Temple. He had been racking his brain to remember what surname his wife had used when working for the Whites. Why had she felt compelled to change it again? He couldn't remember her reasons – and, whatever they were, it suddenly struck him anew as very odd that she would change her name between employments.

"Anyhow, Mr Temple," said Mr White, "we shan't keep you. Best we all get indoors out of this nasty weather. We're staying with my sister in Bloomsbury for a week."

"We like to keep ourselves busy," added Mrs White. "The countryside can be so quiet at this time of year. For what it's worth, we bring his portrait everywhere with us, and show who we can your magnificent work. We've never forgotten you, Mr Temple."

A strange, distant look had come over Temple's face while the woman spoke, as something began to dawn upon him, something unusual, and not entirely pleasant.

"Farewell then, Mr Temple."

"Oh – pardon me, Mrs White. I was remembering … I'm so pleased that I could offer some relief to you in your hour of need. I wish you both the very best."

He tipped his hat, as did Mr White, and Mrs White nodded in return.

Then, the Whites beaming and excitedly chatting to one another about such a coincidental meeting, they parted ways, leaving Temple alone where he stood, unmoving.

It was something that Mrs White had said ... '*a little bottle in her pocket*'. His hand suddenly flew to his own. It was still there – a little bottle in *his* pocket. *Arsenic*. The bottle retrieved from his wife's room. Thoughts – recollections – suddenly began to nudge at him. A conversation – the night he had asked Bridget to be his wife – "*Indeed*," she had said, "*I should begin to think that I had something to do with it ...*" 'It' being the death of Adeline Brown – the girl who couldn't stop herself from eating. "*It must have been something she ate or drank*," Bridget had observed. Temple's mind flew back to another scene from their association – the miniature rooms of the dwarf, George Osborne, with his secret bottles of hard liquor. It had been her job to keep them full ... he, too ... it had been something he had consumed ... isn't that what she had told him? He, too, had died all of a sudden – like the others – the others who he, Temple, had photographed. To whom *she* had led him – all of them different – broken, she called them.

And again, his mind strayed back to the night they were engaged, when first he saw a true glimpse of the woman she would become. Or was it the woman she had been all along and he, the fool in love, had admired her figure so that he had entirely failed to notice?

"*When something is broken, it is broken*," she had told him firmly. "*And unfit for purpose, and should be disposed of ...*"

He thought of her visceral reaction every time she saw what was left of Maud's arms. Maud, also broken – and Bridget despised her and despised her deformity. He raised his head but saw nothing on the street before him. The broken things – the broken people – there was no place for them in Bridget's world. And so ... had she ... was it possible? Truly possible?

He felt again for the bottle in his pocket. Surely not?

A sick dread forming in his stomach, he turned for home.

Chapter 38

2018

Tash yanked back the curtains with as much power as she could summon. The curtain rings rattled and scraped their way along the metal pole but hadn't the desired effect. She glanced over her shoulder at the sleeping figure on the couch, but there was no sign of movement. Joe wasn't waking up any time soon.

So far she had tried stomping into the room loudly, shaking his shoulder, calling his name directly into his ear and banging the empty brandy bottle off the floor – but nothing had worked. "You've really done a number on yourself," she sighed as she looked at him with disapproval and rolled her eyes. It's not that he didn't deserve a night off – could the previous evening have fitted that description – but how the bloody hell was she going to get him home?

She wandered into the kitchen and put the kettle on, glancing at the clock as she did. Almost eleven o'clock on Saturday morning. Early for her. She could have stayed in bed longer, but she'd been awake quite a while – thinking over the extraordinary events of the night before.

She made herself a cup of tea and drank it, gazing

through the window at Louise's overgrown garden, frosted white. So much had happened – such extraordinary things. It all hardly seemed real. The sound of the chair rolling on its castors at such speed along the hallway played once more in her mind. In the brightness of a cold January morning, drinking warm tea, it seemed impossible that such a thing could have ever happened, yet it had.

Finally, after all those years of reading, and taking ghost tours and immersing herself in everything about the paranormal that she could lay her hands on, she had *proof* that something else existed beyond death, evidence that there was more than just existing in *this* life – more than being a college student who still lived in a sensible, ordinary home with her sensible, ordinary parents. She had always hoped – known – there was more than this, and now she was sure.

She rinsed her mug at the sink and turned to survey the kitchen, marvelling at how ordinary it looked in the daylight. And there, on the table right in front of her, was the cause of it all. It was just too good. Imagine that little, innocuous-looking box being the cause of an actual haunting – audio, visual manifestations, poltergeist activity – how *delicious* it was going to be to discuss with – *nah*, to show off to the gang.

She sat down at the table, sliding the box closer to her. She rubbed her finger over the roughness of where Joe had drunkenly attacked the lock, before opening it reverently, with both hands, and surveying the contents in wonder. They were originals – she had no doubt of that. Imagine – images preserved for what – one hundred and fifty years or so? Unthinkable. As for the subject matter of most of them – she had come across this before in her studies – Victorian post-mortem photography. Commemorative portraits – sometimes the first, last and only pictures – of a person. The mortality rate amongst Victorians was extremely high, so they weren't a bit squeamish about it and it wasn't uncommon for an individual to be immortalised in death. How creepy by today's standards, she thought, to have such pictures floating about on display. She shuddered. So ghoulish today, but things had been different then.

She braced herself and withdrew them from the box to study them. They were so artfully done – bodies posed to perfection, the costumes, the flowers, the lighting. They must have required hours of composition – who had done that, she wondered. The family? Or the photographer? How comfortable they must have been in the presence of the dead – to dress them up and manipulate their lifeless corpses until they found the perfect angle. What an extraordinary way to earn a living – and how much of a living? Were they rich or poor? How were they regarded by society? The more Tash thought about it, the more questions she had.

Of course, the biggest question of all couldn't be answered by any amount of searching online or visiting the library. She wondered if there were anyone alive who could answer it, and strongly doubted that there was – but there had to be a reason, had to be some explanation, some history behind *why* some of the people in these photographs, these poor, immortal souls, couldn't pass over to the other side peacefully. Why where they still here, attached so strongly to the photographs of their own dead bodies? Maybe that was the reason in itself – maybe they felt violated, disrespected in death – she could certainly understand that being the case for Adeline (and yes, Joe was right, there was a resemblance there to herself, but she'd never admit to him that she'd spotted it) laid out in her shift, or for Baby – still called 'Baby', even though he was a grown man – posed with his grieving parents, infantilised – by parents or photographer? And what of Maud? Who was she? Was she born that way, or had she suffered an accident? And why was she posed with a musical instrument that she could never hope to play? Was it something she had done before she'd lost her hands, or something that she'd always wanted to do – or was it a mockery of some form? Doubtful, she mused. The Victorians were very respectful of their dead, even though they had a love of the macabre.

An idea came to her and she paused to think it through. It wouldn't answer any of her questions immediately, she imagined, but it could set her on the right road, lead her to someone who might be able to take her back through history. And Louise had said it herself, hadn't she? That she wanted help from anyone or anywhere? And if she now did what she was thinking, then the photos would be out of the house. Problem solved for Louise.

She'd have to explain away the broken box, of course. The man from – where did Louise get that camera again? Church ... Chapel ... *Temple* Antiques – that was it. He might look for money for it. She'd just pay with her student credit card, she supposed, and get Joe to reimburse her – he'd broken it after all. But maybe that man might be able to tell her where he'd got the camera from – she cursed herself for not looking at it more closely when Louise had had it, in case there was anything to identify the owner in the contents of the box. Maybe he'd let her take a look at the camera in the shop though, and he'd be pleased, she was sure, to get the photographs back, so maybe he'd entertain a few questions and she could start to piece together her puzzle? It was certainly worth a shot – and she wasn't doing anything else today. She'd have to give the photos back, of course.

Cocking an ear to listen for any movement from either Joe or Louise, Tash pulled her phone from her pocket and snapped each of the photos. There. She'd just keep her own copies for evidence. That done, she carefully replaced the prints into their case and picked it up. And with a final glance at her still-sleeping brother on the sofa as she passed, she slid into her coat in the hall and let herself out, very gently, into the bright morning and headed, determined, for town.

Chapter 39

London, 1867

Samuel Temple paused on his own doorstep.

His back ached from bending and lifting and carrying, and his brain ached from the effort of consoling and cajoling a mother who insisted on posing with her son on her lap. A child, taken in his sleep, while holding his favourite toy boat. Temple had sympathetically used the selfsame boat as a prop for the portrait. Then, he had tripped back and forth at least ten times, it seemed, to secure the boat as if the child held it, only for the mother to sob or heave and disturb it again and require words of reassurance.

His heart ached too. Absentmindedly, he toyed again with the empty arsenic bottle in his pocket, as had become his habit, again making the dreadful connection in his mind that he simply could not ignore. It was three days now since his chance meeting with the Whites, three days when he had kept his counsel, avoiding his wife as best he could – even avoiding Maud, as if the darkness of the theory should somehow sully the time to be spent with her in any way. What if it were true? What if the deadly purpose of the bottle in his pocket had been to ... he could not even bring himself to use the words ...

cruelly *expedite* the passing of all those people? Those mysterious, different souls who he intended to memorialise for his gallery? What fearsome plot was he caught in, if that truly had been the cause of their deaths? Is that what he had paid her for at the time? Not a finder's fee, as she called it, but a ... a *bounty* on their heads? It was simply unthinkable. Steeling himself with a deep breath, he entered his home.

As he did, it seemed that the boy with the boat was not to be the only troublesome child to shatter his fragile peace today. The screeches of his own son assaulted his ears from upstairs. Bath-time then, Temple concluded, and slipped, as quietly as he could, into the relative silence of the drawing room, to pour himself a restorative drink. He assumed that Bridget would busy herself with Samuel Junior for as long as it took to sufficiently restrain him and remove the layers of filth that accumulated on him over the course of any given day. Why she insisted on doing it herself, he couldn't understand. He didn't pay a housemaid for his wife to act like a domestic, but she insisted on being present for this shrieking, splashing calamity every evening at this time.

He closed the door firmly behind him, blocking most of the noise save the most high-pitched of objections. Was there to be no peace in this house anymore, he wondered, sinking into his armchair beside the fire, his shoulders heavy under the weight of his worry and regret.

What had he done? His mind strayed to the same question he posed to himself at least once a day. *Marry in haste, repent at leisure.* No truer word indeed.

Making Bridget his wife had been, at best, a misfortune, at worst an utter failure – and possibly worse, if his fears were to be found true.

291

The siren who had been the Widow Watson had wrecked him on rocks of banality – life as a husband, a father and a working man. His head had been turned by her at first, her firm jaw and neat waist, her wiles, the admiration of her employers, her contacts, her very capability. But underneath, had she truly a desire to ... *dispose* of the broken, useless things, as she called them, that she encountered – that he then unwittingly reclaimed for his own use?

Was it really possible that the woman he had married was a murderer? He shuddered. He did not want to know.

He lost himself as he gazed into the flames, slipping into a rueful reverie, until the sudden opening of the door roused him, and he looked up to see none other than the very woman enter, her now-ample figure straining against the purple silk of her dress, her hair escaping from its fastenings and floating, frondlike, about her ruddy face.

"My dear," he said, by way of greeting.

She responded with a frown. "And how long have you been home, Samuel Temple?" she barked. "And your son asking for his father?"

Temple looked up at her, catching for a moment in her haughty stance a shadow of the woman with whom he had once been so infatuated. "Bed and baths," he sighed. "Hearth and home. Mother and child. What has happened to us, Mrs Watson? Where did we go?"

Bridget harrumphed. "Mrs Watson? Is my first husband, who left me so cruelly childless, resurrected from the dead then? The last I knew I was Mrs Temple, your wife, sir."

Temple looked down at his feet. "Oh Bridget," he groaned, "have you nothing to speak of but the bitter past, the drudgery of the here and now? Have you no mind to the future? No dreams to speak of?"

292

She fixed him in her stare. "I have made no secret of my dreams, Samuel. This here and now of which you speak – that – *that* is my dream – part of it anyhow. Those things that you speak of with such a derogatory tone – wife, mother, mistress of her own household – those are the fulfillment of some of my life's ambitions. The rest? Well, you put paid to that with your refusal to so much as consider the purchase of Redtrees Hall."

Temple ran his hand across his face. "That again. But what dreams of the future? What legacy do you wish to leave behind? What do you wish the world to say of Bridget Temple in the future?"

"Are you drunk, Samuel? What utter poppycock you talk this evening."

"Answer me," he demanded. "You are my wife, now act like one – you vowed to obey – now answer me."

Eyebrows raised, she lowered herself onto the chair opposite and sat on the edge. "Very well, *husband*," she replied bitterly. "The world will say of Bridget Temple that she had no time for what might never be."

Samuel sat back and eyed her suspiciously. "And what is that supposed to mean?"

She glared directly back. "Exactly what it is," she said coldly. "Sometimes, Mr Temple, I wonder at how *soft* you are, and I conclude that these dreams of which you are obsessed are the product of your softness."

"I am not *soft* – how dare you!" he said, indignantly.

"Oh, but you are – would you like me to explain how? Your upbringing for starters – a mother and father who considered you, food every day, clean water and a place to piss that didn't involve squatting in the street."

"Mrs Temple!"

"No – you asked, I shall answer. You shared your bed with neither siblings nor your mother's tricks, and armies of fleas and lice besides. Your beatings were administered at the hand of a smartly dressed schoolteacher and only when deserved. You saw the seaside, and the countryside, and had your trade and this house handed to you by your father. You wore clothes that at their very worst had a stitch in the seam, and you owned shoes and your future was never a worry, never a struggle. All of this made you *soft*. Imagine being *you*, Samuel Temple, so fulfilled by life that you could think beyond what you had or required, to imagine things like art and beauty and greatness. Your dreams, sir, are born of softness and even if they are to remain forever unfulfilled, you will still be safe and warm and fed in your bed. And that is where we differ. Because everything you had that made you soft, I had the opposite, and it made me hard, as you well know. And it made my dreams different than yours – instead of portraiture, I dreamt of survival, in place of a longing for posterity I longed for enough to eat, and the bruises to heal, and the disease to stay away from our door and to live long enough to see the sun rise the following morning. That is what I mean when I say that this – this house, this status, this security ... these are *my* dreams."

Samuel blinked. "So ... this? This dull house, that screaming brat? That is where your satisfaction lies? What happened to you, woman? It was not *that* I married – *that* woman you speak of I could have found ten times over anywhere in the city – but instead I found *you* – wise, and intelligent – my Athena. Surely this is not all that you can want? Surely you could not leave yourself so low?"

Bridget's eyes narrowed. "I am growing tired of this conversation, Samuel. I know low. I came from *low*. I have seen sights you could never imagine, and I got away from all that by fair means and foul." She leaned closer to him. "And at this time in my life, I am tired of dreaming and waiting and quite like the having – and, indeed, the wanting more, if you please. So if that should displease you, I could show you low, if you really wanted."

A silence fell between them that felt like a sheet of delicate crystal, ready to shatter at the slightest touch.

Bridget glared at Samuel, whose heart thudded and whose stomach turned over.

"Like you showed Alistair White?"

There. He had not wanted to do that, but he could not stop himself.

He was aware, despite the spinning sensation in his head, that this – more than any other – this was the moment he had changed his life forever. He slid his hands into his pockets to conceal their trembling where, of course, one of them met the cursed glass vessel.

His mind raced ahead of himself. She would deny it, of course. She wouldn't so much as understand what he meant. She would frown, and make some remark that would degrade him, but still it would be better than the truth. Because it simply couldn't be true.

Instead ... good God, no ... her face went pale for a moment, then there followed the most fearsome expression on it. The blood rushed back to her head as quickly as it had drained out – a tide of momentary astonishment turned, rushing back to shore as sheer fury.

"I was thinking more like I showed my first husband," she replied, her tone quiet and chilling. "Mr

Watson. The one who left me penniless and childless and once raised the poker to me. The one who liked a tipple or ten in the evenings and a wager on a game of cards. He always said it would be his downfall – and I was happy to oblige."

He swallowed silently as she allowed him time to grasp her meaning.

"The arsenic ..." The word emerged in a ragged whisper.

Bridget raised her eyebrow and nodded. "You have heard me say often enough that I have no time for the broken and the downright wrong. Perhaps now you have an inkling that I mean it."

"But *why?*" His voice trembled with distress. He felt as though he had stepped out of his own body, and into a nightmare not of his own creation. Not only were his worst fears now realised, but this woman ... she was admitting to it ... and she was *shameless.*

"All of them ... the dwarf ... the fat girl ... my God, the *child* ..."

"Not the eyeless child." She shook her head forcefully. "I will not be accused of that which I have not done. Death came for her himself. I happened to be there at the time. But the rest – it seemed that I was to be always in charge of the afflicted – one position led to the next, experience led to recommendation – I could not turn them down but, my God, I could not take it sometimes. The reminders ... the places my mind would go ..."

"To worse places than the dying?" He rose and stepped away from her.

"They were not all dying," she chided him, as if he had made something as simple as a grammatical mistake.

"Why, Bridget? I cannot believe I am hearing this!"

She sneered at him. "You cannot believe it, eh? Well, I am tired of keeping it from you. You, you, you, Samuel. It is always a matter of what *you* think, or what *you* want or don't want, or what *you* believe. Did you ever think of me? *Do* you ever? Or is your head always full of that artistic nonsense you rant about? There are more people in this world than you, Samuel Temple, in your soft little world where care has never so much as knocked at your door!"

He was angry now. "And what of it, woman? What of it?"

An expression of disbelief formed on her features, as she fixed him with a stare.

"What of it, indeed. Do you know my name, Mr Temple?"

"*What?*" he blustered.

"My name. What is it?"

"Why, it is Temple! Bridget Temple! My wife."

"And before that?"

He shook his head in exasperation. "Damned if I know! Fields you called yourself one minute, Watson the next – and now that I know your true nature, I finally understand why you flitted from one alias to another. Were there more? More names? More poor souls whose lives you took?"

She smirked. "Whose pictures you never got to take for your special collection? Before that again ... what was my name before my first marriage? My maiden name?"

"*How the devil would I know?*" roared Samuel.

Bridget remained absolutely calm. "It was O'Dowd. Bridget O'Dowd. What do you make of that?"

Bemused, he stared at her. "That name is Irish, is it not? But you're not Irish – and surely this is by-the-by – what has this to do with anything?"

"You wouldn't think it for a moment, but yes, it is an Irish name, and I am – I *was* Irish – cursed by God to be born onto that wretched island which he forsook. You'd never tell by my accent now, nor any of the names that I chose since, nor by my spiritual habits, but yes – Bridget O'Dowd, born in the county of Mayo."

Again, his tone turned disdainful. "And what of *that*?"

She took a deep breath, as if to cleanse herself. There was something about it made him tense, to give her his full attention.

"Have you ever been truly hungry, Samuel? Not just peckish for a sandwich, say, or a piece of bread and dripping. But *truly* hungry – so hungry that words like '*ravenous*' and '*famished*' do not begin to do it justice? Have you ever, literally, starved? No? I thought not." She paused, glaring at him. "Well, I have. And I have seen everyone around me starve too – some of them to death. There was a famine in Ireland, Samuel. When I was a child. You did not know that, did you? Or if you did, you have paid it no heed your entire life – am I correct? *An Gorta Mór*, we called it in our language – because I spoke a different language once, Samuel – does that surprise you too? The Great Hunger. Years and years, the people of that godforsaken country had nothing to eat. Our potatoes failed – but what sort of country relies on potatoes, I hear you ask? Well, we had other crops too – corn and so on. But you English made sure that you had that for yourselves, did you not? And your landlords threw us from our homes when we could not pay their rent, and then burned them down so we could not return to them and so we lived where we could – frozen and barefoot and filthy and poor and all the time starving, *starving* with the hunger, and no help in sight. And we died, Samuel – some of us died. Our loved ones – and we left them where they fell because we had no means to bury them. Bodies littered the countryside – you have no idea. The stench! The disease! You might check a bush in a ditch for berries, only to be greeted by the wide, lifeless eyes of the last person to go under it for shelter. The animals starved too – but sometimes they did better than us because when we would drop dead to the ground, they could find food ... can you imagine it, Samuel? No? I'll wager you could never for as long as you live conceive of what I have seen and smelled and breathed. *You* have never lain out on the freezing ground without blanket or pillow and stared at the stars and wish to the high heavens that you might never wake again so that the feeling of hunger is taken from you. I see your face, Samuel, and you look at me as if I still speak in a language that you cannot understand – and you never will, you great soft Englishman. You never will."

"But ... but ... why ...? All those people – if it is true that you have poisoned them all? What has any of this to do with what happened in Ireland twenty or more years ago?"

Bridget squeezed her eyes shut, exasperated, a desperation coming over her that Temple had never seen, that made him wary.

"It is not those *people*, Samuel," she whispered. "It is the *memories*. The pictures that I cannot banish from my mind – a feral dog making off into the dusk with a man's arm – my *father's* arm ... a child looking at the heavens with empty sockets because the birds took its eyes – I cannot bear the memories, seeing it all over again." She rose to her feet, suddenly furious. "And as much as that, I cannot bear the sight of the gluttonous – all of you who filled your bellies, especially those who cannot stop – the greedy fat – disgusting! The priests who denied us food if we did not atone for their imaginary sins, if we did not beg for their mercy – the debauched drinkers and gamblers – the profligate who took what little my family had – our last hope – and made off with it. All of them! Broken! Unfit for purpose! *Now do you understand?*"

Samuel stared at her, dumbfounded. A stranger stood before him, her eyes grown wild, spittle caught on the corner of her mouth. Her chest heaved and her fists were clenched, the knuckles whitening as she flexed them.

"You ... you are quite *mad*," he whispered. "You make no sense ... you must be ill ... ill in the head – you simply must be!"

He was taken aback at her response – a snort of disbelief.

"I am ill?" she repeated. "Ill in the head? Me? Yet there is reason and logic to my actions – what reason is there for yours?"

"What ... whatever do you mean? This is more of it now – more of your deranged nonsense."

"Your photographs, Samuel, eh? What kind of sick mind does it take to form an obsession such as yours? To seek out the maimed and the disfigured – I've seen the way you look at them – slavering over the corpses of the unthinkable. Do they excite you, perhaps? Do you draw a pleasure from them that you cannot draw from anything normal? Anything alive?"

"That is quite enough, Bridget!"

"Is there some thrill in the arrangement of them? Touching them, posing them?"

"I said that's enough!"

"Playing with them as if they were toys?"

"*Stop it!*"

"And more thrill still in the profit to be made from them? Or is the biggest thrill of all this dream you have of *collecting* them in one place. Your gallery, as you call it? Who on earth will come to view pictures of dead misfits and grotesqueries of all kinds? These plans you speak of all the time – what kind of mind formulates such notions? And I am the sick one?"

"*Stop this at once!*"

Samuel's voice was forceful, more forceful than his wife had ever heard, and she drew back, as if slapped. The stunned silence that followed his order, however, was suddenly sharply broken by a sound – a piercing scream, from up the stairs. A child's scream. Bridget's head whipped around in the direction of it.

"My son," she gasped. "He is hurt." She shifted, as if to run to him, but froze and turned again, back to her husband. "I warn you," she said, agitated by the continued screaming from the child. "I will go to the boy now, and you will be here when I return, is that understood? There is more to be said, before all is well again, do you understand?"

He said nothing in return. Instead, he watched her go – utterly bewildered by the revelations, the accusations – the very fact of the conversation in which he had just participated.

And had she not cautioned him so coldly, so firmly, to stay put, then he might have. But her very warning to

301

him was what made him suddenly realise that he could do the very opposite. Without thought or hesitation, and with his feet moving beneath him as if they belonged to another man, he took a step ... and another ... and another until he fled from the room, grabbed his coat and hat from the stand, and, with a final glance up the stairs, he let himself out of the house and into the street. And once there, he continued to move, half walking, half running, on hasty, clumsy feet, a great well of emotions bubbling suddenly inside him the further he got from that dread house. Relief – horror – grief for what had become of him – worry – not for the child, Bridget adored the wretched boy – but – oh dear God, there was another ...

He slowed, dazed, as a thought above all thoughts struck him.

Maud.

He had not yet done as Bridget ordered and sent her back to the countryside – damn himself for a fool! If he had just done what his heart would not let him do, then she would not be in danger – but she was there – alone, with Bridget, who despised her. His poor, defenceless Maud – at the mercies of a madwoman. He turned in a circle, unsure what to do. A passerby appeared as if from nowhere and bumped against him ... something was shouted at him ... but he could not hear, could barely see. He should carry on, his head told him. Find a constable – explain everything – have her taken away – to Bedlam, for she was clearly unwell.

But his heart – again, his cursed heart – his heart told him to turn, and turn now – to go to Maud, to save her, and then keep her safe. His mind filled with a picture of her, framed in light like an angel, her hair aflame. His knees all but buckled at the sight of it, and the thought that she might be in peril.

Without a moment's further hesitation, he turned. And as fast as he had conveyed himself away, he conveyed himself back, faster even, for he ran, breathless but without care other than to be with her, to get to her on time ...

A fruitless journey, if ever there was one.

Chapter 40

2018

It was close to noon when Joe shuffled into the kitchen, his face ashen-grey and covered in rough stubble. His clothes were crumpled, his gait unsteady.

Louise turned as she heard him.

"Top o' the mornin' to ya," she said wryly.

He avoided her gaze. "What time is it?" he asked, his voice thick. He cleared his throat.

"Just midday," replied Louise. "I wasn't sure what time to expect you up."

He collapsed onto the chair opposite her at the table as she poured a mug of tea from a pot kept warm under a knitted tea cosy which was half unravelled.

"It's fresh," she assured him. "No judgement, by the way – I'm up only about twenty minutes myself."

He accepted the mug gratefully and wrapped his hands around it. "You certainly look fresher than I feel."

"I won't dispute that. You seem to have slept solidly enough, mind, although I dread to think what state your head's in."

He nodded, then winced. "I would say that I don't know what came over me, but I know *exactly* what came over me – but why I chose to deal with it with *brandy* of all things ..."

"Hey – don't worry," Louise interrupted. "Gin – remember? And at least you haven't puked in a basin, nor do I need to take you to Urgent Care. I don't, do I?"

Joe managed a laugh. "Fair point. Sorry, all the same. I can handle a few pints, in my defence – but brandy! I just passed out on your couch – how embarrassing." He flushed red and sipped gingerly at the hot tea.

"I think you had a fairly understandable response to a bloody weird night."

"I don't remember all that much of it, to be honest," he admitted. "At least not after I opened that box ... those pictures ..." He set the mug down and rubbed his eyes, as if to erase the memory. "They're fuzzy, but I remember enough ... what else happened?"

Louise avoided his gaze and sipped her tea, thinking, as she stared out the window. So much – the picture of Maud's face flashed again in her mind. *Maud.* Such an easy name to think, to say. As if she were real, as if she and Louise knew each other. But, of course, she *was* real ...

Joe coughed, and Louise returned to herself with a start. What was she thinking?

"You didn't miss too much," she said. "Me and Tash had a look through the pictures, Tash decided to stay in the spare room and I ... I just went to bed."

"And ... and everything's ... okay, is it? I mean, you're not in danger from any of those ... *things* that we saw."

Louise bristled at the use of the word 'things'. She shook her head. "It's weirdly fine," she replied. "I just have to decide what to do next. Tash will be able to give me a dig out with that, hopefully."

"Sorry she's a bit forward about things," said Joe. "She's been steamrolling you into tons of weird stuff – she's been virtually obsessed with ghosts since she was a little kid – I'm not sure she gets that they're actually real. Well, you know what I mean."

"She's been an enormous help, actually," Louise assured him. "If it hadn't been for her, I'd still be here terrified of shadows and thinking I was going mad. I'd probably have done something stupid at this stage."

"Like asking Ros to move back in."

Louise snorted, and Joe managed a smile as he took a deep slug from his tea.

"I think I'd rather live with ghosts forever than have that happen," she said.

"*Shhh*," urged Joe. "Don't let them hear you."

Louise giggled and glanced around. "It's funny, but I think I know what ... *who* they are now. And everything that's happened – knowing you've seen things too, doing that séance last night, although I thought I'd die of fright – even finding those photos, although they're pretty grim, but they've helped me face up to it all, made me feel less afraid somehow."

"Lucky for you," Joe retorted. "Guess I'd better pull my socks up on that front."

Louise studied his wretched face. "You don't always have to be the responsible one, you know," she said, softly.

Joe frowned. "What do you mean?"

"Oh, just something Tash said."

"Tash seems to have been saying a lot," he replied drily. "Maybe she can tell me all about it too when she finally surfaces – what time did she go to bed?"

"She's up already – apparently feeling fit – bed made,

gone out. I guess for milk or something?"

Joe replied with a snort. "That would be a first," he replied. "I've seen her have Ribena on her cornflakes rather than nip out."

"I take your point. So what *would* she go out for?"

"Most likely she just went home, probably to get stuck into something on the internet about more ghostly shenanigans." He paused, thought for a moment, and then addressed the air around him. "No offence meant!"

"Don't joke," giggled Louise. "Right, in that case, I'm going to go for a shower and get dressed. Feel free to help yourself to anything – there's paracetamol in the top of that cupboard there – or I'm sure I have one of my painkillers left over somewhere if you really need it?"

"I might," replied Joe, rubbing his temples as Louise left the room and made her way upstairs.

She returned, feeling more refreshed than she had done in weeks, to find Joe looking for something on the countertops, lifting papers and checking behind the chopping-boards.

"Looking for the plot you've lost?" she asked playfully, and he turned sharply.

"Jesus, you gave me a fright," he said. "Although what's new around here. Sorry if it looks like I'm snooping, but I was just looking for something."

"For what?"

Joe paused and sighed deeply. "Those photos actually. I thought it was time to man up and actually look at them – get myself up to speed, I suppose. See what you and Tash saw."

Louise's eyes strayed to the table. "They were on the

kitchen table last night when I went to bed," she said. "But they weren't there when I got up. Maybe Tash moved them – I'll go check." She turned and headed into the studio but emerged moments later.

"No sign in there," she said.

Joe stood, hands on his hips, scanning the kitchen. "They're not in the sitting room either – I checked while you were in the shower," he said. "You don't think something happened to them ..." His voice trailed off and his eyes widened.

Louise stared back at him, mirroring his expression but not understanding what he meant for a moment. "Oh, you mean ... like ... *supernatural,* or something?"

Joe looked awkward. "Well, yeah – it sounds silly but, you know, with everything that's been going on."

"Maybe Tash took them upstairs," she said. "Probably did. I'll go check."

"I'll do it – even with my head I'll be faster than you with your foot." He rolled his eyes.

He headed up the stairs and returned a few minutes later.

"I did a thorough search – even in the bathroom – no sign."

A thought struck her. "You don't think Tash took them, do you?"

"*Steal* them? No!" Joe looked shocked. "I mean glasses from pubs, yes – a jacket at a party once – I made her take it back –"

"No – not *steal* them, you idiot! *Borrowed* them, I mean ... she was keen to show them to her friends." The thought dismayed her. The photos could get lost – or Tash could lend them to someone and they could go astray. She could imagine her doing just that.

"Her spooky mates at college? I'd swear she fancies one of them. Let me ring her and see. Just let me get my phone."

Louise leaned against the countertop by the sink as she waited for Joe to retrieve his phone from the sitting room.

"There's a text from her here," he said, re-entering the kitchen and reading from the screen. "Sent at a quarter past nine. '*Have taken death pics back to antiques shop. Want to ask some q's and hopefully it'll get rid of whatever is in Louise's house. Will call back there l8tr so u can drive me home, once u've sobered up, u drunk x*'."

"Taken them back?" Louise was dismayed – somehow the thought disturbed her. "How could she do that without asking me? She shouldn't have."

"She's crazy. Haven't you gathered that by this time? That's her style. Jump right in. Don't think first. Here, I'll try and give her a ring."

Louise gnawed anxiously at her nails as Joe lifted the phone to his ear and the distant buzz of it dialling was audible from where she stood.

He let it ring for a while, then shook his head. "She's not answering. I'll try my mum, see if she's home by now."

It rang again, and again, and then Louise heard a distant voice just as Joe cut off the call.

"*This caller has their unit powered off. Please try again later*," he said, imitating the automatic voice response and rolling his eyes. "Bloody Mum – she's supposed to be resting but she always goes to the library on Saturday mornings – she'd rather die than go without a book. Bet she's got her pal Betty to give her a lift *and* she's turned her phone off – not just put it on silent, mind, but fully off – in case the vibration interrupts someone –"

"That man Temple," Louise interrupted. "He was creepy. He found my address somehow, knew exactly where to come, to knock directly on my door. He kept calling the camera 'she', like it was a person. And he knew that something was missing from the case, so he knows about those photos. He scared me, Joe. If Tash went back to the shop – well, I just don't like the idea of her going on her own."

"I'm sure she's fine," he said, furiously tapping out a text. "There. I've ordered her to make her whereabouts known the second she sees this message. She'll be back to call me more names before we know it."

Louise chewed her lip. She should trust him, he knew his sister best after all – but she just couldn't shake the feeling that had grabbed hold of her, the feeling that something wasn't right.

"But what if she's not?" she blurted out.

This time, he didn't reassure her. Instead, he raised an eyebrow. "You really have a bad feeling about this, haven't you?"

She nodded. "Maybe I'm overthinking this like I do with everything, but ..."

"Give her the time it takes for us to have another cup of tea," Joe said. "If she hasn't called me back by then – she probably can't hear or feel her phone in the bottom of that knapsack thing of hers, remember? – we can go in search if you makes you feel any better."

Reluctantly, Louise nodded and flicked on the kettle. And all the while, worry clung to her, growing heavier and heavier by the minute.

Chapter 41

Tash's eyes shot up as the flicker of movement registered just above her head. A birdcage, suspended from the ceiling, swung gently as the budgie inside warbled and hopped from its perch to grip the bars of the cage with tiny claws, studying her with a sideways look. Tash grimaced. Already she didn't like this place.

The warmth of the shop was welcome, but the gloominess was not. It felt as if it somehow defied the glorious winter sunshine outside, holding on desperately to as much darkness as it possibly could. It was also completely silent, save for the occasional chirrup from the bird, and she found herself holding her breath against the air which smelled of must and damp spores and something else that she couldn't identify. She contemplated leaving and was in the midst of making her mind up when more movement, this time from behind the counter to the rear of the shop, startled her.

"Can I help you at all?"

She turned to see a man – in his fifties, she guessed – emerging from behind the counter. He was a funny-looking thing, she thought, with his ill-fitting pistachio-coloured shirt, burgundy tie and tan slacks, worn with a pair of thick-soled white runners. His full lips dominated his face, drawing attention away from a pair of small dark eyes and aquiline nose. He smoothed down his hair to one side as he approached her, cautiously it seemed at first, but when he stepped into her light, an odd smile flickered across his features.

Instinctively, Tash took a step back.

"Well," he said, "a sight for sore eyes this fine morning – a customer. What can I do for you? I'm Adrian Temple, proprietor."

Tash returned his handshake loosely. So maybe he was doing a whole 'you've stepped back in time' experience. Fair enough, she thought. "I'm Tash – Natasha."

"*Natasha!* Oh, *gesundheit*!" he replied, chuckling. "I'm very sorry, Natasha – my little joke. It's a beautiful name, meaning 'Birthday of the Lord', I believe. Were you born at Christmas?"

Tash stared blankly at him for a moment before shaking her head. "March, actually," she replied, shrugging her shoulders.

Temple nodded. "Wonderful. A spring baby. The best kind. Now, how can I help you?"

"Actually, I might be able to help you," she replied awkwardly. "Or at least we can help each other."

"I've no doubt of it."

Tash hesitated for a split second before rummaging in her knapsack.

"I think this might belong to you." She withdrew the wooden photograph box and held it aloft. "I'm a friend of Louise Lacey and we found this – well, it's a long story – but she returned a camera to you a little while ago? A sort of Victorian box thingy? And she was certain that everything was with it when she brought it back, but then this turned up in her house – she's mortified that she missed it the first time around ..."

Her voice trailed off as it became clear Temple wasn't listening. Instead, he was looking at the box with a mix of wonder and reverence. And excitement. His face lit up, his eyes widened. The hairs on her neck stood up.

"Now, there's been a little damage to the lock – another long story – but I'm more than happy to pay for a new lock – you take cards, do you?"

He shook his head and dismissed the idea with a "*Pff*", instead holding his hands out for the box. She offered it to him as if it were a precious relic. He gasped as his fingers closed around it and he lifted it from her hands, like a father taking his child for the first time.

What a weirdo, thought Tash as she relinquished it. *Louise was right.*

"The vessel is replaceable," he declared. "But the contents are not. I'm sure you've had a peek inside, Natasha, am I correct?" He regarded her with a raised eyebrow, as if sharing a secret.

She nodded uncomfortably.

"You're aware then, that what is contained inside is ... *unusual* ... by today's standards?"

She nodded again. "They're Victorian post-mortem photographs, am I right?"

He was looking at her afresh, eyebrows raised. "Top marks," he said. "How unexpected ... that anyone would know what they were, I mean. I commend you for your knowledge, Natasha. Are you a historian? A student of Victoriana, perhaps?"

"Not quite. I am very interested in –" she stopped herself, "*history*, however. In fact, I wanted to ask if you knew anything about these? Their origin, or the name of the photographer maybe? I'm interested in knowing a bit more, I suppose."

"Did you *like* them?" He looked at her expectantly.

Taken aback, Tash searched for the right response. "They're very well ... composed, I guess," she answered diplomatically. "Actually, that's sort of what I wanted to find out about – I know they were commonplace at the time, but I'm sort of intrigued by the photographer, by the type of person who worked at this for a living."

Temple stared at her, a sudden flush rising to his cheeks. She noticed that his breathing had quickened. He gulped and swallowed hard, in an effort to control it.

"Please forgive me, Natasha – but, truly – I'm speechless."

"I'm just interested from the point of view of history," she said quickly, defensively. "I'm not, like, fascinated by the subjects – although, actually, I'm *very* interested in them too, but that's sort of another day's work."

"No, no, you misunderstand me," he protested. "I'm just speechless that you should turn up here, unannounced, looking so *glorious* – forgive me – and announcing to me on my own shop floor that you are interested in a subject which also fascinates me – a subject that, again in today's world, I scarcely dare to mention in polite conversation lest I'm called ghoulish or freakish."

"I get that a lot too." Natasha laughed in an effort to diffuse the intensity as it dawned on her that the man maybe found her attractive. The idea repulsed her a little, but if he was interested in the same thing as she was, then maybe she could use that to her advantage? He'd never dare make a move on her, would he? Anyway, if he did, she was probably twice his size, and hurting his odd little feelings really didn't bother her too much. It was no big deal. "That's so cool that you have that interest. Maybe you can tell me a little bit about these photos then? I'd love to hear more. Do you know who the photographer was?"

"Do I know?" His eyes lit up with glee at the question. "Do I know? Yes. I *do* know as it happens. Because his name was Samuel Temple." He beamed broadly, as if he had declared something very obvious.

It took a moment for Tash to spot what it was. "*Oh,*" she said. "Your name – Temple."

"Yes. Family, Natasha, that wonderful, fateful cobweb, connecting us through time, whether or not we know it. Samuel Temple was my great-great-grandfather. The camera, which was sold in error to your friend, was *his* camera, passed down through the generations to me, and the photographs in this box are some of his life's work."

"*Oh, wow!* So do you know who the people in the photos are? And how he worked? The mechanics of taking shots like these?"

"I do. Would you like to see some more?"

Tash hesitated. "Well, I was mainly interested in these ..." She saw disappointment flash across his features. "But a few more won't do any harm if you have them?" *Softly, softly, catchee weirdo*, she told herself.

"You won't regret it," he huffed excitedly, placing the box gently down on the counter and headed to the door behind the counter.

Tash smiled politely, turning to look at the bird which was watching them, twitching in its cage. A moment later, she turned back and jumped, startled. He hadn't gone through the door at all, but was still standing there, watching her with a fascinated expression. She frowned.

"The more I look at you ..." he whispered, as if to himself.

He snapped suddenly out of his reverie.

"I *am* sorry, Natasha," he said. "I must be coming across as strange, but you remind me of someone – seeing you turn your head there, I was struck by the similarity. Anyway, that is, as you say yourself, another story. Apologies. I'll get back to the task in hand. I'll be right back. I have more wonders for you. What luck! You can't possibly imagine ..."

He was true to his word this time. After a while he reappeared, bearing a large cardboard box and setting it on the counter with a grin.

Tash returned the grin, although her heart sank at the size of the box. The portraits were fascinating, but there was definitely a limit to how many she could consume at once.

"How did you come to learn about post-mortem photography?" he asked, breathlessly excited as he unpacked items – leather-bound diaries, sheaves of paper, yellowed envelopes – from the box. "Oh, I just stumbled across it while I was reading. I'm interested in the paranormal." Tash was sure that she saw him freeze for the tiniest second in his search. "And I came across the subject along the way."

"These must not be confused with spirit photography, you understand?" he said sternly.

Tash nodded. "Of course not – completely different thing. I just end up on a tangent sometimes when I'm reading or browsing online, and I just happened on some of these pictures. There's a lot of fakes out there, am I correct?"

"Not in Samuel's work, let me assure you. And he was prolific!" Temple virtually glowed with pride, and a touch of outrage that his ancestor be accused of such a thing. "Ah, here we are!" He withdrew a small bundle, wrapped in crumpled, waxy paper and unfolded it to reveal photographs inside. "Take a look at these," he urged.

Tash began to slowly flick through them.

"Ordinary Victorians," he said, "captured so beautifully at the end of their lives. Sometimes it was the first and last photograph that a family would have of their loved one."

Tash inhaled sharply at the sight of a toddler, cradled by her mother who gazed into the distance, her eyes filled with sorrow, while what was presumably the child's father stood behind her, hand on her shoulder, looking directly at the camera.

"Always makes me sad, that one," Temple said. "I feel an odd connection to these ... souls ... for whom I've been awarded responsibility. Because that's what my uncle Samuel did – captured the very souls of his subjects ... before ..."

Tash's eyes widened and she looked at him in disbelief. "Some cultures believe that, of course," she prodded. "That a photograph will rob the soul."

Temple nodded. "Perhaps they do, Natasha, perhaps they do," he said.

For a second, the two of them were frozen in time, Temple's words weighing heavily on Tash. Did he know? Was he aware of the strangeness that surrounded his box of photographs? Her heart thudded.

"Of course," he continued, in a lighter tone, "the portraits also served as Memento Mori."

"*Remember you must die,*" she translated.

Temple rewarded her with a coy look of surprise. "You are really impressive, Natasha. Remarkable. *Remember you must die.* Indeed."

"So, tell me a little about your great-great-grandfather – is that enough greats? Although he is, clearly, absolutely *great.*" She wondered if she'd gone too far with that.

Temple's response indicated otherwise. His face crumpled and his mouth opened wide as he gave a long, silent, helpless laugh and then applauded. "Excellent, Natasha," he said once he regained control. "And correct, in my opinion. I think the man was a *bit* of a genius."

"For sure," replied Tash, as sincerely as she could manage.

"So, to tell you about my forebear – where to begin? He plied his trade in Queen Victoria's London where death was as much a part of life as life itself. Respectful etiquette was observed – the wearing of black, mourning periods – appropriate time was spent indulging in grief, I believe. Unlike today where it's a case of get 'em in the ground or burn 'em, wear bright colours and play rock songs, and family-only flowers." Temple shook his head in disapproval. "In Samuel's day, the time was taken to *mourn* and to do it correctly. The dead were many, but they were *honoured.*"

Tash raised an eyebrow and continued to flick through the gallery of death which he had just handed her, growing a little weary of the subject matter – predominantly children, depressingly enough.

"Beautiful, aren't they?" interrupted Temple.

She nodded as enthusiastically as she could and handed the pile back. Immediately, Temple tried to swap it for another similar bundle withdrawn from a tattered brown envelope.

"Gorgeous," she said, deflecting his attention by pointing across the counter. "But what about these ones in the box I returned? They're quite different, in a way, from the others. The subjects – a dwarf, a priest, a girl with no hands ... they must all have interesting stories?"

She looked back at Temple and was surprised to see a change in his demeanour. He had stiffened and grown serious, with a glint of something she couldn't quite recognise in his eyes. "And my buxom girl ..."

Tash regarded him sharply.

He seemed to wait a beat, then gave a half smile and reached out a hand to pat her arm.

"Yes, the pictures in there, I have to admit, do feature rather a rich gallery of life. They're my favourites, you see, and special to my great-great-grandfather – that's why they were stored separately and kept with her – the camera, that is. I liked to have them all together – it sounds odd, but perhaps I'm a little bit ... OCD, if that's the right term? It just made me feel calmer to keep them with her, like a mother with her children. There's a sense of order to it that I find fascinating. I'm ... I'm also working on a special project that involves those pictures, in fact, which is another reason I'm so very grateful to you, so happy that you stumbled into my little shop today."

Tash smiled awkwardly. "That's alright," she said. "So what sort of project are you undertaking? An exhibition? Do you know, that's something I'd be really interested in, and I know some people at my college who'd certainly come along."

"It's not really an exhibition ... Listen to me! I shouldn't have said a word!" Temple rolled his eyes and made an odd little gesture of smacking his own cheeks. "Actually, as you're here, would you mind awfully if I asked for your help?"

"Oh, I'm not sure I have the time," said Tash, glancing at her watch.

"It'll only take a minute – it's just, I've never met anyone who had even heard of the practice of post-mortem photography, much less showed as much appreciation for it as you. I promise I won't keep you, but it would mean the world to me if you'd have a quick glance at something I'm working on and gave me your opinion?"

Tash shifted her weight from foot to foot and thought for a moment. "Alright then, but I really have to get going after that. I've some things to do today."

"Of course you have. You're a busy woman, I'm sure," Temple replied. "Wait there a moment. Actually, let me just pop the 'closed' sign around for five minutes so we won't be disturbed. Saturday's my busy day, you know."

Tash turned to look over her shoulder at the empty shop while Temple scurried to the door and back again.

"Now. I'll just pop through here for a second – I won't be long."

Politely, she smiled as he unlocked a second door directly behind the counter, a smile that dropped as soon as he disappeared through it. With a sigh, she slid her backpack to the floor and rotated the shoulder on which it had been hanging. This was turning out to be a complete waste of time, after all. The history – the stories she'd hoped she might glean were all in the hands of a weird little man with orthotic runners who liked to ramble on about how the Victorians did death right, and how saucy dead Victorian fat girls were. "*Jesus*," she whispered at the thought. When she put it like that …

"*Natasha!*" The call came from somewhere distant.

She rolled her eyes. "*Yes?*"

"*Just come through – I'll be with you in just a sec!*"

Tash gave another quiet little groan to herself, and then did what she was told. She really wished he'd hurry up – she was starting to get hungry now on top of the aggravation. Passing through the door, she found herself alone in a musty-smelling hallway, a flight of stairs leading up from it, and another leading down.

"*Won't be long!*" came his voice from below. "*The bulb's been gone here a couple of days! I'm so silly, I keep forgetting to get a replacement. These old houses, you know, the wiring can be very … aaargh!*"

The strangled cry was accompanied by a couple of loud bangs.

Tash jumped and peered down into the murky stairwell. She couldn't see much beyond the turn in the stairs.

"*Are you okay?*" she called.

There was no answer at first, and then a groan. "*I'm fine*," the call came weakly. "*Just had … a shock. Tripped … I've bumped my head and twisted my ankle. I'll be fine in a minute … I'm sure …*"

"*Can I help at all?*" Tash called, alarmed. What if he'd given himself a concussion? What if he was bleeding, or had broken something and she was going to have to call an ambulance?

321

"*Actually ... you can,*" he replied, groaning again. "*My glasses ... I'm forever leaving them off, like a fool. They're in the top drawer underneath the counter ... could you bring them down to me? If I'd only had them on ... I really have to start wearing them ...*"

"Wait there," Tash replied, and rushed to find them. They were exactly where he had described, and exactly the sort of thing she imagined he'd wear with thick tortoiseshell rims. She peered through them and watched the world swirl and distort. His eyesight must be abysmal, she concluded. No wonder he'd fallen over.

"*Coming!*" she called, as she carefully descended the first set of steps and then turned.

To her surprise, Temple was nowhere to be seen below. Odder still, it wasn't very dark at all. Instead, a pale, bare bulb cast a weak light by which she could see down the bottom flight of stairs to a dimly lit corridor with a couple of doors leading off it and a large blacked-out pane of glass along one wall.

"*Mr Temple?*" she called, pausing where she stood, her heartbeat quickening.

"*I'm in here ...*" he called from somewhere, his voice alarmingly weak.

"*Where?*" Tash asked, descending the remainder of the steps, worried by how feeble he suddenly sounded.

"*The door to your right, beside the big window,*" he croaked. "*I'm so very sorry – I really should take better care ...*"

"*It's fine!*" replied Tash, "*I'm here now!*"

She reached the door to the room from where Temple's voice came. How was she going to get him up the bloody stairs, she wondered. What if he'd broken his poxy leg? It was pitch black in here too – this must be where the bulb was gone. Bloody little freak of a man – why had she agreed to stay and see his stupid project?

"*I've got your glasses here, Mr Temple – can you walk at all?*" she called into the gloom.

No response came. *Shit*, she thought. "*Mr Temple?*"

She took a tentative step over the threshold ... heard a groan ... took another ...

At first, she thought that a flash of lightning had somehow gone off in the dark room.

It took the briefest second, however, before her brain could understand that no, it wasn't a light from without, it came from *within* – from inside her own head. Then the sudden thump of the blow registered, and she cried out, a great gasp of shock and pain. She staggered forward, unable to see for a moment, half-falling to the ground, before she managed to turn, raising her hands in defence. She tried to call out, but words wouldn't come – her brain raced ... Temple, he was hurt ... no, *she* was hurt ... and falling, down to the ground, putting out her hands to stop herself ... the room, it was so dark, she couldn't see ... save for the light coming from the open door behind ...

And then that, too was gone.

And she was alone, stunned, on her hands and knees on a cold floor in thick, thick darkness.

Tash gasped, tried her best to register where she was and what had happened, if it had *really* happened – if this were true ... could it be? Had she really been so stupid? Rage bubbled up inside her, and she staggered to her feet.

"*No!*" she cried – even her own voice sounded strange

323

and distant. "*No!*" she cried again, tried to find the door, but staggered and keeled over, the floor coming up to meet her head. She lay there, stupefied, staring into the dark, the only sound her ragged breathing.

And the shuffling.

She gasped, and held her breath silent as she heard it, clear, even in her dazed state.

And she heard it again. Shuffling movement. Approaching her in the darkness.

Her entire body went cold and she opened her mouth to scream.

She wasn't alone.

Chapter 42

"I'm sure she's gone home or gone to meet up with her mates or gone to the library at college or something ..."

Louise gritted her teeth against the frustration rising inside her. It wasn't entirely directed at Joe, despite the constant babble that he had kept up the entire way into town – trying to reassure her that there was no need for concern as to Tash's whereabouts, that everything was fine, that they'd laugh about this later. She was well aware that she came across as overreacting – she hoped she *was* – but something gnawed relentlessly at her gut and she was simply unable to let it go.

Her crutch – she still didn't feel confident leaving the house without it – beat a repetitive tempo along the pavement as she thumped with as much speed as she could manage along the Quays.

Joe strode along beside her, flashing worried looks at her now and then. He was more worried at how worried Louise was, he realised, than he was about his sister.

When they reached Temple Antiques, Louise stopped dead, and studied the front of the building before steeling herself with a breath and mounting the steps. As she climbed, she cast a glance over her shoulder to make sure Joe was still there before pushing open the door into the familiar cocoon of the shop.

Temple himself was standing behind the counter, packing old books and papers into a large cardboard box. He looked up suddenly as they entered, and went red, his expression slightly alarmed, even more so when he recognised Louise. It transformed as suddenly, however, to the smooth, insincere smile that she had seen on her doorstep. *How had he known where she bloody well lived?* she asked herself again. With a great force of will, she fixed her own smile and made her way across the shop, the sound of the crutch muffled against the rug on the wooden floor.

"Miss ... *Lacey*, isn't it?" Temple asked, closing over the cardboard flaps of the box, before turning very suddenly and shutting the open door directly behind him.

Louise studied his face. She could tell that he was only pretending to hesitate over her name. A strong desire burned inside her to demand of him how he had found her, and what the real story was behind the box of photographs of dead people that he had so desperately wanted to retrieve. She suppressed it, however. Tash was her concern now. She couldn't relax until she knew where she was.

"Mr Temple," she replied. "How are you?"

He closed his heavy-lidded eyes and shook his head. "Swamped, Miss Lacey," he said. "All work and no play, and on a Saturday too. This Jack is a very dull boy, I'm afraid. How can I help you? Are you here with a purpose, or just browsing with your gentleman friend?"

The tone of his voice made her skin crawl.

"Here with a purpose," she replied. "I was actually

looking for someone, a girl – a friend – I told her about your lovely shop and she mentioned that she might call in while passing today ... I can't get hold of her by mobile phone ..."

She broke off the sentence. Temple's eyes had flickered involuntarily downwards, to something behind the counter at his feet, but then immediately back to her. The movement was tiny – had she blinked she'd have missed it – but it struck her as odd.

"Do you need your friend urgently?" he asked. Also odd.

"No," replied Louise. "I just ... have something belonging to her that I need to give back as soon as possible, and I can't seem to get hold of her. I said I'd pop in on the off-chance you'd seen her."

Temple nodded. "Let me see ... I've had quite a few customers today – what does your friend look like?"

Louise glanced at Joe, frowning slightly. "She's in her early twenties. Long dark hair, dressed in black – a long skirt, boots, knitted green scarf, carrying a floral canvas backpack."

Temple seemed to search very hard through his brain before shaking his head. "No, I'm afraid that there's been no one of that description through this morning at all," he said regretfully. "I'm so terribly sorry, but ... no, definitely not ... I'd remember that." He gave a creepy, unnecessary chuckle.

Louise stared at him. "You're sure?"

He nodded vigorously. "Afraid I'm no use to you this morning. Unless you have a desire to purchase an antiquity, a collectable, a curio –"

"No, thanks," Louise cut him off. "Okay then, thanks for your help."

"My absolute pleasure," fawned Temple. "Until our paths cross again, Miss Lacey. Enjoy your day."

He waved as Louise and Joe turned and made their way back out onto the street.

"So, she hasn't been in then," observed Joe, once they were a few feet clear of the shop door. "I'm telling you she's just doing what it is that Tash does at a weekend – our main concern is getting those photos back before she and her friends ... I dunno, *lose* them or something. Can we go get a coffee actually? I think I really need a caffeine hit."

Louise stopped abruptly and turned, looking back at the shop.

"Sure," she replied, only half paying attention.

"Are you alright?" Joe's voice was suddenly blunt. "I think ... you're very ... *het up* about something that's ..."

"What? *All in my head?*" Louise snapped.

Joe flushed. "I'm sorry, I don't want to come across like a total prick, like I'm doubting you or something ..."

Louise sighed, still staring at the front of the building that she knew so well. "You don't," she replied. "Yeah – let's go get a coffee. But there's something ..."

"What? What's in your gut?" asked Joe. "I don't doubt you, but you have to let me in on your thinking."

Louise shook her head. "I don't know," she said, turning away from the shop and starting to walk again. "I can't put my finger on it. All I know is one thing for certain."

"What's that?" asked Joe, falling into step beside her.

Louise turned and glanced over her shoulder again.

"I don't like that man," she said. "I don't trust him one bit."

Chapter 43

London, 1867

He wept as he photographed her, when he was finally allowed.

She was, as was to be expected, as beautiful in death as she had been alive. Her hair, the colour of autumn, arranged around the winter whiteness of her skin. The contrast was breathtaking. Had she been simply a subject, she would have delighted him. But it was Maud. His purest love, his heavenly being.

He had, of course, been too late.

The blur of it all in his mind now – he had turned to run home to her, he remembered that, sick with fear. And then ... it was all confused ... there had been a constable, summoned from somewhere – who had met him along the way, by chance?

He recalled stumbling on the stairs – the last memory from before he found her. Her horrified eyes had been open and she lay on the floor, as if she had been crawling when death overcame her. And the stench too – the ordure – he simply couldn't bear to think of it – poor Maud's body had tried its best to expel the poison as it attacked her in the gut with the ferocity of a thousand knives.

There had been no need for an autopsy. The arsenic in the tea which Bridget had undoubtedly made Maud drink as soon as she had heard the front door close behind her husband was still easily detectable.

The doctor estimated the time of death as being about teatime that evening – but that was impossible, reckoned Temple. He hadn't fled from the house until almost seven ... unless ... dear God, no ... unless she had been dead all the time, all throughout his wife's – he could not think of her as such now – insane revelations. Had it been true? Had poor Maud truly been dead all the time? Lifeless, upstairs, as he listened to Bridget's wretched admissions? Alone, in bitter agony, her life expiring in that most hideous fashion as she, incapable of walking or even standing, had expired there, on the rug of her bedroom, her whole life yet to be lived, and all her love to be given still?

Samuel had commanded that they take Bridget away – to Bedlam, to Newgate, he had told them – to Hell – he cared not what became of her. All he cared for was Maud, and his regret at not knowing, not checking – not sending her away to safety when he had been *told* to do so – consumed him. He wished he could cut it out of himself with a knife, like a tumour. But he could not, so instead he took it upon himself, and himself alone, to care for her – to lift her from the floor onto her bed, where he commanded the housemaid – that stupid girl – why had *she* not known anything? – to wash Maud clean, and to dress her in her nightgown, as if she were going to sleep. And when that was done, he told the maid, she was to leave, and take the boy with her overnight – he cared not where, but the child could not stay under his roof now, not for a minute on this dreadful night. Had he his way, he would have sent him away forever – simply forgotten about him, erased him from that most dreadful chapter through which he had just lived. A niggling sense of duty would prevent him from doing so, he knew that much, but for the moment he wanted the child out of his sight. He would decide what to do with him later.

For now, alone, he would mourn for Maud. Watch her through the night, make his grief his sustenance, his rest, the very air that he breathed. He would lock the doors and close the shutters, just as it was in all of those houses where he photographed the dead, and simply be with her, before he had to say goodbye.

And then on the day after tomorrow – when it was light again, and when the dreadful stiffness of death had left her body, he would photograph her. For her poor mother, he told himself – it was the least he could do to apologise to her for not keeping Maud safe. The portrait would be a keepsake, a memento mori, to console the woman who had shown him such hospitality. Yes, that is what he would do. He would restore Maud to the very innocence of her baptism, he told himself, as he planned how he would place her in his most wonderful – and fitting – portrait yet.

And when the time came, he picked her up in his exhausted arms and carried her down to the chaise longue in his studio and surrounded her with lilies. The very scent of them – he fancied it to be the aroma of angels as they bore her virtuous soul heavenward – threatened to join with his grief to overpower him as he arranged the flowers carefully – most carefully of all across the porcelain smoothness of her stumps to look as if she held a vast bouquet – in the first of the photographs he took. That one was for her mother.

Then he slid a second plate into place for the next photograph: the one where he placed upon her a small prop – yet another that he had acquired to perfect the scene.

And a single, long tear rolled down his cheek as he stood back to take her in, posed as if she were playing a small harp, strumming on an instrument as she had so desired in life.

That photograph he would keep just for him.

Samuel heard the knock, just as he emerged from the developing room. At first, he ignored it, waiting for someone else – as was usually the way – to hurry past him along the hall and admit whoever it might be.

It was at the second knock – a more insistent pounding – that he suddenly remembered that he was alone. All who shared his household were dead or gone. Best that they should never return, he thought. He would stay here forever now, alone, mourning the loss of the most beautiful soul the world had ever known.

"*Samuel Temple! Open up!*"

A heavier hand indeed beat upon the door now. Whatever could it be, wondered Samuel, as he hastened his step. Perhaps it was the Constable again, come with word of what would become of Bridget.

"*Temple! It is the police! I advise you to open this door or I shall have to enter by force!*"

Gracious, thought Temple. It *was* a policeman – whatever could he want?

It was three policemen, in fact – in they stormed, a

blur of rough serge and shining buttons. He was forced to stand back to admit them – and to admit a fourth member of the party who did not meet his eye as she swept through the door, pulled to her full height. His stomach lurched at the sight of her.

"*What is she doing here?*" he roared. "*Why is she not locked up, where she should be, so that she cannot kill any more innocents?*"

The Inspector who led the group gave Temple a hard look and nodded at his constable to close the front door behind them.

"We have some questions to ask you, Mr Temple," he growled. "Where can we speak?"

"This way!"

It was Bridget's voice – lilting and sweet. It shot through Temple's head like a steel bolt. How dare she! How dare she show herself in and then proceed to act like the lady of the manor in *his* house, when she was no more than a lowlife criminal and had admitted as much to him?

He had opened his mouth to say so when she swung around to face him.

"Where is my son, Mr Temple?" she demanded.

He looked at her, taken aback. "Safe. Samuel Junior is with Dolly's family," he replied, with as much authority as he could muster. "It is best that he is not in the house at this present time."

He steeled himself for her response – rage-filled, no doubt. She would launch into a tirade against him, demanding the child.

It astounded him when, instead, she nodded her head.

"Quite," she agreed.

The small group shuffled their way into the drawing room, much to Temple's continued bemusement.

"Mr Temple, can you sit down a moment," ordered the Inspector, leaning against the mantel while his constables took their positions either side of the door.

Bridget was seated already, in the armchair in front of the window. Temple looked at her properly as he sank reluctantly into a chair opposite. The light shone in behind her, yet it gave her no beatific beauty as it had her victim. Instead it highlighted her grey skin and dishevelled hair. She was still in the clothes she had been wearing when she had left the house. All of it should have served to make her look wretched. Yet there was something about her – something that did not sit right with Samuel. She had been arrested, brought here by the police – she should have been meek, diminished somehow. Yet her back was straight, and her eyes alert. And he was sure that a hint of a smile played around her lips as the policeman turned to address her husband.

"Mrs Temple here has informed us that you might have something to tell us about the death of her niece, Miss Maud Hodges," he said.

Temple frowned and looked blankly at him. "I have no more to say other than that you have the perpetrator in that seat in front of you, a hideous and depraved thing that she is – and what's more, it is a great mystery to me why she is sitting in my chair, instead of a cell with four sturdy walls and a steel door with a heavy lock. Poor Maud is not her only victim, you know – she told me herself."

Temple was astonished to see the Inspector roll his eyes, and the two policemen by the door exchange a glance.

"Well, it is interesting that you say that, sir," the Inspector said, "because Mrs Temple here has told us something quite different. Can you repeat to your husband what that is, Mrs Temple?"

Bridget cast a demure eye at the Inspector and straightened her shoulders.

Temple shook his head at the performance. What could she say?

"Well, Inspector, as much as it pains me such a great deal to say it, it was in fact my husband who killed poor, darling Maud – and the others. And I have proof."

Temple shot to his feet. "*I beg your pardon?*" he bellowed.

"Sit down, Mr Temple!" barked the Inspector. "Can you tell us where we might find this proof, Mrs Temple?"

"Indeed," replied Bridget, clutching at her chest, as if Samuel's outburst had shocked her.

"First – if you check Mr Temple's coat pocket, you'll find something. And then, in his photographic studio, there are pictures – he keeps them in a wooden case in the bottom drawer of his desk – he kills them all to photograph them, you see – he is quite ill in his mind ..."

"*Poppycock!*" interrupted Temple, agape at her words.

"But the most important piece of evidence ... I should have gone to you months ago when first I found it ... had only I done so, then darling Maud, my sister-in-law's beloved child, would still be here with us ..." She broke off to emit a little sob before seeming to compose herself and carry on. "On that dreadful day – I took it and concealed it lest he try to destroy it – it is in the drawer of my desk in my room – you will need to unlock it."

She reached her hand to her throat, and from underneath the collar of her dress, she pulled a small key on a chain into view, removed it, and handed it to one of the policemen.

"I pray that when you see it, you'll know full well why I couldn't possibly have done this hideous crime of which I am accused. I am so grieved that it is, however, my very own beloved husband."

And with that, there were more sobs, which continued intermittently into the handkerchief which Bridget was handed by the Inspector.

Temple watched the charade in a state of disbelief, until the first policeman returned, white-faced.

"This was in Mr Temple's pocket, sir," he addressed his superior, opening his palm to reveal what he had found there. Temple made a "*pff*" sound as he recognised it.

"What explanation might you have for an empty bottle of arsenic concealed in your coat pocket, sir?"

"It was my wife's," Temple, answered. "Not mine. It was Maud, in fact, who found it in Bridget's room some days ago and brought it to me – the poor girl could not read enough to identify it from the label. I thought at first that we might have had rats but Maud assured me that we did not. I put this bottle in my pocket then simply forgot about it. It is no proof whatsoever that it was I who poisoned Maud – in fact, I was out of the house wearing that exact coat when she was so cruelly killed."

"I see," said the Inspector gravely. "What else have you for me, Perkins?"

The policeman handed over the case to which Bridget had directed him.

"They are my work," said Temple dismissively.

"There is not a photographer in London who does not take commissions to photograph the deceased. You will find nothing unusual about them."

"Except they are all deformed, as I told you," interjected Bridget. "All of them – these ones he keeps in a special box, separate from all of the others – the healthy and the normal. He has a sickness, sir – a sickness of the mind to keep such things for himself, for his own private perusal – it is not natural, I tell you – look at them! All of them charges of mine from my time as a housekeeper – I had a way with special cases, you see, and he inveigled his way into my good books to gain access to the lot of them, but this was his intent all along – to kill them and make private portraits of them – ghastly things!"

"*That is preposterous!*" yelled Temple. "All of those portraits – there are copies to be found in the possession of the parents of each of those people ... it was you who called me to photograph them, Bridget, once they were dead – once you had killed them because of their imperfections – you told me so yourself!"

"Sir, there's something else," added Perkins quietly.

The Inspector looked up at him, disgusted at the box of photographs. "What's that?"

"Perhaps you should go and take a look, sir ..."

His face like stone, the Inspector closed the wooden case, and, casting an eye on both Bridget and Samuel, strode past and off in the direction that was pointed out to him by the constable who remained in the room, his eyes cast to the floor.

Then silence. Silence in the drawing room where the air felt thick and smothering, silence from beyond, throughout the empty house ... then the silence was shattered by a loud exclamation – the Inspector had seen something. Then, a door slamming, and footsteps storming across the hall – then an exchange in low voices. It was a moment later before the Inspector re-entered, his cheeks red, and his chest moving rapidly.

"Where did Maud Hodges die, Mr Temple," he demanded. "In what room?"

Temple frowned a little. "In her bedroom, sir," he said. "Crawling along the floor, her dignity lost in death thanks to this woman."

"*That'll do, sir!*"

Temple stopped abruptly, his confusion suddenly replaced by anxiety at the sight of the Inspector's expression.

"And if I went upstairs to Maud Hodges' room now, I would find her laid out there, am I correct? In her room, where it is natural for a body to be kept before removal for burial, is that not so?"

Temple flushed and squirmed in his seat. "Well, actually, now that you mention it, sir ..."

"*So I will not find her there,*" hissed the Inspector. "And I know that for a fact, because I have just this minute found her – lying in a – a – *provocative* manner, on a chaise longue in what I assume is your photographic studio!"

Bridget gasped.

"Posed in an entirely inappropriate and disrespectful manner!"

"It was her wish," blurted Temple. "To play an instrument ... I could not get the light in her bedroom ... the photograph is for her mother ... a keepsake, I swear it ..."

"*Enough!*" roared the policeman. "Your wife brought me here today and I confess I did not believe her at first.

Such accusations to be thrown at a respectable member of society, or so I thought were inconceivable. But no – every word she told us is proven true. It was you, sir. You who murdered Maud Hodges, and the others too. You'll hang for this, Temple – I swear!"

"*What proof do you have?*" shouted Temple. "An empty bottle of rat poison in a city infested with vermin? Some portraits that are not to your taste – none of these things conclusively prove that I killed anyone – because it was not me! It was *her*! Show me your proof!"

"I will then!" replied the Inspector. "I will! The proof is written here – an account of every one."

And with that, he turned to the second policeman and pulled something from his hand, something that Temple did not at first recognise.

And then he did.

It was a ledger. One of so many that Bridget would crowd before him as he tried to work – household accounts, stock lists, supplies needed ... good God, she hadn't ... it was *unthinkable* ...

"I think you'll find that anything written in those ledgers is in my wife's hand," he said. "All her writing, all her doing ..."

"All *printed* – neat and tidy in a hand which clearly does not match that of your wife – she has kindly provided us with samples when she realised that she simply must tell us the terrible truth. An indistinguishable hand – yet what is that underneath the entries? Why it is a *very* distinguishable hand that signs all of it with your signature," said the Inspector coolly.

Temple looked, aghast and disbelieving, at Bridget who lifted her face from the handkerchief long enough to catch his eye. Long enough to curl one side of her face into a sneering grin meant only for him.

"And yes," continued the Inspector, "the arsenic alone is not sufficient, nor the photographs, but together with what appears to be a signed confession and your eagerness to lay the blame at the feet of a woman – a sex, in my belief, which nurtures life, not cuts it short – paints a picture more vile than those sickening portraits of yours, a picture which no judge in the land could ignore. You are under arrest, Mr Temple, in the name of Her Majesty on suspicion of murder."

Chapter 44

2018

The world lurched around her as Tash tried to push herself into a sitting position. Everything spun – everything and nothing, all around her was in utter darkness. But she had to sit up, had to gain control – had to get away from whatever else was in here.

The shuffling noise was punctuated by a groan, and she whimpered as she tried to push herself backwards with her feet and hands, as far away from the sound as she could. Her head spun, and she lost her balance yet again, her elbow buckling and causing her to keel to one side, just as another loud groan rang out into the darkness and what sounded like thick, garbled words.

And then light ... sudden light. The space around her was illuminated by a weak, yellow glow coming from a bare-bulbed lamp on the floor opposite. After a moment, her eyesight adjusted and the room came into focus. On the floor where she sat were blue carpet tiles, and the wall was red ... and also carpeted, which she didn't understand ... where the hell was she? What sort of place *was* this?

And then, from the shadows just to her right, came

sudden movement. She scrabbled backwards again, away from whatever it was ... something that slid across the floor... dragging itself along ... her mind raced and terror surged through her as a dark shape loomed, filling the space around her with a stink of filth, and something rotten ... breath ... fetid, warm breath right next to her face ...

Tash groaned, suddenly helpless, and turned her head away just as a voice filled her ear, words carried on a wave of stinking breath.

"*Help me!*"

A cloud of stink enveloped her, and she gagged.

"*Get me out ... I'm hurt ... he hurt me!*"

She couldn't bear it. She twisted the entire upper half of her body away and rolled over onto her knees. "Get away," she managed, pushing out with her left hand against the surging odour. Her fingers connected with something, and she recoiled, shrieking, before attempting to crawl away as fast as she could.

"Get *away!*" she sobbed as she began to register what it was ... an eye first, the side of a head ... an entire face, grey and haggard, large, weeping red eyes, a nose scabbed and crusting, dried lips, scraggly filthy hair.

"*Help me!*" it begged again.

She couldn't bring herself to look at it, didn't know if it was living or dead or if it wanted to harm her ... when suddenly it slumped back and the sound it released changed from pleading to wailing. She turned her head and focused on what could make such a noise – it was like nothing she had ever heard – plaintive, both child- and animal-like – it was despair, pure and utter despair. She struggled to control herself to take it all in, to fully see what sort of creature could make this most pitiful and terrifying sound ...

And then she saw ... and she, in turn, screamed – loudly, uncontrollably ...

Because the face of the boy – because that is all that it was, a teenage boy – was terrifying enough.

But it was what he had pressed to his face that made her blood turn to ice and fill her with a terror so pure that her entire body felt as if she had been electrocuted. The bandages ... the filthy grey of them, contrasting against russet stains – she could scarcely take it in.

Still wailing and keening, gulping for air, so desperate, so deserted and afraid, the boy held his hands to his face. Or rather he held what should have been his hands to his face.

Instead, he pressed the two bloodied, bandaged stumps that remained of his hands and lower arms into his eyes and wailed loud and long.

Tash pressed her hands to her ears and buried her head against her knees. Anything to block out the dreadful sound. What the hell was happening to her? This couldn't be real – it had to be some sort of nightmare – she'd wake up – she *had* to ...

When he finally fell silent, slumped against the wall, in some pitiful state between consciousness and unconsciousness, she studied him as best she could. He was young, she realised. Fifteen? Sixteen? And *dirty* – it looked like there were *weeks* of dirt ground into his body. He was so thin, too – what was left of his arms appeared to be little more than bone and sinew, and his body was feeble beneath a dirty T-shirt and grimy jeans.

His hair – reddish-brown – hung, limp and matted,

over his shoulders, and the scraggle of a soft beard had formed on his face. His head rolled back, exposing his face to the light – sharp cheekbones with gaunt hollows beneath them, rheumy eyes and a scab-covered face. Now and again, an involuntary whimper escaped him, and his frail chest would contract with the force of it. The poor boy, she thought. A part of her wanted to comfort him. Instead, she stayed where she was, frozen to the spot, as far as she could get from him and the stench that came from him.

It was stronger now that her senses were coming back to normal – not just the rank odour of his breath, but of urine and faeces too. An enamel chamber pot sat not far from the lamp, covered over with a small piece of plywood, but she knew that much of the smell came from the boy where he had soiled himself. It disgusted her, but he couldn't have helped it – it wasn't his fault. And neither was the other faint, worrying undertone of an odour in the air that she suspected came from beneath the bandages. She looked away and focused on the red-carpeted walls. She couldn't bear to think what was under those bandages and what might be happening to him.

How long had he been here? And who was he?

And why ... why was *she* here? How was she going to get out of this?

What did Temple want from her?

Tash suddenly pushed herself to her feet. Other than herself and the boy, the chamber pot and the lamp – which she saw had a long cable with a switch fitting halfway along that rested on the floor near where the boy sat to enable him turn it on and off – the room was empty. She looked up at the ceiling, across which rippled some sort of spongy styrofoam. She looked down again, and around the room, locating the door through which she had come. Beside it, running the length of the wall, was the huge window which was blacked out. She went to it and tapped the glass. It made a dull thud against her hand – wow, but it was thick – thicker than on any window she'd ever come across – and the door – out of sheer habit, she tested it, pulling at the handle. It was extremely heavy but – to her amazement – it *moved*.

Tash's heart gave a huge leap, and excitedly, she grabbed the handle with both hands. Incredibly, it opened – she could leave – she could get out of here …

Sure of escape, she pulled harder, everything inside her lifting, only for it all to sink again back down to despair as, on the other side of it, instead of the dark passageway to freedom, was another door.

She stared at it, then, propping the heavy first door open with her body, she grabbed the second handle with both hands and pulled, then pushed, with all her strength, but nothing happened.

Locked.

Of course it was. In desperation, she turned back into the stinking, hot room allowing the inner door slide shut with a gentle *thunk* behind her. Double doors, an unbreakable window, carpet on the walls, foam on the ceiling – her stomach dropped as the logic clicked into place.

It was soundproofed.

No one could have heard the desperate wails of the boy, and no one would hear her either if she called for help. Panic suddenly flooded through her, and she turned sharply, pulling open the inner door, and propping its heavy weight against her leg to keep it open, she began to pound on the outer door and yell, calling for help, calling Temple's name.

But no one heard her.

Or if they did, they certainly didn't come.

Tash's entire body trembled as she gave up, and she looked around her once more.

What was she going to do?

Worse still, what was he going to do to her?

Chapter 45

Louise's coffee sat, untouched, while she stared blankly out the café window at the river.

Joe watched her across the table, and contemplated saying one of roughly five different things, but decided against each one.

"How did he know where I live?" Louise demanded suddenly, turning so swiftly to look at him that she startled him and he rattled his cup against his saucer.

He looked at her, wide-eyed, unsure if she actually required an answer.

"I can't figure it out," she sighed. "I never gave an address – never gave anything more than my name for the receipt to that girl when we returned the damn camera."

"There's a lot you can do with a name," offered Joe. "Everyone's got an online footprint nowadays."

"But I'm really careful about that," she replied. "I keep my profile completely private, I never accept friend requests, and I have a policy of never ever posting pictures of my face – I mean, I'll do vague stuff, like scenery, or flowers – my foot even, but that's hardly an identifying feature – and my address isn't anywhere online – I mean, maybe it is, but there has to be fifty or a hundred Louise Laceys in Dublin – it's not like it's a highly unusual name – even *I've* met another Louise Lacey – so how did he find me? How did he narrow me down in such a short space of time unless he's got some creepy way of doing it?"

Joe shrugged. "Maybe he's really good with computers? I assume he'd be used to, I dunno, tracking down antique stock and what have you – maybe he just used some of his same techniques?"

"Exactly," Louise replied. "Creepy stalking – not very GDPR friendly, is it? I mean he called to my house – if I'd let him in, who knows what he would have done? That's why I'm worried about Tash – there's just something so *off* about him."

Joe worried a piece of bacon from between his teeth with his tongue as he stared out the window and thought.

"What if he's just a bit strange?" he suggested cautiously. "No, hear me out – what if he's just an odd little man with an odd little way of presenting himself to the world but, in fact, he came to your house to get the photos back and maybe spare you from what – you know – what's been going on? What if the ... *spirits* ... or whatever, are dangerous? And he knows about them – maybe that's why he didn't want the camera sold, because it's dangerous? Maybe he's their – I dunno – *wrangler*, or something?"

Louise seemed to think about it. "I don't know," she said, slumping against the back of her chair. "There's so much absolutely crazy shit going on in my life at the moment that I just ... I don't know up from down anymore. I mean, you're probably right – Tash probably went home to her own comfy bed, or she's having a lovely laugh with all her mates, completely unaware her phone battery's dead, or she's deep in analysis with her fellow ghost hunters and charging it up ..."

"Using spirit energy," quipped Joe.

"Using spirit energy," she repeated, allowing herself to smile.

"I've gone and got myself in a tizz now," she said. "Which is typical me, and I won't be able to rest until I know what the deal is, except I'll probably never figure this out ..."

"Unless we just go back to the shop and ask him."

The suggestion hung in the air.

"Ask him what?" said Louise. "Hello, Mr Temple, can you tell us what system you use for stalking women so effectively? And would you like your ghosts back?"

"And where *exactly* do you get your trainers?" Joe continued, smirking as Louise rolled her eyes in an attempt to appear as though she wasn't laughing.

"No – how about we just ask him out straight how he found you? If he's doing something illegal and we spot it, *then* you can jump to, and call the gardaí. We can, however, also let him know that, by the way, we found his photos and wondered if he knew there was anything strange about them at all, *nudge nudge, wink wink*?"

"And what if he ends up calling the Guards on *us*?" snorted Louise. "We don't even have his bloody photos, not on us anyway."

"Well, then, we just promise to drop them in next time we're passing – I'll improvise – I need to work on my improv. I'll just use Temple for a rehearsal. Look, I'm with you – and he's not that scary – he's only the same height as you for heaven's sakes, you could take him with one hand behind your back! What's the worst that could happen? Maybe he'll do one of those smiles again but you've made it through before – you can face that again, can't you?"

Louise grimaced. "Not sure about that," she smirked. "Oh, I don't know – it's a bit ... *brash* ... or something to just wander in and demand to know how he found out where I lived."

"So, be *brash* then," urged Joe. "What happened to the girl who wasn't going to be afraid of anything anymore? You've stood up to bloody *ghosts* – surely one creepy little man who's *obtained information about you illegally* is easier than that? It won't do you any harm to mark his card and let him know you're onto him – ooh, you could even blackmail him a bit – he doesn't get his photos back until he promises to leave you alone or you go to the police on him?"

Louise chewed her lip.

"Fine. I suppose. Now let's go do this before I change my mind."

They blinked in the sunshine as they left the café, and made their way around the corner and along Quaker Lane at a steady pace.

"I wish I'd never gone in here in the first place now," muttered Louise as she clunked along. "Me and my stupid, misguided sense of nostalgia. Just wanted to check the old place out again, trip down Memory Lane – confront the old demons and all that. I felt ... I dunno ... *drawn back* or something ... aw, *shit* ..." Louise stopped dead just as she reached the bottom step and saw the sign hanging on the door. "It's bloody closed." Carefully, she limped to the top step, peered in through the glass and tried the handle. "*Dammit!*" she spat. "It doesn't say when he'll be back or anything ..."

"Louise."

"He could be gone for ten minutes, or closed for the whole bloody day, for *feck's* sake!"

"*Louise.*"

She turned at the urgency in Joe's voice. "*What?*"

He was down on one knee on the pavement, staring at something on the ground. He looked up at Louise, his face suddenly white.

"*What?*" she urged.

"*This!*" he gasped.

"What's that?" she asked and came down the steps to get a better look.

When she did, she wished she hadn't.

He picked it up and held it out to her.

Her stomach flipped. "Is that ...?" she asked as she took it from him and laid it across her palm for them both to examine.

"It is," he managed.

The plastic fingernail was painfully familiar, gleaming like a penny.

"It's Tash's," he said, looking from the nail to Louise; "She's been here. He lied to us. You were right."

Chapter 46

"It's Dylan, isn't it?"

The name had come to Tash out of the blue as she had stared at him in his half-delirium. He lifted his head at the mention of his name and turned in her direction, trying desperately to focus.

"Dylan Fogarty, right? People are looking for you everywhere – you've been on the news, and all over social media. Your picture's on posters, and lampposts and stuff."

The boy didn't reply. Instead, he allowed his head to flop back against the wall and his eyes rolled. Tash wasn't sure if he understood her at all.

She glanced around the room for what felt like the millionth time, painfully aware that it was now forever burned into her mind, that it would be not just a memory but an *imprint*, seared there for the rest of her life, however long that would be. She shifted position and pressed herself against the wall, trying to get away from the thought. That couldn't possibly happen. This ... *this* was impossible, all of it. That she should be locked in a basement room like this with a half-dead kid whose hands had been *butchered* by an absolute fucking madman. None of this was believable – it was fiction. It couldn't happen to her.

She felt a rush of rage at herself. Why on earth had she gone down the stairs after Temple? It was the most basic bloody safety rule in the book – don't go into dark spaces with strange men – but she had – *why?* Why had she been so *stupid?*

"*My freeend …*"

The words were slurred and drawn out. Tash looked back at the boy and was filled again with pity and revulsion.

She studied his face which was barely recognisable from that which she had seen on social media and the news reports, but undeniably him. He was striking – tall, slightly feminine-looking, with long red hair and high cheekbones – he'd done some modelling, she remembered. In the pictures they'd used of him everywhere he'd been looking moody and windswept in tweeds and Aran sweaters by the sea. They'd caught her attention – he was from a good part of town, middle-class, nice parents, nice school – how he had ended up like this?

"M'freeend," he mumbled again.

"Hi, Dylan," Tash said. "Yes, I'll be your friend if you want."

He shook his head as best he could. "No," he said.

"No?" repeated Tash. "Okay. You're the boss."

Her reply seemed only to agitate him. "*No. M'freeend … here … gone.*" With great effort, he tried to sit up a little straighter and open his eyes to look around.

Tash, confused, followed suit. "No, Dylan, there's no

one else here. Did Temple put you down here?"

He nodded, exhausted, but trying desperately to focus. "*Me. An' m'friend*," he managed. "*Daddy Long Legs*."

Oh, for fuck's sake, thought Tash, rolling her eyes in exasperation. Just as she thought she was getting sense out of him. She reminded herself that he was sick, injured, probably suffering a massive infection – no wonder he'd befriended a spider.

"No spiders here today, Dylan," she said, and rubbed her hands over her face.

"*Noooo* ..." His response was emphatic. "*Big fellah, he was here. Patrick sum'n.*"

Tash looked at him again. That almost made sense.

"*The fellah upstairs ... pulled him out ... haven't seen him since. Who're you?*"

So, he was more lucid than she'd thought. "I'm Tash," she replied. "Are you saying there was someone else here, Dylan?"

The boy nodded and leaned back against the wall again, exhausted. "*My head ... I can't think ...*" He gave another gentle sob.

"How long have you been here, Dylan?" Tash probed.

He shrugged feebly. "*Dunno ... m'hands ... my fuckin' hands ... look ... it hurts so bad ...*"

Shit, thought Tash. "I know, Dylan," she said gently. "Try not to think about that. We have to figure out how to get out of here, don't we?" She regretted saying it as soon as the words were out of her mouth, but she'd had to say something – she hoped she hadn't given him hope that she couldn't deliver on.

"Actually – my friends know I was coming here," she remembered. "Once I'm gone a while, they'll check – I'm sure they'll find us then." Would they, though? Would anyone look for her? Would anyone even imagine her being in a bloody soundproofed basement, led there by her own bloody stupidity? She squeezed her eyes shut and groaned.

"*Thirsty*," moaned Dylan.

"Me too."

"*Water ...*"

She clenched her fists. "I don't have any, Dylan, I'm sorry."

"Water," he repeated, more insistently.

"Stop asking me for water," she said crossly.

"No, there!"

She opened her eyes and looked at him. He was nodding at something in the shadows over by the wall beside her. She turned to see a bottle of water, lying on its side against the wall.

"Kicked it ... rolled away ... my water."

It seemed he was growing more lucid as time passed.

"Oh, I'm sorry. I'll get it now."

Tash picked it up and approached him, her stomach churning as she got closer.

"I'm sorry," he said. "I stink."

"It's no problem," she managed, holding her breath.

"No – so out of it ... I'm not like this ..."

She looked into his eyes which looked directly back into hers. He seemed so helpless.

"I know," she whispered, crouching down in front of him.

"So thirsty," he said.

She made to hand it to him, then stopped – realising as she did that her own mouth was dry. She glanced at the bottle in her hand.

She knew, ashamed, that once Dylan had taken it, she wouldn't be able to stomach drinking from it herself. She unscrewed the lid. She took a long slug, and then held it out to him.

"Sorry," she said. "I couldn't help myself."

He didn't reply, just opened his mouth and she held the bottle to it, holding her breath as she poured in what she could, save for what ran down his cheeks and chin.

"My mate ..."

She winced as he swiped a bandaged stump across his lips.

"Was here. Took him upstairs, said he was gonna take a photo. He musta let him go. Maybe he'll let us go too."

"Maybe," Tash said, closing the lid on the bottle before retreating back to her patch of the floor. She considered the fact that someone else had been here – but who? Another missing person? She racked her brain – there were missing persons notices every day on Facebook – it could have been anyone, or no one – she couldn't remember anyone else. Only Dylan had stood out, because of how he looked. A sudden chill descended on her as she thought of something.

"Dylan, how long was Patrick here with you?"

He gave another of his shrugs. "Long Legs? The whole time, I think. Only gone ... could be a coupla days ... I don't know anymore."

"Why do you call him that? You said Daddy Long Legs earlier?"

Dylan gave a snort that might have been laughter. "Nickname. Tall fellah," he said. "Really tall. Sold gear to the lads at school."

"Dylan, did you say that the man upstairs wanted to take his picture or something?"

He nodded.

"And Patrick – Daddy Long Legs – didn't come back after that?"

There was no response this time.

"Dylan, you have to stay awake!" Tash tried her best to inject urgency into her tone, but it was becoming so hard ... she was starting to feel so tired herself. "Was it the guy upstairs who ... hurt your arms?"

He responded with the faintest shrug.

"Did he ... say anything about ... taking *your* photo? Thish ... is ... 'mportant, Dyln ..." She was slurring her own words now.

Again, the boy didn't respond. His head had slumped onto his shoulder.

Tash, too, felt weak. She needed to think, but it was so confusing ... this seed of an idea ... a tall friend of Dylan's – another boy? Surely not – if two schoolboys had gone missing together then they'd both have been in the news. No – the Daddy Long Legs character – Dylan said he'd sold gear – drugs. Tall – and Temple had taken his picture – and let him go? Her eyes strayed to Dylan again. Feminine features, high cheekbones, long, thick hair – at a glance, he could pass for a girl.

And now he had no hands.

Jesus, no, thought Tash, her head starting to spin with the force of the realisation.

A girl with no hands.

And a tall man.

And a buxom girl.

My buxom girl. Temple had skipped over it deftly, but

357

she'd known it wasn't right when he'd said that. *A buxom girl.* She'd thought it herself, and Joe had seen it too – and Temple – he'd looked at her and said she reminded him of someone ...

Tash thought she might vomit suddenly and made to scramble to her feet. She had to get out of there – had to get them both out of there. *Special pictures.* The special box. She had to get up ... but she couldn't ... her head spun, and her legs turned to jelly. Something ... something powerful drifted through her veins ... this wasn't right ... what the hell?

She glanced over at Dylan who appeared to be unconscious, and then her eye caught the bottle of water – they'd both drunk from it. Panic gripped her, but there was nothing she could do about it.

She moaned as she slumped against the wall and the world turned black.

Chapter 47

"What are we doing here?" Joe asked.

He had followed Louise down the lane that ran alongside the Temple Antiques building – Quaker Alley, the sign read. She had stopped at a set of iron railings across the entrance to a small underground parking space to the rear of the building.

"The radio station had a couple of cars – branded Citroen Dyanes – which they kept in those parking spaces through there," she said, peering through the bars. "Here ... just let me try something ..." She brushed past him to a keypad set into the wall. "I'm pretty sure this won't work ..." She punched in a four-number code.

There was, however, a sudden, loud squeak, followed by a clink and Louise stood back in surprise as a section of the railings popped open.

"*Shitting hell*," she observed, shocked. "The station's been gone for years – and they never changed the gatecode? How stupid is that?"

Joe looked from the gate to Louise in alarm. "Pretty stupid. Speaking of which, you're not going in there, are you?"

She pushed the gate open and stepped carefully through. "I just want to see."

"See what?" hissed Joe, following her.

"I don't know ..." She glanced behind her and then proceeded to make her way down into the parking area where a small navy-blue van was parked in front of a heavy fire-escape door.

She rattled the handle, but nothing budged. "Not stupid enough to leave the back door open though," she said with a sigh.

Joe raised an eyebrow. "No. I wouldn't imagine so. Look, Louise, we need to go back out there and wait for Temple to come back –"

"*And what? Talk to him?*"

Joe was taken aback.

"*So he can lie to us again?*" she went on. "He's the one who told us Tash hadn't been in when she had – unless there's another woman in Dublin with identical acrylic nails who just wandered past and happened to lose one right outside the very shop Tash told us she was going to, coincidentally at the exact same time that Tash told us she was going there?" She paused and searched his face. "This man stalked me to my house to get back photographs of dead people. A sensory-deprived gnat could tell he's a creep. I don't like him and I don't trust him – talking to him will get us nowhere."

"Okay, okay!" said Joe, studying the lane behind them to see if they were being observed. "But what do you suggest we ... *Jesus Christ!*" He whipped around sharply as the sound of a loud thump echoed around the car park, followed by a second thump and a smash.

Louise stood back and let some of the glass of the

window she had just shattered with her crutch fall to the ground.

"*What in the name of God are you doing?*" he hissed.

"I don't know. I actually haven't a clue, but I've done it now." She used the crutch to knock out the jagged pieces of glass that remained around the frame. "It's just the toilets," she said calmly. "The gents', I think."

Joe pressed his hands to the top of his head. "*Just the toilets*," he mimicked. "It's breaking and entering – if anyone rings the Guards ..."

"Then we just tell them the truth and see if they'll help but, in the meantime, I've broken this now and I may as well be hanged for a sheep as a lamb. Luckily it's a fair-sized ordinary window, not one of those tiny little high-up ones they often have in toilets. Right – I'm going in for a look around – you don't have to come if you don't want to."

"*This is insane!* What if Temple comes back and catches you? What if an alarm goes off?"

"If there was one, I'm damn sure it would be going off by now. In my day, the alarm never worked. The overnight staff dismantled it once because it kept triggering and knocking the station off air at night. If the gate code hasn't been changed, I hope the alarm hasn't been fixed either. But listen – not a peep – so far so good."

"But Temple –"

"Jesus Joe, you're sounding like me now." Louise even managed to smirk as she glanced over her shoulder at him. "Give me a leg-up on the sill – I'll be in and out in no time. I just want to see."

"I don't even know who you *are* anymore," he replied, his eyes wide with alarm, but he boosted her up onto the sill.

"Good stuff. Wait there – I'll be back in a minute."

"You've got to be kidding me. I'm not letting you go in there alone."

He held her steady as she leaned in, observed her surroundings, then withdrew and put her good leg in, before following through, aided by her crutch.

"We'll get it done twice as fast then," she said as he followed. "We'll be out in a flash, no harm done, and I'll be able to rest easy."

"Well, that's the most important thing, isn't it?" sighed Joe sarcastically.

"They called this *Basement Jacks*," she said. "After the band. The jocks – the presenters – all thought that was hilarious."

Joe wrinkled his nose at the yellowing sinks and urinals as they made their way out into a dark passageway.

Louise fumbled in her pocket and held up her phone, tapping it to activate the torch. Across the corridor from them was a large blacked-out window and a heavy wooden door.

"Production 2," Louise continued. "Used at busy times, or for Comm Prod during Station Re-Imaging and stuff ..."

"I don't actually understand a word you're saying."

"Sorry. It's one of the studios. I'm babbling. Nervous."

"We *could* just leave."

"We're here now. There's the lift – I think we're best avoiding that. Those stairs there lead up to the antique shop and then there's two floors above – it won't take long to have a quick look."

"For what, though? You don't really think Tash is still in here, do you?"

Louise sighed in frustration and stopped on the bottom step of the stairs. "No – I don't know, Joe. I just want to see. Can we just do it quickly, please?"

He didn't respond, and she turned and resumed her ascent of the stairs regardless.

At the landing on the ground floor, she raised a finger to her lips, and they paused for a moment, listening for movement in the shop itself.

"No one there," she whispered.

"You're sure?" he mouthed, glancing nervously at the closed door.

She nodded. "Okay. To speed things up, I'm going to head up to the top floor – the old studios, Production 1, the Chief Exec's office. Why don't you just have a glance around the first floor – it's just offices – accounts and S&P?"

"What the fuck's S&P?" hissed Joe.

"Sponsorship and Promotions," she replied crossly. "Not that it's even those things anymore – look, it doesn't matter – let's just do it and get out of here. I'm not sure how much longer my nerve will hold."

"It's lasted longer than mine," Joe replied, as they turned and began to climb again until they reached the next floor and faced a door painted bright green.

"You're heading through there," she instructed him softly. "I'll do upstairs and come straight down again and meet you – there should be plenty of places to hide if you need to – the offices are interconnected all the way around leading back to the reception area so you can even go in a circle if someone comes in – does that make sense?"

"*None of this makes sense*," hissed Joe in return. "You owe me for this."

"I owe you for a lot," she replied, and flashed him a smile. "Now go!"

With that, she disappeared upwards.

Joe watched her go for a bit, before doing as he was told and pushing open the door to the offices.

The smell of damp was the first thing that hit him – that earthy wetness. The space he stepped into was bare, the floor covered in what had once been a bright-green carpet. The outline of some long-gone lettering – '*Emerald FM*' – could be read on the wall opposite. It was dim, but not entirely bereft of natural light which came through glass panels in the doors to his left and his right from the rooms beyond. He hesitated as he chose which one to enter, momentarily stumped as he wondered again what the hell he was doing here at all. His hand found its way inside his jacket pocket however, and he ran his thumbnail over the smoothness of the tip of his sister's acrylic nail, his stomach suddenly giving a lurch. That was why, he told himself. At least Louise thought it was a valid why. He didn't know if he agreed or not but, as she said herself, he was here now. May as well do what he was told.

He chose to go through the door on the right, for no other reason than the nail was in his right pocket. Did it really make a difference, he wondered, as he opened the door into a much brighter room with long sash windows that overlooked the street below, through which sunlight streamed. He looked around – the only sign of furniture, the occasional indentation in the carpet, and the darker rectangular patches over by the windows that indicated the presence of a now-departed desk. Hopefully all the rooms would be as bare as this, Joe thought. He didn't have to do any of this, of course. He was only the sodding painter, after all – so why was he here running round after his sister at the behest of a tiny, angry, confusing woman whose house he was simply supposed to freshen up? Well, precisely *because* of the angry, confusing, lovely little woman, if he was honest. He rolled his eyes at himself. His crushes never got him anywhere, never had. And this one seemed to be heading toward even more trouble than usual.

He pushed his way through a door at the back that led into the parallel room – a mirror image of the one he had just been in. Nothing to see here either – literally nothing. Right then, he'd go back out and wait for her.

He charged back out to the reception area, half hoping that she would be there already, but he was disappointed. He tutted impatiently and leaned against the door he'd just come through. How long was she bloody well going to take up there? Surely their luck couldn't hold out much longer – and if they were caught, exactly how much trouble would they be in? Would he need a solicitor? Jesus, but his dad would *murder* him.

It was then that he spotted a door that he'd missed – easily enough, in his defence – as it had been to his back when he'd walked into the reception area. He tried the handle, assuming that it would be locked, but he was wrong. A bolt of fear shot through him when it opened easily in his hands. *Shit*, he thought. What the hell was he going to find in here? With trembling hands, he fished his phone from his pocket and shone the torch in.

It must have been a stationery cupboard once, he

reckoned, the walls lined with shelves from top to bottom and just enough space for a person to walk between them. There was no stationery there now. Instead, it was a sort of stock cupboard, he surmised, filled with a host of oddities. He tensed as he moved the light around and tried to take it all in – on the top and middle shelves, masks – huge, terrifying tribal things fringed with feathers and straw – a long, metal arm with a claw-like hand gripping the edge of a shelf – the artificial eyes of a stuffed cat flashed as he slid the light over it – a pair of small dolls with open stomachs, revealing tiny, anatomically correct organs inside – empty bird cages containing dark, fossilised shapes – a bell jar within whose dusty glass a yellowing ferret stood on its hind legs, eye to eye with a stuffed finch on a twig – a wooden leg – a box, its lid ajar, in which what appeared to be a glass eye glinted. This was where all of the stuff that was too terrifying to sell in the shop was kept, then.

He lowered the torch beam to floor level, illuminating more practical, mundane things – cardboard boxes and plastic tubs with lids, tucked in out of the way. He peered closer – what a bizarre collection of things – a couple of transparent five-litre containers of a clear, yellow-tinted liquid, a toolbox, a tray of bottled water with five or six plastic bottles remaining, what looked like the blade of a circular saw, a suitcase ...

Joe slammed the door shut suddenly, not wishing to see any more. Maybe Louise was right and there really was something disturbing about Temple. He stood with his back against the door, waiting for the hammering in his chest to subside. Where *was* bloody Louise anyway? It was ridiculous, this entire endeavour. What did they think they were going to achieve? That was it. He was finished.

His head down, heart still thumping, he made for the door that led back out to the stairs, determined to just go up there, get Louise, and get them both out safely. There was no need for anyone to know who had been there – as for the broken window, well, he'd just have to have that on his conscience. There was nothing could be done about it after all. But that was it – that was all the harm they were going to do, and those ... things in the cupboard – well, that was all he was going to see – no more.

He had grasped the door handle firmly, and tensed himself to pull it, when something made him stop, something that chilled him far more than what he had seen in the cupboard.

The sound of Louise somewhere above. Screaming.

Chapter 48

It was dark on the top floors. It hadn't always been – Louise remembered that windows had looked out over the city, letting light flood through what had once been attics and servants' quarters. So what had happened? She had to use the torch on her phone from the moment she turned at the top landing and entered through the heavy green doors. There had been a keycode panel here once too but it was gone now, and the door had swung open easily. She hesitated for a moment, fearful. Then she took a deep breath and forced herself on.

She knew this place like her own home – every inch of it familiar in her mind. Just a quick look, and then she'd have done it. It occurred to her suddenly that this whole fool's errand had become about her, not about Tash, nor about Temple – not entirely. It was as if she needed desperately to prove something to herself. But what? That she could do something illegal? Creep about in the dark? Invade the space of someone who had invaded hers? There were easier challenges she could have picked, she admitted to herself.

She shone her torch up and down the corridor where

she stood and turned first toward the office at the end which had belonged to the Programme Director. The torchlight lit her path along the familiar bright-green carpet – garish, but in keeping with the company logo and artwork.

She wrinkled her nose again as she walked. It absolutely stank up here – a sort of sweet rot, like bags of food waste left to ferment. It was a possibility, she supposed. Another was dead rodents, gross – although unfortunately very possible.

Nothing was decomposing in the former PD's office, at least, she observed gratefully as she shone the light around. It was completely empty, the carpet continuing through from the corridor, the white walls cracked and peeling. She shone her torch upwards toward the skylight to see that the glass had been painted over with black paint – so that explained the darkness – and that it was circled with ring of black mould. She grimaced again, wondering if Temple had responsibility for the entire building or just for the shop? It had certainly come a long way from the crisp, well-maintained decor that she remembered on this floor – how quickly it had all decayed.

She slipped from the room, and doubled back on herself, heading toward the office at the opposite end of the corridor. The territory of the big boss – the station owner. His had been the deluxe suite – a much bigger office, with a small area out front for his PA, and his own comfortable space partitioned off for privacy. Now it was bare, stinking and damp too.

The former conference room was the same, as was the small office that the show production teams used, the windows all blacked out – a crude attempt at keeping the sun off the carpets, perhaps? There was nothing to see up here, after all. She decided she'd glance into the remaining studios anyway – almost as much for old time's sake as anything, really, and then she'd just go, get Joe and get out.

She wondered how he was doing downstairs as she made her way to the smaller of the two studios – Production 1 – and took a moment to mentally appreciate him. He had no need to be there – he could get into tremendous trouble for it too – yet he was there, and for her. For Tash too, of course – a flash of worry crossed her mind as she pictured the fingernail they had found.

It took her a moment to balance her phone in the same hand as her crutch as she put all her strength into opening the outer door to the first studio – now that was proper soundproofing – she'd forgotten how heavy the doors were. She stood against it while she pushed the inner door open.

She had happy memories of this room – the red light over the door indicating that recording was in process and no one should enter, although Amy had never minded when Louise ignored it. Sometimes, Amy would flick the red light on so that she and Louise could enjoy a chat and a coffee undisturbed. The thick-glassed internal window that overlooked the corridor and the offices which she had just checked was now too painted black, as were the specially soundproofed windows that overlooked the roofs of the buildings the opposite side of Quaker Lane, with a glimpse of the Dublin Mountains beyond. Of all the rooms, this was most like it had used to be – the walls covered in red carpet, the ceiling with its layer of hard soundproof foam – even the wooden frame of the old production desk, bereft of equipment of course, still stood in place.

Then her heart skipped a beat as the light hit something in the corner opposite, beside the recording booth which still stood there, unoccupied. Something white hanging in the corner. She was relieved to see that it was simply a piece of fabric hung on a metal clothes rack. She crossed the room for a better look – an old-fashioned, high-necked dress hung there. Just old clothes, then. Probably stock for the shop – so Temple did use these rooms after all.

She returned to the door and let herself out carefully, turning next door to her final destination – the broadcast studio. One more to go, she told herself, and pulled the outer door toward her.

The foul smell in the air immediately grew stronger. *Oh wow,* she thought, her hand flying to cover her nose. *Someone's left rubbish in here – and not recently either.* For a moment, she pondered just leaving this one. Instead, she held her breath and entered, shining her torch in to light her way. This room was different from how she remembered it.

The first thing different were the curtains that had been pulled across the window. Louise frowned. They had never been there before – deep red, heavy velvet drapes.

The bed was next, right in the centre of the room, covers rumpled. So someone slept here – was it Temple? Was this where he *lived*?

She hurriedly swung the light back across the room, toward the back wall, where a trestle table stood, laden with items – bottles of water, dirty towels – and ... how strange ... an incongruously modern, expensive camera.

She moved the light again – back toward the centre, just a little in front of the trestle table – what was that there? She felt the colour drain from her face as she recognised it – another camera, *her* camera – the antique – all set up as if it were to be used with the bellows extended and aimed at the cast-iron bed. She felt herself starting to tremble as she followed its direction.

The tremble became uncontrollable – how had she missed it at first glance?

The bed ... the covers weren't rumpled at all ... it was a shape ... dear God, no – there was someone *on* it ...

She tried to convince herself it was a dummy at first – it couldn't be a person ... couldn't *possibly* be ...

But it was. A man – a tall man – lay on the bed, completely still, dressed in black – a priest's soutane. Beside him, on a table, a wilted rose dangled over the side of a bud vase, a thick book – the Bible presumably – sat beside it. Beads were wound around his fingers.

It wasn't an exact replication, but it was close enough ...

A tall, young priest – at least, a man dressed as a priest – had or was to have his portrait taken.

His death portrait.

She shone the torch, still trembling, along the body, praying that it was fake – a mannequin for the shop, dressed for display. But when she came to the face, lit by the harsh beam of the phone, looking like he might open his eyes and look at her at any second, she gasped. It was real – it was a real body – and, horrifying, the jaw dropped open in a hideous expression of surprise, revealing filthy brown teeth. And the skin was mottled and discoloured. She could see enough of the hair to know that it was dirty brown and straggly, enough of the nails on the bony hands to make out filth under them, the fingers stained yellow with tobacco.

It was then that she screamed.

For a moment – or a lifetime – everything was a blur.

First, she was in that room, staring at the corpse on the bed, trying to understand what she saw – then she was back out in the dark corridor, still screaming – then Joe was there, and she tried to explain what she had seen, but the words wouldn't come, so she simply pointed at the door of the studio. Then Joe went to look for himself and there were retching sounds in the darkness – then arms around her – safe, warm arms, and hot breath in her hair, and the feel of a living heart next to where her face was buried ...

And then, from nowhere, the smell of lilies. Surrounding her, stronger than ever, stronger than she'd ever smelled them in her house, overwhelming the rotting stink of the body, stifling the panic and the terror and calming her down to enable her to think ... then gone again.

"We have to go," she said, the words muffled against Joe's chest where he still crushed her to him. She pushed herself free. "We *have* to go, Joe. We can't get caught here. We have to go fast ..."

Joe looked down at her, barely able to make her out in the darkness. He struggled at first to speak but finding no words he simply nodded.

She wrenched herself free from his arms, and staggered, slamming her crutch to the floor to balance against. She realised that her phone was gone – she must have dropped it – but that didn't matter now. All that

373

mattered was getting out, calling the Guards – telling them they had found a body – she could worry about everything else then.

She lunged for the door back out to the stairs, worried that she wouldn't be able to make it down as quickly as she needed, when an idea struck her. It was most likely pointless, she knew, but she felt in the dark along the wall beside the door anyway, working her trembling fingers around until they found what she sought. She jabbed at the button of the lift and suddenly – miraculously it seemed – the doors *whooshed* open slowly and a weak light flooded from it out into the corridor. Louise heard Joe gasp, and for the briefest moment, she hesitated. But still she did it. She grabbed him by the arm, and half plunged, half fell into the lift, hitting the button marked B for Basement and praying silently for the doors to close and take them away from that horrendous sight.

To her amazement, it worked. The doors slid slowly shut, and everything was still for a moment – longer than she'd have liked. But then, with a great lurch and a groan, it began to slowly descend. Louise looked at Joe just as a weak smile of hope spread across her features. They could do it. They could really do it – they could get out of there. The number on the wall panel flashed to 1, and the descent continued, slowly but surely ... they were almost there, they had almost made it ...

Until the descent started to slow a little, then a little more. Surely not yet, thought Louise, and glanced at the panel. They were slowing – but that was okay, wasn't it? It would just slow down the closer they got and then they'd be there ... all clear ...

Her brain felt as though it might explode as the lift suddenly lurched to a stop.

G. *Ground Floor.*

They were only on the Ground Floor. The shop. She reached out to jab the button again, just as the doors very slowly slid open.

And outside stood Adrian Temple.

Louise and Joe watched in horror as he stepped into the lift, turned his back to them, and leaned against the doorframe. The lift door nudged him as it attempted to close itself, then retreated, and didn't try again. The silence in the small space was palpable from the faint juddering of Louise's breathing.

"It looks like you're lost."

Louise and Joe exchanged a panicked look.

"I *should* call the gardaí," he continued. "Have you arrested for trespassing – because as far as I'm aware, you two left my shop before I did – yet somehow, here you are, back inside again, but in my house this time. I could have you arrested for breaking and entering – searched for stolen items – you'd would be in a lot of trouble. However, if I'm correct, I've found you on your way *down* in my lift, indicating that you've been *up*, poking your noses where you shouldn't have been. And, I think, unfortunately, you're aware that I won't be calling the Guards to this building any time soon – at least until I've had the chance to ... tidy up a little. So it appears we have to figure out a way to deal with this between ourselves."

He turned slowly and looked them up and down.

"So how *did* you get in? And whatever for? *Are* you here to rob me? There's plenty of stuff on the shop floor – you didn't have to go searching for hidden treasure."

"*There's a fucking dead body up there!*" yelled Joe, unable to contain himself. "*And you've dressed him up!*"

Temple shrugged and nodded. "Dead *vermin*, to be fair," he remarked. "I think there's a special place in hell reserved for drug dealers and their customers. They're certainly not missed here on earth, that's for certain."

"You're using him to copy the photograph!" gasped Louise.

To her surprise, Temple smiled.

"You recognised it," he said. "I am indeed – all of this made possible because of you, actually – thank you very much, Louise Lacey."

"I had nothing to do with it ..." But it dawned on her that she did – he'd told her as much, that returning the camera enabled him to take on a project that he'd wanted to do for a long time. "You're sick!" she spat. "If I'd known – if I'd had a clue –"

"You'd have done what? Called the Guards yourself? I doubt you'd have got very far." At that, he stepped into the lift, and closer to them. The door slid shut behind him. Temple calmly pressed the button marked B, and stood, his hands in his pockets, looking at his feet as the lift clunked down to the final floor.

Joe tensed as they slowed for the final time – he had half a notion to run at Temple when the doors opened, tackle him, knock him aside so that they could get out.

"I wouldn't, sir," said Temple calmly. He raised his head slowly and looked at Joe directly, shaking his head, just as the lift pinged and stopped.

Surprised, Joe froze and watched as Temple withdrew his hand from his pocket, holding something – a sports bottle. He popped the lid open carefully, leaving the nozzle exposed and held it up in the air just as he stepped backwards out of the lift, leaving his foot against the door this time to keep it open.

"I'm not a big man, I know – what is your name, anyway?" he said.

Joe looked at Louise and back at Temple. "Joe," he said.

"Joe," repeated Temple. "Disappointing. I thought you'd be a *Dean* or a *Steve* or something sort of *hunky* seeing as you're the boyfriend character. *Joe.*" He thrust the bottle closer to him and aimed the nozzle directly at his face. "So I keep some of this handy. At best it'll just burn your skin – very, very badly. If it gets in your eye or your mouth though – you might be in a little more trouble then. Don't think I'm bluffing you with Ballygowan, by the way. Now come out here. And please, for your own sake, don't try running off anywhere to be the hero, either of you. I only have to run as fast as whichever one of you is slowest – doesn't matter to me which one I catch up with first. And one of you is using a crutch ..."

He swung the bottle suddenly from Joe's face to Louise's, and she screamed. The briefest smile flickered across Temple's face, and he took a step backwards.

Carefully, he retreated from the lift and out into the corridor,. Obediently, Louise followed – although for a few seconds she contemplated staying in the lift and trying to go back up, but she left it a second too long, and, as her stomach sank, the door whooshed shut, leaving all three of them standing momentarily in the darkness of the basement corridor, until Temple flicked a switch and a bare bulb on the ceiling threw a pale light over them.

Temple used the bottle to herd them, ushering them closer to him, and then indicated that they should stand just outside the room called Production 2, just opposite the door of the toilets where they had entered. It was so close – they could even feel a cold breeze wafting under the toilet door and along the passage from the window they had broken. Escape was so, *so* close – just a matter of feet to get to freedom ... but how?

The urge rose in Louise again to just run, to take the chance, but who was she kidding? She had no doubt that Temple would spray Joe with whatever was in the bottle, and then turn on her. If she could just run fast enough, though ... who was she kidding? Even if she were fast, she wasn't brave enough, and even if Joe had bravery enough for both of them – she stole a glance at his pale face – she couldn't risk it – for either of them.

Instead, they stood, eyes fixed on Temple as he reached for a key hanging on the frame of the studio door. He watched them, the entire time, keeping the bottle trained on each of them in turn, and inserted the key smoothly into the lock.

"What are you going to do to us?" Louise blurted suddenly.

Temple thought for a moment. "I don't actually know," he replied. "I haven't had time to think yet – it's not like I was planning my day around finding two people snooping around my building." His tone grew increasingly annoyed. "And it's not like I didn't have enough to do today already – *and* not like you haven't delayed me enough by taking my great-great-grandfather's camera when it wasn't for sale, Miss Lacey, and then keeping the most vital component from me.

We're all just going to have to wait and see until I figure things out, aren't we? Now – would you both step in there for the time being."

He pulled open the outer door of the disused production studio and nodded at the inner one. Louise froze.

"What's in there?" she demanded. "More women that you've stalked?"

Temple looked genuinely taken aback for a moment, and then laughed. "You mean *you* – you're saying that I stalked *you* ... but you more or less *told* me where you lived – you may as well have drawn me a map, in fact – once my assistant overheard you say where you lived, it was a click and a stroll to find you."

Louise still regarded him in confusion.

"Oh, come *on*," he said, frustrated. "Your neighbours have a very distinctive campervan, Louise, and it made for a lovely Facebook – ghastly thing – profile picture."

The campervan. How could she be so stupid?

"And no, I don't stalk women but if someone has something belonging to me, I'm damn well going to find them to get *my* property back. My blueprints – my templates. Now inside, please – I don't have time to discuss this."

"You hurt the guy upstairs," Louise said. "When did you do that? And how?"

"*Louise.*"

She ignored Joe's interruption. "What's the deal with the photographs in the box? Why recreate one of them?"

"Not just one." Temple snorted suddenly, as if she were an idiot.

"*Louise!*" Joe's voice was more urgent, but she didn't want to stop – she couldn't.

"You're kidding – please tell me there aren't more ..."

"Not yet ..."

"*Louise!*"

"*Jesus Christ!*"

It was only then that she saw what Joe was trying to do – not, in fact, to stop her stalling Temple, but to draw her attention to something else, something behind the man. She watched, fascinated and fearful, as the air at the bottom of the stairs seemed to grow denser, the dimness thickening, lengthening, taking shape.

Behind Temple, the figure of a person manifested. It was a tall man, dressed in a black soutane, with long, straggling hair.

It was the man from upstairs.

And behind him, peeling away from the wall came another shadow, even taller, growing clearer as it took the form of a man in identical dress. The original – the tall priest from the box of photographs.

And then another – in front of them both – the small, stocky shape of the dwarf, Baby – and to the side, the full figure of a large girl in a shift ... and before her a small child, gazing straight ahead through her one good eye.

Louise took a step back, unable to comprehend what was happening before her eyes, just as a familiar scent greeted her nostrils and, at the very top of the stairs, she saw Maud, white and glowing against the great, dark mass that had gathered down along the steps.

"What are you doing?" growled Temple. "Don't move."

Louise ignored him, reaching out instead for Joe's hand.

"Do you see them?" he whispered, his voice a mix of wonder and sheer terror.

She could only nod, trying her best to see them all, to look at every one of them individually, recognise and bear witness to them.

"*Did your great-great-grandfather kill his subjects?*" she whispered at Temple, who was completely oblivious to the gathering behind them.

"*How dare you!*" he bit back, shaking the bottle at her. "Samuel Temple was an artist of his time, journaling grief, recording it for posterity. Some of his subjects were in a state of great suffering, of course, some required assistance to release them from earthly trials and pain ... but that was not Samuel's fault. He worked tirelessly to assist and celebrate and honour the dead in a time when death was not something to fear. To be immortalised in death, restored to how you were, or transformed into what you longed to be ... well, that was something to which one aspired – something that took you beyond your petty, earthly bounds – made you *better, worthy*. Even a filthy drug dealer can be elevated – even vindicated – by such things. Immortality, cleansing of the soul – all can be purified if memorialised in the perfect, proper way .... Samuel could do that – *I* can do that!"

A great surge rippled through the group of phantoms behind him. Still, Temple didn't notice them. They even made a noise now – the faintest whisper, so quiet that it barely existed, but, Louise knew, contained the voices and prayers and accusations of every single one of them. She turned her head a little to hear it better, and as she did it seemed to increase in volume, louder, and then louder still, rising until it sounded like a river rushing over rocks. Louder and louder, until Louise couldn't stop herself and dropped Joe's hand to cover an ear and block out the whispered cacophony of long-forgotten voices.

It was only then that Temple paled, and tilted his own head, as if finally hearing something that was very distant. The hand holding the sports bottle flagged for a brief second, until he caught himself and aimed it again with purpose. It seemed, in that brief second, as if he was somehow determined *not* to hear anything.

Louise stared at him, bewildered. How could he not hear that noise? The rush, like a violent wind through a forest of trees ...

"*Don't!*" yelled Temple.

For a second, Louise couldn't tell if the order was barked at her and Joe for flinching, or at the growing roar behind him. He *had* to hear it now, she thought. It was inescapable, deafening, and growing louder and louder until it reached an unmerciful crescendo ...

And then – sudden silence.

The eyes of the dead all continued to stare at Temple – *into* Temple – but no more sound came. Louise watched, sick with anticipation at what might come next, waiting, waiting ... She blanched as she realised that she was relying on the spirits on the stairs to ... to what? To rescue them somehow? But such a thing was impossible – they were just shadows, intangible – as capable of rescuing two living, breathing humans as a summer breeze. They could do nothing. And still Temple stood there. He had displayed no glimmer of shame, just purpose. "*Not just one,*" he'd said of recreating the photographs. He felt no guilt, no fear of punishment. He would hurt Louise and Joe – by spraying acid, or whatever was in that bottle – in their faces, or by another means – it didn't make a difference whether or not a million ghosts stood and chanted at him – he was resolute in driving on with whatever sick project he imagined he had to complete.

"*Can't you hear them?*" Joe demanded suddenly.

Something flickered over Temple's features, but he composed himself again. "Hear who?" he replied, his voice wavering.

"The dead," Louise said. "The victims." Maybe, if she made him talk, distracted him from forcing them to enter a room from which they might never emerge ...

"*Pff!*" Temple dismissed Louise's words.

But she could tell by him it was half-hearted. He had heard, he had *definitely* heard.

"They're behind you," she added, staring at them, through the crowd, and up at Maud who seemed to float and shimmer above the rest, smiling down like some beatific vision, giving her *strength* somehow ...

Temple burst out laughing. "You're not at a *pantomime*," he sneered, his voice rising as he grew angrier. "I'm not a *fool*, Louise Lacey – the girl who puts pictures on the internet which led me to her neighbour's door in half an hour. You don't think you were going to keep the special photos, do you? Telling me to my face that I wasn't missing anything? From my camera? My prize possession? I know those people like the back of my hand ..."

And so did she.

"Look – they're all behind you," she said. "I can see them ... Maud, Baby, Adeline, the tall priest – what was his name ... Alistair? Your drug dealer – the *vermin* – is there too – all watching you, judging you ..."

Temple paled, and his head twitched, on the verge of turning to look. "*Shut up!*" he hissed, aiming the bottle and stepping closer to Louise.

"*They are!*" she exclaimed defiantly. "I can see them, every one of them .. and ... oh my God ..." She gasped.

At the bottom of the stairs – or just above it – hovered the woman – the tall, fearsome woman with the stern face – the only living subject in the box of pictures.

And then there was another – a man. A shapeless grey smock reached his ankles, revealing bare feet underneath. His hands were bound behind his back, and a noose was visible around his neck. His face bulged red and purple, every feature distorted. And the eyes – blood ran from them in a mess of red tears down the cheeks, spilling from the blackness at the centre of them.

It was Joe who pointed this time. "*There ... behind you ...*" he gasped.

Temple twitched uncomfortably. "*Stop this!*" he said, visibly forcing himself to stay facing Joe and Louise.

"No – I swear – there's a man – he's been hanged ..."

"And the woman," said Louise, "That woman in the long black dress from the photograph ..."

At that, Temple suddenly froze, his face a mixture of disbelief and fear.

"*It's not,*" he said. "*You're lying. Why couldn't you have just left me alone?*"

And with that he turned, no longer able to resist the urge – and he made a noise, a deep strangled senseless sound as he saw them all there, their eyes fixed on him, their tormented souls watching him. Temple turned back, glancing over his shoulder at Joe and Louise, instinctively making sure that they were still there, still under his control. It was then that Joe was gripped with an instinct of his own. Without thinking, he grabbed

Louise's crutch from her hand, and drove it, with as much force as he could manage, directly into Temple's face.

Then he grabbed Louise's hand and ran.

Chapter 49

The hours that followed were blurred and, always afterwards, out of sequence.

Louise remembered the Guards arriving – one car at first, then more, then vans – blue lights and the crackle of walkie-talkies. She remembered answering questions – maybe once, maybe repeatedly. A catalogue of faces, some kind, some harsh, flashed before her.

Then Tash was being helped down the steps of the shop, wrapped in a blanket and taken to an ambulance – and someone else was carried down on a stretcher – it had to be Temple – the man upstairs was well and truly dead, and didn't the dead come out in zipped-up bags? How badly had Joe injured Temple when he hit him in the face with the crutch? There was so much confusion, so much she couldn't understand – and pictures in her head that she could never erase.

It was close to midnight when a man put his head around the door of the private hospital room where Joe and Louise sat in uncomfortable high-backed armchairs on either side of the bed where Tash lay sleeping.

"Sorry to disturb you," he whispered and came in.

Louise studied him as he introduced himself as John Miller, a plainclothes officer. She observed that he wasn't much older than either of them, and was dressed in a tweed jacket and a pair of navy pants that seemed slightly too short for him when he sat down. Stubble had formed on his chin, and his face was drawn and tired – as was Joe's, she noted, seeing him glance at his sister for the thousandth time since they had been allowed in to sit with her.

"I was hoping to have a chat with all three of you, but I see that your sister is still asleep."

Joe nodded. "They gave her something to help her settle earlier on," he said. "She was pretty disoriented and freaked out when they found her – we were so close to her and never knew she was in that room – I could have got her out ..."

"The docs say that she should probably be fine to go home tomorrow," John Miller said reassuringly. "You were right to get out when you did and raise the alarm."

"Do you know what she was given?" asked Louise, reaching out and gently rubbing Tash's hand.

"The search of the shop and house on Quaker Lane is ongoing. We did find some strong sedatives there, amongst other things."

"Like what?" Louise sat up, her eyes wide. "More bodies? Did you find more bodies?"

Miller extended a hand to calm her. "There were no more bodies, Louise – you've had an awful ordeal, but I can assure you there were no other fatalities."

Louise relaxed a little, but soon tensed again. "But who was brought out on the stretcher?"

"Well, this is what I need to tell you about. We found someone else being held with Natasha. A teenager by the name of Dylan Fogarty. He'd been missing for a couple of weeks, in fact – you might have heard some of the appeals on the news or seen stuff on social media – it was very widely publicised."

Joe nodded, a look of comprehension spreading over his face. "So ... you're saying that Temple had held that boy captive for weeks?"

Gravely, Miller nodded. "It appears so. We don't have all the facts yet – we won't be able to speak to Dylan for a couple of days – he's extremely ill. What we do know is that a small-time drug dealer went missing on the same day he did, and we have an eyewitness who spotted the two of them together on the boardwalk along the Liffey talking with a small man who was wearing distinctive white trainers –"

"That was him! That was Temple!" Louise interrupted. "He always wore those white trainers!"

"Probably, yes. The drug dealer – a guy by the name of Patrick Goode, aka Daddy Long Legs – because of his height – has been identified as the man whose remains you found in the upstairs room."

Louise went white and slumped back in her seat, winded. "Oh God," she whimpered. "I just kept thinking of him as 'the body' – I didn't think beyond that, not to him having a name, or ... *Jesus!*" Her head spun.

"Are you okay, Louise?" Miller asked. "Would you like me to get you some tea or coffee?"

She shook her head.

"I'm sorry," Miller said softly. "I know that this is very distressing for you both, but you're going to see stuff coming out in the news over the next couple of days and I thought it best that you got it from us first. The facts will probably get distorted when you factor in Twitter and what-have-you, so I wanted to talk to all three of you as soon as I could."

"Thanks," said Joe, and glanced again at Tash who had stirred and mumbled.

"Do you want to get the nurse?" Miller asked, nodding at her.

Joe watched her for a second, saw her settle, and shook his head. "She's grand, I think. The nurses have been coming around pretty regularly. I'm just glad it was a sedative she was given, and not something worse, considering that Temple … did he really and truly *murder* a drug dealer? Like – I can't get my head around that – it seems so unreal."

"It's a lot to take in," nodded Miller. "We suspect that Goode was poisoned – the autopsy will confirm that. Dylan Fogarty had been very heavily drugged over a long period of time, presumably to keep him out of it – keep him calm and quiet. He'd been seriously injured, you see – here, actually – this is the kid we're talking about – recognise him?"

Miller took his phone from his pocket and called up a photograph which he passed first to Joe, who shook his head, and then to Louise who gazed at it. Long red hair, windswept, on a stormy beach. It couldn't have looked more stereotypically Irish if he was holding up a tricolour.

"Fogarty did some modelling work," Miller explained. "This was the most recent – for an in-flight magazine thing apparently. He's a pretty distinctive-looking kid. He was known to be sort of cocky, had disposable cash, liked his recreational drugs, and hung around with dodgy types to get them. Poor kid won't be getting much in the line of modelling work anymore, I'd imagine."

"Why's that?" asked Louise, her gaze lingering on the distinctive features of the boy as she passed the phone back to Miller.

"Well, that's another thing I wanted to tell you before you heard it elsewhere. Dylan had been ... mutilated, I suppose. The man you're calling Temple had performed a surgery of sorts, had cut his arms off below the elbow."

Louise's hands flew to cover her eyes. "That's what he meant – *not yet*," she groaned. "If Goode was Alistair, then that poor boy was to be Maud ... the long red hair ... it was as close as he could get! This is all my fault!"

Miller frowned and looked from her to Joe.

"I don't follow," he said, a note of concern creeping into his voice. "You know ... you understand something? How? How is it your fault?"

"The motive for the murder –" Joe began.

"Yes," interrupted Miller. "We're working on the basis that it's revenge. He had dressed Goode in a cassock – our guess is that our perpetrator was perhaps ill-treated by a priest at school, or *perceived* that he had been ill-treated –"

"*No, no, no!*" exclaimed Louise.

Miller sat further forward in his chair.

"That's not what Temple was doing!" she said. "He was copying his great-great grandfather – taking photographs of dead bodies ... people with differences ... disabilities ..."

"We found camera equipment alright, but photographs are usually taken as sort of souvenirs in instances like this – they're not the motive."

Louise balled her hands into fists as she tried to calm herself in order to speak coherently, to try to explain. She opened her mouth to begin, when suddenly a voice came from the bed.

"*My phone,*" Tash slurred.

Joe immediately jumped to her side. "Tash – are you okay?"

Her eyes flickered open for a second before closing again. "*My phone,*" she repeated. "*They're there.*" She struggled to sit upright and Joe shot up, hands on her shoulders to make her lie down again.

"*Stop,*" she croaked. "I'm awake. Where's my phone?"

"I don't know," Joe replied, panicked. "Maybe the nurses took it ..."

"*Backpack,*" mumbled Tash. "Drink of water ..."

"I know, I know," sighed Joe. "You drank something but it's fine now ..."

"No, you *thick*. Give me a drink of water."

Despite herself, Louise snorted and Miller bent his head to hide a smirk, while Joe, taken aback, poured water from the jug on the bedside table into a glass, inserted a straw and held it to his sister's lips.

"It was in my backpack," Tash said once she had swallowed and she tried to sit up again.

This time, Louise reached in and rearranged her pillows to prop her up. "We thought you were still asleep," she said, smiling. "Good to have you back."

"I was just resting my eyes," replied Tash wryly.

"Do you mean this backpack?" Miller asked, holding up another photograph on his phone.

Tash peered at it and nodded.

"Okay," he said. "We thought as much. We found it at the scene – forensics have it right now."

"Get them to check my photos," ordered Tash with as much strength as she could muster. "Passcode is twenty-one zero nine."

Miller frowned. "Can you tell me what we're looking for?"

In response, Tash managed to roll her eyes. "They'll know," she said, as Miller pressed the number on screen and held it to his ear.

Ten minutes later, his phone sounded the *whoosh* of an incoming email, and then another and another. His face, when he opened them, betrayed only a hint of horror, but it was there, as the connections began to dawn on him.

A nurse was called and tea and toast was brought for Tash while someone was sent for coffees for the others.

Little by little, they filled in the blanks as much as they could.

When they had finished, Miller sat, nodding slightly as he took it in, clearly thinking hard.

He was disturbed suddenly by the insistent ringing of his phone and stepped outside to take the call. He returned a few moments later, still finishing up the conversation. "Yeah, that's right – briefing in half an hour – we have new leads. In the meantime, I repeat – as much manpower as you can pull together on this. We need everyone we can get out there searching. Yes. Extremely dangerous. Great. Okay. Thanks for the ID, Ger."

He hung up and looked at Louise and Joe.

"Right, you guys, I've got to take what you told me on this to the team. In the meantime, Lisa, my colleague, is coming to get you transferred to a hotel. If you want to give us keys and addresses and what not, I can send someone to pick stuff up for you from home. Tash – you're covered here for the night. There's one of our lads outside for the duration."

Silence fell over the room as Louise, Joe and Tash looked at him blankly.

"Hotel?" Joe said. "Can we not go home? My parents will be in a state."

"We've had a liaison officer with them already," Miller assured him. "And no, I'm afraid that you can't go home – the man you call Temple –"

"Hang on a sec," Louise interrupted. "You keep saying that – the man we call Temple – is his name not Temple?"

"The man at the centre of this isn't an Adrian Temple," Miller explained. "We're still waiting on DNA results from blood on the crutch you used to hit him for confirmation, but we're pretty sure our guy is called Adrian Furniss, late fifties, formerly a vet in Oxfordshire. Up and disappeared from his home and practice two years or so ago – we're still piecing things together but without going into too much detail we're dealing with someone who leaves us concerned for your safety until he's caught."

"*Caught?*" Tash and Louise spoke simultaneously, the unease on their faces turning to shock.

Miller sighed. "I apologise – I thought someone would have told you."

"Are you saying you let him escape?" demanded Joe,

placing a protective hand on Tash's shoulder.

"I'm so sorry, guys, but we haven't got him – yet. The search is intensive and ongoing but I'm afraid by the time we got there there was no trace of him. He simply wasn't there."

Louise swallowed down the nausea that stirred in her gut as she saw it all happen again.

She wasn't in the least surprised.

Chapter 50

London, 1869

Which will I pick, wondered Bridget. She had always relished this moment – the choosing. The trying on for size. What about Jones? It was easy to blend in as a Jones, although it lacked a certain panache. She glanced around her, scanning the books on the study shelves for inspiration – Mrs Dickens – no. Mrs Griffiths, perhaps? Mrs Browning? Mrs Gaskell? Double-barrelled always sounded aristocratic – Mrs Ainscroft-Worthington, for example. No. Too much. It was the sort of name that had a family history attached – property and the likes. She needed something simpler – a name that would not stand out, but one that was all her own. Because that was her lot now. Save for the boy, she was alone. At last.

And it was wonderful.

Yet another reason why it was time to be on the move again. She was simply too happy.

She was doing her level best, of course – into her third month now of wearing only black. The clocks in the house had not been restarted because, despite the circumstances, the head of the household had passed and that was how it was. And in the manner of the Queen,

Bridget had withdrawn from society – which was no great hardship to a woman who had never taken a place in it. The problem, however, was maintaining the countenance of grief, as was expected of her. A woman as versed in deception as she was, knew that this might well be her undoing if she stayed put. She simply could not manage it. How could anyone in her circumstance?

To the outward eye, it would seem as if she should be in despair – the widow of a murderer, of all things. A hanged man, one whose body lay in lime within the prison walls, not returned to her for proper burial or rites. How ashamed she must be, people would think. And how tragic a circumstance – left with no husband – and for the second time at that – and a fatherless child. How could she bear the grief of it all? She would have to hide her face away until the end of her days and never know another moment's happiness.

But how wrong they were. Bridget allowed herself a moment of quiet glee when she thought of it. Imagine – a woman, such as her, with that unspeakable upbringing, and her troubled past – free at last. No man to trouble her – to bully and boss her and interfere with how she wished to raise her child. No man to make demands of her body, or to dull her brain with his endless boasting and lecturing and so-called male wisdom. She – and no one else – was in charge of her life now. She was owned by no one, unfettered by wifely duties – in control at last, of her life and her destiny. And thanks to her judicious planning, and her fool husband's easy pen, and the idiot police who had believed every word she told them, she was independent, there was money in her purse and a house in her name. Shame be damned – for all of it. She was a wealthy widow. How could one possibly keep a countenance of grief with all of the prospects that brought?

And so it was time. She was ready, even though others were not. In the morning, the housekeeper and the maid that she had managed to keep with tearful displays of shame at her husband's terrible deeds, would arise to find their last pay waiting for them, and instructions to cover the furniture in dust sheets and leave the house. The keys would be returned to an agent named in an official letter – the mistress would not be returning.

Tonight, meantime, the boy would sleep, his head on her knee, in the carriage of a train taking them far, far away from this wretched house, and the wretched life she had led so far. Once shadows had fallen, poor, innocent, betrayed Mrs Temple would leave the house where her husband had plied his wicked trade, where a poor, broken girl's life had so cruelly been taken by his warped inclinations. A house of horrors, indeed.

And when the sun rose in the morning, well, who knew where she would be? Or who she would be?

And what matter, so long as she was – at last – free. With a new name, and a new home, it would be easy to forget. For what had come before was past now and would never happen again. By the new dawn, it would all be erased, and she would be reborn. Already she could feel it begin to fade behind her and fall away, leaving her light and clean.

With a shiver of excitement, Bridget took a final look around the room where the business of the house had been conducted. All those documents – diligently and neatly printed with her left hand, the hand which she had taught herself not to use in order to fit in better with the educated around her, all signed and stored safely away in case they were ever needed again. It had been impossibly simple in the end.

She stood and straightened her skirts and walked, head high and hopeful, toward the door for the last time. And as she did, the spine of a book she had missed caught her eye. Another author, another name. We'll try it, shall we, she asked herself? See how it fits. And, as with the others, she whispered it aloud, released it into the world and paused to see how it felt, tried it with 'Master Samuel' before it. And she liked it. That was that, then.

With more hope than she'd ever allowed herself to feel, Bridget strode from the room and away. Tonight, Mrs Bridget Temple would leave this place for good.

Tomorrow, Mrs Bridget Furniss would greet the world.

Chapter 51

"Do you reckon he'll be much longer?"

Tash swung her legs impatiently and glanced over her shoulder at the door yet again.

"He's just doing his rounds ..." Joe began.

"Of what? Canada?"

Joe thought better of responding, biting his lip and gazing at the door, hoping beyond hope that at that precise moment it would open, and in would stride a team of medics who would tell Tash what she wanted to hear and then they could go. She'd been dressed and ready since first thing that morning, terse and snappy as she awaited release.

"I'm sure he won't be long," Louise added in an attempt to calm and reassure from where she sat in the chair where she'd managed a couple of hours' sleep. She longed for a hot soak and to climb into a proper bed – her own bed. Although what awaited her at home? And what about Temple, still on the loose? Secretly, she hoped that the doctor would be delayed indefinitely – by some nice, long brain surgery for example – anything that meant Tash couldn't be discharged and then they could all stay here in this nice, safe hospital room with a guard on the door, all together in one place.

Joe stretched and yawned loudly, running his hands over his face which was haggard in the harsh light.

Tash frowned at him. "I don't know why you two morons didn't go off and stay in a nice free hotel room last night instead of martyring yourselves by my hospital bed. I'm perfectly fine, you now."

"We didn't want to ..." Louise began but Joe cut in, mimicking Tash's whiny tone.

"*Thanks, Joe – thanks, Louise – for being kind enough to stay with me overnight when I was in hospital and make sure my pillows were plumped and my glass of water was held to my lips every time I needed it, and keeping me safe and actually caring enough to make sure that I was alright after my ordeal!*"

Tash responded by rolling her eyes and tutting loudly. She twisted herself around on the bed so that she could see Joe better and seemed just about to launch into a diatribe against him when suddenly the door squeaked open and she swung back excitedly, expecting at last that release was nigh.

It wasn't a doctor who stood there, however, nor any sort of medical personnel. Instead, a thin, worried-looking woman with lank blonde hair and a heavy coat and scarf looked at the three occupants of the room.

"Hi?" said Tash, impatiently.

"Sorry ..." the woman said. "I'm sorry to barge in – I'm looking for a Natasha Davis?"

"That's me," replied Tash. "Have I got to sign something?"

The woman blushed. "Oh no, I'm sorry – I don't work here ..."

She took a tentative step further into the room and, with a glance behind her, closed the door. "The policeman outside the door said it would be okay for me to come in – I've been speaking with Detective Miller, you see –"

"Oh, you're from the gardaí – is there any news?" Tash interrupted.

The woman looked down at her feet this time.

"I'm awfully sorry – I'm not with the Garda either. This is a bit awkward, but Mr Miller said it was probably okay for me to come talk to you." She looked up at Tash again and fixed her with a pair of pale-blue eyes which brimmed with tears.

Her accent was English, they realised.

"I wanted to apologise, you see. I mean, I know it's not my fault – *I* didn't do any of the things that they said he did, but I sort of feel partially responsible – or maybe I don't, actually – I don't know. I'm so ... I mean, I'm just as shocked as you are ... well, not *as* shocked – obviously you've had a far more shocking time –"

"Sorry," interrupted Joe gently. "What did you say your name was again?"

The woman swallowed and again looked around at the three faces looking back her curiously. "Sorry again. I'm Lynn – Lynn Furniss. I'm ... I'm Adrian's wife."

An uneasy silence followed. Tash looked at Joe, and Joe at Louise, and then all three turned back to the woman who clasped the strap of the handbag slung over her shoulder with both hands, her knuckles white.

"I'm not anymore," she added suddenly. "Obviously – I hope. I've come from the UK this morning – Oxfordshire – I stayed there after he disappeared – in case he came back, I suppose, although I don't know why. I mean he was bad when he left – unwell – but I never dreamed ... when the police told me they'd found him it was enough of a shock but when they told me what he'd done ... it's just unimaginable ... actually, it's not really ... I mean, I didn't think he'd actually go that far – not ever, you have to believe me on that ... but there were signs that I should have read, little giveaways in his behaviour ... it's all so clear to me *now*, but I couldn't have known then ... or maybe I just didn't want to see it ... oh, I don't know anymore!"

"Sit down," ordered Joe, jumping from his seat and indicating that she should take it.

"Oh no, I'm fine ..." Lynn Furniss shook her head, but it was clear that she was in a state of some distress. Gratefully, and resignedly, she accepted Joe's offer and sank into it, while he stood, arms folded, leaning against the wall of the hospital room.

"Sorry," she said again, fidgeting with her scarf and making a deal of putting her bag down on the floor underneath the chair. "Sorry for barging in like this and starting to just blurt everything out. I haven't had much sleep – although I'd imagine you haven't either. You must all be exhausted, you poor things, you've been through so much – I can't believe that Adrian ..."

"How long were you married?" asked Louise softly.

"Oh – twenty-five years."

"Wow," replied Louise. "This must all be an awful shock for you too. How long has he been ... away, I suppose?"

"Officially classed as a missing person?" said Lynn. "Two years. Two years last November, actually. Left one day when I was at work. Not a word. Of course, I didn't realise he was gone – properly gone – for quite a few days. He'd taken to sort of wandering off and since he'd started the whole family-tree business he could be gone for a while at a time, all over the country trying to find church records in places I'd never heard of, or visiting towns all over the place. He'd always ring eventually, though. Just a 'Hello, I'm in Accrington, back Thursday or Friday, can you get some fish in for me,' sort of thing. He'd never let it go more than three days without that call though, so when he disappeared – that week – I was terribly busy, you see – I'm a PA to the director of a small company and we had an event on ... anyway, four days had gone past in their entirety before I realised I hadn't heard from him and then ... if only I'd acted sooner ... I simply left him another two before I did anything. The truth was, it was so much simpler and calmer when he wasn't around. He'd been ... difficult, and unpredictable for quite a long time. I was glad of the peace when he went on his jaunts, and that's what I was sure this was – simply another jaunt. By the time I was alarmed enough to alert the police he was well gone – how he did it we'll never know. He simply left no trace of himself – just walked off with the clothes he was wearing. They found his car eventually in Oxford – impounded. He'd just left it in the town centre and when the parking expired it was towed away. The police assumed he must have got a train or a coach but they just couldn't find him, not on CCTV anywhere, no one remembered seeing him – it's as if he was a ghost."

Joe and Tash turned simultaneously to glance at Louise just as she shuddered involuntarily. Lynn Furniss, busy weaving the tassels on her scarf between her fingers, didn't notice.

"You said he was unwell," prompted Joe.

Lynn nodded gravely. "He'd always been really, as long as I'd known him and that was going on for almost thirty years. Up until recently he'd kept it all very much under control but then he started to act rather strangely ... there were so many signs that I can see now ... I should have been so concerned – to think of what he did ..."

Lynn was suddenly overcome with tears, tears for which Tash had little sympathy.

"Like what?" she demanded. "What sort of signs?"

Joe flashed her one of his warning looks, which she ignored.

"The animals," sobbed Lynn. "He was a vet, you see – just a country vet ..."

Her voice trailed off as she scrabbled in her coat pocket for a tissue and blew her nose.

"There was so much trouble – he came close to being struck off once ..."

"*What – sort – of – signs*." Tash was clearly losing patience.

"I only found all of this out after he'd gone – the police told me," replied Lynn. "He had ... experimented, I suppose. A couple of times. With the anaesthetic he'd use when he was operating on the animals – the dosage. On the smaller ones – gerbils, hamsters, eventually cats and small dogs. There was an instance where ..." she paused to take a breath, "more than once, actually ... where they'd wake up – mid-operation – squealing or yelping or doing whatever it is that animals do when they're in pain ..." She swallowed again to quell more tears. "He wouldn't use enough ... or he'd use too much, and they wouldn't wake for ages ... or at all in a couple of instances. The Meadows' cat – he told them it had passed away of old age on the operating table but the truth was that it just never woke up from whatever he'd given it. Sometimes he'd perform an operation when it wasn't necessary – amputations in particular ..."

Louise gasped, and Tash squirmed on the bed.

"I'm so sorry, this is gruesome ... I won't go on ..."

"No, please do," said Tash. "I need to know."

"Well, the pattern was only observed after he'd disappeared, but an animal would be brought in with a simple problem ... something stuck in its paw, for example, and the owner would be told to leave it with him, and come back later and by the time they'd return for their pet, Adrian would have removed the paw or even an entire leg. It was Morgan's Errand that was the last straw, however ..."

"Morgan's Errand?" asked Joe.

"Sorry – yes. Morgan's Errand was a racehorse – belonged to a very wealthy gentleman. He was being trained at a stable near to where we lived. Adrian was no specialist, but he was good with horses and he'd gone there a hundred times for simple things. Morgan's Errand took a stumble out in training – it didn't seem at first to be too big a problem, but Adrian ... he just took it upon himself ... he never even ran it past the boss ... something that valuable, and next thing, Adrian just ... his leg ... the entire leg, just below the – what do you call the joint, the elbow? The knee? For a country vet's wife, I'm extraordinarily ignorant of animals. And I hate horses with a passion. Anyway – Morgan's Errand had to be destroyed, of course, millions of pounds down the drain, and Adrian was suspended and there was all this palaver going on and it was then that he vanished. The pressure of it all, I assumed. Between that, and ... well, Adrian hadn't been taking his medication for some time, quite some time, in fact. When he left, I found it all – he'd carried on getting his prescription filled but he hadn't taken so much as a single tablet in months. No wonder his judgement was impaired, and the family-tree business – well, it had got out of hand, really. It was a juggernaut, with the brakes cut – that's what Adrian's life was, and then ... *poof*, gone!"

"What do you mean by the family-tree business?" asked Louise.

Lynn rubbed her tissue under her eyes and cleared her throat. "Yes. This is where some of the pieces are finally filled in – between his life here and his life at home – although they couldn't be more different. It's like two different men, in fact – I can't believe Adrian went as far as he did. The obsessive signs though – it's so clear now. The first thing that he became obsessive about was that TV show – I don't know if you get it over here – *Who Do You Think You Are?* The genealogy programme?"

Louise nodded. "We do," she said.

"You'll know what I'm talking about then. Adrian loved it – particularly the ones where people discovered that their ancestors were completely different from them – royalty, or subjects of terrific scandal – he thought it was wonderful, and he used to talk about how he wondered if he had someone fascinating in his family, something that would make him stand out from the crowd, he used to say, that would give him a purpose. I never understood what he meant by that. I used to remind him that his purpose was to be a wonderful village vet and be kind to lots of animals but that wasn't good enough for him. Then it got so that he didn't just love the show, he used to obsess about it – recording it and re-watching it over and over, taking notes of all the places and resources that you could go to find out your family tree – it was inevitable that he would go and start to look himself. The connection with Dublin was something that I should have made more of with the police – I can see that now – but at the time, well, it was ridiculous that he should come here. If only I'd known ..."

"So you said," interjected Tash. "What was the connection to Dublin, then?"

"Well, as far as I understood – and the one thing he *did* take with him other than all the money from our savings account, by the way – was all of his notes and records that he'd made about his own family search – he left us with nothing to investigate really – other than what he'd told me which was that he'd traced back to his great-grandmother, or something, who was a Bridget Furniss from Dublin. I should have listened more to him, but he was a dreadful bore when he got started, and he'd go off on tangents and make these great long, wandering speeches – he simply couldn't stick to his point."

Slowly, Tash raised an eyebrow and turned to Joe, who saw but ignored her.

"So what did you learn about this Bridget Furniss?" he urged. "What did he tell you about her?"

Disappointingly, Lynn shook her head. "Nothing much. Nothing other than that she was a widow, who never remarried and had one son who was Adrian's great-grandfather or something – I can't remember, and that she'd first shown up in Dublin on the 1901 census –

strange the things I *did* retain. Anyway, he was terribly frustrated by it all because he simply couldn't go back any further with her. It almost drove him mad – if he wasn't mad already, that is. He kept trying Irish records but I gather they're not all that great, and he even had a poke around English records but he couldn't find anything that fitted. It was almost as if she'd just appeared, fully formed, in Dublin in or around 1901. And that was as far as things got. Then there was the business with the horse – the stress of which, I presume, drove him to disappear. I mentioned the whole Dublin thing to the police but there had been no trace found of Adrian at ports or airports or anything, so they didn't pursue that. They thought he'd simply chucked himself into the sea somewhere, I imagine. And up until last night when Detective Miller called me, I didn't know if he was alive or dead. And now that I know what he did – I wish it were the latter – I know, that's terrible and I'm sorry – actually, I'm not a bit sorry. What I'm sorry for, Natasha – and Louise and Joe – have I got that right? What I'm sorry for is not putting two and two together sooner and somehow preventing all this from happening. And now ... a man is dead, and a boy – that poor boy – if only I'd known ..."

She burst into tears again and Joe patted her on the back.

"You weren't to know, Lynn," he said softly. "It was good of you to come but, really, there was no need."

"Did Adrian have an interest in photography at all, Lynn?" asked Louise suddenly.

Lynn sniffed and shook her head. "Not really," she replied, thinking. "Apart from holiday snaps and such. Why do you ask?"

Louise, Tash and Joe exchanged glances again, a silent exchange where they looked to one another to see who would tell her. An exchange that was interrupted by the door of the room swinging open again.

This time, it was who Tash was waiting for. Her doctor swept in, followed by a junior, and Detective Miller who made a beeline for Lynn Furniss.

The room was suddenly filled with conversation – the doctor checking Tash's pulse and asking her how she was, Miller shaking hands with Lynn, telling her how he wished they didn't have to meet under such circumstances.

Then Lynn stood, gathered her belongings, and was ushered out the door by the detective without a goodbye, just at the same time as Tash's doctor gave her the all-clear to leave and swept from the room himself.

In a matter of minutes, Louise, Joe and Tash were alone again.

"Right then," said Tash, beaming, as she slid from the bed and pulled her coat on. "Time to make like a tree and leaf."

Louise looked directly at her, amazed. "You're so positive," she said.

"That's me alright," replied Tash loudly, glancing at the door through which they would leave.

A little too loudly, Louise realised. So it wasn't positivity then. There, in her eyes, she saw a glimmer of the same fear that was now rippling through Louise's veins, a ripple that would turn to a torrent the second they filed out the door.

"So," she said, hesitantly, making no move to exit. "Furniss's wife – all that stuff – what do we do now?

Where do we go from here?"

For a moment, no one answered. All three simply stood in place, staring at the door, each imagining what might be on the other side.

"Away," said Joe, aloud, but almost to himself. "As far away from here and all this shit as we can get."

Reluctantly, he took the first step, and the others followed.

Chapter 52

Dublin, 1913

The bereaved man watched his wife ascend the stairs ahead of him, her head bent to watch her step, framed in the halo of light from the lamp she carried. Her mourning silks swished gently as she disappeared around the turn in the stairs, and he sighed, wishing that he could go with her and simply lay his head down to sleep on the pillow beside her.

Instead, with heavy feet he entered his study where the fire needed stoking, and, upon closing the door behind him, locked it, for fear that he should be disturbed. He was exhausted, but he needed to be alone, to reflect and think.

He turned and surveyed the familiar room – his desk and chair, the mantel and the ticking clock, and over it, the portrait of the woman he had thought he knew. It had hung there his entire life, the photographer unknown, and now, in the space of a few days, the subject too. He had always felt comfortable with every feature of her stern face, every fold in her dark skirts but today it was a stranger who hung there. No longer the mother he had loved his entire life. Looking at it made him almost glad she was gone.

He poured himself a whiskey, and sat down, sighing with the weight of the day. The funeral had been enormous – he must have shaken a thousand hands and listened to half as many people tell him how much she had meant to them – how she had clothed them, fed them, sheltered them. The societies and guilds and charitable institutions at which Bridget Furniss had been the heart or mind seemed endless. Tearful women spoke to him of how she had provided sanctuary when their husbands had grown too ready with their fists, prosperous adults credited their very existence to her intervention when they were starving children – the list of her good deeds seemed never-ending, as he'd known it would be. Such was the life that she had lived. 'Philanthropist and Benefactor' to the poor and needy of Dublin, she had been called. When the news that she had passed in her sleep had reached the citizens of the empire's second city, a great wave of grief had rippled through it. Yes, it had been a long life, but to see it pass marked the end of an era. They would never see her like again and so on.

To listen to the commiserating and see the tears on even the most hardened faces – well, you'd think she was a saint. And she'd have loved it, too. Samuel drained his glass in one drop and smiled ruefully at nothing. "Sam," she'd have said, "don't go making any fuss." Which of course meant that he should. How well she'd had him trained.

He stood and poured himself another glass, placing it back on his desk before reaching up and removing the framed photograph of her from the wall, and holding it out from him the better to study the dour, handsome woman. It was as if he beheld a stranger, and it struck him that it always had, because he had no memory of his mother looking like this. Tall and straight and slim, but strong. Her hair pulled back in a modest style, her attire so plain that it might be easily be mistaken as that of a domestic. Her eyes were fierce and cold, her jaw set, her lips tight, yet there had been something striking about her – a power to her that he had never known. This woman was of a different time, a different place and a different life than he had ever known. And now, today, he knew that to be true.

He had wondered – he had, indeed, asked her – who had taken it and where? What year? How old had she been? What had been her station in life?

And never, once, in all his years of life, had she given him a straight answer. More often than not she would dismiss the question and replace it with one of her own, distracting him sufficiently to change the subject. At other times she would make things up – playfully suggesting that she had been a lady's maid to royalty, or a spy or – if she was especially imaginative, a Duke's mistress. She had never given any true indication of what her life had been before his memories of her began. She had always, to her son, been a woman of independent means. They had lived a comfortable life the entire time in their house on Quaker Lane near the River Liffey, with a cook and a nanny and, when he was old enough, a series of tutors who had taught him well enough to facilitate entry to Trinity. He had never left home, even then, even when qualified, even when working in trade, even when his marriage to Helena had taken place. And

413

there he still lived with his family – his son James, his daughters Annabel and young Bridget. And never once had he questioned any of it. Until now. Until he had made the shocking discovery in his mother's room.

Setting aside the photograph, he buried his head in his hands. What sort of a foolish, pampered idiot had he been this whole time? Never once pushing her to find out. But then again, how *could* he have found out? She would never have told him and now – knowing the truth – he understood why. But it meant that he, his whole life, had been a lie, every moment of it. From the history that he thought he knew to the very blood flowing through his veins. To his name – his identity. Every shred of himself was untrue.

If she had only, just once, told him truthfully how old she was.

That was all he had gone in search of – something that told him the year of her birth. He needed it for her death certificate. It was such a simple thing, but it had never struck him as truly necessary until he was asked for it in an official capacity. And then – what a fool he felt for not knowing. Age had not seemed relevant throughout her life – she had defied it – right until the very end she had seemed ageless and timeless – she was always moving forward, never pausing to take stock or indulge in nostalgia.

"She must be a good age by now," people would say to him as they asked after her once she had retired and he would reply that yes, yes she was, indeed, but still strong. They did not need to know that her memory had all but failed her – that she did not recognise her own son, nor her grandchildren – that she knew not her surroundings and rambled incomprehensible nonsense about wild dogs and priests – and that she woke in the dead of night screaming that a girl with no hands was at the end of her bed, watching her, and waiting. No one who respected the legacy of Bridget Furniss had any need to know that she had taken leave of her senses, had forgotten every last detail of her long life. And that death, when it soon arrived, would be a welcome release for her from the land of nightmare in which she was trapped.

When the time came, she had woken only for the briefest moment to trouble Helena for a drink of water and to announce, rather strangely and solemnly – and in a manner most lucid – that she regretted none of it, before she lay back down on her pillow and promptly passed, her eyes wide open as if looking at something on the ceiling. And there it was, a ferocious life snuffed out like a candle flame. A life that had been how long – seventy, eighty, ninety – a hundred years or more? He had no idea. And so he had gone to the attics, where he never went, in search of something – anything – that would finally reveal the secret of his mother's true age. It had been almost exciting – a mystery to be solved, sealed boxes of hers to be opened at last – how naughty this felt – snooping in his mother's things. So formidable had she been, and so clearly had she made him aware that they were forbidden, that he had never gone near them, as child or man. A trained lapdog, he now realised he was. A puppy that has been smacked on the nose with the newspaper so often it instinctively does not go near the larder. But now she was not there anymore to admonish him or – God forbid – punish him as she might have done when he was small with a sound spanking. And he was free to finally explore the treasures that have been kept up here, locked away his whole life.

And so, he had taken her keys – those which had never left her belt – and gone to the smallest of the attic rooms, and inside he had gone to the treasure trove of secrets she had kept from him.

Unopened packing crates, still sealed shut, marked 'London', filled with trinkets and ornaments from the last century – signs that there had been another house, another life. From time to time, he almost fancied that he recognised some of them, as though they nudged far buried memories of his, memories that brought him almost, but not quite, to the cusp of remembering something ... someone ... a fleeting image of a girl with red hair and a beaming smile ... gone again, an ephemeral vision that slipped away almost before it had formed.

Into another crate then – what would he find here? Books – novels that had been fashionable before he was born, and underneath them, business ledgers and journals – whatever might they contain? And, like a fool, he had opened them and begun to read.

And still he read when, hours later, Helena came in search of him to tell him that the undertaker waited downstairs to discuss the plans – a discussion that felt as if it happened without him fully present. And then, when that was done, his mother washed and laid out on her deathbed with candles burning at the four corners, and his presence required by her side – he returned to his reading, and the desperate secrets that he had uncovered when he had wrenched open that dreadful box.

That which he found in the journals was terrible enough – his father discovered – his fearful crimes, his grisly end at the hangman's hands in Newgate. This was truly terrible beyond belief – no wonder his mother had kept it all from him his whole life. It had been to protect him from the truth – he understood that now – and finally he wept. It was there again, on the floor of that tiny attic room, his lamp burning low, that Helena found him, and bade him come away from these recollections that made his pain all the greater. She bade him dry his tears and come away from it all – it was another day's work for him, but for now he needed to watch through the night at his mother's side, as a good son would.

And tearfully he agreed with her and allowed himself to be led away from the dreadful discoveries he had made.

But not without one last item to keep with him through the night, the smallest of the journals that he placed in his pocket, he knew not why, and forgot for a while in the haze of chanted prayer and commiseration. Until in the small hours, when Helena and the children slept, and he sat alone beside the stiff corpse of his ageless mother, he remembered, and withdrew the journal, holding it close to the candlelight in order to read. And as he did, her true nature, her history, finally became known to him as the more horrible revelations of all became clear.

Some of it was illegible, and some in a code of sorts that he thought at times he could decipher but not always. Enough of it was comprehensible, however, scribbled in fading pencil in a hand that he knew as well his own, a hand that had composed lists and letters and notes through the entirety of his life. A hand that now curled around a bible, waxen and stiff. A hand that had described events, and emotions and responses, secretive thoughts, notions that should never have seen the light of day. All of it comprehensible enough for him to understand one thing – that it was not his father, one Samuel Temple, photographer and eccentric, who should have hung for those deeds of which he was accused.

It was his mother.

How tainted everything now seemed, thought Samuel Furniss as he took another mouthful of the bitter whiskey. His childhood, all that he remembered of it, his mother's fearsome, undying protection. What would he do? How would he tell Helena? The children? How would they bear the shame of it? It was unthinkable that they should – they were innocents in all of this. And, come to think of it, so was he.

Unlocking the drawer of his desk, Samuel reached inside and retrieved the volume that he had concealed in there, safely locked away from the comings and goings of the past days. He weighed it in his hands. Such a light thing, yet such heavy content. The weight of life and death, of good and evil, of justice and injustice; the weight of history – and the weight of his family's future. Surely his mother had never intended this to be found but was betrayed by her own memory which had been fading for so much longer than he had been prepared to admit.

"*Mother,*" he sighed, "*what on earth have you done?*"

And with that, he tossed it into the fireplace where the coals shifted beneath it, and flames licked at it, gently at first, and then more insistently until finally, and forever, the admission of Bridget Temple's guilt was no more, and her son, Samuel Junior, could carry on with his life, as best he could.

Chapter 53

November 2018

Louise stepped out the doorway of the shop, looked left and right and then turned for home. Winter had come and an icy wind buffeted her back as she strode sharply along the road. She'd have liked to pull her hood up against it but wouldn't have dared. It would have interfered with her peripheral vision. These days, she didn't even wear a hat pulled over her ears which stung with the cold in case it meant that she didn't hear something – anything – the tiniest shuffle, the quietest step.

She'd be home in a matter of minutes, walking briskly. Her mind flashed back to when this simple trip around the corner had been an enormous deal for her, limping along on her crutch, an out-of-date bar of chocolate in her pocket as a gift for Joe. She tried not to let the memory go any further. It didn't do her any good to think about him. The pangs of missing him were still frequent, especially since the day he had sent his dad to collect all of his stuff from the house – the paint and brushes, everything that had been left behind, the job unfinished, all those weeks ago. The old man had been polite but hadn't mentioned Joe at all and his gruff

419

demeanour had led Louise to keep the questions about his son's welfare that she had hoped to ask well in check. Mr Davis Senior had not been happy at all with Joe's sudden departure to Spain ... what was it, six months ago now? Ever the dutiful brother, he'd gone with Tash when she had suddenly decided to drop out of college and go to stay with an uncle who owned a bar near Marbella. She just couldn't remain in Dublin, she'd said, not with everything that had happened and especially not with so much unresolved. And as much as Louise didn't want either of them to go, she completely understood why.

She could have gone too, of course. Tash had pushed for it in her typical blunt way, and Louise had thought about it – just packing a case and getting on a plane and away from it all – the house and its shadows, the threat of Furniss, still out there despite the best efforts of the gardaí. But there was a bigger picture to consider – work – she just couldn't up and leave that, not when she relied on a hard-built client base, not when she needed to be close to agencies and studios. And while she missed her new friends more than she'd ever have thought possible, what good – really – would it have done their relationships to go with them? What bound her to Tash and Joe was all so strange, so unreal – how could they ever, truly, get away from what had happened if the three of them were constantly together? The idea of being far away from home, in a strange new place, with only a terrible bond to unite them – it simply didn't feel right. Louise had assured them that she'd be absolutely fine and that she'd see them whenever they got back. Which would probably be never, she reminded herself as she turned the corner into Maryborough Gardens and the wind sliced at her face. Why would they ever bother to come back to this?

Without thinking, she scanned the area around her. Eyes out over the Green, checking for movement behind the trees or in the gardens. Just a few more feet and then home. Louise readied her keys, and her stomach tightened as she prepared to open the front door – the sensation of her nerve-endings tingling as she prepared to go into her home was her normal now – the great build-up of fear just at the moment of entry. Defying it, she held the keys up, her hand trembled and then dropped as she came to a stop just at the gate. She couldn't do it. She simply couldn't. She grabbed the gatepost as she felt her knees weaken and took a deep breath. It had got her. The fear. The nerves. Overcome, she stood there for a moment as her head swam and her anxiety reached a crescendo. This would pass. It always did. She just had to wait it out. Breathe in for five, breathe out for five … touch something, listen for the traffic in the distance, breathe in and smell the night air. Slowly, it began to pass.

With a great sigh, she let the last of the panic attack go, and straightened, facing her greatest fear of all – her own home. How could it have come to this? Her refuge, the place that she had dreamed of transforming into her refuge, her forever home – how could it terrify her so? How could she keep living like this? How could she go on being on constant alert for any sound or smell? How could she live being afraid to close doors behind her for fear of what would be on the other side when she opened them again? She hated it. She wanted to love her little house – her own small space in the world – but she simply couldn't allow herself to in case it … it *turned* on her again.

What made it almost worse was that *nothing* had happened since that terrible weekend – the confrontation with Furniss ... don't go back there, she warned herself as her mind began to stray and images began to flash into her head – the nozzle of the bottle aimed at her, the air on the darkened stairs shimmering, distorting, the *crack* of her crutch against Furniss's face – *stop!* Put the thoughts away.

But her house – what certainty did she have when she went inside that all would remain quiet? Nothing could convince her that all was well in there, that suddenly, despite the quietness of the past weeks, a shape wouldn't emerge from a wall, or a pan wouldn't fly across the room. She listened always, without even realising she was doing it, for the whispers, and sitting down at her desk to work made her sick at the prospect of a voice in her headphones, or mysterious skips in the waveforms.

Louise straightened and allowed herself to let go of the gatepost. The ground didn't lurch beneath her, nor did she crumple to the ground. She was getting there.

But still, there was always a possibility – the chance that they'd all be standing on her stairs, like they had done in Furniss's basement. Again, she urged herself to stop. But she couldn't, not without closure and, in the absence of the photographs that were the source of all this – the gardaí had never found them among Furniss's possessions – finding that closure seemed as though it would never happen.

With a final deep breath, Louise began to move, taking tentative steps, one by one, toward the steps, then up, and then the key in the door – every movement considered and careful. *It's all fine*, she reassured herself.

She turned the key, then pushed, and opened the door wide, looking inside before she entered, grateful as always that she had left all the lights on before she had gone to the shop.

As always, it felt like an achievement that she had made it at all. She closed the front door behind her and took a moment to ground herself – touching the wall, sniffing the air which smelled of the toast she'd eaten for dinner. All was fine. All was as it should have been. Feeling somewhat restored, she slid the chain into place on the door and locked the mortice from inside, before taking off her heavy coat and hanging it over the banister post, finally releasing a long, relieved breath.

Which she could see.

Louise's eyes widened in alarm, and she exhaled again. This breath, too, formed a cloud. Which it shouldn't have. Goosebumps prickled on her upper arms as she looked around in alarm. It was freezing in here alright, despite the fact that she'd had the heating on all afternoon. Perhaps it had finally broken down – yet even if it had, there was no way it should have been this cold, this quickly.

Her stomach sank. Here it was, happening again. They were back. Despite her reassurances to herself. It had finally happened. She wasn't alone. *Again.*

She turned toward the kitchen as a shuffling sound came from it. They were in there. Which one would it be? What on earth was she going to see this time? She longed for Tash suddenly, the brave, curious Tash who had pushed her way in through the front door and announced that she loved ghosts. Why did she have to be so far away?

A gust of wind outside made a sudden whine through the keyhole, and, at the same time, Louise was hit by a cold draught coming from the kitchen. She turned toward it and sniffed. It was cold night air, blowing through from the back. The door to the garden was open, she realised. There was nothing supernatural about it. *Someone had broken in.* Her heart skipped a beat. An intruder. Something real and tangible – not harmless, of course, but something alive. Maybe she stood a chance against that. She looked around and picked up her umbrella from the hallstand and extended the handle. It was the best she could do. Swallowing deeply, she crept toward the kitchen door and entered as quietly as she could. Maybe she could scare them off ... maybe ...

She didn't expect the enormity of the surge of shock that went through her as she came face to face with the person in her kitchen. A yell exploded from her at the sight of the trespasser – a bearded, filthy tramp. Her first thought, oddly, was relief. It was just a vagrant – in search of money for drugs, or food, or just cash – common or garden – this was a standard break-in. She almost laughed.

And then she recognised him, and the urge to laugh dissipated. Of course it was him – who else would it be? She'd been expecting him all this time so naturally it made sense he'd finally turned up. She'd known – deep down, she'd known. Every time the Guards tried to tell her he was far away and not coming back, she'd known in her gut it made no sense. And here he was, in her kitchen, her every fear come true.

"*Get out!*" she yelled, raising the umbrella over her head.

He looked at her defiantly with wild contempt-filled eyes.

"No," he hissed. "*I will not.*"

Stunned, she stepped backwards. What now? What should she do? What should she say? Trembling, she stared at him, and he stared back, an arrogance to him, as if she were trespassing on his property again and not the other way round.

"How did you get in?" she demanded.

He curled his lip and sneered at her.

"Is that all you have to say to me?" he growled. "What's your next question going to be? How am I finding the weather? Have I any holidays planned this year? All that you have seen and done and that's the best you can do?"

Louise shook her head, dumbstruck. What was he doing to do next? Was he going to try to hurt her? Was he armed? Jesus, what was she going to do here? She tried to think, tried to map out what best to do – run for the front door? But the chain, and the lock – by the time she had them open – no – he'd get to her way before then. There had to be something else ... run for her studio ... barricade herself in somehow – phone the gardaí ... but there wasn't time – he would get to her too quickly and her phone ... *shit* ... her phone was still in the pocket of her coat on the banister. She stepped back again.

He stepped forward.

She caught a hint of the smell of him – stale urine and ... worse ... dear God, where had he been all this time?

"I've been hiding in plain sight," he said, as if he could read her mind. "I watched them looking, your police buddies. And they looked everywhere but in the right place. They were sure I'd left, that I'd get out of Dodge, wouldn't stick around. Well, they were wrong. And I knew they'd be wrong because I can think their thoughts before they do, do you understand? They won't catch me. Ever."

His conviction terrified her. "How ... you're sure of that?" she asked.

He nodded slowly. "They won't."

"They ... they check on me from time to time – I never know when," she said, timidly. "If they find you here ..."

"Again, you're talking to me as if I were stupid, Louise Lacey. Like you did before – thought you were so smart with your beefy boyfriend bodyguard. I don't see him here now. I'm pretty sure you're alone. And you're locked in that a-way," he pointed in the direction of the front door, "and I'm between you and escape this a-way – so I think conditions are ideal for what is going to happen between you and me."

Her stomach churned and she spasmed with terror.

"I'm here you leave you a memory, Louise Lacey. Something you'll see until you shut your eyes for the last time on this earth, do you understand? From the day you walked into my shop and got your hands on my camera and then stole from me – well, you had no idea what you were doing. But there were wheels in motion and you stuck a stick through the spokes, do you understand? So I'm here tonight to do the same for you. Fair's fair and all that."

"Don't hurt me."

"Did I say I would? Well, I might. You hurt me after all – Beefcakes and that hefty swing of his. Not sure my profile will ever be what it was ..." He emitted a high-pitched giggle and thrust his hands deep into the pockets of his grimy overcoat. "Speaking of hefty, by the way, was that his sister who was kind enough to return my photographs to me? The ones that you withheld from me when I went to all the effort to retrieve them?"

"She's not in the country," retorted Louise. "You can't get to her. She's safe."

He rolled his eyes. "There would be no point in her now anyway," he said. "She was part of the plan and then you ruined it."

"*What* plan?" Louise spluttered. "You keep going on about this plan of yours – what plan made you kill a man and cut a kid's arms off? What kind of plan is that? You're sick!"

He twitched, and Louise instantly regretted opening her mouth.

"You're so stupid, Louise Lacey – there's no other way of putting it. I'll tell you who was sick though. Temple. That's who was sick. Sick in his head and in his heart."

Louise frowned. "But you're Temple? At least you were ... was Temple different from you now? Are you not him anymore?"

"Jesus *Christ!*" he yelled.

Louise jumped and cowered.

"My great-great-grandfather! Do you know nothing? *That's* who was sick. He killed them all – the people in the photographs – you guessed that he did, and you were right for once. He poisoned them! And then he tried to blame my great-great-grandmother for it. They were all innocents, all of them! And he took their lives! Don't you understand? I was trying to make it all better – make it right! I was never *Temple* – I merely took his name because that is what I need to do, to play my role. I was *fixing* things!"

Louise stared at him, on the verge of tears now. She still didn't understand – not really anyway – but she was terrified of angering him even more. He was ill, his wife had said. Delusional – that much was clear.

"The diaries and journals – the damn gardaí have them all now, I'm sure – Bridget Furniss – my great-great-grandmother – she had copies of them all, signed accounts of what he did – and the photographs in the box – his souvenirs, his trophies – they were his victims, do you see now? He wrote it all down and signed it – he wanted to exhibit them – domestic freaks, he called them. Too conventional for the carnivals and circuses yet too unusual, too *abnormal*, for polite Victorian society. They existed, of course, but they were not celebrated – not the ones that he captured anyway. And capture them he did – their very souls went into his work ...."

"Into the photographs," interrupted Louise. "Their ghosts – I saw them ..."

"You wouldn't have if you'd just given me back the box, can't you see? I was making the exchanges ... a soul for a soul, so that they could rest in peace. All I had to do was replace one that didn't matter for one that did, don't you understand? The replacements even presented themselves to me in turn – three of them I had. Three! I was almost there and trusted in the universe and the spirits and fate and serendipity and coincidence and *destiny* that I would find them all – that they would walk across my path. That is how it worked. But *you* had to come and interfere."

Louise's eyes widened. "You thought – you really

thought that you could ... sweet Jesus, you're insane! Who did you think you were?"

Furniss fixed her in his gaze – his eyes wide and calm. "I was the saviour, the redeemer. That's who I was. Just as Samuel Temple wished to redeem the outcasts of his time, the unthinkables, I was here to redeem the unthinkables of a different age. The dead. The gone. The forgotten. Except to him, and to me. It was my purpose in life to release the souls that were spirit-bound to those photographs, the souls that he had taken. Thanks to you, those souls are now forever lost – they will never find peace, never find justice."

His beatific tone suddenly filled Louise with anger.

"*None of that had to happen – do you know that?*" she shouted. "Do you know that or are you actually mad? Your wife told us all about you – maiming fucking innocent animals – you just liked to chop things up, to hurt things – you're ill – you need medical help, or at least you did but now you've gone and murdered someone – you didn't have to do that. And you didn't have to ruin a kid's life by hacking off his arms, and you didn't have to ruin my friend's life by scaring her to death – you're poison, do you know that? You're sick and, instead of taking responsibility for that when you could, you've spread your sickness around so many lives – your wife, those people you hurt – *me!* Why are you like this? What gives you the right to do that? Why can't you just ... just give yourself up to the police and do the right damn thing for once – get treatment, get help or something? Why have you done this? Why have you done this to *me?*"

"*You did this to yourself!*" Furniss yelled. "*And all I*

429

have left is to make sure that you don't forget that! That you will never forget that! Do you hear me?! You took everything else from me, all that remains is this ..."

Louise saw his hand emerge from his coat, holding something – not again, no – not this – a different bottle this time – she could see it plain as day. It was an ordinary water bottle this time – she watched, frozen, as he hastily unscrewed the top and held it up. Instinctively, she cowered, covering her face and turning her back to him as quickly as she could, waiting, waiting for the impact – for the burning – this was how he would make her remember. In anticipation she screamed, just at the precise moment that she felt an enormous force *pushing* her, propelling her forwards, knocking her off her feet like an explosion. She screamed even louder as she hit the floor, curling herself rapidly into a ball at first and then, terrified, scrabbling to stand, to look behind her, to see how close Furniss was, to simply get away from him ... and instead of seeing him coming after her, wanting to hurt her, to mark her for life, what she saw was indeed something that she would never forget. It was simply her own kitchen door slamming shut, with such force that she heard doors upstairs rattle and felt the floor beneath her reverberate.

Slamming shut. By itself.

And as it did, the instant that barrier was formed between her and Temple, the air was flooded with the familiar scent of lilies, like a shield, a forcefield of protection, keeping her safe from the sight in the kitchen. She was spared that at least.

But she would never, as long as she lived, be able to block out the sound of the horrendous scream that rent the air, that Furniss made as he drank from the bottle, the final act that he had meant for her to see and never forget.

At least she had been spared that.

Chapter 54

April 2019

Louise set the jug of water down carefully on the small cast-iron table and slid into the chair opposite her companion.

It was the golden hour, the evening imbued with that hazy blush that made her wish it would go on forever. She could feel it spreading across her skin, the flaxen light of the low sun. She closed her eyes, tilted her head back and felt the last of the unseasonably warm sun on her face. There was a poignancy to it all, her desperate bid to savour the moment, to absorb it so that she might not forget it. This would be one of the last – if not the last – of these evenings in this garden. And there had been so few.

She opened her eyes at the gurgle of water into her glass and smiled in gratitude at the girl across the table who poured it. Thinner, dressed in white, her skin still pale, her fingernails short and neat and free of lacquer or varnish. With her once wild hair pulled back into a neat ponytail, she looked both younger and older than the last time Louise had seen her. Freer. The eyes were still careworn, but they did not dart anxiously from left to right. Instead, they were cast to the cloudless sky, travelling across it as if exploring its expanse with a single gaze. Louise knew that in her heart her friend pined for somewhere else, but was also content to be here, for now.

At the sight of her wistful gaze into the heavens, Louise felt a tug at her own heart, a longing to bring her back. She picked her wineglass up and clinked it against the other on the table, as if to ground her. It worked.

Tash pulled her eyes from the sky and focused first on her own glass, then on Louise's face. "Cheers, m'dear!" she smiled, picking up her wine and holding it aloft by way of a toast. "Million miles away there for a mo. Bit sleepy after the grub and the grog."

Louise tutted. "You can't go to sleep now," she warned. "We're going out – proper out, out. I haven't been out out in –"

"Your entire life," Tash said dryly. "And it shows – what's with the Nana sandals? Did she leave you *everything*? And even if she did, do you have to wear it?"

Louise frowned and glanced down at her feet.

Tash brayed. "Made you look," she said, and took a long swig of water. "I'm rallying, I'm rallying!" she announced, adjusting her position in her seat, while Louise rolled her eyes.

"What are you – six?" she asked. "You come home for one week, having been sunning yourself in Spain and I'm kind enough to cook you dinner and you repay me with insults!"

"I wouldn't call it cooking so much as assembling –"

"Watch it!" warned Louise, smiling.

"And I work very hard in Spain – look at me, I'm still as white as a sheet." She held up her arms for Louise's

433

perusal. "Although that might be something to do with the Factor 50, to be fair. I easily work as hard as Joe and he looks like ... I dunno ... David Copperfield or something. The magician now, not the Dickens one ..."

"I got that," said Louise, her heart giving an unexpected kick. "You look great – I barely recognised you at the door. '*What have you done with my friend?*' I was going to ask. Not even a lick of nail varnish ..."

She stopped as Tash winced and balled her hands into a fist, burying her nails in her palms.

"You know yourself," Tash said, her tone subdued. "Different place, different me. Got myself a whole new look when we went to Spain first. Rang my mam and told her to hobble on upstairs and bring whatever was left to the clothes bank."

"How are your mum and dad anyway?" Louise asked, keen to change the subject.

Tash took a mouthful of her wine and thought about it. "Same as," she replied after a moment. "Mam's a lot better with the new hip but Dad's still really cross. I don't think he's forgiven Joe yet for having fecked off on him and forcing him to sell the business on." Her voice dropped deep, as she mimicked a grumpy old man. "'*What's that gobshite doing behind a bar in Spain with that gobshite uncle of yours when he could be making a living painting houses here?*' Oh, I don't know, Dad – let me think about that for a bit." Tash rolled her eyes. "It was all well overdue – if Joe hadn't got out when he did, he'd still have been driving round in that van emulsifying ladies' skirtings – and not in a good way – until he was old and grey. Grey*er*. He certainly wouldn't have got the practice to do what he's going to do tonight – although that could be a complete disaster – but I won't say anything just yet, and he'll be back in Spain before the angry mob finds him."

Louise felt the sting of sadness in her heart again at Tash's words, truthful as they were. What was there to keep him in Dublin after everything that had happened, after the horror that he had seen?

"It's changed us all, hasn't it," she said suddenly.

A thick silence fell between them.

"I guess," Tash said. "You've done a really nice job with the garden. The place is looking well."

"Thanks," Louise replied.

There was silence again, for longer this time. Louise contemplated suggesting that they leave, head for town now to grab a drink somewhere.

"I had to get away – you know that, don't you?" Tash blurted suddenly.

Louise looked at her in alarm. "Of course I know that. I completely understand!"

"No – what I mean is that *I* had to go, but Joe didn't – not really. He just followed the old *stank* of guilt over what happened to me. Couldn't let me go on my own, even though I was only going to Uncle Peadar's for a short while at first. And now I'm stuck with him, both of us working at the bar, and I really appreciate everything he's done for me, but it's time for him to come home and leave me at it. He needs a reason to come back to Dublin that isn't in a tin that needs stirring with a stick."

"Well, it's safe now, at least," Louise said. "Temple – *Furniss*, God, I can never get that right – he's not coming back from the dead."

Tash snorted and glanced up at the back of Louise's house. "You, of all people, are sure of that?"

Louise frowned. "Yes," she stated bluntly, studying her wineglass.

"And what about you?" Tash asked suddenly.

Louise looked up, confused.

"Me? I'm fine. Once I knew he was dead, it was like I'd regained something."

"What about inside?" Tash looked again at the rear of Louise's house, her eyes drifting from window to window. "Are they still there?"

Louise turned to look herself and shook her head. "Not a soul," she lied.

Tash stared at her intently for a few moments.

"So that's not why the *For Sale* sign is up?"

Louise grinned ruefully.

"Can't you bear it anymore? There was a time when all you wanted was to just have your home to yourself and make it a little hermit's haven. What changed?"

Louise laughed again and shrugged.

"Me, I suppose," she said.

"Oh, here we go," Tash smirked. "Voyage of self-discovery. Empowerment. You do you and all that."

Louise giggled. "You're right in saying that all I wanted, so very badly, back then, was to be left alone, doing my thing, getting by, not having to deal with anything – because I was so beaten by dealing with *crap* in my life. But what I want, and what I need are two different things at this stage, and too many things have happened in this house – too many memories – so I'm selling up and pulling up my big-girl knickers and getting on a plane and going far, far away."

Tash's eyes widened. "For real?" she asked. "Where? Bray?"

436

"Close," Louise replied. "Australia. For starters, to see my friend Amy for a holiday, and then I'll decide where to go from there."

"*Holy Bravery, Batman!*" exclaimed Tash.

"Well, not really, I'm absolutely shitting my pants, but I'm not coming home until I've been to at least six different places and done three things that I'd never have contemplated previously."

"Are you suffering delusions too? Are they catching? What's brought this on?"

Louise shook her head. "You're going to think that this is ridiculous ... but ... it's Maud. The reason I'm doing all this is because of Maud."

Tash racked her brains for a moment, before remembering. "The girl with no hands?"

Louise blushed, and her gaze flickered to the house and back again. "I sometimes see her ... I mean, I see the image of her again," she stumbled. "She was so young, and so pure and innocent and there was probably stuff that she couldn't do because she had no hands and it was the eighteen hundreds and, I dunno, then she was dead, having her portrait taken by one nutter and then with another one wanting to resurrect her. She just feels awfully *dishonoured* to me. She'd have loved a life – I'm sure of it. And I *have* one – and two hands, and the whole of my health and I think I owe it to her to go and embrace it, fears and all."

Tash lifted her glass and raised it, first to Louise and then to the house, over which the sun had slid while they spoke, the glorious golden moment before dusk gone in an instant.

"To Maud," she said simply.

437

"To Maud," replied Louise.

They drank in solemn silence.

An hour later, they drifted out of the house and down the front path, arm in arm, heading toward the bus stop.

"Whatever you do, just laugh at his jokes, okay?" instructed Tash. "He's been doing this set at the bar for the last three months at least, but he's probably going to fluff it all when he sees you, but if you laugh he'll get it together. And then maybe he'll move home and leave me to live a life, got it?"

Louise nudged Tash away. "Why would he fluff it when he sees me?" she asked scornfully. "I think it's great that he's doing this – imagine being that brave to go and book himself a slot at an open mic night just like that?"

"Or that stupid," retorted Tash. "And you know why he'll fluff his lines. You'll probably go all red too and bashful, and shuffle your feet, or faint or something."

At that, Louise blushed immediately.

"See?"

"Tash?" Louise asked, as they strolled away.

"What's your question, caller?"

Louise stopped.

"I'm only getting it now – when you said to give him something to come home for, you meant me, didn't you?"

"Genius."

"Except I'm going to Australia and Asia or America or wherever. Does that ruin everything, do you think?"

Tash harrumphed. "Not in the slightest. I'm pretty sure they have coffee shops in those places where he can scamper out in the mornings to get you a cappuccino. And everywhere needs good painters – and bad stand-up comics, but don't tell him I told you that ..."

Louise smiled, and listened to Tash chatting aimlessly, cutting barbs here, sardonic asides there, just the way she remembered.

As they crossed the road, she turned to take a look back at her house, her little universe for so long, for good and for ill. The *For Sale* sign loomed large in the garden. It would be so hard to say goodbye ...

And there she saw her, sitting in her usual spot on the chair by the upstirs window, watching over everything. She appeared just as she had in those dreams, all those months ago, which hadn't really been dreams at all. Opalescent, glowing, Louise could almost smell the familiar scent that came with her, every time.

Louise watched as Maud turned, her head moving in a soft blur before coming into focus again and she looked directly at Louise and almost seemed to smile.

Louise returned the smile faintly and, without thinking, waved.

And then, seemingly satisfied, the spirit at the window suddenly grew fainter, and fainter again, becoming more blurred, the figure growing transparent, gradually turning to what looked like a mist and disappearing.

"Wotcha waving at?" asked Tash.

Louise turned. "Nothing," she said brightly. "Thought I saw someone I knew but they're gone now." And with that, she linked arms with her friend and faced forward.

All was well now.

And there would be no more looking back.

THE END

Printed in Great Britain
by Amazon